# CONTINUUM

# CONTINUUM

## French Science Fiction Short Stories

*edited by* Annabelle Dolidon *with* Tessa Sermet

Ooligan Press | Portland, Oregon

*Continuum: French Science Fiction Short Stories*
© 2024 Annabelle Dolidon, Tessa Sermet

ISBN13: 978–1-947845–47-3

Ooligan Press
Portland State University
Post Office Box 751, Portland, Oregon 97207
503.725.9748
ooligan@ooliganpress.pdx.edu
www.ooliganpress.com

Library of Congress Cataloging-in-Publication Data
Names: Dolidon, Annabelle, editor. | Sermet, Tessa, editor.
Title: Continuum: French Science Fiction Short Stories / edited by Annabelle Dolidon with Tessa Sermet.
Identifiers: LCCN 2023023408 (print) | LCCN 2023023409 (ebook) | ISBN 9781947845473 (trade paperback) | ISBN 9781947845480 (ebook)
Subjects: LCSH: Science fiction, French--Translations into English. | Short stories, French--Translations into English. | LCGFT: Science fiction. | Short stories.
Classification: LCC PQ1278 .C66 2024 (print) | LCC PQ1278 (ebook) | DDC 843/.0876208--dc23/eng/20230907
LC record available at https://lccn.loc.gov/2023023408
LC ebook record available at https://lccn.loc.gov/2023023409

Cover design by Laura Renckens
Interior design by Claire Curry

Printed in the United States of America

La science-fiction . . . ne relève ni de la prospective, ni de la futurologie. Elle augmente le présent de son écriture de tous les possibles envisageables, mais aussi de tous les possibles déjà envisagés. Le macro-texte de la science-fiction regroupe la mémoire de tous les futurs passés, présents et à venir.

*Science fiction is not about anticipation or futurology. It feeds its present writing with all that is conceivably possible, and all the possible that has already been conceived. The macro-text of science fiction brings together the memory of all past, present, and forthcoming futures.*

—Simon Bréan

Est-ce qu'on peut être fière d'avoir envie de rêver?

*Could we be proud to want to dream?*

—Sabrina Calvo

Oui ! *Yes!*

# CONTENTS

# INTRODUCTION

*by* Annabelle Dolidon and Tessa Sermet

## WHY THIS ANTHOLOGY?

THERE ARE TWO COMMON REACTIONS when talking about French science fiction in the Anglo-American context: it starts with someone saying "oh, I didn't know there were French science fiction writers besides Jules Verne"; and this statement is most likely followed by the question, "then how is French science fiction *different* from other types of science fiction?" The first comment says more about how globalization affects the publishing world than anything else; indeed, very little fiction originally written in foreign languages gets translated into English, science fiction or otherwise. The dominance of Anglo-American science fiction and the saturation of Hollywood mainstream science fiction franchises (Marvel, DC, Star Wars) falsely gives the impression that *this* is what science fiction is, and pushes everything else towards categorization such as "global" or "world" literature.[1] Nonetheless, France has a long tradition of science fiction, from Voltaire's philosophical tale, *Micromégas* (1752), to Jules Verne's *Extraordinary Voyages* (1863–1905) and beyond. For example, did you know that the very first science fiction film, *A Trip to the Moon* (1902), was written, produced, and directed by Georges Méliès, a French magician converted film director? Or that the *Planet of the Apes* movies are adapted from the novel with the same name written

---

1    We refer you to Istvan Csicsery-Ronay's article "What do we mean when we say 'Global Science Fiction'? Reflexion on a new nexus." *Science Fiction Studies,* vol. 39 (3), Nov. 2012, pp. 478–493.

by French author Pierre Boulle in 1963? With this anthology, we aim to show you how this tradition is continued by many authors to this day.

The second question, "How is French science fiction different from science fiction written elsewhere, especially science fiction written in English in the US?" requires a more nuanced response. As Ken Liu stated about Chinese science fiction,[2] it is difficult to give a neat answer to this question because, as is the case for American (and Chinese) science fiction, French authors have different styles and interests. Moreover, science fiction is a literary genre marked by common tropes across cultures and languages, such as cities under domes, rebellious robots, climate catastrophe, or faster-than-light space travel, that you will find in all national productions. There is still a dose of "Frenchness" in the texts in this anthology and the best way for you to experience French "sensibility" in science fiction is perhaps to start with the stories in this book, and to discuss them with fellow readers.

This is not the first collection of French science fiction short stories in English translation, but you will be hard pressed to find the others unless you turn to eBay or used bookstores. You will find a few French science fiction short stories in anthologies such as *The SFWA European Hall of Fame* edited by James and Kathryn Morrow (2008) or *The Big Book of Science Fiction* edited by Jeff and Ann VanderMeer (2016), including stories by Jean-Claude Dunyach, also represented in this anthology. However, the last anthologies entirely dedicated to French science fiction were published in the 1960s and 1970s: *13 French Science-Fiction Stories* edited by Damon Knight (1965 and 1972) and *Travelling Towards Epsilon: An Anthology of French Science Fiction* edited by Maxim Jakubowski, (1976). In the latter, Jakubowski starts his introduction with these words: "Science fiction does exist outside Britain and America! Not a surprising claim in itself, but one the average reader has, in the past, had little chance to check out."[3] Have

---

2  Ken Liu. n.d. "China Dreams: Contemporary Chinese Science Fiction." Clarkesworld Magazine. Accessed June 1, 2021. https://clarkesworldmagazine.com/liu_12_14/.

3  Maxim Jakubowski. *Travelling Towards Epsilon: An Anthology of French Science Fiction.* London, England: New English Library, 1976. p 9.

12 • CONTINUUM

things changed since then? A few contemporary French authors have published short stories in English in science fiction magazines here and there. Jean-Claude Dunyach, mentioned above, has published collections. Yet, most stories are either difficult to trace or just not on the radar of many readers who are not die-hard fans.

It is important to note that not all the stories in this anthology were written by authors from France, so when we say "French," we mean in the French language. Jacques Sternberg was Belgian and Laurence Suhner is Swiss, but they write in French and share the same readership of Western Europe as French nationals. Of course, many writers write and publish in French in other Francophone countries; but, apart from Quebec, science fiction isn't as popular there as it is in Europe. As author Nalo Hopkinson lamented in an interview talking about English-language science fiction back in 2011, there is (still) a "relative lack of voices of color and postcolonial voices in science fiction."[4] This is also the case in the French Caribbean and French-speaking African countries. This absence is unfortunate because many authors there publish wonderful and successful novels and short stories, just not in the science fiction genre. In the end, selecting nine science fiction stories was difficult enough, and we found it more meaningful and relevant to stay within the European borders—which doesn't preclude a later *Continuum: Francophone Science Fiction Short Stories*!

## A (VERY) SHORT HISTORY OF FRENCH SCIENCE FICTION

In 1516, Thomas More wrote *Utopia*, subtitled "A little, true book, not less beneficial than enjoyable, about how things should be in a state and about the new island Utopia." More placed his story in Utopia, a place where everything is perfect and a place that doesn't exist, to criticize contemporary England. More's novel, alongside the discovery of "new" lands and popular travel narratives written by colonists and missionaries, gave birth to a new genre: extraordinary

---

4 Jessica Langer. *Postcolonialism and Science Fiction*. New York, NY: Palgrave Macmillan, 2011.

travels. For centuries in France, authors privileged travels to mysterious, unknown lands and the discovery of strange places and people. They created utopian societies, imaginary or programmatic, to better comment on their times, criticize them, and sometimes suggest alternatives. Thus, maybe the history of French science fiction started in the seventeenth century when poet-soldier Savinien de Cyrano de Bergerac, surfing the utopian wave, described life on the moon and the sun to satirize the religious and astronomical beliefs of his time. Or maybe it started in 1771, when Louis-Sébastien Mercier wrote *The Year 2440* (*L'An 2440. Rêve s'il en fut jamais*). Shaped by the philosophy of the Enlightenment, this utopia takes place not in a faraway land but in the future. Mercier's utopia is considered one of the first novels of *Anticipation*, a term often used to describe early French science fiction.

Origins might not be clearly defined, but French science fiction gained momentum in the nineteenth century with the *Extraordinary Voyages* of Jules Verne (1828–1905), probably the French science fiction author most famous outside of France. In the nineteenth century, technological advances ignited other narratives around disease, machinery, or extraterrestrial life. The mid-century saw the rise of socialism and dreams of a new society based on the collective good. Jules Verne's entire work is strongly marked by positivism,[5] with the exception of "The Eternal Adam" (1910), a posthumous short story that might have been co-written by his son Michel Verne. But if Verne is the most famous, there are other French authors publishing at the turn of the century and beyond, such as J.-H. Rosny aîné (1856–1940) whose 1887 novel, *Les Xipéhuz,* is considered one of the first novels of the *merveilleux scientifique* genre, another term for early science fiction. The short story "The Horla" (1887) by Guy de Maupassant (available in English) encompassed many of the fears born out of knowing more about the world, and thus facing the fact that there was, and is, much we don't know. Maupassant was influenced by

---

5  At the end of the nineteenth century, in the sciences, positivism refers to a methodology that rests on what can be "positively" observed, quantified, measured, and verified. Positivism is anchored in a strong belief in human progress and in a future when all questions can be answered through the positivist method.

hypnosis techniques, advances in astronomy, and Darwin's theory of evolution. During this era of positivism and great faith in the progress of technology and human civilization (before it all collapsed with WWI), this story stood out. It is usually categorized as a *conte fantastique* or a horror story rather than a science fiction story, but it is a good representation of the tropes that science fiction was privileging at the time.

At the turn of the century, France's intellectual, political, and scientific communities were, for the most part, seduced by the optimistic promises of positivism and industrial expansion. This seemingly contradictory atmosphere of capitalist (and colonial) expansion and aspirations of *vivre ensemble* (living together) found its way into socialist utopias as well as dystopic tales of machines gone mad, which retrospectively foreshadowed the monstrous weapons that killed millions in WWI and again in WWII. The collective imagination that gets expressed in these stories shows great optimism next to a real concern for the ways in which "progress" is accelerating and profoundly changing society, not just in France but globally. Distances shrunk with new modes of transportation. Periodicals, catalogs, and department stores introduced people to a world of local and exotic manufactured artifacts never seen before. The cinematograph made objects move on two-dimensional planes that people couldn't touch.[6] Freud discovered the unconscious. A law by Jules Ferry made school mandatory in France for children who then did not have to work before they turned twelve. French people generally believed that humanity was on a linear path to better days, to a higher civilization, while remaining oblivious to the terrible misuse of science for many at home and abroad.

These ways of relating to a determinate world changed with the onset of WWI and its display of violence on a global scale, crushing optimism, fragmenting time, and demonstrating the terrible destructive capability of a different kind of collective "us." As Natacha Vas-Deyre puts it, "The First World War will disrupt the materialization of the imaginary, of progress rendered dynamic by utopian

---

6  Again, check *Journey to the Moon* by Georges Méliès; it is available on YouTube and only fifteen minutes long!

literature, and give a terrible blow to this optimistic ideology."[7] The authors of early science fiction or *merveilleux scientifique* became pessimistic; utopia was abandoned. According to Natacha Vas-Deyre, authors even turned away from science fiction altogether as science became not a source of knowledge but of doubt and fear, and it was in the United States that science fiction fully developed.[8] In 1926, Hugo Gernsback[9] founded the first magazine dedicated to science fiction, *Amazing Stories*. The first issue contained texts from Edgar Allan Poe and H. G. Wells, but also Jules Verne.

Jumping ahead, the 1950s marked the start of several collections of science fiction in France, including Anticipation novels and short-story collections at several large Parisian publishers like Gallimard and Denoël. Magazines like *Fiction* and *Galaxies*, modeled after American publications, were launched. Space travel and extraterrestrial encounters were popular themes, but some stories (as you will see when you read "The Bubbles" and "So Far From Home" included in this collection) still stand out for their ability to question modernity as well as entertain. The world wasn't the same after Hiroshima and the contemporary philosophical and social movements of the 1950s and 1960s (the philosophy of existentialism, the rise of consumer society, the feminist movement, and decolonization to name a few). These developments became a new source of inspiration for authors who questioned (again) the use of technology to trap, kill, or destroy the planet, rather than to improve people's lives. Yet, science fascinated.

One important author, despite his conservative views (an after-the-fact yet accurate reading of his overall oeuvre), made many young French readers dream of the future starting in the 1940s: René Barjavel (1911–1985). His main novels have been translated, *Ravage* published in 1943 and translated as *Ashes, Ashes* in 1967; *Le Voyageur imprudent* (1944) translated as *Future Times Three* (1958); and *La Nuit des temps* (1968) translated as *The Ice People* (1971). Used copies

---

7  Vas Deyre, Natacha. *Ces Français qui ont écrit demain: utopie, anticipation et science-fiction au XXe siècle*. Champion, 2012, 34. (*These French who wrote tomorrow*—Our translation.)
8  Vas-Deyre, 126, 132.
9  Gernsback also coined the term "science fiction," saying that the stories in the magazine were "75 percent literature interwoven with 25 percent science."

of the English translations are available but not affordably. While *Ravage* is set in a hetero-patriarchal France imbued with Pétainist[10] ideology of returning to the soil and raising large families, and against modern technology (a unilateral means for humans to destroy and be lazy), his later work remained fascinated by the infinite possibilities of time travel (such as the famous science fiction trope of the grandfather paradox) and rebirth after apocalyptic upheavals.

French science fiction cannot be reduced to one trend or vision: While Barjavel is still famous nowadays (you can find his books in almost any French bookstore and *Ravage* is taught in French schools today), various authors published science fiction from the 1940s and 1950s onward, such as Robert Merle, Jacques Spitz, Julia Verlanger, Régis Messac, and Maurice Renard, to name a few. Francis Carsac (1919–1981) excelled at both delighting and writing intelligent science fiction that responded to his time's question of how to better live together, much like Isaac Asimov or Arthur C. Clarke. His excellent, ageless novel *Pour patrie l'espace* (1962) is now available in English translation as *The City Among the Stars* (2020).

Science fiction in France kept expanding in the following decades and increasingly turned to social issues and climate concerns, but also embraced the new world of social media, avatars, and virtual reality. In the 1970s, new collections were launched. Authors stayed attentive to what was happening to US science fiction, carried by a wave of popular sci-fi films, but kept on their own trajectory. Major early names in science fiction prose to keep in mind (whose texts are not present in this collection) are Jean-Pierre Andrevon, Philippe Curval, Michel Demuth, Charles Henneberg, Nathalie Henneberg, Michel Jeury, Gérard Klein. More recent authors include Pierre Bordage, Catherine Dufour, Jean-Marc Ligny, and a pleiad of exciting young authors. Like Anglo-American science fiction, French science fiction has been heavily dominated by male authors, but an increasing number of female science fiction authors publish with the large and small specialized presses that now exist and thrive in and outside Paris. Women have been writing great science fiction for a long time

---

10  This term refers to the political philosophy associated with the Marshal Philippe Pétain, who served as head of the collaborationist regime of Vichy France during WWII.

(see stories by Julia Verlanger and Colette Fayard in this collection). Still, there is more to do to make these authors better known to the younger generation of readers, even in France.

It is important to note the parallel development of comics (*bande dessinées*) that also have much to offer in terms of science fiction. The adult-focused magazine *Métal Hurlant*, co-founded by artist Jean Giraud/Gir/Moebius in 1974, focused on science fiction, fantasy, and horror. Comics have come out of the silo of children's literature the way science fiction is about to become a "respectable" literary genre— we're almost there. The first tome of the comic series *Snowpiercer* by Jacques Lob and Jean-Marc Rochette was released in 1982. Since then, five other volumes, a film adaptation by Bong Joon-ho (2013), and a TV show (2020) have enriched the *Snowpiercer* universe and showed that French science fiction is popular beyond French borders. Today, comics are a good medium for English readers to discover French science fiction because many comic albums are translated—and available in US public libraries—while prose science fiction literature still is not. There are too many French comics available in English to give an exhaustive list, but look up collaborative albums for which author Serge Lehman wrote scenarios or, more recently, all the graphic novels by Mathieu Bablet. Another format in which French artists are very present, yet perhaps inconspicuously so, is video games. The yearly festival *Les Utopiales* always features a video game pole for visitors to experience the multiple universes created by French (and others) game designers. Some authors, like Sabrina Calvo (whose French prose is just gorgeous), are also game designers. If you wish to keep track of current publications in French, check out the selection of new works in competition at the *Utopiales* each year or follow *Bifrost*, a quarterly publication that publishes book reviews. For general information, a great database is *nooSFere.org*.

## THE STORIES

In French, a short story is called *une nouvelle*. It is a genre that designates a narrative shorter than a novel, but it is not its only specificity. The constraints of brevity lead authors to take a different path to tell a story that relies on a particular attention to detail and to language.

Each paragraph in a short story is carefully crafted as only the essential must be said. Often—but not always—a *nouvelle* focuses on an anecdote, a moment, a tipping point in the life of one character or a small group of characters. The short story is by nature an invitation to the reader to fill in the blanks, to jump over the ellipses that necessarily punctuate the text. In this regard, short stories are cognitively close to comics and short graphic novels whose readers must also (re)construct the unsaid, signaled notably by the gutter (the space between two panels). We hope the nine stories presented in this collection will both entertain and challenge you and that they will prompt you to start a conversation about the themes they explore and the questions they raise. Each story is followed by a short text titled "Expansion" about the author and the story to offer further insight into what you have read, and by "Discussion Questions" to ponder alone or in a group. These stories are unique and, as a collection, will introduce you to the breadth of ways in which French science fiction intrigues, amuses, estranges, and challenges readers to look at the future from a critical standpoint on the present. Here is a snapshot of the stories—we don't want to tell you too much.

"The Bubbles" (1956) by Julia Verlanger rings a bell in the wake of COVID-19 and the lockdown we went through, whose effects are still palpable. Unknown diseases and war certainly have not gone away in our time and the story still reads well. Told from the point of view of a sixteen-year-old confined in her house, the narrative evokes the fears that lingered in the post-WWII decades but also demands answers that may or may not be given at the end. It is left to the reader to fill in these blanks.

"So Far From Home" (1957) by Jacques Sternberg takes a different approach to the 1950s than Verlanger and a more philosophical tone. It is the longest text in the collection, and its length mirrors its content to make us feel, like its extraterrestrial agent that landed on Earth and blended into the population, the slow descent into existentialist void. Otherness leads to alienation; for the reader, this story might even feel like a wake-up call.

"That Which is Not Named" (1985) by Roland C. Wagner takes you on a journey into the power and complexities of language. A young man is chosen to become the future guardian of his people's language. However, his role won't be to preserve it but to reduce it to the point where reality and dangers disappear. Does that which is not named exist? Can that which is named be *reduced* to that name? Who decides?

"The Liberator" (1989) by Colette Fayard is one of the most bizarre of the stories presented here. Reminiscent of Maupassant's frightening tale "The Horla," it holds some uncanny and some disturbing moments that will only be explained at the very end, if one can consider the ending an *explanation*. Is the narrator crazy despite his constant recourse to science? If you imagine life out there, what shape do you think it takes? How far do you think fascination for what you don't understand can take you? Content warning and spoiler alert: this story evokes an adult-minor relationship. However, it turns out the minor is not a human being; it is an alien that took on a human appearance to trick the narrator.

"Nowhere in Liverion" (1996) by Serge Lehman offers a twist on the classic *Utopia* by Thomas More by merging history with a future world engulfed in virtual reality. When everything is data and simulacrum, the battleground moves from Earth to geo-satellites. The power of utopias does not reside only in their possible existence on a different plane of truth but in the resisting force they represent in a monolithic society run by faceless regimes and corporations. Read this story to know if the place is real, but then again, which reality are we talking about?

"Inside, Outside" (1999) by Sylvie Denis picks up where you left off with Lehman's utopia and takes you to a different kind of dreamland, one that exists, but not one the main protagonist cares to emulate. In this cult-driven, surveillance-obsessed, dystopian enclave of modern comfort, brainwashed children perpetuate their community's ideals. The heroine, of course, knows better and wants to get out. The premise might seem familiar but Denis's original take on some science fiction tropes might surprise you.

"The Swing of Your Gait" (2009) by Sylvie Lainé explores how a man overcomes losing his girlfriend in a pure science-fictive universe. The main character lost the woman he loves and seeks to *know* her through technology. You will be charmed by this story that mixes gravity and humor. Like other stories in the collection, the use of technology is never devoid of ambiguity but Lainé, a very talented *nouvelliste*, never takes our eyes off the characters and what they are going through. What we might take for a tale of transformation is in fact a story of love for the other and the self.

"Beyond the Terminator" (2017) by Laurence Suhner takes us far, far away, to another planet, but it is not a classic tale of colonization or terraformation. New encounters are recast in twenty-first century reconsiderations of human-animal relations. Suhner, a Swiss author and graphic designer, writes in parallel with the scientific discoveries of her time, whether it is the identification of new celestial bodies or the explosions generated in the Large Hadron Collider. With this short story, she takes off from astrophysics findings to craft a tale about encountering beauty, and the need to respect what we do not know.

"The City, That Night" (2019) by Jean-Claude Dunyach renders a gothic-like atmospheric world in which characters seem to silently glide. Is this *fantastique*?[11] The short story diffuses an ambience that evokes vampire stories and builds upon a boy's need to belong. Is it science fiction? Yes, read carefully. Dunyach is a versatile master writer who has published a lot, including texts available in English translation (a new collection of translated short stories is forthcoming as we write this introduction). This story is unique and weird—a little twist to end *Continuum: French Science Fiction Short Stories* on an overarching question: what is science fiction?

Many articles and books by science fiction scholars propose definitions of the genre of science fiction: it is a literature of wonder and estrangement; it often revolves around a *novum*, an element that marks a story as science fiction through the introduction of a technological device or another narrative element that oversees the internal logic of the story. Our favorite approach is that of Istvan Csicsery-Ronay Jr. who wrote *The Seven Beauties of Science Fiction*: it is "a kind of awareness, a mode of response".[12] Science fiction raises

---

11    The term *fantastique* refers to the intrusion of the supranatural into the realistic frame of a story. It is often used to describes the works of Edgar Allan Poe and nineteenth century French writers such as Guy Maupassant, Théophile Gautier, or Villiers de l'Isle-Adam (all found in translation).

12    *The Seven Beauties of Science Fiction*. Wesleyan University Press, 2008, pg. 2

fundamental questions about how we use new technology, how we treat others, how we relate to our own body, how we build community, and how we care or not for our planet *through* creative fiction. These fictional worlds cannot but reflect our reality and, more importantly, our perception and interpretation of what reality is—what we love and what we hate about it, what we hope and what we fear about it. Through the fictional detours of space travel, post-apocalyptic upheaval, authoritarian regimes, and the overall confrontation with the unknown, science fiction helps us make sense of our social and physical environment. Science fiction makes you think. It enchants and gets you out of your skin so you can experiment with other ways of living, working, loving, and thinking. As a species, we have traced the origins of humankind back thousands of years ago and imagined, as well as researched, how people have lived, organized, and believed through the ages. Why not explore what we will become one hundred years, ten thousand years from now? Shouldn't we at least question who we *want* to be, what trajectory humanity might follow? Science fiction does that. Back and forth between adventure and activism, exaltation and fear, in between the elusive limits of this large historical and thematic arch, French science fiction has proven to be, and remains, a dynamic and inquisitive literary genre.

The nine stories you are about to read form an eclectic corpus across time (from the 1950s until recently) and topics (aliens, oppressive regimes, technology, (anti)speciesism...). They were chosen carefully to provide a range of themes, questions, and approaches to the issues French-language authors are interested in. With this new anthology, we wish to (re)introduce readers, especially those who don't usually read science fiction, to an array of stories that address different important themes in the field of science fiction in France in the hope that more translations will be available in the future. It is a first, modest, yet important step to open the door to a more explicit dialogue between productions of global science fiction in different languages, beyond the circle of the insiders; an extended hand to invite you to seek more, read more, connect more with the fabulous conversations that science fiction allows.

# The Bubbles

*by* Julia Verlanger

*translated by* Tessa Sermet

## AUGUST 8

TODAY, I SAW THE OTHER AGAIN. She was waving her long arms in front of the window, and she talked, talked. Her mouth moved non-stop, but I didn't hear anything. Of course, we cannot hear anything behind the window. Then she pressed all her arms on the glass, she pushed. I got scared, I pressed the button, and the shutters slammed shut. Yet I know she can't enter. No one can enter.

Father used to say that in the past, long, long ago, window glass could break. I cannot believe it, but Father knew. He used to say that we were very lucky the bubbles arrived during our time because, in the old days, everyone would have died. The houses weren't like nowadays, and there were no servants. No one would have been safe from the bubbles.

It is Father who said I should write when I was older. He used to say, "One has to write for the future." Because, one day, we would find a way to fight the bubbles, and everything would be back the way it was. He used to say: "One will have to know what happened during the years of the bubbles. That is why you need to write, Monica, when you're older, when I'm not here anymore." My father probably didn't think he'd be gone so early. Oh! If only he hadn't gone outside, if only he hadn't gone outside!

He used to say: when I'm older. I'm sixteen today, so I think I'm old enough and I started writing this morning.

As for him, Father did write a lot. He wrote the whole story of the bubbles, how the world was before. Me, I didn't get to know this world, I only know what Father told me. I was born just after the bubbles arrived.

According to Father, a lot of people died at first, many, many people, until they understood we couldn't fight against the bubbles, and the only way not to die or to become an Other was not to go outside.

As for him, Father understood right away, and that is why we were saved. He used to say that before, it wouldn't have been possible not to go outside, people would have starved to death. Because meat tanks and indoor gardening systems didn't exist, neither did servants to take care of everything. He told me that in the old days, people had to do everything by themselves, plant vegetables in the dirt, and breed cattle, for the meat.

It was funny, I didn't know what "cattle" was. So, Father explained it to me, and showed me pictures in the old books. These things are so weird! I could barely believe all this existed.

## AUGUST 9

This morning, I went to the library to look at the old books, but there's a lot I don't understand now that Father isn't here to explain things to me.

As it happens, I saw an image that looked very much like the Other that came to the window yesterday, with all her wiggling arms. The goddess Kali, the picture indicated. Were there already Others, back in the old days? But Father used to say that there weren't, that it was because of the bubbles that people became Others. Before, there were none.

I cannot stand the Others. They make me shiver, especially when they come close to the window, like the one yesterday did. She comes often, this one. It looks like she wants to tell me something, her mouth moving nonstop.

Father used to say: "It's strange, we're a lot more scared of the Others, who aren't very dangerous, than of the bubbles. I suppose it's because the Others outrage us and make our skin crawl, while the bubbles have some sort of perfect beauty." It's true, they're quite pretty, the bubbles. I often watch them floating outside. They shine gently, streaked with colors, looking like the soap bubbles I used to make for fun, when I was little. But they are much bigger, and harder, so hard that nothing can destroy them.

But they break on humans, who then die.

I saw it, once, when Father was still here. A man. He was running as fast as he could, his mouth wide open. He must have been screaming, but we couldn't hear anything. And an enormous bubble sliding behind him. Fast, so fast. It caught him, and she broke right on his head. He was entirely covered in this iridescent slime.

I started shouting, and Father came running and pressed my face against him. He said: "Don't look, don't be scared, honey." He held me very tightly, and when he let me go and I looked again, there was nothing outside anymore, only a large shiny puddle of the bubbles' blended color.

Father said: "He is dead, poor man, he was instantly dissolved. And that is better for him than becoming an Other." Of course, Father was always right, but I do wonder if it is really better to die than to become an Other, because I'm quite sure I really wouldn't want to die.

But the Others are so horrifying!

## AUGUST 15

The nanny circled around me the whole morning. She kept asking if I needed something. She gets on my nerves, oh! How she gets on my nerves sometimes. I sent her to the vegetable garden, and when she came back, I chased her away from the room.

If only Father was still here! I've been alone for three years now. I know it because I still mark down the days, like Father used to do. Sometimes we would say that he himself didn't really know why he kept doing it. He thought it was because we keep clinging to the past. But me, I don't know the past. I do it because Father did it, and it seems that it's almost like he never really left.

I've always known the world as it is, with the bubbles, and the empty street where no one ever walks besides the Others.

Father told me so much about the world from before that I'd like it to come back. To be able to go out and see people who aren't Others. Father used to say that outside the city, there is the country, where everything is green, with grass and trees and flowers and animals, too, in the reserves.

I saw the pictures, in the old books and on our screen, but Father used to say that it wasn't the same. He would talk about how marvelous it was to feel the sun on one's skin, or the rain. I often see the rain dripping on the windowpanes, but I wonder how it would drip on the skin. And apparently there is the sea, big stretches of water, and salted. And people used to swim in it, like me in the caves' swimming pool. I think I'd like to swim in the sea.

Father thought I'd see the world from before, maybe not him, but me, I would. Apparently, there are a lot of people trying to find a way to kill the bubbles. Father thought that there was no way they wouldn't succeed, one day. But it's been a very long time since I've been waiting, and there is still nothing other than today's world, with only bubbles and Others outside, and me inside.

I'm bored, and I miss Father terribly. I only wish he were still here. There are the servants, and the nanny, but they get on my nerves so much, sometimes. Of course, they're not humans. Father called them machines, a weird word. He would say that before there weren't servants. Those we called servants, then, were humans who worked for the Others.

It seems weird, but Father always knew everything. He had read all the old books, and he could talk about the old world for hours. I try to read them nowadays, but there are so many things I don't understand. What does it mean, for example, "to be in love," or "to take the metro"? Oh! Father should be here to explain all this to me.

## AUGUST 23

I went into Mother's room. I opened the wardrobe; it smelled vaguely like perfume. At first, I didn't dare touch anything. It seemed that Mother was going to arrive behind me and look at me with her empty eyes. I was scared. Then, I became more daring, I took one of her dresses. It was soft under my fingers, and all green, like the big stones in her jewelry box.

I put it on. I must have grown a lot because it fit me well. I looked at myself in the mirror. It was pretty. The dress's green color made my eyes sparkle like my mother's stones.

I think I must be beautiful, because I look a lot like Mother, and Father used to say that Mother was beautiful. He also said our hair was like a wheat field in the summer sun. I don't know what it is, a wheat field in a summer sun, but Father looked like he was dreaming when he said it, so I'm guessing it's pretty.

My hair is very long, I can use it as a coat. It seems that, in the old days, women sometimes cut theirs under the ears, like Father. What a funny idea, to want to look like Father! Because Mother was a lot prettier. But I liked Father a lot more, oh I did!

Mother scared me a little. She had this habit of staring at you without seeing you, with eyes turned to the inside. She never took care of me; she didn't even speak to me. Sometimes, she would start crying for hours, then she would run to the door, and pound it with her fists while screaming: "I want to go outside, I want to go outside, let me go outside!" Father would then hold her against himself, and talk to her, nicely: "shush, honey, be patient, my sweetheart." Father loved her a lot and it was for her that he went outside. I know I shouldn't say this, Father wouldn't have liked it, but he shouldn't have! He shouldn't have!

Once, I was mean. Father was comforting her, and I said: "Let her go! You see that she doesn't understand anything!" Then Father looked at me, sad, and later talked to me for a long time. "You shouldn't hate your mother, my little girl, it's not her fault if she is like this . . . Yes, I know, she doesn't take care of you, and she doesn't have any interest in anyone, but she wasn't like this before the bubbles. Her mind didn't resist what happened to us. She lives in an imaginary world and refuses to see reality. But she is the way she is, and you must not hate her, Monica, you should pity her . . . If anything were to happen to me, you'll have to take care of her, as if she were the little girl, and not you. You do know that she sometimes wants to go outside, and we can't let that happen, she doesn't know what she's doing . . . Promise me to be good to your mother, to watch over her if I'm not here. Promise me, Monica." He seemed so sad, and so unhappy. But I couldn't keep my promise.

She died when he went outside.

# AUGUST 26

Today, it is raining.

This morning, I went to the window, and there were lots of drops falling on the street. I wondered what it would do to my skin, and I wanted to open the window. But we can't. Father explained to me that he blocked all the exits. To open anything, I would need to go deep in the caves, behind the tank room, and the vegetable gardens, and close the circuit breaker.

He had shown me how to do it, he said that it was for when liberation would happen, in case he wasn't with me anymore. He had blocked everything to avoid the temptation of opening it up, exactly like me this morning, and for Mother who always wanted to go outside. But he closed the breaker when he went outside, and I went to open it back up a few days later.

Because it looked to me like everything he had said was right and that I would have loved for this circuit breaker to be completely defective, that way Father wouldn't have been able to leave. I've never closed it since. And it's much better this way, because when I want to open the window, like this morning, I can't; and by the time I'd get to the circuit breaker, I would remember that I might die if I moved it, or become an Other, and I'm very scared of both.

I went to the swimming pool in the caves because I was bored at the window. I remembered that Father had said that, if the bubbles had come in days past, there wouldn't have been any water, or light, because there weren't any servants to make all of it work. It was humans who did all that. Then the bubbles would have killed them, and nothing would have worked anymore. Meanwhile, of course, the bubbles can't hurt the servants, and they are built to last a very long time. Father even used to say that if humanity were to entirely disappear, servants would keep making everything work for centuries on.

He would explain that, for example, if I grew very old and died, the nanny would stay there, waiting. Almost for eternity. Because the nanny was synchronized with me. She protects me all the time and does what I ask her to. She must guard me from any harm. If the bubbles were to enter, she would try to remove them and save me. But she wouldn't be able to do so for very long, poor thing, because there are so many and they always reach their goal, which is to kill us.

# SEPTEMBER 1

It's funny, no one knows where the bubbles come from, or why some die, and some don't but become Others.

I've heard an old man, once, on TV. It was the day after Father went outside.

From time to time, Father turned the TV on, but the screen was always black. He told me to keep trying to make it work, if he wasn't there anymore. He used to say he was sure there were survivors, and that someone must have been trying to find a way to kill the bubbles. He used to say that if liberation was close, the TV would announce it.

Father explained that until now, nothing could destroy the bubbles. Not even a flamethrower, and that was a very, very powerful weapon. Apparently, we had tried everything, at first, but the bubbles were resistant to it all. They'd break only on humans, who would die. And when they didn't die, it was worse. They became Others. The Others transformed. Instead of being dissolved by the bubbles' slime, after a while they get up, and initially they look like nothing happened. But, after a few days, they start growing stuff! Multiple arms, like the woman who looks like that old book's goddess, or a bunch of legs, or eyes everywhere, or two heads, or a series of mouths on the neck and the chest. It's horrible!

The old man I heard on TV was, as it happens, talking about the bubbles and the Others. The TV had been all black for days and days, and suddenly the screen turned on. This old man was sitting at a table, in a big white room. He looked very tired. The room was full of servants, but much more complex ones than those in my house, with a lot of buttons and little lights.

I was happy to listen to him. His voice was warm, a little bit like Father's. I felt less lonely.

He was talking about battles and hope and waiting. One mustn't lose courage. The day would come when the bubbles would be defeated. I didn't understand all he was saying, there were very complicated words, but I listened until the end. He looked nice, that old man, but so tired. Yet, when he'd say "courage," his voice would be warm and young again.

He explained that it would take a long time because no one knew where the bubbles had come from, or what they were made of. We couldn't understand the phenomenon that transformed the humans into Others or killed them. We had tried everything against the bubbles, everything we knew, but nothing could destroy them. Many men had given their lives in this fight, and many still would. Even a few Others had offered their help because they hated what they had become. They could go outside with impunity, which in many cases made them very useful. We needed to thank them for fighting with us.

The old man also said that some believed the bubbles were formed over a long period of time, maybe centuries, before appearing in this era. That we might be paying for our ancestors' mistakes, as they had scaled up atomic experiments and undiscerningly played with forces they knew so poorly. That we might be victims of their stupidity because they used only for killing what was meant to give to future eras a pleasant life. They'd released radioactivity into the world, in that time, and some thought the bubbles had slowly been born from that. As for him, he tended to agree.

But the fight was still going on, and since we had used all the current knowledge without any success, we were now going to use the old sciences again and try to find a solution.

Then he said that broadcasting took a lot of time and money that would be better spent on the fight against the bubbles, so he would rarely talk to us, only to keep us updated with potential progress. And he repeated not to lose hope. And the screen became black once more.

I often think about this old man. I've never heard of him, or anyone else. The TV doesn't turn on anymore. I wonder if he was right, and if the old world will come back. I'd like that.

## SEPTEMBER 5

The Other, from the window, came back. It's strange, with time she horrifies me less. Besides, she isn't that hideous, despite all her arms. It isn't like those with many eyes, or a bunch of mouths, or noses everywhere.

I actually pity her. Today she really seemed to want to tell me something. She was holding a tiny baby, folded in her arm, and she kept showing him to me. She was shaking and moving a lot, her long black hair flying in all directions.

In the end, she tried to hand me the baby. It looked like she wanted me to take him. It was weird, the baby didn't seem transformed at all. He was very cute, exactly like my toy-babies. Suddenly, she undressed him, and showed him to me once more. I could see there weren't any transformations—he was completely normal. Chubby, pudgy, he was waving his little legs. He had his mouth open; he mustn't have been happy to be undressed like that, this little one.

I didn't want to close the shutters. I signaled to her to leave, but she stayed there. She was crying. I could see tears on her face, and she kept showing me the baby. It really looked like she wanted me to take him. What a fool! As if I were going to open and let the bubbles come in! And yet, there were no bubbles at all in the street at the moment. I motioned to her to leave, and as she wasn't moving anymore, I left the window.

I haven't been able to stop thinking about it since. It upset me how distraught that Other looked. I couldn't truly take this baby, raise a little Other. Besides, I wouldn't know how to raise a baby. I've only known toy-babies, and Father had told me babies don't eat like we do. Maybe the nanny would know? But I'm crazy. Father would be furious if he knew. To open! To an Other! And to take in a little Other! I shouldn't think about this any longer.

Yet, the fact that this baby didn't have any transformations was strange. Maybe he was too little? But transformation doesn't usually take time when one is outside and doesn't die. Maybe he was only a few days old? But he looked so much like my toy-babies, and Father had told me they were like a two-year-old little human. I wonder why this Other wanted to give him to me. Maybe to save him from the bubbles, and she wanted to save him before he'd become an Other? But you can't stay safe from the bubbles. No one can.

## SEPTEMBER 7

I was scared, so, so scared. My belly was hurting, and I thought I was going to die like Mother did. I screamed, and the nanny came running.

She palpated my belly and then reprimanded me and said I didn't have anything wrong; I was simply eating too many apples. It's true, but I really like apples. She gave me a pill and my pain stopped right away. The nanny can heal almost everything.

Father also always knew what to take when not feeling well. But not for what Mother had. He couldn't do anything for her, and neither could the nanny.

This is why he went outside, to find a doctor. He said calling on the phone was pointless because no one would agree to go outside. But he took a flamethrower and said he would bring a doctor back no matter what.

It was foolish because of the bubbles, yet he left all the same. He couldn't stand hearing Mother screaming while holding her belly. He loved her so much. I think it made him crazy because he knew there was no point in going outside.

He gave Mother an injection, to me as well to make me sleep, and he left. I know very well that I shouldn't think this way, but it would have been better to let her die; he never came back, and she died anyways. It was the nanny who woke me up and told me. The servants had already removed her body, and Father wasn't there anymore.

It caused me so much grief that I couldn't stop crying, and the nanny had to force me to eat. He should have let her die, yes. He should have. See! Where would he have found a doctor? And even if he had found one, I'm sure the doctor would rather have been burnt than face the bubbles.

Sometimes, I wonder if Father got dissolved, or if . . . I wonder if he's still outside, with a bunch of arms or legs, or if all his hair fell out and a bunch of eyes grew on his skull, or if . . . but I don't want to think about it. I do not want to. I'd rather think that Father is dead.

And yet . . . if he came back one day, to the window, like the goddess Kali? What would I do? Oh! Father, what would I do?

## SEPTEMBER 10

The phone rang the whole day, but I didn't answer.

When Father was still here, he'd always answer, and sometimes, he would call himself. He used to say that it wasn't good to live without human contact, so he'd look for survivors. Only, so many people had died at the beginning of the bubbles' time, that he could almost never find any. The Others had broken into plenty of houses, and besides, entire families had been transformed; so it was Others we would always see on the telephone screen. And they were mean, Father always had to end the call.

I remember that the old man from the TV said a few Others were helping us against the bubbles. That really surprised me because Father used to say the Others hated humans. Father thought that it was because they were so different from us, and that they hated us because we were normal.

In the early days after Father's departure, I would still answer the phone, but it was always Others showing off their arms or multiple eyes on the screen. And they would insult me or invite me to go outside and join them. They scared me.

And then one time, a human appeared on the screen. A woman.

At that time, I already almost never answered the phone, but the bell rang so long and was so insistent that I wanted to know.

The woman on the screen was old, and her eyes looked absolutely crazy. Her hair, of a nasty, dirty grey, dangled in her face, and she was wringing her knotted hands. She started talking in a rush the second that she saw me:

"I beg you, sweetie, do you know where I could find a doctor? Please, I absolutely need to find a doctor. I'm calling everywhere, nonstop. Help me, honey, I need someone to help me. My husband is very sick. He's going to die. He's going to die, and I'll be left alone. Please, help me."

She was crying. Then she moved aside, and I saw an old man lying on a couch at the back of the room. His face was all swollen up and burning with fever, and his breathing was jerky, painful, like he couldn't breathe anymore.

The woman came back to the screen.

"You saw? He's going to die, he's gonna die, he's gonna die."

Her voice swelled. I couldn't stand it any longer. I ended the conversation.

And I started crying. I couldn't help her; I couldn't do anything. I kept thinking about Father, who also needed a doctor so badly.

I never answered the phone again.

## SEPTEMBER 18

Something happened! Something happened!

I'm so excited that I keep running from the TV to the window, and from the window to the TV. I can't stay in place.

The nanny is grumbling, saying that I should stay quiet, and that it's not good to get that agitated, but I think she's scolding me as a matter of form. I think she's happy. Maybe she understands.

I hadn't seen many bubbles outside the last couple of days, and almost no Others as well. The goddess Kali and her baby didn't come back.

But I'd never imagined it would be this!

The world from before is coming back! The world from before is coming back!

Father was right, the old man was right! We won!

I turned the TV on, and there you have it, the screen lit up suddenly instead of remaining all black as usual. I recognized the big room, where I had seen the old man, but this time a young man had replaced him. He didn't look tired at all, this one. He was talking fast, loudly, in a clear voice, and his eyes were shining. At first, I didn't really understand what he was saying. It was far too incredible! I could hear the words, but I felt like I couldn't put them together. Then I realized I was crying. Do tears flow when people are so happy, they think their heart is going to explode? Without a doubt, because my face was all wet.

Oh! Father, why were you not with me to hear that? We won! The bubbles were defeated!

The young man was still talking, with his clear and strong voice. He was explaining the weapon that killed the bubbles, and the protective gear that allowed us to go out and that at the present time volunteer teams were cleaning the city.

Then he really insisted. Above all, no one should go out at the moment. It was way too early. There were still quantities of bubbles in the city. Some patience was needed. After having waited for so long, it would be stupid to rush and lose everything, wouldn't it? Someone would come to us, teams that would bring us the protective gear. For now, we needed to stay in that sheltered position, and wait. It wouldn't be long.

After that, he showed us a working team. I saw a street like mine, and a dozen men walking. They were wearing some sort of stiff black bag that covered even their heads, with a transparent visor. They had big gloves of the same color, and they were all holding a tube that looked a lot like Father's flamethrower, except bigger and thicker.

At that time, three or four bubbles appeared floating quickly toward them. The men pointed their tubes at them and something blue and so shiny it hurt your eyes came out of it, and the bubbles broke. On the ground, not on them.

It was wonderful to see these horrible bubbles destroyed! I started to shout to encourage them.

The nanny came to make me eat. I chased her away. How can anyone be hungry when they are living through such events, and when they're soon going to know what the world from before was.

## SEPTEMBER 21

That's it! I saw other humans, and I talked to them!

I couldn't contain myself anymore. I would be at the window the whole day, and it was always the same empty street, except for the small number of bubbles, and no Others at all.

I had heard the same young man multiple times on TV, but he'd always repeat the same: "Patience, someone will come to you." He was starting to annoy me, that one. I was sick and tired of waiting. I was making the nanny run all day long. She was grumpy.

But she's the one who called me. I was watching TV again.

"Come see, Monica."

I ran to the window. There were men in ugly black bags in my street!

I started to scream, I forgot they couldn't hear me. But I was gesticulating so much through the window that they ended up seeing me, and they came towards my house, gesturing to me.

For three days already, I had lowered the circuit breaker, I was waiting for this so much. I rushed toward the door, I opened it wide, and they entered! They quickly closed it behind them, and they took off their black bags.

There were two of them. A tall one and a small one. The tall one had black hair and brown eyes radiating playfulness. When he smiled, his face would suddenly light up. The small one was all round, with very, very curly blond hair and tiny blue eyes in a chubby face.

The tall one said, "Well, well! The Lorelai with her long hair. Green eyes undine with a golden coat."

And the small one said, "Oh, shut up! You're going to scare her, this little one, with your nonsense that no one understands!"

It was true that I didn't understand, but I wasn't scared at all.

They said their names. The tall one: Frank; the small one: Eric. Me, I said: Monica. And then we shook hands, and they wanted me to hug them.

The tall one said, "After all, this is quite an exceptional day."

I hugged them, and I had a funny feeling because I had only hugged Father until then.

Frank asked, "Where are your parents, Monica? Are you alone?"

I answered very quickly, "My mother is dead, and Father . . . went outside."

He looked at me, sad, and put his hand on my shoulder.

"Was it a long time ago, Monica?"

"Three years."

He sighed, then said, "You don't need to think about it anymore, you will be very happy now. How old are you?"

"Sixteen."

There was a moment of silence, and they stared at each other.

Frank said, "Only sixteen? I should have guessed; you look so young . . ."

And Eric asked quickly, "Sixteen since when?"

"Since last month."

Then, they both kept quiet. They were staring at each other. They seemed weird, embarrassed. I didn't really understand. Because I was only sixteen? They thought I was too young? A little girl? But they looked like they were regretting it, a lot.

Frank caressed my cheeks, but Eric was turning away.

Suddenly, I felt embarrassed too, uncomfortable, and a little sad, without really knowing why. I wanted to ask them what was going on, but I didn't dare.

# SEPTEMBER 22

I'm waiting for Frank, who is coming to pick me up.

I dragged the little table to the window to be able to watch out while writing. Surely, I won't need to keep this diary anymore, since the era of the bubbles is over. So, I think this is the last time.

To think that I'm going outside! I can't believe it. I asked Frank, "And you'll show me the world from before?"

He seemed puzzled, then he replied, "Of course, little girl, of course I'll show you the world from before."

But he didn't seem happy at all. Why? Was the world from before not as beautiful as I believed it to be? Or maybe it's that it'll never quite be like that again?

It doesn't matter. I'm leaving, and no matter how, it will be marvelous.

Yet, I would be much happier if it weren't for one thing... it's that I understand, now, why this Other wanted me so much to take her baby in. Oh! I should have, because I heard what Frank and Eric were saying yesterday, and today I saw it on TV.

I had left them for a moment yesterday, because I wanted to make myself beautiful, and I had gone to put on one of mother's dresses. They were sitting in the library, and the nanny had served them this drink she would always give Father, and that she never agreed to make for me.

I came back softly, to surprise them, and this is when I heard.

Frank was saying, "We shouldn't do this. It's inhuman! After all, they have the right to live as much as we do, it's not their fault. It seems to me that we could have done things differently, I don't know, settling them in reservations for example."

And Eric replied, "We cannot do 'differently,' you know that very well. There is no cure, and they might be contagious. There is no other solution. There is no way around it!"

Frank said with anger, "You might like it—you—but me, I can't shoot. I just can't! It's monstruous to do so! I'm ashamed."

Then Eric started to reply with his hasty, high-pitched voice. It was odd, it looked like he was justifying himself. Exactly like me when the nanny reprimands me, and I know she's right, but I don't want to admit it.

He said, "It's the law. There's nothing else to do. We can't let ourselves be contaminated..." Frank interrupted him, "We don't even know if they're actually dangerous! And these children! All these kids!"

"We can't take any risk! The Others' children don't transform. Try figuring out which ones are normal! It's impossible to choose."

"But they might be immunized! We didn't even try to find out. And here, at least, you see, well, that this is not an issue."

"The Counsel decided, good grief! The bubbles have been here for sixteen years and two months. And the numbers are the numbers!"

The house made a little creak and they both jumped.

"Shut up," said Frank. "If she came back..."

Then I entered the room, and I could tell they thought I was pretty, but it didn't please me as much as it should have, because I felt like I understood. And this morning, I was absolutely sure.

I was watching TV, and it was showing once again the teams cleaning up the city. Except, this time, we saw another scene.

An Other, running. He had multiple legs, and he couldn't really hurry because he kept stumbling. But we could understand how desperately he was trying to save himself. And one of the men held up a flamethrower, and the Other shriveled to the ground into a little black mass.

They changed the scene right away and talked about something else. Surely, they hadn't wanted to show us all this. But I understood very well all the same, especially after having heard Frank and Eric.

They kill all the Others. There it is.

Oh! Frank was right, it seems to me that this isn't good. The Others scare me, but still...

This is why the goddess wanted me to take her baby in so badly. She knew, without a doubt. I wonder if they burned her. I could never have killed Kali, that's for sure. And her baby? He looked so normal!

It seems to me that this is mean, what they do. Father wouldn't have liked this.

But I shouldn't think about this any longer. I shouldn't be sad. It's a wonderful day. I'm waiting for Frank, and I'm going to go outside! I'm on the lookout at the window, and...

There he comes! He's getting here . . . no. It's Eric. Frank probably couldn't come and asked Eric to replace him. I'm a little disappointed. Eric is nice, but I'd have preferred Frank.

It's crazy how slowly he's walking. And he's lowering his head. It's weird, he saw me at the window, but he didn't answer my wave. Why?

He's holding a flamethrower. For what? And why is he taking so much time?

He's getting closer. I'm going to open the door for him.

Finally, I'm going to see the world from before.

# EXPANSION

Julia Verlanger: "The Bubbles"

French title: "Les Bulles"

First published in the French magazine *Fiction* (vol. No. 35, October 1956) and more recently, after appearing in several anthologies, by the French publisher Bragelonne in the collected volume *La Terre sauvage* in 2008 (and again in the tenth anniversary edition of the same volume in 2019).

*Translated by* Tessa Sermet

Julia Verlanger is the pen name of Éliane Taïeb (1929–1985). Verlanger published her very first short story, "The Bubbles," in 1956 and kept publishing short stories in French magazines dedicated to science fiction such as *Fiction*, *Galaxie*, and *Satellite* until 1963. She then remained silent until 1976, when she released a post-apocalyptical trilogy (*L'Autoroute sauvage*, then *La Mort en billes*, and *L'Île brûlée*, now together in the collected volume *La Terre sauvage*) under the name of Gilles Thomas, with French publisher Fleuve Noir's *Anticipation* collection. Founded after her passing by her husband, the "Julia Verlanger Award" is now allotted yearly to a science fiction, fantasy, or *fantastique* work during the Utopiales Festival.

Verlanger's work often doesn't describe the background story of what leads to the worlds she describes—"The Bubbles" is a perfect example of this—which is also a regular feature of short stories as a literary genre: all the information the reader gets from this post-apocalyptical world is distilled through the journal entries of Monica, a naïve teenager who has lived all her life inside a house-bunker and has never had contact with the outside world.

The story was published during the Cold War, in the wake of WWII, at a time when the fear of the atomic bomb was at its highest. Still, Verlanger's short story feels contemporary, and not only because people retreating inside their homes for an indefinite amount of time to remain safe reminds us of the COVID-19 lockdowns. The way mutants are ostracized and dehumanized for being different yet harmless; the interrogations around whether humanity's past lifestyle is to blame for the bubbles; and the questioning of what makes someone human—all these elements seem more than relevant nowadays.

## DISCUSSION QUESTIONS

What are the possible uses of atomic energy and which ones are criticized here? Does this story have a moral? If so, what do you think it is? If not, what do you think readers should come away with after reading it?

Monica's father used to say: "It is strange, we are a lot more scared of the Others, who aren't very dangerous, than of the bubbles." Why do you think that is? What does it say about people's behavior towards the Others?

This story is told in the form of a personal diary. How do you think this choice impacts the way you relate to the main character? Further, how does it limit the scope of knowledge that she is exposed to?

Why does Frank call Monica the "Lorelai"? What does Monica have in common with that mythical character? Why is it relevant to the story?

What is the core disagreement between Frank and Eric?

What do you think Frank and Eric will do in the end?

# So Far From Home

*by* Jacques Sternberg

*translated by* Brian Mather


## SO FAR FROM HOME...

### DAY TWO.


SO FAR, so very far.

Only now do I measure the distance, the abyss of nothingness that fills up and hollows out that distance. Up there I didn't think about it. What's the difference, in the infinite void of space, between a few centimeters and millions of kilometers? But now that I'm on solid ground, back in a stable universe, I think about the unfathomable distance that separates the world I come from and the world in which I now find myself. How am I to get back across that expanse? Is going back even part of the plan? It's only now that a wave of dizziness washes over me.

I've been on Earth for two days.

♦ ♦ ♦

So much time had been spent perfecting the plan; there was no possibility of error. So why do I feel so certain that there's a flaw somewhere, much more serious than we could have imagined? There's no evidence to support this feeling since everything up to now has gone exactly as it should. Even the timetable has been perfect.

I landed in an area that was completely deserted. I destroyed the ship that had ferried me across space. Then, keeping to unpopulated areas, I managed to reach the capital without being noticed and blend in with the crowd. I feel safe here. Nobody will take any notice of me. I'm just one among millions of passersby. This is where I'm to meet Agent 001, exactly one hour from now.

◆ ◆ ◆

I've sat down on a park bench in the center of town to rest. I think about what awaits me. A future that's less than reassuring. For though the landing was part of a meticulously crafted plan, everything that lies ahead belongs to the unknown.

This agency was created years ago on Fylchride; its sole purpose, to prepare for secret landings on Earth. For what reason? We don't know. We are nothing more than agents. All we know is the mission we've been secretly assigned to carry out. The motives are none of our business. We know only the facts: we are to live among the Earthlings as Earthlings for months, maybe years without being noticed, isolated, each one of us on his own. Agent 001 has been here three months already. I am Agent 002. Three months later Agent 003 will come. Then others. Maybe hundreds of others, thousands. We don't know that either, not with any precision. Just as we don't know whether we will ever be able to go back to Fylchride someday. Our mission is to blend in with the Earthlings and make detailed reports on everything that we had observed, experienced, and deduced.

For the moment there's no point in starting my reports. Agent 001 is sure to have meticulously noted everything that I've experienced since my arrival. Redundancy is not tolerated on Fylchride. I'll need to read Agent 001's report before beginning mine.

Besides, I haven't yet had the time to be surprised or worried. I haven't gotten close enough to really experience this world, to make any observations. I've done nothing but act. And the things that I've accomplished I practiced so much on Fylchride that now they inspire a curious impression of banality. I know the area in which I land as if I have lived here all my life. I can do everything with my eyes closed. The terrain holds no surprises for me. It is almost identical to the models constructed on Fylchride. I am only slightly surprised to find it much softer and spongier than I had imagined—repugnant as well under this riot of green smothered by the absurd blue of a cloudless sky.

From the natural world, I journeyed into the precarious and hostile world of men: the city. We had not constructed any models of this world. The real adventure begins here at this crossroads. At the edge of this mass of beings I know almost nothing about, in the very center of this capital whose secret laws are almost entirely unknown to me. And though I've spent years learning the theory of this adventure I'm destined for, I know nothing of its practice. Yet here I am, suddenly cut loose, placed at the beginning of still-inchoate events that rise up around me like a gathering storm. What's to be done?

Behind me, between my worry and any impulse to flee, is a vast interstellar void. I can only move forward. I must remember all the years spent cultivating my composure and proceed step by step, discreetly, feigning a complete relaxation of my nerves.

In the park where I've stopped to rest, I look at the beings that surround me. I look at them without much curiosity, without the air of somebody who is observing. Nobody pays me any attention. Nobody stops to stare. It's strangely intoxicating to know that I was born on another planet, that I could trigger a revolution by proving it, and that all these people take me for one of their own, an anonymous passerby. There's nothing about me that would indicate otherwise. My strangely transparent eyes would only barely strike as odd those who had the time to take a hard look. But Earthlings do not seem to have much time to lose. And in any case, there are most likely men whose eyes are as light as mine. As for my particularly bronze complexion, this doesn't worry me any more than my eyes. It seems that the sun here produces exactly the same effect as does the one on Fylchride. It is astonishing to think that from strictly different causes we arrive at identical consequences.

Finally, whatever happens, I must never betray my feelings, nor anything that could reveal my true identity. There isn't much to worry about though. I've had years of training, like all the other agents destined for Earth. I was chosen from among hundreds of candidates. I wonder, why were there so many? The training is tedious and exhausting. The mission is exciting perhaps, but extremely uncertain. Which means that the official title so graciously bestowed upon us ultimately counts for very little. *Agent 002*—that has a nice ring to it, but it couldn't be more misleading. In reality, we're guinea pigs in an experiment whose secret purpose is unknown to us. Guinea pigs, nothing more. As for why we had accepted this mission in the first place . . . on Fylchride, it wasn't a question of accepting or refusing. We were drugged with the will to accomplish what needed to be accomplished, and that was that. Regrets, like every other reaction, were excluded.

It will be nightfall shortly. It's getting colder; I feel heavy, opaque. From the noise, no doubt. That had been anticipated as well. The actual experience is not so easy to bear, however. Perhaps Agent 001 has found a means of remedying this inconvenience. And all the others. It's time I met up with him.

## DAY THREE.

Alone.

I'm the only one left. I'm now alone among several million strangers. Agent 001 is dead. I learned of it yesterday. He's been dead for weeks now.

I was on my way up to his apartment when an insufferably loud voice roared inside my head:

"Where are you going?"

I turned around. I had to make a terrible effort not to show my surprise. This was the first contact I'd had with a human being. An elderly woman, an enormous pile of flesh. It must have been her job to guard this building. I remembered just in time what I had learned, that on Earth, everything is closely monitored, that nothing escapes the ever-watching and mistrustful eye of man. I also remembered that I must smile, though the echo of that shattering voice still throbbed inside my head—smile and speak with courtesy. I gave her the name of the man I had come to see.

"He will have been living here for a few months," I told her.

"He was here," she responded, "but he died."

My shock must have seemed a normal reaction. On Earth, death is most often unexpected, and thus my surprise seemed entirely plausible.

"He got sick. Then he died. Four weeks ago. Why did you want to see him?"

This question was expected. I'd been warned about Earthlings' insatiable curiosity. Their unquenchable thirst for information. I told her that he was a friend, that we hadn't seen each other for a very long time.

Then, I left.

What else could I do? There is no more Agent 001. It is no use looking for his reports; he is sure to have destroyed them. He got sick, then he died. How simple it is. Sickness, a concept that means nothing to me. On Fylchride, we had no notion of what sickness might be. However, I'd been told that on Earth there are viruses and microbes that can devour the human body and sometimes lead to death. Does this mean that we can die on Earth as Earthlings die? Carried away by the flu, pneumonia, or perhaps even a simple head cold? Or had he been contaminated by a sickness that we alone are susceptible to? I don't know, I can't know. And I certainly am not allowed to ask around for information. Asking questions is likely to arouse suspicion. I have to be careful about the law, about interrogations, about judicial networks. Cities are riddled with them. They are one of the biggest dangers to avoid, I know that too.

So here I am.

Asking myself questions that I'll never be able to answer. Life or death questions. Maybe Agent 001 was a victim of chance? Or maybe he died because it was inevitable, because it couldn't be otherwise, which means that I, too, will die, in the same way, most likely within the same amount of time. In order to be certain, and since I cannot carry out an investigation, it would seem that there are only two pieces of evidence I might recover: Agent 001's journal and his body. But there's no point in thinking about it. The journal has been destroyed. And the Earthlings bury their dead in public parks. How could I open the tomb of Agent 001 and take his corpse without being noticed? It's not worth thinking about. I'll have to wait. Answers will come in time. Wait calmly, mastering my fear without the least amount of effort. No effort is required; before my departure I was inoculated with the will to fulfill my mission, a perfect mastery of my reflexes, and an unassailable sense of calm.

That being said, I am still alone.

I've become Agent 001, which means that I have to start from the beginning. Note down in my reports the obvious details of my first moments here as if Agent 001 had never existed. Take notes while haunted by the specter of an unavoidable question: will this mean anything? Will I not also be forced to tear up my reports as I feel death approaching?

And yet, specter or no, I must focus on playing my part. Just surviving would be a good start. I was counting on Agent 001 to give me some advice in that regard; now I'll have to get by on my own. And without delay. I have valid papers and excellent letters of recommendation, but very little money. And though we might previously have had some doubts about this, I can now attest that one must pay for everything here, absolutely everything; everything is for sale, and everything can be bought. One needs a constant supply of money, much more than I would have believed. It is difficult to fully accept this new myth when one comes from a world where it is unknown. And yet, months on Fylchride were spent forcibly instilling in me the concept of money and teaching me the complex system of buying and selling that governs every civilization here on Earth.

Training notwithstanding, I feel a bit unsettled. The brutality of it surpasses, by rather a lot, the circumscribed nature of the simulation. I hadn't realized that every action would be subjected to the laws of transaction, that one must continuously give in order to receive in turn.

The money I have won't last long. Two days were enough for me to understand that I cannot count on the inhabitants of this city for material aid in case of distress. The Earthling has but one ideal: possession. His most instinctive action is holding out his hand to collect money.

I rented a hotel room downtown yesterday. As soon as I walked in the door I was given a form and told to fill it out. Requests for information—I had been warned—are indeed constant. Even regarding the smallest details. It would not have surprised me if there had been a question on why I'd been born and in what circumstances. What would have happened if I had put "from the planet Fylchride" in response to the question "place of origin"? It's a relief to think that nobody would have believed me. Though I'm sure they would have been suspicious all the same. Here, a sense of seriousness seems to be compulsory; its lack must surely be punishable by some law or other. I had only just finished filling out the form when I was asked to pay. I had to turn over a full half of my budget. I was dismayed. Clearly, without realizing it, I had chosen one of the more luxurious hotels. For in this place, even the ambiance, the décor, the light, the amount of scent in the air that one breathes, all of it has a price tag.

Since that mistake I hardly dare attempt any purchase whatsoever. Yet it is not for lack of temptation. The entire city is nothing but an enormous mass of objects thrown one on top of the other. On our planet, everything is reduced to a few invariable prototypes, but here, each object, no matter how preposterous, has thousands of variations, thousands of derivations, thousands of imitations. An object as banal as an ashtray convulses into the most eccentric forms; it would be impossible to list its innumerable metamorphoses.

Must we then conclude that man is hopelessly allergic to everything seen the day before? This hypothesis is most certainly false, since he gladly keeps an acquired object for decades and never grows tired of it. Must we then conclude that each man has very particular tastes, different from those of his neighbor? No more true, that hypothesis, for nearly all men have the same tastes and, above all, a violent passion for the hideous. So why this infinite proliferation of variants? For love of business. The Earthling is a born salesman, and he's been taught that he can sell anything. It's just a matter of producing. Producing what? Anything. And this explains the hellish congestion on this planet.

There's hardly any place left to live. Little by little, objects have consumed the space of the living. Men lavish their objects with the finest accessories, luxurious cases and coverings; they put them atop pedestals in the most flattering light. Objects are spared no refinement; they are coddled in every imaginable way. Each and every object has a dozen men at its disposition, teams of creators, salesmen, technicians, and employees: all of them slaves. Objects control the world. They alone are maintained, improved, cherished, continually reinvented. Man is so obsessed by his lust for lucre that he has almost forgotten himself in the midst of it all. He's done nothing for himself.

He knows nothing of the essential secrets of his life and of his death. The Earthling will eat anything, live in any conditions, often in miserable slums. Like an animal, he doesn't know why he is brought into this world, and death unceremoniously takes him from it, most often by accident, never with any warning. He has learned to master neither his beginning nor his end, which is to say that the truly crucial problems escape him entirely. The trivial problems, on the other hand, have, all of them, been solved. He is not master of his destiny, but he is the undisputed master of the ham-slicing machine and the inventor of the can opener. That is enough for him. He draws legitimate pride from it and, in exchange, will accept anything, including a ridiculously premature death. But then, the Earthling possesses an unassailable will to submit.

Truly, death is the principal myth of this world. Even for objects. Indeed, back home, nothing wears out because nothing ever decays. Here, everything wears out and decays with alarming speed, which explains a continuous rumbling of supply and demand in this aggravated babel. Upon this hysterical exchange rests an entire civilization eternally chasing its tail and dragging millions of beings into a race without end. A demented and fatal race, I should clarify, for human beings wear down much faster than objects. This, however, does not seem to preoccupy them. It doesn't prevent them from running faster and faster, as if their only fear were arriving late to their own death. How do they manage to deny the absurdity of it all? How do they live with it? A question without an answer.

Those most concerned have, themselves, neglected to hazard a response.

What can be said about the millions of numbers and price tags that scintillate in this world? I am at a total loss. Simple objects without any apparent value are worth a fortune while other, infinitely more complex objects are worth almost nothing. What's more, despite my years on Fylchride spent cataloging objects commonly used by Earthlings, there are a number of them whose significance or function seems to me absolutely devoid of sense. There again, we underestimated. Excess and exaggeration have made Earth their home.

Of course, there is a constant risk of exposing myself. But this is easy to avoid. All I must do is ask continually, "What do I owe you?"

A common phrase; one hears it constantly, pronounced with every inflection. And who could suppose, upon seeing me wander around a department store, that half of the items displayed there are wholly unknown to me? Exactly as if I were a five- or six-year-old child. This actually is not too far from the truth: my studies on Fylchride lasted only a few years. I've noticed with some bitterness that they have not sufficed. I am yet ignorant of a great many things, and here I refer only to the world of the senses. Undoubtedly there is also abstract—and thus secret and as yet unthinkable—information. And much more than I could imagine. That's without mentioning the fact that I have to endure life here, and this presents other problems. Perhaps the most serious.

In any case, whether I like it or not, I'm forced to follow the directive laid out in the plan: in order to survive, I'll need to find work right away. My skills were defined long ago, limited by the basic rules of the trade I'd been given—I know how to bind and stitch books. Agent 001 had been trained as a mechanic; I was trained as a bookbinder. I hadn't chosen this trade; it was assigned to me with assurances that it was no more or less absurd than the other trades commonly practiced on Earth. How could I have objected?

Fortunately, the subject of food will never be a tragic one. I will not die of hunger; this much, at least, seems clear. A single meal per week is more than sufficient for me, whereas Earthlings require three per day, and their entire budget is calculated on this basis. Truly, the geometrical center of a human being is his stomach. In order to sustain himself, each inhabitant of this city must spend twenty times more than I do. But it still remains to be seen whether I will be able to tolerate the food here. The tests conducted on Fylchride had been conclusive. But they had been carried out on a much smaller scale, just like everything else. In order to prepare us for Earth, no expense had been spared on Fylchride. An entire facility had been created; every question had been asked, analyzed, reanalyzed, resolved. Earth's environment had been recreated in a secret location, completely off limits to visitors. For years already, over the course of multiple missions to Earth, we had been bringing back documents, objects, maps, scraps of this world we intended to visit one day.

That day had finally come. I can see that nothing was neglected, nothing in particular at least. Yet something isn't right. In reality, on Fylchride we had solved every problem in terms of plane geometry. On Earth, these problems suddenly appear in three dimensions. Under the withering light of reality, the facts take on an unexpected form, a new dimension: that of multiplication unto excess. This was something we had not anticipated as, day after day, we submitted to our frenzied training program in a limited, linear space. Here, space is neither linear nor limited. And this new dimension could very well prove fatal to us.

I mustn't forget that Agent 001 is dead. I haven't forgotten. I was injected with calm on Fylchride; I was injected with prudence as well; I am positively brimming with marvelous qualities. A perfect agent, tailor-made for the mission I've been assigned. I mustn't forget that the circumstances leading to Agent 001's death are entirely unknown to me. Was it the food perhaps? We had long ago accustomed ourselves to common Earth-foods, but there were perhaps certain foods, seemingly innocuous, that we must avoid entirely. Which ones? We have no way of knowing. We know, by experience or by inference, that we are capable of withstanding Earth's climate, its temperature, that we can drink its water and breathe its air. But the rest? What do we know of the unseen reactions that result from our contact with the incessant noise of this world? Are we strong enough to survive in the middle of this sea of aliens? How can we know that we aren't allergic to the totality of this never-before-seen environment, to its true density?

The more I think about it, the more I'm convinced that our training cannot have been enough to prove we can survive here, that we've really only solved a part of the problem.

That's the real reason I'm here. To find out for sure. A guinea pig taken from a preliminary experiment and thrown into a conclusive one. I've already discovered a part of the conclusion: the death of the first guinea pig. And if that conclusion doesn't frighten me, it's only because nothing can frighten me. On Fylchride, science has worked miracles in this regard.

But are these miracles equally valid on Earth?

This only occurs to me because I'm feeling tired this evening. It's taken some time for me to accurately identify this sensation, which is almost entirely foreign to me. There can be no doubt however, even if I have some difficulty accepting it: it would seem that I need to sleep. And yet I slept more than four hours last night. On Fylchride, one hour is more than sufficient. And this fatigue I feel overtaking me is more intense than what I felt on a mission long ago when I went without sleep for twelve days.

It's the noise; that's what's so tiring. It must be the noise. Truly much more taxing than I ever could have imagined. Our training failed us in this respect as well. A few hours of deafening noise per day seemed an excellent exercise. In reality, it was only a pitiful imitation. The noise is more intense here, and constant. Constant, that changes everything.

I have to sleep. To escape. To forget. Stop seeing, stop hearing. I begin to understand why Earthlings are so fiercely attached to their sleep.

Tonight, I value it as they do.

## DAY FOUR.

I had a dream last night.

This is very unusual. On Fylchride I dreamed only rarely. Sometimes haunted by some happening or other. But again, only rarely.

I dreamed that I traveled to an alien planet, and that I came, not from the sky, but from the bowels of the planet, the surface of which gave way like a thin membrane. I couldn't manage to land my vessel. Everything in that world was geometrical pits and silence, with large, sunken, crumbling, metal rhombi in the distance. Then, I felt suddenly that I was falling. I woke up, surprised to find that I'd sat up in my sleep. What I felt was even stranger: an indescribable anguish, like the fear of finding myself surrounded by a maleficent and formless circumstance that I couldn't identify.

What I feel this morning, having just woken up, is no less disappointing. For one thing, I'm tired. The exact sensation is that of my organs having grown heavier, of their having doubled in density, while my muscles, on the other hand, feel as if they have atrophied. The sensation of weight, that's it more than anything. I haul my body around like an unwieldy piece of baggage. And then there's the inexplicable indifference I feel contemplating the day that lies ahead. This is even more worrying than the rest of it. But there's no use ignoring it or denying reality: this world that I've only just arrived in, a world situated millions of kilometers beyond our wildest dreams, leaves me with a curious feeling of déjà vu, of dull and uninteresting things erupting in an enormous explosion of meaningless babel and vain agitation. There is nothing in this alien world that appeals to me. On the contrary, I feel rising within me a nascent fear at the idea of having to tread upon it. Fear not of meeting danger, but rather of wandering about vainly in a day with no salient features or points of reference.

Perhaps it's time to pause for a moment and ask myself why this world seems so dreary, so totally bereft of interest. I get up, I walk over to the window, I try to collect myself. I suppose there are many things about this world that disappoint and weary me.

For one thing, there's the color. Or rather the lack of it. At night, everything is black. During the day, everything is gray. The sky is almost always gray, the buildings are gray, the ground is gray. The air is gray, just like the wind, the light, the faces, the clothes, and the bodies of the inhabitants of this gray world. Everything has been contaminated by this color without color, everything dissolved in its mist. Some nuances cling on here and there like pieces of wreckage. A red roof here, a strip of green there, a patch of yellow or an island of blue, but the tide of gray continues to rise; it attacks from the inside, pitilessly eroding everything it infects. Little by little everything has been affected, and blue, like red and green, has become gray, like a dirty white or faded black. A world like a gigantic cocoon woven in the filth that it secretes, sprouted in the dust that it engenders, and each day that passes turns to dust, increasing the dimensions of the cocoon, making it denser, drearier, more opaque.

How exactly should I feel when I think about the fact that I—inhabitant of Fylchride, where all was luminosity, brilliance, purity, radiance—managed, with practice, to fill up my eyes with the will to withstand the spectacle of a universe of gray without risking blindness or insanity? For my eyes have withstood it, I must admit. And I, too, have withstood it; I've withstood even the acrid, insipid odor of this gray. For this stew of rocks and living things, slowly decomposing in the dust and ennui, gives off a constant odor of decay that I shouldn't be able to bear. And it surely would be unbearable if I were limited to my own natural abilities. But greater abilities have been added onto me; my potential has been increased. New potential has been grafted into me. My perseverance and all the practical exercises have paid off. I endure; and without even a trace of disgust, no shudder of revulsion. Not yet at least.

And what can I say about the noise? We now have confirmation. It was definitely the most difficult thing to deal with. Are Earthlings deaf? Or is it our senses that are abnormally acute? It doesn't matter which side the anomaly belongs to; the disparity, however, is undeniable. What amounts to light background noise for Earthlings is to us a racket of unbearable density. I'll have to get used to this as well. It's certainly difficult, at night when everything becomes calm, having to hear the dull, viscous grating of the microbes that saturate the air of this world. It's just as difficult, when it so happens that man consents to lie still, hearing the gargle of his body, the precipitous bellows of his respiration, the liquid sound of life that always seems on the verge of death. It's even more difficult getting used to the crashing thunder of voices, of the most trivial utterances exchanged unceasingly on this planet. The city itself vomits out an infinite variety of noise, and I have to summon every reserve of self-control to endure it. What would it be like if I hadn't had the hearing in one of my ears destroyed before leaving Fylchride? I would surely never have been able to cope. But now I must take steps to protect the ear I have left. Otherwise, deafness will be my fate, which is hardly appealing. Truly everything in this world is sound, amorphous music, a constant onslaught of words. Even inanimate objects groan and appear to be alive, as if there were tiny beings living inside of them who carry on, especially at night, with their interminable pursuits.

The dust is no less noxious. It covers and permeates everything, and all throughout the day you can see it dissolving into the air. It germinates outside of things and then settles on every surface, covering everything with a fine layer of mildew. As if each minute is removing a number of atoms from the things of this world and converting them into millions of particles of transparent dust. Or maybe that dust is really only one of the multiple forms of that living gray which infects the entire Earth. But men must harbor a secret passion for that rancid color, since they coat everything in it, themselves as well as their possessions. And their passion for dust is just as strong, for smoking is man's greatest pleasure, and he vomits forth clouds of transparent dust that dissolve into the surrounding grime, gradually weaving the cocoon of vermin into which this world is sinking.

For these reasons, leaving aside the myriad others, I feel uneasy as I look out upon the city I must go into this morning. And it doesn't look as if I'll get anything today in exchange for it all. Neither today nor tomorrow.

This morning, I saw a man die.

It all happened so simply. To see something as frightening as death clothed in such simplicity—it gave me chills.

The man had fallen five stories into the street below. It was an astonishing sight. We had not been mistaken in concluding that Earth's inhabitants are extremely fragile creatures, constantly exposed to death. One false step is all it takes. Fatal accidents, almost unheard of back home, are quite frequent here. Failing to get out of the way of a vehicle, a bad fall, a slip with something sharp, and it's death in minutes. Or even immediately. I should add that man is brimming with an astonishing amount of blood, which, at every opportunity, gushes forth in a hemorrhage that's impossible to staunch, that his bones are extraordinarily fragile, that his body is entirely unprotected, and that his flexibility is non-existent. This is why falling a few stories had reduced that man to mush, just as if his body had been crushed under the weight of an entire building. I mustn't ever take such a fall; if somebody were to see me getting back up without a scratch, which would inevitably happen, that person would think it very strange. I should also avoid getting hit by a car while crossing the street. To come out of that unscathed would seem just as unusual.

Clearly, then, the Earthling is a very fragile thing. But, paradoxically, though conscious of this fragility, he has delighted in placing innumerable snares in his way, risks of all kinds and countless possibilities of sudden death. This entire world is bristling with machines of enormous power that can bring about the death of their owners in a matter of seconds. Can it be that man makes it a point of honor to die before the things that he has so patiently created? And why this enthusiasm for risk? Man certainly doesn't believe in life after death; as a rule he does not look to commit suicide or to end it all as quickly as possible. Quite the opposite: death terrifies him, and clearly life is very dear to him. But every man is more than willing to imagine that he is immortal, and the evidence that this is an illusion is not enough, it would seem, to shake his conviction, unless we must accept that man is driven by an unbridled impulse to heroism and that he is proud to consider crossing the street a genuine adventure in which he gambles his life in the simplest of terms, as one might flip a coin. But I believe that man is simply little disposed to confront head-on the only really significant problem: death; he has settled it once and for all with a few platitudes. Then with infinitely more interest, he turns toward the many ridiculous problems of everyday life. For us, who have spent centuries working on the means of delaying death for as long as possible, the Earthling's attitude seems that of a simpleton. Which indeed he is.

◆ ◆ ◆

This morning, I found a job.

It's in a large bindery that employs over a hundred and fifty workers. Man is obsessed with centralization, and his love for stacks and piles never wanes. I have been accepted without difficulty after a trial period of one morning. The head of personnel is impressed by my knowledge of the trade and my dexterity. Of course, I have to feign a certain clumsiness and above all slow my reflexes down as much as possible. That, too, has been part of adapting to terrestrial laws. If for a few minutes I should let myself go and perform my work at my natural rhythm, it would immediately provoke a genuine revolution. Perhaps they would understand that these abilities cannot possibly belong to an inhabitant of this world. Or rather, more simply, they would consider me a prodigy, worthy of immediate promotion to shift supervisor.

In any case, I begin tomorrow.

"I hope you like it here," said one of the managers.

Not likely.

Here, more than anywhere else, the gray dominates, crushes everything under its law. The tables, the machines, the windows, the ground, the walls are all gray. The employees are swaddled up to their necks in sheaths of gray. The sun, through a gigantic glass roof, mercilessly pursues the leprosy eating away at this place. The paper lost its color long ago. Having taken on a grayish hue, it gives off an appalling odor of decay. In this world, nothing is deodorized as it is back home; every object has its own peculiar stink.

Substances as innocuous as glue or hemp, ink or paint, produce an odor that is alive and belligerent, and so oppressive that I find it terrifying. Is it possible that Agent oo1 was killed by a particularly insistent odor? That hadn't occurred to me before. But how am I to identify it? And if I identify it, how am I to avoid it? Doubtless it kills slowly, insidiously, unbeknownst to its victim. But this is really just a guess. And I have so many guesses. It's better not to think about it. Be careful, that's what I need to do. Be careful about everything. Move forward one step at a time without being rash, without ever forgetting that this world is certainly much less innocuous than it seems. If only I could find the body of Agent oo1. Or his journal. A single sentence, a single fact would be enough. Somewhere in that journal there must be a short note revealing why Agent oo1 died. A word that names what killed him. But what use is there in thinking about it? That word, I'm sure to find it eventually. The question is whether it will be too late.

◆ ◆ ◆

Tonight, once again, I feel tired. Like yesterday, I have the same need to throw myself onto the bed, to collapse into sleep. Yet I've done nothing extraordinary today, just a few trivial things of mind-numbing simplicity. Even so, my entire body aches, as if I had done it all underwater, crushed under fathoms of pressure.

Is it the food I ate at the restaurant this evening? That had been my first meal on Earth. What a relief to think that I won't have to eat more than one per week. I couldn't possibly eat three every day in the cloying excess of their gigantic feed houses. I already had to fight desperately to bear, for just half an hour, the violent agitation of these ravenous creatures, their lust and laughter ringing out thick and rancid in a stifling odor of frying fat. For eating ranks among the Earthling's greatest pleasures in life. The mere thought of food and drink excites and arouses him beyond anything we could have imagined. He pounces on a glass of wine or a piece of meat as he would pounce on a woman. And in those moments, his eyes and his expression have something dreadful about them. Now I understand why their newspapers are filled with stories of rape and murder. Man, seated before his dinner more than at any other moment, appears such as he is, his essence laid bare: a being who tirelessly seeks to seize and devour and, more than anything, to possess, a carnivore and a drunkard, excitable and consumed by nervous tics, obsessive and irritable. In a word, dangerous. Weak, extremely vulnerable, but dangerous.

As for the food, it was what I'd expected. Bland, repellent, but nourishing. As if Earthlings lived exclusively on vast quantities of odors reduced into a mash and served in a sea of colors dissolved in water or grease. Man's capacity for food is staggering. For me personally, a single meal is sufficient. I wasn't even able to finish it. And though the food is already bloated with liquid, men take on even more of it by ingesting vast quantities of water and wine. This is why they all look like enormous casks filled with flaccid meat, marinating in a mixture of blood and water. This is why shaking a man's hand always feels like grabbing onto a clammy, boneless piece of flesh.

From now on, I'll just eat cookies. I don't require anything else, and the risks are certainly fewer.

But what does the word "risk" actually mean? It seems so ridiculous when I really think about it. What meaning could it possibly have? Where is the risk in this world? What piece of information holds the key to finding it? I really don't know. I simply know that it exists. But for now, it's invisible, impossible to identify.

To forget, that's all I want right now. To sleep and, after drifting in the oblivion of night, recover my resilience, my strength, my calm and composure.

◆ ◆ ◆

I am at the point of falling asleep when, suddenly, I get up from my bed. Brusquely, as if thrown out by a force of irresistible power.

Anguish. It can only be anguish. Suddenly, as if I've gone into a tunnel with no issue, the thought comes to me, if I let myself fall asleep, I will never wake up again. That at the other end of that tunnel, there can only be death.

I don't understand. I've never had such thoughts before. I should never have such thoughts. Doubtless, it's a simple question of color once again. It's in the impenetrable black of this night, pressing in like a tomb, that such thoughts come to be. How I miss the translucent, green nights on Fylchride. They were so gentle and calming, as light as the air, and with vast open spaces. Here, the filth of the day is followed by the suffocating weight of the night. A sticky syrup into which everything subsides. No more dimensions, no more shapes. Nothing. Night and sleep are really nothing more than a dress rehearsal for death. Until daybreak, everything sinks down and mingles with the kingdom of the dead. And dawn, on Earth, breaks upon a world of corpses. A pallid world, lifeless and frightening to behold. Perhaps this is why human bodies aren't able to regain any color or vitality during the day. They wake up, emerge from their tombs, come back to life, but they're still gray, already half consumed by vermin, too bloated and lethargic to reach their full potential, too anemic to really flourish.

This anxiety isn't normal. It wasn't part of the plan. It wasn't in the injections I received before my departure. On the contrary, I'd been injected with reserves of strength and calm. Where are they now? It's almost as if they've been diluted in the air of this world. And what if contact with this world is causing me, little by little, to undergo a transformation, to adapt, to lose my strengths and acquire the Earthling's natural weaknesses? To become like them, to become one of them. How can I know for sure?

And still the weariness rises up inside of me. Like strange, thickened water seeping out of the ground and up into my feet, and then higher, higher, and higher, heavier and heavier.

Sleep. This is the task I've given myself tonight. I barely have the will to carry it out.

# DAY FIVE.

The wheels, well-greased, have been set in motion without a hitch. The objective I needed to attain has been attained; henceforth, I am no longer an anonymous visitor in this city; I am an anonymous employee. I've been taken on at a legitimate firm. I'll be earning a union wage for practicing a legal trade during union-sanctioned hours.

I'm going to adopt the human condition. But what words could possibly express everything that's humiliating, dull, and terrifying about this condition?

Man really only has one true function: that of a tool. He makes use of a multitude of bizarre objects, forgetting all the while that he is himself an object, a living object, but only half alive. He himself can be used. For anything, to accomplish the most ridiculous and degrading work. And sometimes he doesn't even know exactly what his function is, which doesn't prevent him in the least from keeping up the pace. And what a frenzied pace it is! For one of the principal myths of this world is maximum yield and the automatic investment of profit toward the purchase of new profit-making machines.

That's why every man must have a well-defined specialty, and that's why his work is just an endless repetition of the same movements, the same utterances. He becomes a simple link in a chain with no end and no beginning, eternally shackled to his clocks, which affirm, all of them, that time once lost is lost forever. He spins around like a belt or a gearwheel in a turbine; he goes along with the frenzied agitation of it all, infinitely less efficient than his machines, doing everything he possibly can just to keep up with them, haunted by the terrifying prospect of being considered obsolete, that is to say, utterly useless.

This is why, on my very first day at the bindery, I am placed at a table with a brush in my hand, a pot of glue in front of me, and a stack of cardboard book covers to my right. My job is of disconcerting simplicity, like all the other jobs in this place. You'd think we are in a rehabilitation center for cripples or simpletons. I dip my brush in glue; I apply the glue to one of the book covers. That's it. As soon as those steps are complete, a different employee attends to the next one.

And the hours pass.

The worker to my right prepares stacks of book covers. I apply the glue; I pass them to another worker who affixes the flyleaves. And, step by step, what was nothing more than stacks of paper becomes a book. Always the same book. Always the same steps.

Always the same movements. Always the same rhythm. And the hours go by. And the stacks of books reach ever higher. More and more books. Without end. And the movements unfold in such a stifling ennui that, in order to escape it, we work at greater and greater speeds. The towers of books rise faster and faster. Productivity increases; profits pile up. And the final book never comes; after the last in a series, the first of a new series automatically appears. Exactly the same one. And the same movements, following the same assembly line. And, finally, the ennui expands outward; from time it falls into space, from resignation into terrified silence, from panic into the need to have done and reach some kind of an end. That's when our movements reach the height of efficiency.

The stacks of books reach the ceiling. The ceiling creaks, the lunch bell rings. Work stops instantly. And everything starts over again two hours later. In the same way. As if all memory of that morning has been magically erased.

This morning, the worker who glues on the flyleaves asked me some questions. Now, this afternoon, I ask him some questions:

"Have you worked here long?"

"About ten years," he responds.

"And you've always had the same job?"

"Oh no!" he says, "before this I mixed the glue."

Before this, he mixed the glue. But, as a reward for his years of service, the company accorded him the honor of applying that glue. And make no mistake, this man is proud of his advancement. Here, they call it assuming one's responsibilities, building a future for oneself. A future in which one endlessly stutters out the same lines in a play with only one act performed over and over again. How do they do it? What inner strength stifles their screams? What keeps them from deciding that they don't want any part in this horrifying production and refusing to continue any further? What drugs cloud their eyes so that they don't see the dread billowing out like smoke from that infinite repetition, repetition that can only lead to one thing, death? And why is it that men sometimes sit bolt upright in the middle of the night, bathed in sweat, terrified by some nightmare, but that they never sit bolt upright at work, in the much more horrifying nightmare they live every day?

But no, there's none of that.

What will it take for them to understand? What proof do they need? It's all right in front of them; in this very room, they have a panorama of what twenty years of working with glue and paper will make of them: larvae, pale larvae stuck in a mindless stupor, with contorted limbs, fingers bloated and gnawed away by the scourge of the working class, eyes swollen from the plodding spectacle of each new day, forever identical to the one before. But human monsters do not frighten man. He's filled with revulsion at the sight of a snake, a rat, a fly, a spider. But the monster, what he's to become has no effect on him. He's resigned to it. He accepts it.

And his hands detach from his body to accomplish by themselves the work to be done. His head, his body are checked at the door, withered, useless, inept. For man passes for a thinking being, yet rarely is he called upon to think. Why is he not simply reduced to two enormous pairs of hands? Or a mass of twenty hands? One wonders. Clearly, nature has not done things very well on this planet.

Perhaps I must acknowledge that, from time to time, man does use his head to utter a few words. These words, are they worth it? Do they justify having a head? They're always the same words it seems. And here again the same obligatory repetition. Man's words are in sync with his movements. And, like the movements, they're infected with the ennui and monotony that hang thick in the air of this place. Just as downy and gray as the dust, they seem like echoes of words spoken that morning, or the day before, or a week earlier, or last year. Endlessly repeated, never changing.

Men speak like their machines. Always the same tone, always the same cadence, endlessly repeating the same refrains. Why do they speak? Perhaps in order to prove to each other that they're still alive, or perhaps simply because the babel is as necessary to them as the fouled air that they breathe, because the silence would surely drive them all mad.

This is why they engage in a constant exchange of questions and answers. Always useless, always ridiculous. This is also why there are supervisors whose only job is to move through that slough of ennui from one table to the next, from a machine of steel to a machine of flesh, asking questions, carrying out mournful interrogations without end or beginning.

"You think you'll get that done today?"

"Wouldn't that go faster if you switched hands?"

"When's your shift end?"

"Why weren't you at work this morning?"

"How many did you finish today?"

"How many did you finish yesterday?"

All of these questions must be answered. For a supervisor is someone who commands respect. It would seem, according to their history at least, that slavery on Earth has been abolished. On what basis do they make this claim? These employees, condemned to forced labor, forced answers, forced smiles, to unflagging civility and zeal, what are they if not slaves? Yet man wants nothing more than to look the other way. He was taught that slavery is no longer practiced. He believes it. He's proud of it. It would never even occur to him that he has been duped. His credulity is rivaled only by the strength of his resignation.

Clearly, man is to be pitied. Is that the reason I was sent here? I doubt it. Does contempt exclude all pity? Probably not. Man does repulse me, without question. Yet he does not leave me entirely indifferent. Perhaps because I'm obliged, at least for the moment, to share in his condition. All of a sudden, while reflecting on my lack of any information regarding the length of my stay here, I'm seized by panic. What if I'm forced to live here for years, under the same conditions as the Earthlings? Constantly watched, interrogated, imposed upon, monitored. Forever subjected to a regimen of suggestions, orders, counter-orders. Subjected, willingly or not, to the laws, facts, paths one must follow. Having but one single and unique liberty: to die of hunger and destitution if I should refuse. The thought of it makes me flush with panic; how can this be possible? I won't do it. I refuse to live such a life, to suffer through this nightmare year after year.

One way or another I'll get out. They'll come get me and take me back home to Fylchride. All of this is just a mission after all. And if by chance I were to be forgotten here, I'd focus on one thing and one thing only: how to die. As quickly as possible.

◆ ◆ ◆

This evening, I went to a movie theater.

There are hundreds of them in this city, which is to say far too many. But anything with a small chance of success in this world triggers an avalanche of overproduction. Greed has neither scruples nor limits here. And movies certainly are a very popular distraction. A genuine drug for some. For just as there are drunks, lechers, addicts, and collectors, there are also those who have a consuming hunger for entertainment. But regardless of how he chooses to go about it, man is really only looking to forget. Forget what? Everything. The fact that he was born and that this means that between life and death there is no solution, that he is forever reduced to himself, to the proportions of absolute banality. Does he really succeed in forgetting? It would seem so. And yet the truth of his condition is staring him in the face. How does he manage to deny it? The diversions offered by this city seem to be so completely ineffective. But man contents himself with little. Food, a roof to shelter him from the rain, a floor to keep out the damp, a few worthless antiques passed down from generation to generation, a modest employment so he can buy his daily bread, a Sunday in compensation for the weekdays, that's life, while there's life there's hope—hope is the poor man's bread, beggars can't be choosers—just a bit, moderation in all things, enough is enough, you reap what you sow, get used to it. Small maxims for small ambitions. This, too, he needs. With this, too, he is content. Man does not care to uncover the secret and terrifying side of things; appearance is enough for him. As long as the appearance is reassuring, all is for the best.

This is why everything in the movie theater is a façade, a mirage. Comfort, elasticity, balmy warmth, celestial music, glowing light, hideous paneling of enormous dimensions, velvet and carpeting, all of it is put at the disposal of the spectator. The most important thing is that, for two hours, sullen, dejected human beings can come experience the illusion of a better world, at the threshold of that fourth dimension that everybody talks about but nobody can define: happiness.

Since price is determined according to the height of the ceiling and the padding in the walls and seats, the ticket wiped out half of what I had earned in an entire day. Four hours of slavery in exchange for a two-hour show is quite expensive. That said, I found the show even more boring than the work I'd done earlier that day. It was even darker, grayer, flatter, and much noisier. Added to the already interminable dialogue were disembodied explanations that sounded like announcements from heaven and, on top of it all, a constant soundtrack droning in the background, an absurd contrivance that I'm happy to report is absent from real life. That's how it is, as disconcerting as it may sound. What do men do to relax and recuperate after playing their part for eight hours at work?

They go to see that same part played by another and watch this performance with a smile, delighted, pensive, drunk with wonder, hardly recognizing themselves, wholly subjugated, genuinely moved by the veneration in which they hold themselves.

And just what do the actors do in this movie I suffered through tonight? With much dramatic display, they appear to mimic what every person in the audience has either already experienced or will surely experience at some point in the future. Specifically, the movie tells the story of a man's struggle to leave his wife, wed his mistress, advance his career, and find happiness by improving his station in life. This is, in reality, what every single inhabitant of this city desires. But then, the Earthling is a great fan of what he's already familiar with. He loathes imagination as he loathes dreams. He only takes pleasure in that which he has already experienced or thought, or at most, that which, one day, he hopes to experience. Consequently, the characters in the movie talked a lot, rushed around frantically in all directions, ended up actually doing very little, and evinced a narcissistic greed that doubtless reassured everybody.

Is this what passes for entertainment here? Is this what they call diversion? Does man, then, have an unlimited capacity to put up with himself continuously at every hour of the day, even after work? Can he not do without gazing upon his own reflection, the projection of his own dreary presence? Naturally, some adjustments had been made for the film in order to put the audience at their ease; characters had been scrubbed down, fixed up, stripped of every imperfection, and carefully draped in artful chiaroscuro; luxurious sets seemed to throw off sparks under the bright lights; sequined dresses shimmered and flashed and every pleat in the clothing was perfectly fashioned; the plot and dialogue had received a good deal of tidying up as well. But the core of mediocrity remained untouched. It is impossible to remove the mediocrity that, on Earth, seems to be a law as natural as the freefall of a body in space. At the core of the movie, there was also ennui, as well as ugliness. The sets hadn't been scrubbed clean of their gray color, and even if they seemed freshly painted, the space of a year would see them sullied once again, just as a single day would betray, under the actor's foundation, the eternally devastated face of man, just as a few hours will snuff out the lights and crumple and crease the formless sacks that pass for garments here.

How can they believe such an illusion even for a second? Are they blind? Are they unconscious? Has somebody slipped them a bottle of anesthetic? Can't they see that whoever made the film has gone to great lengths to recreate events that could be observed in the real life of absolutely any human being? Can't they see that the spectacle in the actual movie theater is much more enthralling than the one projected on the screen? Can't they see the squalor already gnawing away at the plaster and stucco of that theater which they are meant to take for a dreamlike oasis of delights? Can't they smell the stink of the tomb wafting up from those hundreds of bodies pressed in one against the other? Don't they know that no amount of silver or gold or disinfectant could remove the putrid grayness that preys and feeds upon this world?

No, they don't know, and their satisfied smiles affirm that they don't want to know. They have squandered the day trying to solve insoluble problems, but they consider their evening well spent and savor every single moment, proud to have the means to treat themselves to it. They actually consider it fair compensation. They are able to make a living, and have a bit of time left over for leisure. They are getting the very most out of life, taking full advantage of the present moment, of what civilization has to offer. They are existing prudently.

I left that place completely numb, as if anesthetized by the tepid warmth in the theater, nauseated by the ennui that hung thick in the air, my head bulging with lifeless shadows and dark chasms. All of the vigor and elegant delights to be found on Fylchride wouldn't be enough to stem the crashing tide of ennui and mediocrity that smothers this world. One lesson learned at least: never again return to such a place. In the end, this kind of entertainment might be fatal to us. Ironic to think that maybe Agent 001 died because movies had become a drug to him, that some masochistic impulse had caused him to cast aside all caution and gorge himself on one film after another until it finally killed him . . .

I have to walk around for a long while to regain the certainty that I am still really and truly alive, unharmed, able to breathe.

◆ ◆ ◆

I didn't spend the night in my hotel room.

I got into bed, but then a terrible certainty that I am going to die in this place coursed through my veins, twisting and writhing into a more and more unbearable feeling of dread until I leapt out of bed and ran from my room. I had to escape, to flee that place, to go anywhere as long as it was somewhere else. But the phrase "somewhere else" means nothing now. Every block, every corner of this city represents an eternal "here" with no exit, with no escape.

Wandering through the city streets in the middle of the night, I understand that I must be wary of women. Or rather that I must be wary of my disgust for them. I've realized that women look at me with more attention than men. At times I can even see, written in their faces with strange intensity, the need to speak to me, to get closer to me. It's something to avoid at all costs; I must keep them at a distance. Never does the desire to rise up, lash out, and kill take hold of me with greater force than when I think about the fact that one can make love to these flabby, liquid things, these fat, fleshy hands without muscle whose acrid smell of sweat, of filth, of desire evokes a subtle venom of insidious power, slow-acting, but fatal. I assume that having a murder on my conscience wouldn't help matters. It's important to be aware of this risk. I mustn't forget.

I've just gotten back to the hotel.

It must be five o'clock in the morning. The sun is rising, as they say here.

No doubt this is the time to go out—now, when all the streets are deserted—in order to really understand what a wondrous seed of sorrow is nurtured and fed by this city, as if it were an enormous concrete incubator producing nothing but decay and corruption, which it slowly exudes in subtle exhalations. Store fronts, sidewalks, and the rare passerby all look to have just risen up from the waters of a marsh. The grayness is no longer that of the dust or noise of the daytime, but a glassy, almost pallid grayness of the drowned. The cold itself has lost its color. And the city has finally fallen silent, hopelessly overcome. It pulls into itself, cold and lifeless as a stone, haggard, like an addict struck down by an overdose.

While walking, I happen upon a dog: a fat, mangy larva covered in miserable clumps of hair. I'd been told that dogs possess a singular instinct. Sure enough, it approaches me, eyes full of rheum and discernment, begging for affection, bursting with that servility common to a great many humans. It crawls. It scrapes the sidewalk. Then, as it gets closer, it suddenly begins to snarl, curls up its lip and runs away with a howl. It must know. It must have smelled me. What it doesn't know is that its disgust is no greater than mine. A nearly irresistible desire courses through me, the need to crush that repugnant animal, the most repugnant to my eyes of all the monsters that populate Earth.

The air does me good.

Absent the noise, the odors, the grayness, without the ridiculously colored sky, walking in these streets is probably the easiest to bear here of all things. I'm not as tired tonight as I was the night before. Maybe it's because I haven't slept? It's bizarre to think that, for us, sleep could be exhausting on this world and staying awake restorative. But who knows? And yet, my normal vigor is lacking something. But what exactly? I feel vulnerable despite everything. I'm certain that I could never do, in this particular moment, the things that were within my power on Fylchride. As if a fine mist has seeped into my body and wrapped around my abilities, diminishing them, sapping them like a poison.

Perhaps I need more exercise. It's a good thing I'm walking, then. But there is nothing exalting about this walk, I have to admit. It's impossible to shake the feeling that I'm underwater. I walk several meters in a bleak landscape without a single remarkable feature. I move slowly, lacking any real desire to move at all. Lacking impetus. What's the use? Why walk a hundred meters, a kilometer, ten kilometers? The streets all crowd together, one inside the other, in a single circle. They all look alike; not a single one stands out among them.

Everywhere the shutters are closed, the stores are closed, the doors are shut. The city is nothing more than a ghostly wall. Everything has been packed up and taken inside.

Garbage cans alone remain out on the sidewalk, undoubtedly the excess that couldn't be crammed behind the façades. Façades that contain millions of compartments where a mass of objects have been stacked and strewn: lifeless bodies, layer upon layer of dead wood, countless old rags, mounds of clutter. The night has retreated behind the pale walls of its mausoleums, and the city is suddenly nothing more than a mournful necropolis. But a necropolis is linked by its cellars to incredible driving forces. A single alarm clock will be enough to set everything in motion. Gas will squirt into pipes, electricity will leap from one bulb to another, a low groaning will pass from turbines into human throats, life and death will rush out through the vast network of pipes. And men—connected to the sounds, to the glow, triggered by the slightest sign of activity—will get out of their beds. Like sleepwalkers, they'll grope around aimlessly until, without giving it a second thought, they find themselves living the very same day they lived the day before, in the same places, at the same times, already doing the same things.

Even inanimate objects follow the rhythm, attached by secret roots to this implacable network of inscrutable laws. Nothing and nobody are exempt from it. Except for cats, that is. Indeed, the cat is the only thing on Earth that really interests me. Probably because it doesn't seem to belong to this world. What is the source of that indolence it alone possesses, that insolent laziness that seems to thumb its nose at commerce, that ability to live life at such a languid pace amid a frantic world of fits and starts, that pleasure it gets from curling up into a ball, complacent in its apathy, opening an eye from time to time to look out on the madness of the world around it, a world that couldn't possibly concern it? Who knows? Men have often asked themselves the same questions. Strange to think that they tolerate cats. No doubt because they don't understand them.

They only understand dogs, their devoted brethren, always craving affection, always ready to perform a thousand clever tricks. In any case, cats are truly the only things on this planet with which I feel some affinity. To me they evoke the universe, the mystery of the void, the long nights of hibernation in space, Fylchride, my home world. The cat is the sole exception in a world where exceptions can only confirm the horrifying rule.

For it's nearly nine o'clock, and when that hour comes, not one man will think to go somewhere where he isn't supposed to be. Not a single man will head toward a place that's unfamiliar to him. Man's memory is the only law. It is his greatest capital. He remembers; he lets himself go to that fateful place where memory meets monotony.

It's as if man only learned to make a few basic movements as a child, then spent the rest of his life mimicking those same movements, seated in front of his own reflection. Man, it is said, descends from the ape. It's safe to say he's not forgotten it.

## DAY SIX.

This is why I, too, find myself back at the book bindery. But at least it was an effort for me to come here. At least I had to fight against the instinct to run in the opposite direction. I've only come here to obey the orders I've been given; or more precisely because, stagnating within me, stronger than anything else, is the artificial will to obey.

Here in this workshop, I find myself once again in front of the same table and the same pot of glue, always half full, in front of a pile of book covers that never gets any smaller, just like yesterday morning.

It's five after nine.

I was just informed that work begins at 09:00, not at 09:03. For a moment, I was speechless. How far can one go beyond the limits of the absurd? Then, accepting that man's pettiness knows no bounds, I acquiesce. Once again, just like earlier this morning with the dog, something rushes through my veins like a throbbing torrent: the desire to crush that man in a single blow, in an instant. Am I losing my composure little by little? I absolutely must make every effort to control myself. It goes without saying that violence is strictly forbidden.

Five after nine: already the rhythm is taking hold of everybody's hands. Nothing about today is different from yesterday. The employees are all the same. They haven't aged a single day. They don't seem surprised at the idea of finding themselves in front of an exact copy of the day before. They don't even think about it. And their reactions, the expressions they wear, they're always exactly the same, as if they are all permanently etched into a record that is played back at the beginning of each day. Perhaps it's just a coincidence? But no, something more serious must be going on, because they always say the same things, exactly the same.

"How you doing today?"

"Did you have a good night last night?"

"Kind of cold this morning."

"This new glue really isn't very good."

"Boy, did I oversleep this morning."

All of this and more. And it's always the same. I can't be fooled on this account. My people don't forget. I remember every single syllable. No, what I'm experiencing right now can't be real. I'm still asleep in my bed. I believe I'm at work, but I'm really wandering around in a nightmare whose horror is its terrifying banality. Or maybe I'm awake but I've unwittingly taken a false step and fallen through a crack in time. Nothing serious after all then. This isn't the present I'm experiencing right now but the past, yesterday all over again. I've already lived every second of it; I remember perfectly. Why doesn't anybody stand up and ask to see a supervisor so this can be brought to the attention of management? Have they all lost their memory? Or maybe I'm the only one living this day over again and everybody else is living it for the first time? In any case, I object. I refuse. There's no point in taking up my brush and performing the assigned movements because I've already completed them all. And if I acquiesce today, that means that I accept this demented reality and then tomorrow I'll accept it with even less resistance, and for days, weeks, years, I'll have to repeat these same movements. Maybe I'll even make my peace with it: Agent 002: book cover specialist. I mustn't be taken in by this reality, perfectly recreated, yes, but absolutely false. The trap is in the flawless appearance. Though it remains to be seen what this trap was intended for. Refuse to cooperate for a start, that's all I can really do.

But hold on, I'm not dreaming after all. I haven't slipped backward through time. Yesterday the calendar showed the twenty-third of March, today it reads the twenty-fourth of March. Twenty-three plus one, that makes twenty-four. This is definitely the same day in terms of space, but a different one in terms of time. Men accept this fact, they're habituated to it, resigned to it; not me. We hadn't envisaged this kind of reiteration back on Fylchride, not even during the most intense parts of our training. It was spoken of, but only vaguely. For thirty minutes a day, I learned my trade, as odd and ridiculous as it seemed, but nobody had ever told me that I would be reduced to painting glue on with a brush and that this monotony would persist, not only throughout the morning, but for eight full hours, and then again the next day, and the day after that. Impossible. I'll never be able to do it. On Fylchride, where monotony never extends beyond an hour, we would never be able to repeat the exact same thing over and over again, in the same place, for the same reasons, only interrupted by a few hours respite per day. How could we when our entire existence was predicated on the myth of variety, when our entire world—dynamic, unstable, and in a constant state of flux—revolved around this principle? I realize now that even the training I'd received for life on Earth, as grueling as it was, hadn't escaped contamination by the Fylchridian love of variety. There's been a mistake. They thought I was ready to survive on Earth, to endure life here, but nothing could be further from the truth. I'm unable to do what's required of me. Between the brushstroke I should be making and my body, there's an invisible wall that stops me cold, a barrier that I can never cross. There's just no way.

This is it. It's still morning and already I can't take it anymore. Every fiber of my being tells me to flee, to drop everything and run.

And here I sit, brush in hand, its movement suspended in the air mid-stroke.

And the man next to me grows impatient waiting for me to pass him the glue-covered cardboard, as if every flyleaf he slapped on earned him a fortune.

"What's the hold up?" he says. "We're wasting time."

I'm going to attract attention, I can feel it, but it's no use. I can't move. Has it really come to this? To the point of forgetting my orders, the exhortations to prudence, the directives against arousing suspicion? I don't know. I can't seem to recall exactly what my orders were anymore. And since, in theory, they should haunt my every thought without my even being aware of it, since my entire body is supposed to be saturated with them, it would seem that this fluid has evaporated, completely leeched away. All that's left is a profound sense of unease, which isn't normal either. Something's not right. What happened to my composure? Where's my sense of calm? Has it all evaporated? Leeched away? For the moment at least. I desperately try to convince myself this isn't happening, that I'm overreacting, but I'm still unable to move; I can't seem to bring the brush down to the cardboard, it hangs frozen in the air, as if encased in a block of ice. And we're wasting time, as my coworker has just pointed out. Three minutes already. And second by second, drop by drop, the time flows in like so much money, collecting and pooling around me. Three minutes, that must be several liters' worth of it. Another minute goes by and time spills over and flows into the room. Wonderful, that's all I needed, now I'm causing a flood. And still, it's impossible to free my brush from that block of air that grips it like a vice. The other employees start to drown, everybody except me. They gawk, they point their fingers, they start to ask questions. So I can live underwater? They find this strange. Another fact I was supposed to keep hidden from them. I must have forgotten.

How was I going to explain, without arousing suspicion, that I could easily remain underwater for up to two hours? But now they're demanding an explanation. They're shouting questions at me; I try to answer but the words won't come. They're stuck just like the brush. They decide to dissect me. But I'm still alive. Which seems stranger and stranger to me. Who are you? Precisely the question I must avoid at all costs. I finally manage to make a tiny movement to save myself. I open my hand, the brush finally comes free, falls to the ground.

"Don't you feel good?" somebody eventually asks.

"Not very good, no. And you?"

A stupid, pointless question. Of course, he feels good. He doesn't understand. Neither do I for that matter. How do they do it? Are they somehow immune to all the terror and oppression they have to face each day? Do they not have the impression, as I do, of eyes clouded with a grayish ink, an ink that grows thicker as it reaches the throat, dries out everything it touches, and finally bursts into a thousand nightmares, all of them rooted in the same vision of that brushstroke eternally suspended in the air? Have they never felt the panic that comes from working, not in front of a pot of glue, but inside of it, inside an enormous pot of it, where air, light, and life all run together in a nauseating mixture?

Frightened, not knowing what else to do, I find the supervisor; I tell him that I feel faint, that I'd like to go home.

"That's really too bad," he tells me. "You've only been here a few days. It won't make a good impression. But if you really don't feel good."

What can I say? That I don't plan to make a career in this company anyway? Or in this city for that matter, or even on this planet? I just thank him and leave.

I've come back to the hotel. I'm lying on the bed.

What should I do? Indecision once again, something that's so foreign to me, so completely unknown. On Fylchride I would never have had this problem. It would never have been possible. But here I find myself confronted by a complex tangle of possibilities, all of them negative, all of them hostile, forbidding.

After leaving the bindery, I was going to take a walk, but I quickly realized I wouldn't get far. I'd walked around the city for several hours that morning, and the thought of walking any longer fills me with disgust. Better just to go straight back to the hotel. But there is no escape to be had there either. Noise passes through the thickest walls, odors pullulate in everything, each object having been sullied by millions of hands; and then there's the ennui, which constitutes the space and time of this world. The hours of the day, geometry, the basic principles of life, all of civilization rests upon thousands of corollaries that all follow from a single theorem defining ennui.

I'm afraid.

There's no denying it. I've only been here six days, but in the air of this world, all the properties I was injected with on Fylchride are slowly fading away. I'm afraid, and everything within me yearns to call out for help. To escape. To return to Fylchride. To leave this place before I sink too far into the sea of gray. To do something while I still have the strength. Why were we ordered to destroy the ship that brought us here? Why were these ships only designed for a one-way trip, from Fylchride to Earth, with no possibility of return? Had we been sent here to die? If so, why not simply let us die at home? Surely death was less horrifying on Fylchride.

Death. I'd never given it a thought. I had so many years ahead of me. At least I did back on Fylchride. Was it really I that wanted so badly to go on this mission to Earth? An expression of my will alone? Or had the will of another been foisted upon me? I can't be sure. Nothing makes sense anymore. I'm afraid. It feels like my thoughts are foundering, along with my composure, my reflexes. Everything in me is submerged. The pressure at these depths squeezes my head like a vice; the water blurs my vision. I feel walled in by ennui, as if in a bell jar filled with viscous liquid. Everything in me is lifeless and limp. Everything seems to move in slow motion, hopelessly adrift. At times I could almost believe I no longer had a body and that the only thing left was a strange consciousness floating in the dark void behind my eyes.

Maybe I just need sleep. If I got a good night's sleep, I might feel better. But how can I wish for sleep when every time I awaken, I have to face the terrifying reality of this world, grayer than ever as it emerges from the night? If only my room would erupt in a brilliant burst of light and strident colors, just for an hour or so. What I wouldn't give to be able to hide myself away in a tunnel of purple! What I wouldn't do to be able to look upon a silent explosion of colors that would eradicate the colorless babel that's paralyzing me little by little!

What will I do, as my strength is gradually slipping away, when my fear turns to panic?

What was it that killed Agent 001? Am I really going to die in the same way he did? Or perhaps I'll find the courage to choose my own death? Six days. In twenty-four days, one month. Only two more months before Agent 003 arrives. At present he's making preparations to depart. How can I warn him? If I only had the strength to scream *no* back across that vast distance. No, no, NO. Do you hear me? Stay where you are. But it's already too late. Agent 003 is falling through space like lightning. And already Agent 004 is taking his place, just as eager to leave. Drunk with life, brimming with confidence, immune to all fear and worry.

What was there to worry about? What harm could possibly befall us on Earth? A world of no consequence—noisy, devoid of color, but completely innocuous. After all, we had so much experience, didn't we? And this certainly wasn't our first time on an alien world, not by a long shot.

Would we get to see any others? Will you see any others, Agent 004? To die of boredom. An oft-used expression on this planet. Such a ridiculous expression. Nobody here ever died of boredom. Absolutely nobody, understand? Impossible.

Nobody. I have no right entertaining such an absurd idea.

No right, none. And yet I do think about it; I can think of nothing else. Think, endure, forget, sleep.

Dream? But on this world, even dreams are dull, washed-out, gray.

## DAY NINETEEN.

I've returned to my job at the bindery.

It's already been a week. I go there. I work.

Work, sleep. That's all I do now.

I don't go out anymore. I've changed hotels to be closer to work. I no longer go on walks. I haven't gone to see any movies. I never go anywhere I might run into a group of men who've gathered together for amusement or simply to share their boredom. Getting through work is hard enough already without, on top of that, having to sit through the varied assortment of spectacles offered to employees for their diversion. When I get home, I go to bed. Sometimes I work extra hours, pushing myself to the point of exhaustion so I can fall directly from work into sleep without transition. I don't want to think anymore. I've noticed that after an hour or so, work emits such a stifling cloud of ennui and stupefaction that I become entirely numb, immune from all thought. That's exactly what I want. At this point I only have one goal, a single obsession: hold out until the arrival of Agent 003. After that, we'll see. Flee perhaps, if that's even possible. It has to be possible. I must never let myself suspect it isn't possible. My only chance is to believe that there's an end to all this. And that it's coming very soon.

I've already made it sixteen days. I'm counting them. I have to last for ninety days in all. Work is the only place where I might have a chance because there, all I have to do is relive the same day over and over again. That's why I went back. I'd already done a full day's work and made it through all right, so I figured I should be able to get through all ninety days, since all I do is repeat the same thing, a repetition that excludes all risk and disallows the unexpected. There's too much risk in wandering aimlessly through the street, seeking desperately to relieve my anguish. More and more I think about Agent 001. Most likely he's dead because he fled from work and then crossed paths with whatever it was that killed him as he made his escape. Where? How? I have no idea. Perhaps a particularly noxious night at the movie theater? Perhaps an act of love with an Earth woman that poisoned him? It doesn't really matter in any case. After giving it some thought, I've realized that the ennui isn't going to kill me. Not by itself at least. And besides, ennui is everywhere. At least at the bindery it's not as aggressive because it's clearly defined and out in the open. After a while, I stop noticing it. It's like being buried in cotton wool. I see nothing; I feel nothing. I'm suspended between life and death. I cease to be. I acquiesce because I no longer have the strength to resist.

True, my fatigue is getting worse. But when I do nothing it becomes even more unbearable. At least by coming to work, I can persuade myself that this fatigue is normal. That my work is difficult, that holding a paintbrush must be particularly draining. I have to be especially careful never to think about what I was capable of doing back on Fylchride. That was another world, another universe. Here on Earth, everything is different: the climate, the terrain, the pressure exerted by the atmosphere. All of these things are sure to affect my abilities. Maybe I'll be able to adapt to it. It's possible at least. I've been assured that I'm very good at my job. I apply myself; I'm docile and disciplined, and the brutish nature of the work imparts to my features a permanent air of resignation. I tried to work through the night once. But I couldn't do it. I had to stop around three in the morning. I needed sleep. I'm becoming more human. I'm starting to adopt their habits. Perhaps I'll eventually start eating one, two, even three meals per day.

I follow the rhythm, as if drugged, asleep, knocked unconscious. It really doesn't matter what state I'm in though. I'm alive. I want to make it through this. The rest is unimportant. Besides, I'm afraid that if I stopped making at least some kind of perfunctory movement, my body would calcify completely.

Other than that, nothing ever happens. It's strange really: every morning and evening sees the publication of thousands of newspapers containing descriptions of a great many events—spectacular accidents, tantalizing tales of murder, earthquakes, and tsunamis— affirming that the world is a volcano of uncertainty. Where do they dig up these newsworthy events? I'm inclined to believe that they just make them up, for I've never seen anything of the kind occur in this city. Nothing ever happens apart from a daily migration of millions of human beings who leave their homes every morning and return to them later that evening.

There was an accident at the bindery this morning. Shall I notify the press? Or perhaps a television reporter? One of the workers cut her hand. It was pretty serious. Work at the bindery was completely disrupted. Not only did it break the rhythm but all activity officially ceased for at least ten minutes. And now, nobody can talk about anything else. This topic will dominate every conversation for days. It just proves that they have nothing to say, nothing to see, nothing to feel, nothing to live for in this world. A tiny spark seems like an explosion. None of them can understand that, in reality, nothing has happened. This ridiculous incident changes nothing. Even the woman who was injured will be back to work in a few days; she'll have gained nothing and lost nothing. A day lived for nothing, just like every other day.

It's April. The grayest month of them all. It rains continuously. Rain, as if the sky were rotting and falling to Earth in a billion little pieces. It smells even worse than their so-called drinking water. And more than ever, in the rain, the feeling of decay. It seems to have something oily about it; it gets under the skin, penetrates flesh and bone, and everything it touches shudders like a thousand gongs. It makes things so much worse. It amplifies the daily racket; it turns the dust into mud and the gray into a darker gray. But I've become accustomed to this as well. I know that things aren't going to get any better. Nothing in this world, real or illusory, can palliate the misery of this condition. It's no longer a question of looking for a way out or some means of escape. I prefer to stay where I am, conserving my strength and vital resources. I have only one goal now: Survive. Wait.

It's clear I'm getting weaker though. I'm forced to admit it, despite myself. For I don't want to know, I mustn't know. One day, however, while I was in my hotel room, I felt the need to do something, anything, and brought my fist down upon the table with all of my strength. The blow should have shattered it instantly. It only made a lengthy crack.

Then I understood. It wasn't just an illusion; I was really getting weaker. But I mustn't think about it; that's the most important thing. I can't let myself believe it. My strength is declining, but I still have more than enough to survive here. It would still provoke surprise and astonishment from the inhabitants of this world. I have to work constantly to keep it under control, and it's becoming more and more difficult. Maybe because I sense, vaguely, that it's gradually slipping away, imperceptibly. Yesterday, for example, toward the end of the workday, the employees around me were joking around to pass the time, and I almost gave in to the urge to strike out at random, to snuff out that horrible laughter gurgling in their throats like fat frying in a pan. It is man's laughter that irritates me more profoundly than anything else. The stupidest things will set it off. When he eats and when he laughs, that's when man appears in all his ugliness: hoarse and pleased with himself, disfigured, his open mouth revealing decay and putrefaction; he is a sack of flesh closed up around rotting teeth. But this is his true form. And then there's the shattering noise in my head when laughter erupts close by. And why this mania for laughter anyway? How can it be explained? How can they laugh day after day, year after year, at the same words, at the same jokes?

An outsider, that's what I am. I'll never understand the telos, the secret motives that animate this world. Better just to close my eyes so that I won't be tempted to see and to reason. But since I can't live with my eyes closed, I've made the decision simply not to look at the things around me any longer. The only things I allow myself to look at are the pot of glue, the brush, the piece of cardboard, and the task at hand. I've shut myself up in a single dimension: work. I just want to stay in here from now on.

I should also say that I'm not taking this situation completely lying down. The stress of living in a world that attacks my senses with such hostility compels me to defend myself. And I defend myself as best I can, with the means at my disposal. A few days ago, in order to give my eyes a rest from constant immersion in the gray, I had the idea to buy sheets of purple paper and, in the evenings, hang them on the walls of my room.

Yesterday I found something even better. Glasses that protect against the sun, with purple-tinted lenses. I put them on as soon as I leave the bindery. My vision remains gloomy, drearier than before in fact, but the gray is dampened, altered somehow.

I've managed to dampen the noise as well, by stuffing my ear full of cotton balls.

They've helped things somewhat. It's impossible to escape the smells, however.

It's also impossible to know whether any of this really does any good. Are the smells more harmful to us than the noise? Is the color gray really the source of my disgust? Or is it men and their words, their laughter, the environment they've created? Or, even more unsettling, the sinister conjugation of all these things that, by some secret transmutation, have ended up forming a three-dimensional world?

Impossible to know. And if I die, I'll die never knowing what killed me. So what use is there in thinking about it? And that's the real victory of these last few days, the fact that I don't think about it anymore. I endure, I defend myself, I retreat.

I want to live.

That is to say, I'm no longer concerned about completing my mission. I've stopped taking notes because I'm no longer conducting any experiments. I don't go anywhere. I have nothing to say, nothing to report. I already know the most important thing: that it is practically impossible to live among Earthlings.

And I suspect something else: what I'm experiencing at this moment is not the end.

Something else has to happen.

But what?

# DAY THIRTY-FOUR.

What?

I don't know yet, but certain things are becoming clear. It occurred to me to take my temperature this morning. Normally it should be around 101.6°; I realized with astonishment that it's dropped to 97.7°. How long has it been so low? There's no way to know. But what I feel is entirely consistent with the implications of such a drop in temperature.

My recent weakness for one; it's been especially bad since yesterday evening. I only barely summoned the will to get out of bed this morning. As I lay there on my back, the ceiling looked vast like a sky, and it seemed so low as to almost be resting on my body. Impossible to sit up without touching it, and the thought of coming into contact with that mass of gray was so repugnant that I couldn't bring myself to move. All throughout my body I felt nascent acts swimming in ambivalence just below the surface, so elusive, so sluggish. Every so often they would drift up toward my face, linger a moment, then sink back down like stones. I was one with the moist warmth of the bed. I was an insubstantial heap of infirmity hidden beneath a layer of down. I wanted very much to keep my eyes open, but rivers of darkness poured into them without reprieve. Beneath this deluge, I toppled backward; I felt myself sink down into the warmth of the bed, which was becoming deeper and deeper, and there was no way to get back to the surface. Tired of struggling, I gave up. I fell into a large hole, and when I climbed back out again, it was eleven o'clock in the morning.

As soon as I got up, that's when I took my temperature and realized with dismay how low it was. What's going to happen to me? Will it drop as low as 89.6°, or even 86°?

Where will it stop? Am I going to slowly harden into a block of ice or marble? Is that how this ends? Out of desperation, I attempt to make a few violent movements.

Immediately I'm forced to stop. The effort is shattering my vertebrae; it feels like my body is tearing itself apart. What do I need? More rest or more exercise? More sleep or more work? There's no way to know. Life was so simple on Fylchride. Uncertainty like this didn't exist because there weren't any unknowns to grind our lives down in a slow attrition. My present situation is so complex because I don't understand what's happening to me. The cause, first and foremost, I have to discover the cause. But how? Even a doctor wouldn't understand any of this. And I can never call a doctor, even on my deathbed.

They would have to open me up from top to bottom and send me away piece by piece to a laboratory in order to find out. And it might not even do any good. What I'm experiencing is doubtless unthinkable for the men of this world, just as it is unthinkable for me because I am not of this world. There's nothing to be done. Shall I grope around aimlessly for uncertain solutions? Shall I trust my intuition? But I have no intuition in particular at the moment. Only a few vague hypotheses come to mind. Maybe I should drink some alcohol to put some fire in my veins? Or take ice baths? Or hot baths instead? If I gouge out my eyes and destroy the hearing in my good ear, would I be able to cope then? Or perhaps I should really start by destroying my sense of smell? Is it possible that sleep is harmful, fatal? Or is it being awake that's killing me?

But the truth is even more horrible, and though I try to deny it, I know there can be no doubt: everything here is harmful to me. Everything, absolutely everything. The dust, the color, the air, the rain, the heat, the ennui, the noise, the filth. A veritable coalition that grows more aggressive, more dangerous with each passing day. And the dust, it seems to be coming down thicker and thicker, like snow; everything is turning grayer before my eyes, growing dirtier and dirtier, exactly as if I were slowly sinking down into a world identical to the world of yesterday, but buried deeper in its mist and in its cocoon. And all of this without mentioning the hidden snares that one isn't expecting and that one discovers all of a sudden, impossible to uproot or destroy. For example, yesterday at the hotel, my neighbor acquired a radio, one of those home sets. Nothing can deaden the noise, which passes through walls as if they were made of air. What can I do? Nothing.

Just put up with it: the static, the chatter, the explosions of sound coming out of this appliance that demonstrates just how desperate man's need is to fill his head with noise at all hours of the day.

No, I'm going to have to change rooms. I have to be on the defensive at all times, continuously fleeing and evading. Most often in vain.

Who's to say I won't end up in a room with a radio set on either side? Or in a room that, through a generous addition, is equipped with a gigantic loudspeaker?

I don't know.

I'm too weary to make the effort to know.

I might as well use what strength I have this morning to transport myself to the bindery, despite everything.

Besides, I urgently need to get out of this room. Somebody's preparing a meal on the ground floor. The odor wafts up to my room, creeps under the door, knocks down the walls, flattens everything in its path and assaults my face like an invisible wave. How does one stop an odor? What can be done to defend against it? If I opened the window, I'd merely be trading the odor of food for that of gasoline and sewage, or worse, the enduring stench of the filth that weeps from every object in this world.

Then, the maid knocks at my door.

"Housekeeping. Is this a good time?" she asks.

She tugs vaguely at the sheets, hurriedly passes a rag over a few surfaces, collects a few particles of dust. If only she could strip the hazy color from this place, change the awkward form of the objects within it, take away the gray light that pervades everything, wrap it up in the thick veil of odors and discard the whole thing in some far-off place, kilometers from here. What she's doing is utterly useless. All of her bustling about is in vain. And so is the way she's moving her thighs and hips around in a dress that's much too tight, hoping that I might screw her on the bed. But the fetid smell of cooking food in my throat is bad enough without having to endure the odor of raw flesh, the stink of this woman's desire. If I had to make love to her at this very moment, I think I would kill her without hesitation. Just to do something. Just to finally know how it feels to hold within my grasp a cause of my terror and to be able to grind it into dust with my own hands.

Fortunately, nothing happens.

The maid collects her rags and her broom; she smiles, pleased with herself, and says, "There you go, the room's all clean."

Yes, of course it is. The room is clean. It's sunny outside. The weather's mild.

There's a pleasant smell of spring. A pleasant smell of flowers, of fruit, of women. The air is pure. The sun bathes the city in vivid colors. The sidewalks are washed clean by the rain, and the façades are like new. Everything shines with a singular brilliance. The world itself breathes joy, purity, light. It's good to be alive.

Man has never left his world. He doesn't know how lucky he is: he can live in a world of mirage and illusion. He has faith. The naïve strength of faith. Yes, they'd thought of almost everything back on Fylchride before I left for Earth. But they forgot one detail that could very well kill me: they forgot to take away my lucidity, my ability to see, to remember, to compare.

Ah! To believe. To believe, if only for a minute, that it really is bright, beautiful, and clean here.

## DAY FORTY-TWO.

I can't take it anymore.

I'm going to have to quit my job. I'm only just managing to perform the limited number of movements my work requires. Endlessly maneuvering my brush up and down for hours on end plunges me into a nauseating vertigo, and I can no longer claw my way back out of it.

More and more I feel as though I'm working in a vat with towering walls, deep in the bowels of a stagnant gray, and every movement I make must fight against the roaring current of glue whose rising tide has infiltrated every facet of my existence. There's not an ounce of strength left in my muscles; they're crumbling away, isolated, cut from my tendons, and the will to reattach them has fled from me. I just let it happen; I can't fight any longer.

I need to leave this place before I get into serious trouble.

Just yesterday I almost caused an incident. It could have turned out very badly. It must have been about five o'clock. I was trying in vain to pass from the next-to-last hour of work into the final hour. In vain because each second took on an approximate value, thrust into a zone where duration had no more seconds at its disposal with which to traverse the hours. Out of strength and out of patience, trying to keep a calm exterior, I was lurching from one action to the next, yet nearly immobile, staring into nothing, letting my hands busy themselves so far away from me—independent and reduced to hideous marionettes gesticulating wildly, reassuring everybody that all was for the best in the best of all possible worlds. And the worker sitting next to me who'd been drunk since noon was talking to me. Talking incessantly. Talking about food, women, things he'd said, things people had said to him, what he'd said in return, what he'd done. So many words that all smelled of sex and rotting meat, of wine and the marsh. And it all combined with the nauseating odor of work, and it all sank down into the torpor that filled me to bursting and inspired a deep-seated feeling of malaise; and I, too, was swept up in that turbulent muck; I was spinning around in slow motion; the words tossed me about violently like a gigantic mixing spoon; I would sink far below the surface, and then at times, I would make it back up again, but the words met me there; and the disgust took on a greater density, submerging everything else. My fear of being swallowed up was so great that I stood up and flung my brush violently against the wall.

"Stop!" I yelled. "Shut your mouth! Stop!"

He stopped talking, out of surprise more than fear. He'd only narrowly averted disaster. So had I. All the strength I'd lost, as if rising up in one last convulsion, had come rushing back to me and gathered into my hand, which was already squeezed into a fist. Had I raised that fist into the air and struck, it would have shattered the man's face. But he fell silent, and all fell silent around his silence. And I collapsed to the floor in slow motion, like a pile of old rags only slightly heavier than the air. It was decided that I had fainted. I was told to go home.

I returned to work this morning.

"You're still very pale," somebody remarked.

"You've really lost your tan," noticed another.

Pale? Impossible. We cannot blush with shame, turn white with anger, or pale due to some fainting spell. These are so many terms that do not apply to us. We are born with our tan and remain that way permanently. I knew my coworkers were spouting nonsense, yet it shook me up. It shook me terribly. I rushed outside; I went to look at myself in the mirror of a store window in full daylight.

I saw.

I stood there for several minutes, stunned. I saw, I understood, I recognized the truth.

It's impossible, of course. But true nonetheless: I am dreadfully pale. My complexion has changed. It's become like ash, like dust, colorless and coated in grime. Almost like a man's. My eyes seem to be losing their clarity. They're glazing over, as if a drop of smoke had been injected into the pupils. My face, my vision, everything is fading away. I'm clouding over.

It staggers belief, but I have to believe it; there's no denying it. The grime, the gray, the smoke, the mist, they bleed me of color, encircle and besiege me so relentlessly that I'm losing myself in the washed-out palette of this world. My native properties are disintegrating little by little and gradually being replaced by something else.

The end? Is this a sign of the end? The gloomy color of the end?

I try to think about it. But already my thoughts are as blurry as the images that detach themselves from this world and crowd into my eyes, rushing in violently like a torrent or wafting in gently, slowly, like an insidious gas—poisonous in either case.

Still forty-eight days before the arrival of Agent 003. I must hang on for forty-eight more days and then . . . and then what?

The circle can't be broken. When Agent 003 finds me, dead or alive, he'll have gained nothing but the certainty that he too is going to die. Like Agent 004. And Agent 005. And the others, all the others. Until back on Fylchride they finally decide to send a representative to Earth whose sole task is to make contact and return home with a report. But that was the problem. Such a thing would never occur to them. Reaching Earth was all that mattered. Getting back home was never part of the plan. What exactly were they thinking? What could have led them to act in such a way? Perhaps they had decided that life on Fylchride was too simple, providing an ideal existence completely disconnected from the death that we would never see coming, that was so far away. Perhaps they wanted to know how we would react when faced with a slow, incomprehensible death, a death that killed gradually, drawing closer and closer, looming greater and greater. Could this be the secret goal of our mission, the goal they'd kept hidden from us?

To know and yet to be unable to even cry out for help. Unable to say anything.

Unable to do anything. Except wait. Endure. And feel the life weeping out of our bodies from an unknown wound. Feel death drawing near; feel it slowly draping over us like a pall, quietly, gently, as a matter of course.

Wait. Bound, gagged, drugged, in the middle of a bizarre organic chemistry experiment.

Wait for how much longer? How many more days? How many more weeks?

## DAY FIFTY-FOUR.

Only one month left. Only one enormous day of a month's duration. Only one interminable month-long second.

How will I know when I've reached the end of it, or gone beyond it? How am I to make such an assessment? By counting the seconds? But am I still able to count? Am I still able to discern without error when I'm sleeping, unconscious, or awake? Can I still tell the difference between dreams, hallucinations, and reality? Between minutes and days, yesterdays and tomorrows, height and width, smells and sounds? Did I ever know the difference? Perhaps I've been mistaking sounds for images or different perspectives for variations in temperature. I don't know; I can't be sure of anything anymore.

I think I remember having changed rooms. I chose a hideous room whose red wallpaper set everything ablaze. But the color has already faded; the red is bleeding away and slowly being replaced by the gray. I don't ever leave my room now. I don't want to see, or hear, or endure anymore. I simply wait. Most often I lie on the bed with the shutters closed, with the window closed, with my eyes closed.

I am nowhere.

I am in an enclosed space of uncertain dimensions where what life I have left wheezes and gulps for air. I am outside of time. I am disconnected from everything else. I'm nothing more than a substance without form that, from time to time, soaks up a spurt of sensation like a sponge soaking up water. One glimmer of awareness remains, inescapable, more dreadful than anything else: that of absorbing the gray, continuously, no matter what I do. The gray, as I had foreseen and inferred, molds itself to any form, works its way in by the subtlest transformations. Every place is its lair, and everything a syringe that injects it into something else. I can't escape it. When I plug my ears, it gets in through my eyes, pouring in from all sides. When I close my eyes, it creeps from one sound to another, flattening itself against the softest rustling. When, blind and deaf, I think I've escaped it, it transforms into an odor, becomes invisible, abstract, just long enough to pass through my defenses, whereupon it immediately turns back into a thick noxious flow of gray. And when I manage to expel all of the air and create a perfect vacuum inside of me, then it comes in through my pores, like dust, impossible to keep out; it filters into every part of me, impossible to spit back out. There's no stopping it now. I am its prey. The more gray I absorb, the more it rises up around me. No doubt I'm now just a mass of gray. A great, living mound of gray. Still alive. But not for much longer. Soon I'll be nothing more than a block of gray. Then just a flat gray surface. Once I've lost a few pounds and a few dimensions, then I'll finally have adapted fully to Earth. And with such skill! I'll actually be a part of this world, its environment, its civilization. I'll have accomplished my mission in a way that goes beyond what anybody could have hoped for back on Fylchride.

Sometimes I try to determine exactly what it is that has contaminated me the most. The ennui? The environment? The noise? The living creatures? The filth? The stench? There's no way to know for sure since each is a root in a tangled mass of roots, all of them converging at the very heart of my existence. All of them secreting the same color, the same poison, the same mortal corruption. But why do I have the feeling that there's even more gray entering into me? What part of me has it not yet corrupted? Where has it not already gone? Am I still too soft? Too spongy? That must be it. I need to grow denser. To have not only the ashen color of the gray, but its density as well. The mineral density of pumice.

I don't want to look at myself in the mirror anymore. No more need. I know I've turned completely gray, as if I were nothing but a pillar of ash. Or a cocoon. The cocoon. The beating heart of this world. It's haunted and tormented me for so long, now I myself am becoming a cocoon. I weave my walls. I'm nearly complete. I draw upon every square centimeter of this world, extracting from it a new substance and feeding patiently upon it. Everything contributes to me, willingly or no, and my death secretes itself with boundless ingenuity. It germinates and I germinate within it, swallowed up little by little. All of the fluids in my body have already turned gray. My saliva is gray. The air I exhale from my lungs is gray. And yesterday, I sliced open a vein to confirm what I already suspected: my blood is gray. Just like my nerves, my bones, my muscles, my heart, my skin, my eyes. Everything.

I am the color gray.

Living my last gray hour in a gray room, hemmed in by thousands of gray façades built atop a gigantic mine of gray whose emanations have laid waste an entire universe.

Even my terror has succumbed. Now gray and colorless, it is nearly imperceptible. I can no longer scream. I can only be silent. But this silence, just like everything else, is gray.

## DAY FIFTY-SEVEN.

Only for a moment.

If only for a moment I could sit up in bed and talk to a being of my own race. Tell him that I know; for I know everything. I've slogged far and wide through the ennui and senseless agitation in which man contends, trying to discover what goal he could possibly be pursuing. I know now. I finally understand: it's death, death alone, the entire secret is there. Earth is the antechamber of death. That's all it is. Men are just walking corpses.

They live only for death. They prepare for it all their lives. That's why, from childhood to their last hours of life, they inure themselves to ennui, to the void, to the infinite repetition of a single act, to long hours of sleep, to everything that approximates death.

Their whole lives are just a dress rehearsal for death. They learn how to become perfect corpses, perfectly conditioned and perfectly submissive. Life for them is so brief, and death so long. Perhaps they're right to act as they do. And that's also why everything is gray. To accustom them to the color of the void. To be ready for it. To pass seamlessly from a cataleptic life in the gray to an eternal rest in the gray. There's hardly any transition at all; I've finally seen things clearly; I know. But it's already too late. Far too late.

If I could just transmit this secret and, at the same time, let somebody know that there had been a mistake. We Fylchridians, we were made for life. Everything on Fylchride was life, duration, brilliance, power, and triumph. We had no need to prepare ourselves for death, and in any case, our eternity couldn't possibly be gray.

A mistake, do you hear me?

I can't be part of this funereal game, in this world that stinks like a tomb. I have to tell them; I have to find a way out of this situation. But whom shall I tell? To start with I'll call the maid, ask her to bring cleaning supplies, brushes, a shovel, to clear a path through these enormous barriers of gray so that I can at least get to the door of my room. But what's the point? That door leads nowhere. There's only one door I need: the one I passed through when I came to this place. Was it really a door? I don't remember.

There's so much that I can't remember anymore. There's cement in the gray that I've accumulated. My past has hardened into a solid mass from which nothing can be extracted. What's happened to me? I used to be alive; that I can still remember; I lived a life akin to that of fire or ice, light or the wind. I was renowned, adored, feared. How is it that I'm currently so dense, like a stone sinking into a bed of sediment, half-sunken into it already, in a kind of fish tank, surrounded by its walls, stuffed beneath its ceiling, deprived of light, hunted by everything around me, and devoured by everything within me? Why am I not capable of shattering these walls, of throwing off the ceiling? Why does my tongue refuse to pronounce even a single word? How can it be, in passing from one world to the next, that I've lost all the qualities I once possessed and slowly acquired all the qualities that will lead to my death?

Lost . . . that's what I am. Lost with nowhere to go, with no possibility of clinging to some piece of debris. Everything I touch sinks down into the numbness that has already half-digested me. When my eyes and mouth slip beneath the surface of this bog, that will be the end.

If only, just for a moment, I could get away from this dampness, this feeling that I'm in an aquarium. Have I unknowingly betrayed my identity? Perhaps they've placed me in a display window filled with water in the middle of the city, fully exposed to the stares of stunned onlookers. They have finally realized that I didn't come from this world and put me in a fish tank labeled "space creature," like some kind of monster. But why would they think I'm a sea monster? Why have they put me in the water and mud of an artificial marsh? I really need to let them know that really, I ... but wait, where are they? Where are the passersby, the onlookers, the voyeurs ridiculing me from the other side of the glass? I can't see them anymore; the glass has become as opaque as stone to my eyes. No doubt they're still there, somewhere beyond this gray smoke that envelops me on all sides. But it's impossible to know where. Impossible to know what they want from me, what they intend to do with me. There's no use worrying about it. They can't possibly dream up a death more sadistic than the one I'm already dying at the hands of a million little invisible things.

I have one last request. I won't ask for anything else. Please take me out of this swamp. Let me die in the sun. Somewhere dry. For pity's sake. It doesn't matter where, just somewhere dry.

They did it.

They took me out. When? I couldn't say, but they did it.

I ought to make an effort to sit up so I can thank them, but that's no longer possible. Thank them with what? There's no expression left in my face; I've no more sounds at my disposal. Nothing. I have only a vague awareness that I'm no longer underwater. They've moved me somewhere else. To some other place, this one filled with air and warmth.

I'm dry here.

They put me in a gigantic dryer. Left me in too long actually; I'm certain there's not a drop of blood or saliva left in my entire body. I'm just a desiccated husk full of air, heat, and void. For my protection, they've wrapped me in cotton. In a protective case of pure-white cotton, that's where they've put me. Under a cotton ceiling, between cotton walls, at the center of the sterile, exsiccating warmth of an enormous ball of cotton. And surrounded by beings made entirely from cotton as well. They're really quite attentive. They float around me in a fog, distorted, transparent, ghost-like, but distended in their movements, so very fluid, imbued with such a strange impression of tenderness and precision. They take care of me. They have but one concern: how best to serve me. They come in and out; they split apart their bodies, break them into pieces, pull themselves back together, grow additional hands and fingers. All to better fly to my aid. To better care for me.

Care for me or kill me? Maybe they don't even know. And what does it matter? Even if they really want to keep me alive, there's nothing they can do about it now. Their actions will lead to my death all the same. That's something else I really should try to communicate to them, but how?

I need to tell them, for example, that already they're doing the wrong thing. How absurd it is filling that little syringe with a dose of liquid gray. Can't they see I'm already drowning in an ocean of it? Can't they see it vomiting out of every pore? Are they trying to hasten my death, as an act of mercy perhaps? I need to tell them that there might be a chance of saving me with that syringe: dump out the gray and fill it instead with a brilliant purple or scarlet and inject liter after liter of it into my veins. Then and only then do I stand a chance, a slim chance. But man knows everything. They know better. They act because they know; they act without hesitation.

"Do you think that's a sufficient dose?" one of them asks.

"Yes, I'm certain it is. We'll administer another injection in an hour," another responds.

The needle comes toward me, disappears into my body, but I don't feel it. The only thing I can feel now is the rising tide of gray, covering me, trickling steadily into my eyes. I start to choke; I sink beneath it. I swallow myself up, disappear into myself.

But it's not over yet. Now they're forcing me to drink a glass of water. They're forcing gray into my body by every means at their disposal. First with an injection, now with a drink. I try to turn away, but they force me to empty the glass. The liquid pouring into my body meets the pool of gray I've just been injected with. There's a muffled explosion. I fall backward. What is it they want exactly? Where is my head? How can I know what they want if I don't have a head?

"He's going to fall asleep," says a voice.

Fall asleep. To what end? To escape the ennui perhaps. Is it possible to escape it then? In any case, I was wrong; it is possible to die of ennui. And die I will. Until then, I choke and drink it to the lees. Fine. I'm not in pain; I now feel only the most vague sensations; I've nothing in particular to contend with. Except for the ennui, and that to the very last drop. I'm drowning in ennui; that's the one thing I can still be sure about. Even if they could pump out of my body everything that's rotting it and eating it away from the inside, the ennui would remain. Men have vigorously sought to eradicate cancer, tuberculosis, madness, rheumatism, but they have never thought to find a cure for ennui. What possible explanation could there be for this? Have they really not understood that so much gray could only have been secreted by ennui, and that so much ennui will ultimately kill them? Unless that is their cure for ennui: death. They haven't found anything better; they're just waiting for death. Must I die to escape the ennui? Die here? While far away from here, on Fylchride, there are so many other means of escape, but so far away, at the uppermost of the pit I've fallen into . . .

If only something would happen. Even though I'm dying, there is the terrible certainty that nothing is happening, that nothing will ever happen.

"It's baffling . . ."

"Really, I must say . . ."

"Perhaps blood poisoning? I just don't understand it."

I understand, but I can barely make out what they're saying. The noise is fading away, withdrawing from my body, leaving me for dead. This world no longer thinks it necessary to attack me in force. The damage is done. Even if man doesn't understand—the things here, they know everything. The unliving things and objects of this world are sometimes more discerning than the living. I am at their mercy. The babel has stopped attacking me. The smells stopped long ago. In the wake of their relentless assault, the fog has grown so dense that I could never get free of it now. The only way would be to dig myself out. With the right tools I'd surely manage it. I'd dig a tunnel straight through to the other side, crawl back into a world full of light, color, air, and life. No use thinking about it since I haven't got the tools. With my teeth perhaps? But it's no good. I can feel them rotting away in my mouth. They would crumble away like clay. As for my hands, they no longer exist. They're out there, somewhere, so far from me, amputated, with no wrists and no arms, or perhaps they've only been severed internally. They're so far away that I've lost sight of them. Unless somebody took care to place them neatly on a table, like a pair of gloves. So considerate, so attentive to my needs. So far from me, my hands and body. So far that it would take weeks to reach them. Weeks. But I have only a few hours left to live.

"And not even a low fever. Nothing, barely 97.3°"

"It's incredible."

Incredible, as he says. But patience, gentlemen, patience. You needn't ask so many questions. In a few hours, tomorrow at the very latest, you'll have your answers; you'll understand everything.

Understand . . . how is it I'm still lucid enough to understand that, ultimately, they'll understand? That they'll understand everything once I'm finally dead and they really start looking for answers, when they grope and probe me with their fleshy, bloated fingers, when they . . . I don't want to know. Mercy, please. I beg of you. I don't want to know what I know anymore. Why has all this gray not driven me mad? Why am I still able to think, anticipate, reason? Have mercy! I won't ask for anything else, only take away my reason before allowing my life to drain away drop by drop. It doesn't make any sense. How is it the gray ball of dust I've become can still think? But think it can, and feel as well, feel the cold panic rising up inside of me. For I know now; it's only just dawned on me. But I know.

I'm a traitor. It's as simple as that. So much effort and all of it wasted. Because I'm going to betray everything. My corpse is going to betray everything. While alive—floundering, suffocating, suffering, dying—I'd managed to be silent, dissemble, evade. But after I'm dead, my corpse will give up its secrets. Oh, how they seem so far from suspecting what they're about to learn. But perhaps they won't understand. Or perhaps, because of the corrosive air of this world, my body will turn to dust immediately after I've taken my last breath, and nothing of me will remain. If only it were possible. What can I do to make that happen? Already I can feel their eyes boring into me. They're suspicious. Of what? They sense the end approaching. They're impatient. They want to know. What will be their reaction when they find that my heart is on the right side of my body? That my stomach is so oddly shaped and ten times smaller than theirs? What will they do when they see that there's no water in my body, no arteries, no liver, no ganglia? What will they infer from all of this? That I'm not of this world. The only possible explanation. I will have betrayed, betrayed my secret, betrayed everything. I can't accept that. I have to find a solution, set the room on fire, blow it up, turn my body to ashes. Not possible. Where will I get the matches? You wouldn't have a light would you please? But I don't smoke. More than enough smoke in me already without the added . . . How does one come by a case of dynamite? You wouldn't have a bit of dynamite would you please? How indeed, when already . . .

When already . . . already what? What was I thinking about? No doubt I was thinking about how I'm still thinking. So futile. In vain. It's all been in vain. They never should have sent me. But they didn't know. Nobody knew. Nobody will ever know. Scream. I have to scream. Sit up, open the window, and scream loud enough for them to hear me back home on Fylchride. Scream *never again, it's impossible, stop everything!* But there's someone guarding the window. They know everything. They're watching me.

They know I can still get up and try to make one last appeal across the void. They've got it all figured out. They're trying to foil my plan. If only I had my strength back, just for a fraction of a second. But never again. So far . . . so far from home . . . farther and farther. So terribly far, suddenly so deep. As if all the water in the world were opening up to become. Become what? So deep in so much gray and grayer and grayer beneath a gray sky toppling down, becoming earth, water, liquid gray, wells of gray, gray of gray without end without blemish with nothing but so much nothing as far as the eye can see, so far, so far, or so close . . .

At that moment, one of the doctors walked into the room.

"He's dead. It just happened," said the nurse.

"Fine. Have him moved to autopsy."

# EXPANSION

Jacques Sternberg: "So Far From Home"

French title: "Si loin du monde"

First published in Sternberg's collection of short stories *Entre deux mondes incertains* by Denoël (1958) in the collection "Présence du futur," and later in various anthologies.

*Translated by* Brian Mather

Jacques Steinberg was a prolific writer of novels and short stories both in the science fiction and the *fantastique* genres, as well as scenarios—he even acted in a few films. He also illustrated several covers of *Fiction*, a French magazine that specialized in stories from "Le monde de l'étrange" [The Strange World].

There is a short entry on Wikipedia France about this story that says that "So Far From Home" is a sarcastic tale that aims at criticizing consumer society. That might be true and in that, Sternberg joins Roland Barthes, who published *Mythologies*, a collection of essays—not devoid of sarcasm—about French culture at the same period, in 1957, and filmmaker Jacques Tati, who offers a funny look at a country in transition in *Mon Oncle* (*My Uncle*, 1958). But Sternberg's story is so much more, also drawing from a long French tradition of mocking the dominant system behind the disguise of alternative reality. Cyrano de Bergerac imagined traveling to the moon to caricature his time in the seventeenth century. Montesquieu invented Persian visitors in Paris who offered a sharp criticism of French aristocratic society in the eighteenth century. Where Sternberg's tale differs is in the tone of his satire. Existentialist melancholy permeates the soul of the main protagonist and—where Barthes analyzes, with a Mona Lisa smile, the way the French eat and vacation in the 1950s—Sternberg drowns his character in utter puzzlement, faced with the ways in which modern society seems to drain itself of all joy, slowly and voluntarily.

The translation of this long short story/novella (seventy pages!) was done by a Portland State University student for his MA thesis. Brian Mather subtly captures the protagonist's descent into the numbness of the human condition ruled by daily chores, meaningless conversations, and moot materialism. The language is clear, yet subtle. The ideas in this text will linger in your mind long after you have finished reading it.

## DISCUSSION QUESTIONS

How do you imagine Agent 002's home planet, Fylchride? Compare it to the Paris he describes.

Do you think Agent 002's account of the Western world in the 1950s is exaggerated? Accurate? Too depressing? Thought-stimulating? Could it apply to society today?

The text also talks about how one may feel estranged in a new environment, a new culture. Can you imagine ways in which Agent 002 could have felt more welcome and gained a better understanding of life on Earth (circumscribed to Paris as it is) that would have led to a different ending?

Why is this story in the form of a journal instead of a more traditional account in the first or the third person? What are the effects of this choice on the reader? If you read "The Bubbles," can you compare their diary approach?

# That Which Is Not Named

*by* Roland C. Wagner

*translated by* Annabelle Dolidon

WHITE SUNRAYS CRUSHED the Interior Sea and the foothills whose steep slopes plunged into the transparent water of a cove. The city nestled there was called Shôr-Aën—which meant, in the local language, "Man's Harbor" as well as "Woman's Slit,"[1] or "Living Valley." Of the fortification that protected it long ago, only a few sections of eroded walls remained, but it didn't matter much because Shôr-Aën's residents didn't fear foreigners since they didn't even know they existed; only the peaceful nomads who lived in the middle of the desert visited them on the occasion of the seven traditional holidays of the year. Even then, these nomads were not exactly foreigners since they belonged to the Shôr ethnic group.

Laëny squinted. Although the teenager was the result of thousands of years of adaptation to the climate conditions of Shôr-Eneng, the bright luminosity of the sun bothered him. He scanned the vibrant horizon. That very night, the opening ceremony of the Sâala-N'Esoël, "the Seaweed Festival," would take place. It was to last three days. This year, the harvest had been so bountiful that Shôr-Aën would be able to arm its last dhow able to sail to take the surplus to the siang, protector of the Shôr people. It would be an opportunity for the dëongs, these lifelong idlers, to drag themselves away from their relative inactivity; offerings to the siang were actually their responsibility.

Laëny made out some movement at the far end of the deep valley. Nomads were approaching. Laëny counted a dozen y'faëngs, each

---

1   This translation renders the intent in connotation of the original, whilst also preserving the (garish) reduction of language.

carrying three or four figures in the shelter of their dorsal skinfold. The massive animals, domesticated since the dawn of the current local civilization, moved rapidly and could live without water for months. Contrary to other species living in the desert, they didn't suffer from heat or solar irradiation; their metabolism, in a way similar to that of plants, functioned by some form of photosynthesis.

Laëny got up and waved his arms. One of the y'faëngs left the caravan. Laëny ran down the rocky slope. For the third time, he had been delegated to welcome the nomads; it would also be the last. This honor was only for adolescents, and Laëny would soon undergo the suën-llôr, the ritual test for young Shôrs to enter adulthood.

The animal stopped, his wide mouth open. The wavy membranes on the internal walls of his cheeks sucked the slightest traces of humidity from the atmosphere.

A nomad let himself down along the rough backbone. Laëny recognized Uëll, the s'uol of the desert people—or Shôr-Eneng. (The disadvantage of the Shôr language was that each of its two hundred words had multiple meanings that all depended on the context; Shôr-Eneng was both the name of the land—"the Land of Men"—and that of the nomads—"Men of the Desert.")

Uëll greeted the adolescent, first with ceremony—performing various codified gestures before spitting on the ground to signify the gift of water, which was also the gift of friendship—then, he warmly hugged him with his skinny, rock-colored arms. Laëny let him; it was up to Uëll, who was eighteen, to guide their reunion.

"How are your parents?" asked the old s'uol, pulling away from Laëny.

"They are happy," said the teenager, performing at the same time the symbolic gestures he had learned out of friendship for Uëll.

In the desert, talking often turned out to be through sign language to avoid swallowing dust and wasting saliva.

"Let's go. We are expected in Shôr-Aën."

The rest of the caravan joined the two Shôrs who climbed on the y'faëng using the ruggedness of its powerful thighs. The procession headed toward town, following the river that had been dry for thousands of years. Shôr-Eneng had once been a rich and green land—unbeknownst to its inhabitants whose ancestral memory was fading alongside the disappearance of now useless words. Then, climate conditions had changed and the vegetation had withered— until it disappeared. No drop of water had fallen on the territory for so long that the Shôrs didn't have a word for rain.

◆ ◆ ◆

The only intact fragment of the old wall, the door stood on the edge of the desert, as high as twenty Shôrs and large enough to let in two y'faëngs walking abreast. The caravan passed the door and entered the city to the acclamation of the population gathered on both sides of the only avenue that ended at the abandoned port and broken-up piers and docks taken over by the sand.

Although it separated the city in two, this artery was in no case a division; instead, it symbolized union. It had been planned to allow the fifteen hundred residents of Shôr-Aën to gather for the banquets that inevitably accompanied each sâala. Long tables would be lined up end to end from the port to the door, and the Shôrs would gorge themselves on food and drinks from dusk to dawn, taking advantage of the coolness of the night.

To the northeast of the city rose the reddish walls of the s'uol's residence, in front of which the nomads stopped their mount before setting foot on the ground. The master of the house stood on the front steps, dressed in the toga inherent to his functions. Uëll walked up to him carrying a block of amethyst. Liëng, s'uol of Shôr-Aën, was a great lover of minerals. He owned a splendid collection that all could admire whenever it suited them. The house of a s'uol was first and foremost a public place, but at the same time a museum, palace, and administrative center.

"Welcome," said Liëng as he received the irregular block with purple reflections. "May forgetting set you free."

"May knowledge get lost," answered Uëll as he bowed, awaiting the s'uol's gift.

Liëng extended his arms, palms facing the sky, and uttered a very ancient word, the use of which was only permitted in very rare circumstances. Neither Laëny nor any of the Shôrs present here knew what it meant; they only knew that this term implied a unique concept that no other word could express and that only s'uols and siangs understood.

Uëll froze, an unidentifiable expression twisting his features. He put his palms on Liëng's.

"I understand you and I assure you of my support. It is time for us to set up our camp."

He joined the nomads and, leading the way, left the city. Soon, big white tents would be erected on the edge of the ruined wall. The nomads would only come back at nightfall to partake in the meal accompanied by libations given in honor of the Sâala-N'Esoël.

But the peacefulness that normally succeeded their arrival was absent. The unknown word uttered by Liëng had troubled the Shôrs and raised an endless series of questions. What was happening? What was this expression that had appeared on Uëll's face? Why hadn't Liëng made an offering? Was the forgotten word a form of offering? Luckily, the Shôrs could feel neither anguish nor worry because these concepts were banished from their language. They were just asking questions that they knew would remain unanswered.

Laëny, like the other suëns—a term designating children and adolescents, as opposed to llôrs, or adults—wasn't attending the celebratory meal. He was getting ready to go to his bed stuffed with dried seaweed when his father came into the bedroom.

Aëff, a strong Shôr with a massive face, was the niëng, or second husband, of Laëny's mother. Among the Shôrs, one girl was born for two boys; this peculiarity had engendered a complex matrimonial system which allowed two male spouses, between whom the woman shared her time when she didn't seek adventures elsewhere. The family was the basic unit only because of children and their need to be raised by their parents; fidelity was in no way mandatory, even if certain triads respected it.

"Son, your suën-llôr will take place tomorrow."

Aëff refused to use circumlocutions with which too many other Shôrs cluttered their sentences. Despite an impoverished vocabulary, the local language had multiple structures of a studied emphasis and uselessness, and formulas of sophisticated politeness that actually tended to disappear.

"Tomorrow? It was supposed to—"

"S'uol's decision."

Laëny suppressed the questions on his lips. An adolescent was not supposed to challenge the words of a s'uol.

"I won't have much time to prepare."

"It is the same for your *opponents*."

Laëny quivered. The word that Aëff had used to designate the three adolescents destined to complete the trials with him—the so called "foëlls"—made no sense in this context; it was only used to describe another city when they discussed the seaweed harvest, the only context in which it was deemed possible to venture an idea that vaguely evoked competition. Aëff should have used "saëngs," a word which meant "those who walk side by side" and that nomads used to refer to members of a caravan.

"I don't see how *opponents* . . ."

"Become a dëong, Son, and your future will be bright."

It was no use trying to find out more. Aëff had already left the room. In only four sentences, he had managed to sow confusion in his son's mind. A nice example of concision.

Laëny had trouble falling asleep.

◆ ◆ ◆

Dëongs of both genders were busy cleaning the central avenue when Laëny and his parents went to the house chosen as the venue for the suën-llôr. To call dëongs idlers was quite inexact. While they had nothing to do with essential works like harvesting seaweed or fishing, they performed very specific tasks, all related to sâalas—preparing receptions, distilling strong alcohol, transporting the harvest surplus to the city of Shôr-Siang. The rest of the time they devoted themselves to the few surviving artistic activities: jewel carving and clay modeling. In all cases, men and women worked side by side, among both the dëongs and the faëngs, these workers who were their indispensable complement. No gender segregation existed among the Shôrs.

"Are you ready?" asked Aëff.

"I didn't sleep much," mumbled Laëny.

"Too much sleep numbs the mind."

Three adolescents and their parents were waiting in front of the designated house, looking up to the naënôl with its terracotta canopy. All the houses were built on the same model: the kitchen, communal room, and parents' bedroom on the first floor; on the second floor, as many bedrooms as there were children; then a low tower, the naënôl, to host various ceremonies—including the suën-llôr with adolescents foreign to the house.

Parents entered first, invited by the fuoll—or first husband, who usually played the role of master of the house—to drink water tinted with the juice of gray seaweed that had soothing effects. Laëny observed his foëlls. Each of them kept their distance, unable or unwilling to talk before the test; being rare, words proved to be precious, as precious as saliva, or even water. However, the four adolescents studied each other secretly, trying to guess what tricks could be hatched under the short crest of white hair, estimating the strength of the muscles stretching their copper skin.

Laëny knew his *opponents* by sight—this word obsessed him, fascinated him with its improper use. Ordaël was a smooth talker, but his small size was a handicap; Sanaol, tall with a broad torso, would have difficulties finding convincing arguments—the stubborn type, who would die of hunger and thirst before giving in to his interlocutor, which happened sometimes; finally, Dëol combined strength and intelligence. He was certainly the most dangerous.

Laëny sighed. He would have to focus his will, to do his utmost if he wanted to know the future his father had promised him.

The fuoll came back and brought the adolescents in. The inside of the house, dry and cool, was permeated with the good smell of dried fish. After they climbed the spiral staircase, they arrived in the naënôl. Each suën went to stand at one of the cardinal points indicated by a protuberance of the parapet. Laëny found himself facing north, contemplating the sea that the Shôrs simply called naël—water.

"Ordaël, Dëol, it is your turn," said the fuoll.

Laëny was suddenly overwhelmed by a disturbing feeling. To defeat Sanaol would be more difficult than one of the two others.

Dëol and Ordaël moved forward until they touched. Before fighting, they had to find balance, the position in which their uneven strength would cancel each other out. Dëol slowly bent the hand of his *opponent*—Laëny couldn't stop repeating this word, unable to discern its deeper meaning—who pivoted around his wrist, wrapping his leg behind Dëol's waist. Dëol, judging his posture unstable, let go of the hand that proceeded to grasp his shoulder, and took hold of a hip while moving his feet to be on a more solid footing.

Then, everything went so fast that Laëny could not appreciate the quality of the victory. The two adolescents' movements were as fluid as a dancer's and as fast as grains of sand carried by a storm. Balance, as soon as it was found, broke. Dëol, triumphant, helped Ordaël up. For the latter, it was all over; he would become a faëng and share his existence between masonry and seaweed cultivation.

The fuoll handed him a carafe of g'naël, a highly fermented alcohol that intoxicated people violently. It was reserved for specific uses; there were no alcoholics among the Shôrs, despite the binge drinking inherent in every party. Ordaël went to sit on the circular stone bench along the parapet and put his lips to the bottle. Dëol, his face in his hands and kneeling facing east, was trying to regain his lost concentration.

The other two opponents stepped forward; without any hesitation, they grappled with each other. From the start, it was obvious their fight would not resemble the previous one. Despite their difference in size and weight, they wrestled hand-to-hand, finding balance in the first moments.

Laëny tried a feint. Sanaol slid to the side, trying to tip him over backward. Standing firm on his legs, Laëny changed his position. Sanaol, ill-served by his own strength—he had to adopt a precarious position during the short preliminary phase—ended up off balance. Laëny, seeing how he could get the upper hand, acted as if he were giving in and took advantage of the fact that Sanaol was intensifying his push, happy to get on what he thought was stronger footing, and let him go. His right shoulder hit the ground; he turned quickly on an elbow and, with one precise move, knocked down his opponent as he was straightening up.

Sanaol got up with a hazy look. The fuoll handed him the carafe of g'naël that he had refilled; Ordaël had emptied it and, dead drunk, was gently nodding his head while contemplating the ravined cliffs.

The fuoll guided both of the vanquished out of the naënôl; there were no witnesses to the final stage of the suën-llôr.

Laëny kneeled facing the desert. Dëol went to stand north, by the port, his face buried in his brown hands. Laëny preferred to look at the old red and brown mountains bedecked with changing reflections under the sun. A meditative thought came to him. The sea and the desert were the foundations of Shôr life and would forever be in opposition. The sea represented birth and the desert death. Every Shôr traveled from one to the other with the city between the two. Symbolically, before the second part of the suën-llôr, those who survived the first one turned their backs, one looking at the sea, the other at the desert. Both had to draw their destiny from the constants of life.

"Why do you need to become an idler?" Dëol started off. "I'm the child of dëongs, I saw what my parents' lives were like; therefore, I know what to expect, but you—whose ancestors, as far as one can remember, are all faëngs—you wouldn't appreciate this role to the fullest, while the status of faëng would suit you perfectly, it is so connected to your lineage . . ."

He had spoken ceremoniously. The Shôr language, on the other hand, was poor in words but infinitely rich in intonations—which had as much of an influence on the meaning of a sentence as the words themselves. Impressed, Laëny inhaled with difficulty; he almost got lost in the meanders of this horribly complicated riposte for a Shôr.

"Art and manual work suit me."

A long silence followed. Dëol was weighing Laëny's arguments—which filled the latter with enthusiasm; a hesitating adolescent is already half defeated.

"Laëny, the harsh work of faëngs cannot be for me; my hands have modeled clay and kneaded bread dough many times already, which has developed their skills. I lived with the dëongs, I acquired their artistic sense, which is perfectly normal since I am their child and thus I inherited their qualities, which makes me a mighty dëong because I was born for this position."

Now Laëny knew that Dëol perfectly personified the gëang—in the past, the dialectician, now, the chatterbox with a heavy pejorative connotation. Laëny had never heard such reptilian reasoning.

"Artistic sense is not hereditary. Although you are the son of dëongs, you are fooling yourself. Simplicity is key."

Dëol went pale. He couldn't find anything to answer. He attempted another sentence as convoluted as a maze, but he started to doubt; he mumbled, hesitated, tried to get back the thread broken by too many detours, failed, and finally, grabbed the carafe with g'naël and put it to his mouth.

He went down the stairs unsteadily.

Left alone, Laëny savored his victory, his gaze embracing Shôr-Aën. Dëol had tricked himself. He thought he could prevail thanks to his convoluted chatter, which would have baffled many adolescents, but the Shôr language was so concise that accumulating words and concepts in a ceremonious fashion only drained it of its essence. Faced with this typical attitude of idle children, Laëny stuck to simplicity, his only weapon.

He behaved like a real Shôr—hence, his victory.

◆ ◆ ◆

Shôr-Eneng, a territory of about one thousand square kilometers, was located at the tip of the southern shore of the Interior Sea. The desert, spiked with worn mountains and sandy hills, took up all its surface. When the Shôrs had come to settle there, a few bushes and cactuses still hung on to the valleys' sides where three cities were built, and tufts of grass survived in dry riverbeds. But there was never enough vegetation to use for nutritional purposes. Luckily, the nearby seabed with a maximum depth of fifteen meters abounded with many species of seaweed, populated by edible, and often delicious, schools of fish.

Land vegetation disappeared even from the Shôrs' memory, who then turned to the sea. Only a few individuals who wanted to escape a sedentary lifestyle ventured into the desert, up to the impassable barrier of the inland high peaks; they became nomads. From time to time, a city-dweller joined them; a nomad could also settle down. Actually, the desert people served as a genetic pool. Because cities had little contact with each other, population exchange remained the exception; this situation could have led to catastrophic consanguinity without nomads.

However, the Shôrs were not aware of any of this. They were content to live not knowing anything about the outside world, the reasons driving the laws to which they conformed, and their history, that they had been unlearning for generations.

◆ ◆ ◆

Laëny woke up. The sun was already high in the sky. The new adult stretched and walked up to the narrow window that was cut into his bedroom wall. He had only vague memories of the hours following the suën-llôr. The excitement, the alcohol, and his first participation in the banquet party had prevented his memory from functioning. Only a few colored and lively images survived, albeit a bit blurry.

He went down to the kitchen and was surprised to find the s'uol there, in deep conversation with his parents. Liëng smiled when he saw him as he sat at the table in front of a seaweed salad with raw fish.

"Welcome to adulthood, Laëny."

"Thank you."

While eating, Laëny listened. Was the presence of the s'uol related to this bright future Aëff had promised him? It seemed to be the case.

When Laëny was done with his meal, Liëng came to sit opposite him and began to speak with a language so simple it was near perfection:

"Laëny, you will go to Shôr-Siang with the harvest. This suën-llôr wasn't like the others. That you came out of it a dëong pleases me because you will not return to Shôr-Aën."

"Is it *that* pleasing?"

"You have a role to play. An important one. Shôr-Siang is as good as Shôr-Aën. Do you agree?"

Confused, Laëny nodded. He had never thought of leaving Shôr-Aën, but now that he was offered to do so, he found the idea attractive.

"We will see each other tomorrow when you leave," the s'uol concluded.

Later, just before the evening banquet, the third and last of the Seaweed Festival, Aëff took Laëny aside.

"You must have many questions . . ."

"Your attitude surprised me."

"Uëll visited me last night because of that word Liëng said. He assured me that your future would depend on the outcome of your suën-llôr . . . So, I remembered one day during my childhood, long ago, when I heard such a word. The day after, a suën-llôr took place and the dëong left for Shôr-Siang and never came back. Liëng's visit confirmed what Uëll said and my memory."

"I must see Uëll."

Aëff rested his hands on his son's shoulders.

"He left. Shôr-Siang is a bigger city but not much different from ours. Maybe . . ." He looked away before continuing. "S'uols could not *lie*."

"*Lie*?"

"An old word, unimportant. It is time to go to the banquet."

◆ ◆ ◆

The dhow sailed along the coast, pushed by a light westerly wind. It carried within its hold a large amount of n'esoël and a few amphoras of dried fish. Sitting in a circle on the deck, the dëongs were singing in harmony to the sound of an instrument whose wood showed the patina of several centuries of use. Wood was precious because it was rare. The reserves could not be renewed because of the absence of trees and diminished year after year. The dhow was made with the wood of six similar boats; as for the instrument that no longer had a name, it consisted of two triangular soundboards held together by a neck along which three fragments of fish intestines were stretched. Only about ten of these remained in all of Shôr-Aën, most of them in bad shape.

Laëny, who had been assigned to the helm, gazed at the coast, amazed by the new world he was discovering over time. At first, the coastline was made of cliffs similar to those dominating Shôr-Aën, then it progressively lowered down to sea level. The desert ended in the Interior Sea in a gentle slope peppered with rounded rocks. The grayish-yellow color of the sand contrasted with the blue—almost green—of the sea under an evening sky painted in dark purple, where stars appeared. Their name was "doal," which also meant eye, look, to look, etc. Shôrs did not follow any cult—they didn't even have the concept of religion—but they thought of the stars as thousands of eyes observing and monitoring them as they persevered in their quest for simplicity. In a way, they were the guardians of the purity of the Shôr's soul.

◆ ◆ ◆

On the fourth night, the dhow passed off the coast of Shôr-Uol, the second city of the region, with twice as many residents as Shôr-Aën. The rust-colored sun glided across the indigo sea. Laëny, who was dozing at the prow, could see a few lights of the port at the end of a large bay.

"Shôr-Uol is like Shôr-Aën," said one of his companions.

"Built on the same plans," said another.

"But it has more people," Laëny whispered.

"Because the valley was wider."

Pensive, Laëny kept his eyes locked on the lights until they disappeared behind a peninsula. To discover that this city was not that different from his gave him the same feeling he'd have if there was a rotten fish on his plate.

The dhow continued north along the shoreline. Again, cliffs of a sinister black color appeared. The dhow had to sail away from the shore because of the many reef banks—the remains of collapsed cliff sides. Waves increased in number and violence. At the end of the following afternoon, a gust of wind almost tipped the boat. During the night, choppy seas continuously sent water across the deck. Laëny was shivering in his frayed blanket.

On the ninth night, the dhow arrived in sight of Shôr-Siang. The city looked huge to Laëny. More Shôrs lived there than in the two other cities combined. The siang's palace, a massive stone building on top of a headland outside of the city, watched over it. Behind the only intact pier of a port where there used to be dozens, two dhows and one galley with the oars raised rocked on the water.

"Why do they need all these boats?" asked Laëny.

"Shôr-Siang does not have seaweed fields close to it. It farms those in the island of Shôr-N'Esoël, one sailing day north. The sea would swallow our boat there."

The dhow docked. Ten workers welcomed the travelers and took them to the siang's palace. Traveling was exceptional, there was no hostel in Shôr cities; the only visitors were usually hosted by the s'uol or the siang, or by friends if they had them.

Laëny was given an austere bedroom with a large window overlooking the harbor. He collapsed on the new mat and fell asleep instantaneously. When he opened his eyes, the sun was rising above the horizon. He went down to the courtyard with a triangular pool—old Shôrs had always privileged this geometric shape symbolizing family. Water was drawn up from the sea through a system of pipes and manual pumps that Laëny found too complicated to be recent.

He dived in the pool and swam a few breaststrokes. His fatigue from the trip was gone. Laëny got out of the water and let himself dry a few minutes in the rising sunrays before going to the kitchens. A young dëong was macerating red seaweed.

"I would like to eat."

"Are you from Shôr-Aen?" asked the dëong as he put a plate of porridge in front of him.

Soon they were peacefully chatting, motivated by a reciprocal curiosity. Laëny told him about Shôr-Aën while the cook talked about his work and, more importantly, about the protector, this enigmatic character who looked after the Shôrs.

"The siang lives alone. I am his only companion."

"He doesn't have a wife?"

"All women can be his."

"Isn't family necessary to the child?"

"Women regularly share his bed without giving him a child."

"Is he old?"

"His hair is white."

"He won't live forever. Who will replace him?"

"No idea. Is it important?"

Laëny pushed this question to the back of his mind. He had so many other things to learn.

◆ ◆ ◆

In terms of biology, the Shôrs were slender humanoids with little hair. Men and women were roughly the same size; a long time ago women were shorter, but the same food and the same tasks as men brought the two genders closer biologically, not to mention that women had at their disposal a unique contraceptive system: they could decide their periods of fertility—which also made it easy to know without a doubt who the baby's father was. Resources in Shôr-Eneng were limited, so three children—sometimes four—would be born in each family; the number of Shôrs had barely varied by a hundred individuals since they had settled on these desolate shores.

The Shôr people were rarely sick. Separated from the rest of the world, they were never in contact with the carriers of harmful viruses. Infant mortality stayed at about one in five thousand—and this death was usually caused by an accident. The Shôr organism didn't need much. Seaweed and fish were enough to keep them in good shape; when it came to water, it didn't matter if it was slightly salty: the Shôrs could digest it without difficulties. Gastronomy was unknown: the Shôrs barely had a gustatory system, and they had no word to describe the taste of food.

It was the same thing with feelings; the closest feeling to love was a fleeting attraction, couples forming and separating with disconcerting ease. Jealousy did not exist. From the beginning, the Shôrs wanted to distinguish between sex and family, which was a social entity separate from the sex life of individuals. Admittedly, the wife and her two husbands conceived their children together—but the act, in this case, was only performed to procreate, though that didn't mean they could not also take pleasure in it.

Having a child with someone outside the family triangle was simply unthinkable, for reasons of balance.

The siang sat on a large, gray stone with his legs under him. In front of him stood the idlers from Shôr-Aën. Laëny stepped forward and put a bag full of seaweed at the foot of the protector who opened it and took out a handful of n'esoël. Then he brought it to his nose.

"It looks like good quality. I thank you, people of Shôr-Aën."

"Several hundred bags are waiting to be unloaded."

"I will send workers to take them. You will dine with me, of course?" During the exemplary frugal dinner, the siang surprised his guests by his mastery of language. He skillfully jumped from one topic to another, without ever being boring. The dëongs answered him, slightly intimidated. Laëny noticed that the siang avoided difficult concepts, limiting the conversation to themes that did not require any complexity. At the end of the meal, when the protector of the Shôr people launched into a philosophical evocation about the past, about this tumultuous period when too many words cluttered the mouth and the mind of Shôrs, Laëny was full of admiration. He would have liked to speak that way, going directly to the point without useless words.

The idlers returned to their rooms while the siang went to stand on the edge of the void, facing the sea that was ablaze with the fire of the setting sun. Laëny approached him with respect.

"Do you like Shôr-Siang?"

"I haven't had time to visit it."

"You will have it."

"Why must I stay here?"

"You will know it when your companions leave."

Then, the siang asked him a few questions about his parents and his childhood, to which Laëny answered as simply as he could. Finally, the siang brought him closer and took him in his arms.

"Do you want to be my son?"

Disconcerted, Laëny apologized with an indecisive voice and went up to bed under the sly gaze of the siang.

Lying on his mat, he turned a hundred times, a thousand times the question in his head, trying to extract from it all its possible meanings. Had the siang asked him to be his son—first meaning of the sentence—or to behave like a real Shôr? Or to become his friend?

In addition to these possibilities, others arose, more vague, difficult to access and understand for a new adult. Old concepts, evoked by aging Shôrs, surfaced in Laëny's mind—but he was unable to identify them and, even more so, to express them.

*How do siangs ensure their succession?* he wondered as he fell asleep.

◆ ◆ ◆

The day after, nomads arrived, guided by Uëll. Laëny was drifting half asleep when he heard the hoarse cry of a y'faëng. He sat, shook his head, and dragged his feet to the window. A caravan with about thirty animals was walking down the central avenue to the port, clearing a path among the welcoming crowd.

Laëny quickly put on his pagne. He skipped breakfast and ran to the port through esplanades of burned earth that separated houses. He arrived at the jetty. Uëll was giving the siang a long, green, and malleable object that Laëny remembered having seen before. The expression that passed over the siang's face reminded him of the expression that, a few days earlier, had deformed the features of the nomads' old s'uol.

"Laëny!" called out the siang when he saw him.

The young Shôr walked forward under the gaze of the crowd. The siang put his arm around his slightly hunched shoulders. Laëny straightened up. Uëll greeted him with respect, but with a certain air of mischief visible in his clear eyes.

"Laëny is now my son," said the siang. "He comes from Shôr-Aën, like me."

The crowd applauded. Laëny felt like he was standing on the edge of a sheer cliff. Knees shaking and a knot in his stomach, he bowed, a forced smile on his lips.

"Our friends from Shôr-Aën will leave soon," said the siang. "Their departure will coincide with that of the galley that is going to the seaweed fields of Shôr-N'Esoël. There will be no shortage of food."

Taking Laëny with him, the siang returned to his palace. On the way, he repeated strange, apparently meaningless words that intensified Laëny's feeling—this feeling that no word could express except "loëng," which was only used to describe the idea of famine.

Laëny's companions had gone to the nomads' camp, so the palace was empty. He would have liked to join them to listen to the old ones talk about the desert, but the siang asked him to retire to his room. Laëny obeyed; one could not disappoint the protector.

◆ ◆ ◆

Uëll visited the young Shôr after his fourth day of confinement. They had a lively conversation; Laëny asked question after question; Uëll evaded most of them. Yes, Laëny was destined to succeed the siang. It would be his turn to look after the Shôr people and he would work on simplifying their lifestyle and language, the two going hand in hand. But the role of the siang did not end there . . . Uëll refused to say more. He left Laëny unsettled—the young Shôr could no longer content himself with questions without answers. Curiosity was the first step toward understanding the role of a siang—but Laëny still didn't know it.

Ten days passed. The dhow had left for Shôr-Aën, carrying many gifts from the siang: dry seaweed from the seabeds along Shôr-N'Esoël that could be smoked for the Sâala-Uol, the Peace Festival; functional pottery that only dëongs from Shôr-Siang still knew how to make; various tools made in the only factory in the land. Several times, Laëny had met with Uëll who taught him some peculiarities of the Shôr's life unknown in Shôr-Aën, like bronze work or butchering y'faëngs. Little by little, the young Shôr realized how much his hometown was kept out of artisanal work. People in Shôr-Aën were farmers, farmers of the sea; they used objects without knowing how they were made.

Laëny's disappointment didn't last long; he soon understood that this lack of interest, this ignorance, was in line with the simplification his people so much sought after. The inhabitants of Shôr-Aën lived close to the sea, while those of Shôr-Siang maintained a close relationship with the desert through the nomads. Laëny now knew why so many y'faëngs accompanied the few Shôr-Enengs who came with Uëll; they transported copper and tin whose deposits showed on the surface at the base of the first foothills. From the desert also came clay that they had to rehydrate with infinite care because it hadn't seen water for thousands of years.

◆ ◆ ◆

"Why did you keep me confined for so long?"
"You needed to dive deep inside yourself and face yourself without shame. Uëll was only here to help you."

Laëny appreciated the siang's response; he mastered the Shôr language perfectly. Laëny couldn't help feeling mixed emotions of friendship and admiration toward the protector.

"Why did you have me come from Shôr-Aën to be your successor?"

"It is in this city that simplification is the most advanced. The siang is not only a protector, he is also the agent of simplification. For generations, they have all come from Shôr-Aën."

"Uëll wanted to teach me forgotten words . . ."

"A siang cannot afford not to know the smallest detail about his people. Many words have disappeared from memory that s'uols and siangs still use. When you understand them, you will be able to succeed me."

"It will take me years!"

"We have time. You must discover complexity to know its weak points. Your role will not be to govern but to monitor the evolution of language. To decide, for example, if a spontaneous simplification complies with the Shôr's spirit . . ."

"Must I sacrifice my right to simplicity so that Shôrs can continue to benefit from it?"

The siang lowered his eyes. He, too, had gone through this; he, too, had refused this truth. Laëny's reaction was natural. It would go away. With time.

"Your role is to look after their happiness."

Laëny retired. Left alone, the siang immersed himself in his thoughts. He remembered when he left Shôr-Aën so many years ago, and the initiation that had followed his arrival in Shôr-Siang: those long days of learning, gorging himself with knowledge, going in a direction opposite to his people, going back in time . . . regressing, in the end . . . because this was about regressing, since progress was, in Shôr's language, the same as simplification.

Contrary to those he protected from the dangers of knowing, siangs forgot nothing. They could still decipher old writings. In the books made with y'faëng skin, the history of Shôr-Eneng unfolded—this history to which each siang added a few lines.

♦ ♦ ♦

In the old times, the Shôrs inhabited the entire coastline of the Interior Sea. They had developed a fairly advanced civilization; they used the wheel, farmed, forged metal, and blew glass. Dhows and galleys traversed the warm waters to carry large quantities of goods from one city to another. Only a few vessels of that time now remained, as well as this odd family structure made necessary by the gender imbalance at birth.

One day, foreigners appeared. They looked like Shôrs, but interfertilization between the two races proved impossible. They immediately behaved like conquerors, pillaging and burning flourishing cities, killing populations. The Shôrs were not completely peaceful—enemy states were often in conflict—but their knowledge of combat was rudimentary. In a few decades, the foreigners conquered most of their territories.

These foreigners were divided into numerous nations, and wars of conquest contributed to creating more of them, each more belligerent than the other. After each invasion of a Shôr nation, people were put to the sword; invaders seemed to not know slavery, and because Shôrs couldn't give them children, they didn't see a reason to bother with women.

Over the years, the Shôrs who survived this genocide gathered on a desolate land that became Shôr-Eneng. When an enemy fleet approached one of the three cities, the residents would find refuge in the desert and come back only after the aggressors had left—the latter finally got tired of attacking an abandoned city with nothing valuable enough in it to justify the trip.

The first siang was a highly sensitive and intelligent Shôr. Seeking simplicity seemed to him an excellent way to insure the survival of his people. Because the Shôrs could stay under water longer than the foreigners, growing seaweed was never a problem for them. Moreover, their enemies would never think of destroying the seabed; thus, food was provided and out of reach in case of aggression. Craft products remained an issue because they had aroused the foreigners' envy. Indeed, when they arrived, they knew neither glass nor the wheel although they carried iron weapons.

The first siang found an unexpected solution to this problem by stating the principle that never escaped the memory of those who continued his work: the Shôr people must possess nothing that could arouse envy. Not even culture.

This last point was only achieved by the fourth siang who contributed to the erasure of words designating or qualifying foreigners. After several dozen generations, while the last blades of grass in Shôr-Eneng dried out, the Shôrs had forgotten how and why they had arrived here. Of course, a few times residents of one of the cities had to find refuge inland under the s'uol's orders, but nothing was explained to them. One of the fourth siang's priorities was to eliminate the concept of curiosity—or rather, to mitigate it enough that no one ever wondered what exists beyond the limits of Shôr-Eneng.

After a thousand years, the foreigners never came back. Shôr-Eneng was undoubtedly considered a cursed or uninteresting land. Legends die hard.

Today, the goal of the first siangs was almost achieved. A two-hundred-word language, that seemed impossible to reduce further than a hundred and fifty words, shaped the Shôr's mentality and prevented them from accessing concepts of hate, violence, ambition, and the outside world. A few traces, a few resurgences—like the idea of competition—still needed to be erased; it would be Laëny's task. As for craft making, its use would be lost. They would forget bronze to make rudimentary tools with the bones of the dead—in this way, these would continue to serve the community, and death would lose all stressful or traumatizing connotations.

The siang took the object Uëll had brought. The long stem had turned from green to gray, its leaves wizened, but there was no doubt: it was a plant. A few drops of rain had fallen, somewhere at the heart of the desert, and a temporary oasis was born. This was the biggest—the only?—danger menacing the Shôrs. If the climate changed, if clouds gathered above Shôr-Eneng and flooded it, the region would regain interest of the foreigners who would eventually invade the last refuge of the Shôr people. If they still lived.

The siang had no worries. He took the unfinished book in which the first six protectors had recorded their reflections and their suggestions for achieving simplification. Using the old language with twenty thousand words, he wrote:

*Year 3097 of the Shôrs.*

*It rained in the desert thirty-four days ago, and a few plants took the opportunity to grow. Thus, it seems the concept of rain still exists in the mind of some Shôrs—nomads, I suspect. One should think about taking it out and, at the same time, erasing the corresponding word from the s'uols' vocabulary. This way, we would be saved from potential climate change because only one person cannot—we know from experience—maintain the persistence of something forgotten.*

*As for the foreigners, I suppose they no longer exist. No chronicle has mentioned them for eight hundred and twenty years; they ceased to exist as soon as we forgot them. My recent conversation with Uëll, the current s'uol of the desert people, confirmed he didn't know the word for them.*

*So, we are safe. There remains a dark point that I believe we cannot eliminate. Our civilization rests on oblivion, on the depletion of knowledge and the modification of the resulting world. I am the last one to know the ancient language and Laëny, my designated successor, would be the only one in his generation to learn it; but I am convinced that, at some point, we will need to break the chain of siangs, cut the cord that—weakly—connects us to our past. The old tongue must be completely forgotten!*

*Until now, no one dared destroy books, no siang ventured to lie to his successor, hiding the truth about the task ahead . . . There lies the danger. What would happen if the Shôrs learned again the lost words, if they rediscovered abolished concepts? Would they become real again? Would foreigners reappear?*

*It rained in the desert because of only one word. The answer to these questions is obvious.*

*I didn't speak much with Laëny, but he seems to love simplicity. No doubt, it is linked to his origins—this city of Shôr-Aën that is generations ahead of Shôr-Siang. The idea of studying to take over after me traumatized him a bit; he cannot, for the time being, get used to the idea. For this reason—and many others—I think he will find the courage to take the leap, to end the siangs' ordeal. I believe he will burn the books and lie to his successor.*

*I think he will end what we started two thousand years ago.*

*We wanted revenge over the foreigners and to live free, without the fear of seeing armed men destroy our cities. But they were too many, too powerful. We were no match for them. So, we decided to forget their mere existence—and they disappeared . . .*

*Of course, we could have brought back a few concepts, some ideas that would have bettered the life of Shôrs . . . no siang took the risk, because simplifying language is irreversible.*

*Let's imagine, for example, that we teach the Shôrs again what rain is. They will soon ask where clouds come from, then if there is something else beyond Shôr-Eneng . . . One day, finally, they'll come to the concept of foreigners! And that day will signal the end of the Shôrs.*

*That's how it is, Laëny. I bequeath you a seemingly unresolvable problem. If you have the courage to do what I could not bring myself to do, you will be the last siang. But always remember: that which is not named does not exist, and the slightest omission can lead to incalculable consequences.*

*May foreigners never come back!*

Laëny closed the book. His predecessor had let himself be carried away by a dream. It was much too soon, much too early to end the role of the siang. In fact, Laëny didn't think it was possible; any society must evolve in one direction or the other. Perpetual stagnation is impossible: once it reached the bottom of the curve, once language is reduced to the minimum, the natural reaction would be to invent new words, to discover new concepts. To rediscover them. Only a siang who knows the past could control this renaissance.

*Words make the world what it is,* Laëny thought. *We will always need a siang to prevent them from hurting, wounding, destroying, and killing. Until now, we simply enjoyed this effect that language—our language?— exerts on the Universe. Now, we must learn to control it, to select the strings of concepts that will lead to a new progression—but, safely this time.*

*How to reinvent rain without the storm, progress without competition, the outside world without foreigners?*

*It is not for me to say. Centuries will be necessary to turn the tide, to rewrite the world. Siangs will follow one another, and each will do his part to add his brick to the wall. Let's hope none of these bricks will be in disequilibrium . . .*

# EXPANSION

## Roland C. Wagner: "That Which Is Not Named"

French title: "Ce qui n'est pas nommé"

First published in 1985 in the fanzine *SFère*, No. 24, this story has been published in several volumes; the latest collection titled *Ce qui n'est pas nommé* was published by La Bibliothèque voltaïque in 2019.

*Translated by* Annabelle Dolidon

Roland C. Wagner was an amazing storyteller who, since the beginning of his writing career in the 1980s, often combined dark humor with pessimism, according to an early introduction to the author by Jean-Pierre Planque.[2] He has received the Prix Rosny-Aîné seven times! Wagner wrote short stories and novels in various genres in what one could call "alternative realities." For example, *Les Futurs Mystères de Paris* (*The Future Mysteries of Paris*), Grand Prix de l'Imaginaire in 1999, features a private detective inquiring in the far future, and *Rêves de gloire* (*Dreams of Glory*), published in 2012, reimagines the history of the Franco-Algerian war—it is an "uchronie," a subgenre of science fiction that plays with alternate history.

"That Which Is Not Named" is more of a pure science fiction story that raises philosophical questions about our relationship to the world around us through language; how language, more than it reflects the world, *shapes* it. In this story, Wagner explores the role of language in community building and conflict, and dissects language in its most basic expressive functions, thus operating a schism between what is essential and what is superfluous. However, when it comes to language, and especially when it comes to leading people and to telling stories (isn't it the same thing?), could it be that, perhaps, the superfluous is what gives language purpose beyond the simple task of *meaning* something, of giving information? You might think that the prose is heavy at times, but it is intrinsic to the meaning of the story, essential to create the tension between excess and asceticism. Another

---

2   "Quand la cigale squatte la fourmi: une approche de l'œuvre de Roland C. Wagner." *SFère*, no. 13, 1984 (https://www.noosfere.org/articles/article.asp?numarticle=152)

important aspect of this story is, of course, the characters' desires for safety and peace. They believe that embracing silence and cultivating ignorance of the world outside the community will make them disappear and keep them safe from the invaders' minds.

Wagner gives us here a condensed space opera of the mind that goes deep into our most basic fears, and a very original and radical way (not) to face them.

## DISCUSSION QUESTIONS

Think of Laëny's suën-llôr, the fight he wins, and of his trip to the place where he will become the next siang. How can you relate to his journey to adulthood? What thoughts does he struggle with? Can you think of other stories you have read that follow the same narrative structure? Can you find personal connections with this story or the main character?

Language is confusing in this alternative world. How does Roland C. Wagner help the reader understand his characters and their environment? What does he explain to us and what are we left to imagine? Can you point to examples?

Who are the "Others" that all the members of the Shôr group fear so much? What do we know about them, and should they be afraid of them in your opinion?

Does not knowing a threat protect us from harm? Can what you don't know not hurt you? (Is ignorance bliss?) What do you think of the siang's way of protecting his people?

What do you make of Laëny's vision for the future?

Language is always changing. We don't speak today like we spoke a hundred years ago, or even fifty years ago. How would you qualify the linguistic changes that have occurred in your culture? Are they positive, negative, a bit of both, a fact of life?

# The Liberator

*by* Colette Fayard

*translated by* Annabelle Dolidon[1]

I ENDED UP GETTING USED to seeing him every day on my way back home, the grandpa, sitting on his chair at the threshold of the house. A polite old man, always smiling, but with an impenetrable smile. Either he was superiorly intelligent, or completely senile; I wondered about it almost until the end. In his right hand, he always had his staff, as if even when seated, he needed to lean on it, and with his left, he fiddled endlessly with a key, probably the apartment key, so he could get home even if his children and grandchildren were absent. He was thin and wrinkled with a white, pointy goatee with almost no hair, and he seemed to fear neither cold nor heat, always there, a pathetic, fragile guardian in this violent world. He somehow represented the stereotype of the old wise man, a myth in which the degeneration into the twilight years has long been concealed in our ancient texts. Actually, everything here resembles a cliché, the cities as well as people who are ordinary ad nauseam. Although the nausea doesn't come right away. It takes time for it to spread, and one day, you feel it inside, surprised to realize it had been there for so long.

I have been here six of our Earth months. I, LC2, intergalactic federal agent. Piggy to friends.

When I arrived on this damn planet, I immediately thought about that holobook I had when I was a child, a travel narrative (I always dug them!) of an English guy who goes to Australia to find another version of England, with the same houses, traditions, everything; he thinks

1   CONTENT WARNING: Adult-Minor Relationship

it wasn't worth going all the way to the other end of the globe to feel like he stayed home. It's only afterward that he notices differences: the desert, natives in reservations after the failure of the great uprising, etc. Well, here, it's the same thing. When you arrive, you think, "Darn! That wasn't worth the trip!" Then, you rush to check if you didn't screw up and if, maybe, you went home without knowing. And then, little by little, you realize that there is something: the houses, the streets, the people are almost the same, but the atmosphere is not (oh! Breathing is okay. I mean the ambiance). Of course, when you're on a mission, the problem doesn't arise the same way. Then again.

I found lodging quite easily upon my arrival, which allowed me to quickly get into contact with the population without having to temporarily camp in the ship, obviously parked in an area away from the city as long as the local authorities would tolerate it. By living in the city, I could quickly fit in. Well, it was a shabby studio on the top floor of a loud building, built on the cheap like the entire neighborhood, but it was close to the center, and this crowd was the dream place for my investigation.

One must remember that the population had grown considerably in a short amount of time, a real demographic explosion. The Intergalactic Safety Services were completely unprepared. Otherwise, of course, they would have intervened much sooner instead of letting this cultural bubbling up of all forms of violence develop. Nowadays, everybody knows these never stay contained on the crisis-stricken planet, no matter which planet, but inevitably lead to dreams of expansion, conquest, and colonization, threatening universal peace. One must also remember, to be fair to the I.S.S., that the first reconnaissance missions had not detected any evolved fauna, much less traces of civilization. Because they didn't explore the entire planet at first, the sudden appearance of a human-type population and its fast development, and its advanced technology, were attributed then to massive migrations, an explanation provided by the locals and accepted by our services. Why on Earth would we have had any suspicion? There was no reason for that. None. At the time. But once official relations were established between urban centers, it became clear that this civilization that seemed so similar to ours was in fact gangrened by both a physical and moral sickness.

Astonishing epidemics would happen constantly, killing a large part of the population each time. I remember the emotion it produced, even if news agencies respected the official directive to minimize the facts to avoid xenophobic reactions... And it was impossible to intervene: local health services had once and for all refused any help from us, even threatening to consider any outside intervention as a form of interference, with all the consequences—in intergalactic law—it would lead to. Local authorities had actually declared they were taking all the necessary prevention measures and guaranteed the bacteriological safety of visitors; indeed, in this regard, there was nothing to report: the epidemics that decimated the local population never extended their ravages to anyone else. Of course. But then, we could neither understand nor act.

As far as the moral sickness is concerned, this time we could do something. And that's why I landed on this damn planet—me, LC2, Piggy, I.S.S. secret agent—with the sole purpose of finding out where such waves of killings and suicides came from. As if diseases were not enough for them. On a regular basis, the planet would suffer enormous losses, then they would make babies left and right, until next time. Again, intergalactic authorities decided to not thoughtlessly spread alarming news. But still, something was wrong. It was up to Piggy to find out what... Of course, it was tempting to explain this by the aforementioned demographic explosion, along with migrations that led to a loss of culture and technological developments that went too fast, in conflict with old values and customs that still determined ways of thinking and behaving. And yet, while all favorable conditions were there for it, there was no unemployment, no racism, no thefts nor vandalism. But murders and suicides in abundance. Gratuitous crimes and unpredictable suicides. Here, too, locals were the only victims. All the investigations said nothing about what caused this because there was no cause, actually, or at least none we could detect. My role, well, was to understand. For the relevant authorities to assess to what degree this rotten planet was dangerous for the rest of the universe, and to take the necessary measures according to the report I was supposed to turn in. In the end.

I started with the neighbors, the local bar, the usual tactic to make contact: "Hello ma'am, sir, how are you, very well thank you, nice weather today, don't you think?" It's not as easy as it looks because, here, people are courteous, nice and all that, but other than that, lockout: you can spend weeks with them, all smiles and excessive courtesies, and in the end, nothing. You realize you don't really know anybody; you know nothing about them.

Still, there were some exceptions. Lucky for Piggy.

The exception was the youngest daughter of a family next door, one of the old man's granddaughters, actually. I ran into her by chance one day when she was coming home from school. She greeted me very politely with a funny look that gave me some hope. Afterward, it was easy for me to arrange a few other random meetings. Children are wonderful informants: they see everything, remember everything, and usually, they like to speak. Scheherazade was exactly like that. My mission, right, was to try to understand behaviors that apparently made no sense. So, I thought, well, this family was after all kind of a concentrate, a summary . . . or a sample, if you'd like, providentially there to be observed. Why look any further? Because I had Scheherazade. Because I was lucky enough to have Scheherazade . . . and yet . . . it took me a while to see that, while she was talking and telling me a thousand and one stories, in fact, she wasn't telling me anything. With her, time would fly by without notice . . . but instead of getting solved, the mystery was deepening.

She developed the habit of coming up to my room after she was done with her homework. At first, she would bombard me with questions about Earth: "Where do you come from? Where is Earth? Is it far? How is it? Is it like here? Is it different?" And little by little, I felt like a weird creature coming from an aberrant, faraway place and I could not find reasons to justify it being that way rather than another. I no longer marveled that this planet looked so much like Earth, but that Earth looked like it. Little girls at home started looking like Scheherazade, not Scheherazade like little girls on Earth.

Even when she babbled excitedly, although she perfectly mastered intergalactic Esperanto, she had a way of carefully articulating each word, which gave the impression that she was constantly in the process of learning how to be a big girl; but don't be fooled: she was happily learning! Like when she would start thinking really hard, all of a sudden—no one could see it coming—and about the most insignificant topics, at least on the surface. She would stop in the middle of a laugh, in the middle of a game, and become pensive. Sometimes, she remained silent; other times, I didn't understand what she meant to say. Maybe that's always the case with children, but I wasn't used to it.

And then, she was so light! When we sat next to each other on my bed, my weight made a hole in the mattress but not hers, so she would always slide against me. Her eyelashes were so long they looked fake; she reminded me of a classmate when I was eight or nine years old whose mother, she had told me, had cut her eyelashes at birth, and they had grown back very long and curved; she wanted to cut mine, but, I don't know why, I thought she actually wanted to pierce my eyes and I ran away because I didn't dare beat her up. Scheherazade's hair was so charged with electricity that it crackled when I touched it; I would say to her, "You have the hair of a witch!"

One day when she was repeating, as if in a dream, "And to think that you come from so far away!", I had replied: "And yet, you see, we are the same." And it made her laugh. I added, curious of her reaction and a bit ashamed of my vulgarity at the same time, "Okay, you and I are a little bit different . . ." And she laughed even more, to tears, and I didn't understand this laughter that supposed a dose of stupidity or perversity that was so foreign to her. I had said to myself, "After all, she's only a child." But this silly scene was the first suffering caused by my dear, my sweet Scheherazade. It is then that I got curious about her body. The desire to know, to check if she was indeed, exactly, in every detail, the same as an Earthling. And I had to control my gaze lingering on the shapes one could guess under her clothes, the neckline, the edges, the imaginary tears of ripped-off clothes. I dreamed of holes in the walls, in doors; I dreamed of key holes through which to look. You understand to what extent I was beside myself (how insane I had become) if I say that the death of a girl at her school made me happy at first, as if it justified to my superiors, for the purposes of my investigation, my frequent meetings with Scheherazade. It is only when I saw a cat sniffing the small body collapsed in front of the gate that I became horrified by my own behavior. I still hear the meowing of the poor animal to which I gave the harshest kick of its existence. Since that time, I know what I'm worth. It comes down to not much.

There was an inquest into the death of the little girl. Obviously, she had been murdered, but not raped or molested in any way, except for the clean razor line at the base of her neck. Still, I got the impression that the investigation was botched, and no one here gave a toss.

On Earth, on the other hand, public opinion was stirred because the murder of the child ushered in a sinister series. It wasn't the first time, but it happened at a time of relative political instability, and of course, no one hesitated to take advantage of the events. Various extremist groups spread a wide range of fantasist statistics, albeit not completely groundless, each more alarming than the last, about the state of mores in this corner of the universe: statistical curves showing the waves of violence that regularly washed over Heliopolis and the neighboring centers, and a study of their amplitude and frequency, hypotheses about causes, and others most eccentric ("Odorless, yet fatal, a gas that makes you mad: a planet is taken over by Swanes as their base for bacteriological experimentations"). All who had dreamed of "pacification" under the leadership of their favorite dictator, but also gangsters of all kinds and good souls with a missionary vocation were interested in Io-Phenix. All kinds of publications, from simple articles to enormous theses, debates, and colloquiums, at times resembling political meetings, multiplied.

I told no one about all this, but I had the distinct impression that the grandpa knew based on the sneer on his face when he said hi each time that I saw him on my way in or out. I thought, maybe he wasn't that senile. When Scheherazade would come to my room, he wouldn't say anything, still courteous and coldly ironic. But I learned that every night he asked the girl to report on all our conversations. This is how I discovered it: one day, she was telling me about her grandfather and the stories he told her. "Everything is the same, he said, only the shape of things changes." She added, "It's easy," and I didn't understand what was easy. It bugged me, and the day after, I wanted to continue the conversation. To my surprise, she got confused and confessed that she had been punished "because you shouldn't talk about these things." Another time, however, she told me again, "Anything is at the same time another [thing]," but she stopped immediately, blushed, and told me in return, in chitchatting mode, "It shouldn't be always the same ones who give answers!"

She had understood that I had not come here as a tourist... I finally told her that I was an intergalactic cop. Probably to impress her. I know I shouldn't have. But she had promised to not tell anyone, and this child, what can I say, with those eyes straight into yours, it was impossible not to trust her, I swear. And also, I thought it would really help me to have an insider accomplice. Anyhow, I explained to her that we didn't want to cause them any harm, but we wanted to understand why people died so much around here, to help them, if we could. I told her about my studies at the police academy, then at the university for psychology, and finally my internship at the intergalactic SOS telephone center where we train to answer distress calls from all over the intelligent universe. I explained to her how we learned to listen to others, to accept different mentalities and moralities, and to make ourselves available to the caller instead of projecting ourselves in the perception we have of their words and the answers we give them. She didn't always understand. I told her about the parasitic life-forms one can find around Albireo, and the funny mentality of the superior parasite that considers human beings, to which it owes its subsistence as a mere source of food, never as a person. I told her about these lands where, out of respect for the elders, one must live all new experiences with them first, and thus sleep first with their mother or mother-in-law before consummating a marriage, because I sometimes forgot I was talking to a child. I told her about hallucinogenic drugs that were mandatory on some planets as the only ones allowing a healthy vision of all things, beyond reductive reasoning, and about the I.S.S. intervention to save entire populations from the slavery to which some laws had reduced them.

"So, you're saying we must respect the way of life of other worlds, but when you disagree, you . . ."

"It's not me, Scheherazade, it's the sworn Intergalactic Council that decides if we need to intervene or not."

"And then, what do you do?"

"We send a civilizing expedition."

"What is it?"

"Well, we talk with people to explain to them that they can't do what they do."

"And if they don't want to change their ways, or they have to do things this way?"

"Well, then the Council sends a purification team, in compliance with the Code of Intergalactic Safety. But we succeed almost every time in making people understand before anything happens."

"Ah? So that's why you came here . . ."

Yes, I know. I should not have told her these things. But you must understand what it is to live on such a planet, that so looks like ours, among people who so look like us, and yet, to be alone with your secret. Among the hairy and slimy monsters of Estrivaran, or surrounded by enemies, it is easy; loneliness makes sense. But here, how do you resist the need for friendship? How do you refuse someone your trust? How do you not look in a little girl's eyes?

Dina's eyes were as dark as Scheherazade's were clear. Dina was Scheherazade's big sister. She was probably sixteen or seventeen years old, and the little one nine or ten. Dina had a boring face, white and ordinarily oval because it was so regular, and a calm voice; in short, you wouldn't notice her, and if by chance you did, you would think she already looked like an old maid. That's what I thought the first time I saw her. Nothing surprised her: she knew I was from Earth, and still, even though her people had never left this planet, a bunch of crawlers who weren't even capable of exploring their own moons, well, she had not been amazed by the arrival of Earthlings who mastered intergalactic travel. That's something, let's admit it.

There was also Jade, the baby. I only saw them once. I never knew if they were a boy or a girl. I asked Scheherazade and she just said, "It doesn't matter." She would often say odd things like that. Jade looked like they were made of porcelain, smooth and firm, with big staring eyes. White skin in a white onesie along with the milky whiteness of the pearl necklace around their neck. I didn't like them very much. But I thought that they would get better as they grew. Did I know what Scheherazade looked like as a baby?

The family's name was Pi. A ridiculous name. I felt sorry for my dear Scheherazade, as if it was an insult to her grace. I kept telling myself we are never responsible for our last name, but all the same. Actually, the parents were charming. Quite insignificant, but charming. This being said, like with the grandpa, I never knew what they were thinking. At home, too, we can't tell what hides behind good manners, can we? Intergalactic Esperanto is a practical language; it doesn't have superfluous complexity and it lacks the necessary nuances for deeper, more subtle conversations... Here, I had the impression it was the only language we spoke. I'm sure they had their own language that I could never learn, but for the time being, on this subject, I was in the dark. Not only on this subject, actually.

After a month or two, I started to see, beyond appearances, what made this planet different from ours. First, the flora and the fauna: in the countryside, like at home, you could see butterflies, cicadas, bats, and tigers (who never attacked people even where they entered their territory), but also the dragons of our legends, in flesh and blood, all undulations and flames—beautiful! Domesticated or wild, eucalyptus, mango trees, and peonies thrived, as well as thousands of other species that seemed familiar to me even if I couldn't name them; but you could also see strange bushes of which no botanist could have justified the eccentricity, for example, the women-flowers; that's the name I gave them, quite fatuously I'll admit. Imagine a tree whose branches carry, instead of leaves, some sort of finely lined lips; that open and close with the slightest breeze, that seem to shiver with the desire for a kiss. I know that for those who haven't seen them it sounds unbelievable. And yet, the diversity of life-forms we have met during our explorations should have cured us of such amazement, the same way the variety of extraterrestrial civilizations should have taught us tolerance.

Should have. In this world where I had been thrown, tasked with an apparently impossible mission, absurdity was at its height, amidst the exquisite courtesy of a serene and delicate population, streams of murders and serial suicides broke out, and—when, finally, peace seemed to be restored—other kinds of epidemics raged: black plague, galloping leprosy, nameless horrors, as lethal as they were repulsive. I trembled for Scheherazade. It was different from the type of nausea that grips me sometimes when faced with universal depravity and stupidity, when the vanity of my job strikes me as self-evident because I know, deep inside, that the stupidest, most primal violence always wins, and that the only refuge against it is irony and detachment with regards to oneself and the whole universe. Ah! Could I remain indifferent to Scheherazade's fate?

But I didn't say how I discovered the women-flowers. One night I was coming home, and I saw Dina who told me, handing me one of these charming branches:

"She's waiting for you. Don't go too fast, she is still so little. Kiss her only with this, for the first time. Please."

Scheherazade, my beloved. I cannot say more.

To sing, to whisper in ecstasy hers mine my sweet and tender Scheherazade:

> *An investigation is not a quest*[2]
> *A stone is not a vase*
> *This is not a . . .*
> *You must polish the stone*
> *And find the red bird*
> *The key . . .*
> *The door . . .*
> *This is not a . . .*

Sang whispered stopped started again whispered sang stopped and softly and tenderly cried. And I would console her, "It doesn't matter, it doesn't matter." And her tears redoubled.

I didn't understand a thing. Of course. No more than I understood Dina's gesture. Dina's eyes on my eyes as she was handing me the branch from the lips-tree.

Instead of making progress in this damn investigation, I was more and more lost. Sometimes, I felt like I was about to discover a network of contradictions and that, with a bit of courage and cunning, I could cut it off. Then I would see Scheherazade again. I said to myself, "This tenderness is the only thing in the world that is worth it." Childhood, the purity of childhood. Out of the mouth of babes . . . I was fooled by all the clichés, me, LC2, despite my perfect training. If I had seen Jade again, I think I would have been suspicious: such an ageless gaze! Then, suddenly, everything started accelerating. Lined up, the coffins of the grandpa, the parents, and in a decreasing pattern, that

---

2   In the original text "L'enquête n'est pas la quête"—the author is playing with the close sounds of the two nouns.

of the children. They had sent backups for the investigation. Fuck! Like I needed that! Nice guys, the I.S.S. colleagues. But I wanted to be alone! Alone!

The funerals were awful. With all the children playing in the cemetery. They went down in the vaults, making the loud metal doors resonate by callously slamming them shut, then they ran up laughing to go run in the alleys where artists were painting sparkling landscapes. All this festive atmosphere created such a contrast with the atrocious reality of the funeral procession! Reality... a lot of people talk casually about it ... here, it was as if there was no emotional bond between the dead and the living, and human beings didn't matter more than the dogs and cats buried in the neighboring cemetery. It was as if the body buried here was nothing more than a mere sheath, the skin of a snake abandoned on a path after sloughing! Ah! What a lesson, what a lesson for us, poor humans! Yes, despite all the religions that fed us, despite all the philosophies we glory in, how far we still are from this haughty spirituality, how basely we remain tied to this perishable body, our home the time of a sigh, the space of this piddly infancy that we call our life, between nothing and nothing! Ah! These beings are no doubt superior to us, I said to myself, to be capable of such detachment! Still, my heart ached in the face of such cruel indifference: the ceremony was rushed, supposing one can call ceremony such hasty formality. I would have liked to see again, the face I loved so much. I wasn't granted it. Worse: when I tried to remember them, I realized I was unable to conjure the features of my little Scheherazade, while in front of my closed eyes, the pale, oval face and the black eyes of her sister Dina formed spontaneously, more clearly than they had when she was alive. I could no longer sleep and not dream of her. Dina. I saw her with the thin line of a bloody razor on her neck, and she was saying to me, "I killed them. It was necessary. And also for me to die." And I knew it was true. And I knew she would come back. Waking up, mixed with this certitude, the disastrous feeling of the absurdity of it stayed with me.

My colleagues didn't find anything. Of course. They went home. They offered to take me: the I.S.S. were ready to give up. I was allowed to stay a few more months: I claimed I was on the verge of discovering something, that I had never gone home in failure, etc. My former reputation earned me this reprieve.

Then, I started gathering and rethinking everything I knew. Snippets.

At any cost, I had to find answers. At any cost, it was imperative, it was imperative to ME to build a system. Yes. That's it. When it comes down to it, isn't that always the case? To invent an answer to fear, a denial to solitude . . . Could I sit motionless in front of my dreams? With Dina's white face in my night? With Dina's white voice in my silence? With Dina's red neck under my finger, as if my caress was the cutting edge of the razor? Could I stay like this, eyes open on the scream of my nights?

Rereading my notes. Gathering my information. Finding. Finding my bearings.

Finding. Finding MYSELF.

Let's see. The first explorers, those that limited their investigations to the southern hemisphere, concluding from their observations that the planet was uninhabited, had to fight during their stay against three or four waves of unknown sickness: it went from eczema to bronchitis without really being one or the other. Whatever it was, it had shaken them, and that's why they came home without trying to learn more. No doubt these diseases had been curbed rapidly. But still, since the planet presented no interest, it wasn't worth risking the health of cosmonauts and waste antibiotics.

Case closed. Very well. However . . . now, I was wondering if it didn't have to do with what Scheherazade had told me: she had told me about a time, before I arrived, when her people were about to disappear; I had assumed they then lived in the northern hemisphere, before the great migration.

"It's difficult to find the right form."

"You mean the right formula?"

"That's it . . ."

"Did your doctors not find the right remedy? Not surprising, considering how everything dies around here, they're not great, these docs!"

She had changed the subject, sounding mocking and a bit cross at the same time. As always, I gave up. As if, on each of my trails, at some point, an invisible net was drawn, an immaterial window, a force field, against which I couldn't go. As if the sweetness, as if the tenderness, as if the little lukewarm body of my Scheherazade would break against it in a thousand shiny and pointless drops of mercury . . . Oh, Dina! Scheherazade! Oh, Dina! Dina!

However, little by little, I had discovered the planet was doomed. I had no doubt about it: the sun was going to die. Okay, fine, in this case, we usually have time to see it coming. Still, one must find a solution. It is worth asking, actually, if the chronically aberrant behavior of the natives wasn't simply due to the frenetic activity and thus, increasing radiation, of the dying star. To which my body was probably more resistant . . . If they knew about it, why on Earth had the leaders not asked other worlds for asylum? Unable to cross outer space by themselves, they should count on mutual universal help. But could they? That's the question! Almost all planets, threatened by overpopulation, were also looking for new territories. It was really strange that here, nobody seemed to worry about this, nor tried to do anything about it. Maybe they didn't know about the threat hanging over them? No, intuitively, I was convinced that they knew; I had come to the point of understanding their detachment from all things like that of a wise person who has been looking death in the eyes for a long time; yes, I think it was the only explanation to this mix of lightness and seriousness in them that first puzzled me, then charmed me. I was still surprised to not detect any attempt to escape mortal danger. But it doesn't mean there wasn't any, after all: what did I understand of them and their world? So little . . .

And yet, I was so close to understanding! One more time, it came to me like a gift from the night . . . one morning, just as I was waking up, when I least expected it, I remembered Scheherazade's confusion and irony the day I spoke to her about other forms of life—parasitic or mimetic—and the strange moral codes developed by polymorphous parasites that are so different from ours they seem inconceivable, abnormal, even monstrous.

And I saw again the little cat smelling the little girl's cut throat. No, I saw again the little cat that SEEMED to smell the little girl's throat in front of the school. And I saw again the still body of the little girl, like an abandoned skin on the gravel . . . and now, without a doubt . . . I shouted: AND NOW, THE LITTLE CAT IS DEAD!

So that was it! Yes, for these people threatened with extinction by the death of their sun, the arrival of first explorers was an unexpected opportunity. Because other planets would never welcome such a large population, they would get rejected everywhere, and at best, parked in camps, eternal exiles or eternal pariahs, irremediably unwanted. The only solution was to invade. Not openly: the I.S.S. were far too powerful! No. By other means, without anyone noticing. Let's check the hypothesis: the first attempts must have been disastrous; Earthlings' bodies colonized by... let's call them... Io-Phenix's "polymorphs"—which are infinitesimal—reacted as they would to a bacterial aggression, and with the help of our medicine, it was a hecatomb among the invaders... who, in all likelihood, never lived in the unhospitable northern hemisphere, but were present when the first ship arrived in some shape that we couldn't see. After several unsuccessful parasitic trials, they must have adopted the mimetic solution. QED,[3] it's nothing new... maybe, still, it was painful, difficult, or dangerous—what do I know?—to maintain human appearance, hence the epidemic, criminal, and suicidal hecatombs, a way to shed their old skin to take on another; to leave the body of a child for, let's say, that of a cat, why not? At this point, I could well imagine that the deviant forms, dragons or lips-trees, constituted here the work of artists or lunatics the way we once believed that "monsters" were the "Devil's" work!

Even so, something wasn't right... What if this multitude of crimes and suicides... had the objective... to... but of course! Once on Earth, it starts again! Survivors would understand too late that all the slaughtered [bodies] didn't come from Io-Phenix. Identity substitutions were an old trick well-known to the police! And one day, Earthlings would be in the minority...

They thought they were so clever, I said to myself! But then again, they had failed. Because the I.S.S. would never allow the immigration of the population, even if they looked human and civilized, if they appeared physiologically and psychologically unstable.

Incidentally, the problem might soon resolve itself: the extinction of the Pi family was only one episode in a long series of similar

---

3    A Latin phrase: *Quod erat demonstrandum* meaning "that which had to be demonstrated."

tragedies of unheard magnitude; soon, I saw buildings with closed shutters, closed shops in the streets, and school gates only opened for a few children. The spaceships of successive missions had all left. I really wondered what I was doing there. I cursed my initial stubbornness to stay, which I no longer understood. If I didn't want to go mad, I had to leave now while the deserted planet was converted to tourism! This was a good vein to exploit: infrastructures were quasi ready; intergalactic travel agencies had time to feast before it became uninhabitable, to be the last ones to come to Io-Phenix before the sun's agony, what an advertising argument! Woe be upon us, all necrophiliacs deep in our heart! Woe be upon us!

I packed my things. I applied for an authorization that was quickly granted, to get from the Pi's house an old holobook the grandpa had asked me to lend him a few days prior . . . It was dear to me. It was a collection of Chinese tales, full of absurdities, but my friend Lao-Yip, with whom I was at the intergalactic university, had gifted it to me. And also, I was thinking about the people, the young women, who had had it in their hands, who had turned around the holotales.

Now I am almost at the end of my journey. In a few hours, I will be back on our old Earth with this damn devilish book! I must say that when I started skimming through it, without thinking, to create a diversion from my obsessive memories, I wasn't expecting that. That shock! This mold between pages. Three big ones, and then three others decreasing in size. To think that I almost wiped them off, by reflex. And then, suddenly, I RECOGNIZED them! A force of evidence, there, turning me upside down. I laughed, and then quickly corrected this silly feeling inside me: of course, it was again nothing more than one of their transitory forms . . . Ah! It made me so happy that they chose to come with me, even if it put me in a funny situation, really happy . . . risky, the book stunt! If I had forgotten it . . . bah, gramps is a fine psychologist. Yes, despite me I continue to give them human names! It's understandable, don't you think?

How will this all end? Sometimes I think I should be afraid. Oh! Just a flash that goes through me, just a flash! It's funny. Really. It's funny. Because I know it would be stupid to be afraid. Afraid! Of them! Still . . . what are we, tiny midges, primitive intelligences, the tired offsprings of aborted civilizations, compared to THEM! Them,

Spirit, Them, Light, Them, sweetness and power together. They who chose me to serve them. Would I close my door to them? No, no, I open wide the door to Earth, I humbly move aside, hand on the handle, sorry, I stand on the threshold, forgive me, I wasn't expecting you so soon, please MAKE YOURSELF AT HOME. Oh, my very dear guests, Oh, my lords, you know, don't you, you know I will never betray you! My report? Come on! For a long time, I have been taking these notes only for myself . . . This is between you and me . . . isn't it? Oh! Tell me, tell me that you trust me! A sign will suffice: a simple sign, no matter how tenuous, I would understand it . . . My love will take the place of my intelligence. Right? Right?

One day, I know it, I am sure of it, one day they will reveal themselves to me. At last. When they deem me worthy. They must. They must. And I will finally know Dina's real form. And I will uncover the mystery of her being beyond deceiving appearances. And despite the staring eyes of newborns. Oh, Dina! My silent one. My unspeakable. My veiled fiancée.

Ah! If it is necessary, may humanity die! This disgusting, shameless bitch that, millennium after millennium, knows only to return to its own vomit!

See, my sweet, see: I laugh! I laugh! I laugh!

Their stinky carcasses will rot in the sun!

Man is finished and I laugh! See, my sweet, come, my sweet: I am waiting for you. Recognize my trembling love, my patient love. Oh, my Dina, come to me!

I am ready. I am waiting for you. Take me.

*Mon amante.*

*Ma mante.* [4]

---

4   My lover. My mantis.

# EXPANSION

Colette Fayard: "The Liberator"

French title: "Le Libérateur"

Published in the collection *Les Chasseurs au bord de la nuit* by French editor Denoël in 1989.

*Translated by* Annabelle Dolidon

Colette Fayard, also a literature professor, has been writing theater plays (not science fiction plays), novels, and short stories since the 1980s. She won the Grand Prix de la S.-F. française (now Grand Prix de l'Imaginaire) in 1990 for her story *Les Chasseurs au bord de la nuit* (*Hunter at the Edge of the Night*) that gives its title to the collection in which "The Liberator" was published.

Her background in literature shows in her writing through intertextual references to canonical texts and characters. In 1996, she even published the novel *Par tous les temps* (which carries a double meaning: *In all times/temporalities* and *In all types of weather*) that transforms poet Arthur Rimbaud into a sci-fi character. In "The Liberator," people familiar with the work of Guy de Maupassant, a nineteenth-century author of great SF/horror short stories (mentioned in the Introduction of this book), will make connections between Fayard's character and the narrator of "Le Horla" (1889) when Piggy "RECOGNIZES them." A series of exclamations follows that is reminiscent of those of Maupassant's narrator "I saw! I know! I don't know! I am crazy!" after doubts and hesitations about what is really going on here. Even the ending that shows Piggy's ambivalence toward the aliens—fear, love, fascination—plays a key part in "Le Horla," both stylistically (exclamation points, short sentences) and narratively (the agony of both narrators over discovering—or inventing—a meaning for what they have been experiencing).[5] Fayard also evokes seventeenth-century

---

5 Piggy's brief attraction to Scheherazade at one point in the story is shocking and he quickly shakes it off. Retrospectively, we understand that he was fascinated with the aliens who are not humans, not the girl. He is, again, very much like the narrator of "Le Horla", attracted to, yet horrified by this new, shapeshifting life-form.

playwright Molière with the famous, enigmatic line "Le petit chat est mort!" from *L'École des femmes* (*The School for Wives*).

Many of Fayard's stories play on uncertainty, and some might look like they belong more to the *fantastique* genre than science fiction because of the uncanny, uneasy feelings she slowly instills in her readers. One critic wrote that this collection was definitively under the aura of painter René Magritte and surrealism. A clear example of this is the scene in the cemetery where children play happily as the grandpa and the parents of Scheherazade are being laid to rest. It is a play on an episode from Magritte's childhood when he used to play with a little girl in a cemetery and stumbled upon a painter at his easel. This reference is cleverly weaved in Fayard's story.

"The Liberator" is a tale about metamorphosis and monsters, as well as a great science fiction story. It will make you ponder, and it will perhaps frighten you, the way the narrator is "horrified by [his] own behavior" (153). It is also in conversation with a great literary history that loves to play with unusual concepts, uncertainties, and the bizarre.

## DISCUSSION QUESTIONS

As mentioned above, Fayard refers to other texts in the French literary tradition that she seems to know well. She also conjures up the famous collection of tales *One Thousand and One Nights* by having her main character name a little girl Scheherazade. By using this name, what might the author indicate to the reader about the girl and her family, her *species*?

Let's talk *genre*. One critic wrote that this story was not science fiction. What do you think? What elements in the text make you think it is science fiction? What elements might contradict it? Can science fiction also be *something else*?

How do the relationships between various characters—the way they are described—work in the story? How may they be essential to the atmosphere of the story and the (at times, disturbing) thoughts of the protagonist?

This story is another take on the "they are among us" trope. Can you think of other stories like this (film or texts) with shape-shifting extraterrestrials?

In this story, we feel the main character's fear of, and morbid fascination for, a possible invasion by living beings we may not be able to detect, a superior species. This is very similar to what happens in Maupassant's "Le Horla." In real life, how do you think we can relate to this?

Did you find some of the elements of the foreign planet surrealistic? Again, you can think about science fiction films and imagined planets in them. What elements signal that they are different, far away, with different fauna and flora, different cultures?

# Nowhere in Liverion

*by* Serge Lehman

*translated by* Jean-Louis Trudel

## 1

THE MOMENT BEFORE, he was alone, sitting on the floor. Sunshine streamed through the windows overlooking the *via* Andrea and filled a pool of pale light around him. There was a knock. Only one, but hard.

He was unworried. When he'd traveled back to Rome, he knew that Saxxon would end up sending his B-men to fetch him. He got up and opened the door.

The men on the landing were not expecting his compliance. One of them hastily stuffed a hammer back inside his sports bag. The dim glow of the LCD glasses they all wore pierced the stairwell's gloom.

"I was waiting for you," he whispered, as if to confess a sin.

In most cases, the B-men were not professional police officers, just middle managers for whom a field operation was enough of a reward that they trained for it daily. When a megacorp—one of the business world's Powers, to use the new buzzword—planned a special operation, it assigned the job to its employees with the best performance reviews. Brilliant men and women who were the corporate world's best businessmen, or "B-men" for short. And who knew how to take care of business . . .

It was quite illegal, but the police forces of nation-states were literally Powerless; B-men operated in parts of the world traditional states no longer tried to control. Lately, though, they were showing up more and more within the bounds of the global Village. Paul put on his jacket, thinking that Marianna was right. Soon, nobody would remember what the twentieth century once called "public services."

The B-men escorted him to the building's roof where a leaper was waiting for them. When it took off, one of the men opaqued the partition. Their destination was to remain secret. Paul shrugged and leaned back in his seat. He was almost certain that he was in no real danger. Even if he was wrong—had he really thought of everything?—he couldn't help smiling.

He hadn't stopped smiling. Not since he'd returned from Georgia. The B-men sitting around him couldn't believe it. One of them peered at him from behind his LCD glasses and he asked at last, "Do you know who we are, Mr. Coray? Do you know what's happening to you?"

Paul mollified him with a nod.

Holding back his euphoria was not so easy.

It was night when they landed. The B-men took him to a windowless room belowground. Thirty or so people were already there, arrayed behind a table shaped like a crescent moon.

They were no threat to him, even if they hoped to inspire fear. He knew some of them. The reality was that they sought to be protected from him. From the force he now carried within.

"You're not in the clear yet," Virtù Jonahsen said when she noticed his smile.

She sat on the board of Saxxon, the industrial empire that controlled half of all air and space transportation companies, with a combined workforce of over two million on Earth and in cislunar space. Her slim, endlessly reworked figure and optimally featured face had ascended to the apex of the megacorp hierarchy in just under five years, moving into ever grander executive suites offering ever nicer views of the world below. Now, she oversaw the philanthropic arm of the Fuller Foundation, named after the company's founder, handing out dozens of millions of marks to NGOs and multitasking laboratories each year.

On the side, she also financed the research of independent scholars, such as medievalist Paul Coray, who formed a loose grouping that was easily controlled and usually escaped notice.

"We could do it, you know. Kill you. Inflict pain."

"You've already made me suffer."

"Not enough. You tricked us."

"I had no idea Wishman was working for you."

Virtù Jonahsen pinned him down with her nearly colorless eyes.

"What would you have done if you'd known?"

"Nothing."

A man seated near the far horn of the crescent moon slapped the table with both of his hands, gazing at Paul with anger and loathing, "You went to Liverion!"

"I went nowhere."

They would get nothing more from him, and they knew it, but they kept talking. If they'd agreed on a strategy beforehand, it was not evident. From time to time, one of them got up, uttered a veiled threat, and left the room with a fierce look, as if they were going to come back with a squad of B-men, before sidling back through another door.

Others referenced the Board, capital B, several times. Paul was familiar with the idea thanks to his fight with Marianna. It rested on the same ideological underpinnings as other high-concept coinings: B-men, the Village, Darwin Alley. Saxxon was showing off to impress him, but Paul had learned, in the course of renegotiating his contract every year with the Fuller Foundation, how to gauge who had the upper hand.

Today, the scales were tilting in his favor.

Jonahsen was the first to leave the room. The others exchanged quizzical glances, as if her exit held some special significance. But no, it was just closing time. Everybody left. Paul remained alone for two or three minutes, in front of the empty table, until the B-men came and delivered him back to his place.

# 2

"What do I want from you? That you stop looking at your screen for all of five minutes, nothing more. That you stop working and listen to me."

It had all started with Marianna's cold anger.

He could have defused her wrath—he'd done so before—but things had gone south in a hurry. Sheer fatigue, most likely. His research on Stephen II and the Donation of Constantine had been hitting dead ends for months. As soon as he tried to figure things out, noting down every element of his topic on cards, he would spread out on the floor to seek unexpected connections; one more time, all the names, dates, and bibliographical references would start to resemble a repulsive collection of dead flies. His mind would start to wander.

*That story with De Lesseps . . .*

No, he should not be thinking of that. It was neither the place nor the time. Breathless from the heat—what was wrong with the AC, anyway?—he abandoned his index cards, turned the chair around, and stared at his wife.

"Can we talk about this later? I'm in the middle of something."

Maria's face was taut, so he cut himself short. Not that it spared him her retort.

"You're always *in the middle of something.*"

She was skinnier than ever. Her T-shirt clung to her ribs and her face was so pale that her hair seemed darker than blond. She was shivering slightly. As the heat was unbearable, he imagined she was scared.

Images from three years back danced briefly in his mind. Fireworks, colorful clothes, people diving into the Seine from a bridge strewn with flowers, eddies floating downstream from the quick splashes. The May 2051 Carnival in Paris. Their dissertations were nearly done, and they'd just spent their first night together, after months wasted checking each other out.

By the windows of their hotel room, they admired the sleek gold-and-black Saxxon long-haulers sliding through the sky like pure geometric shapes. Maria dreamed aloud of Rome, of the Foundation's contract offers, and he let her fantasies wash over him. His head nestled in the curve of her hips, he could have listened to her for hours.

All of that had been over and done with long ago.

"I saw Jonahsen and the people from the Foundation. I found out a few things. I've guessed a few more. Mostly, about the Board. What we talked about."

And how! Three times in two weeks. Why did Maria feel the need to harp on it? Within the Fuller Foundation, she headed an applied psychology research group, while the "Board" was an emerging concept in macroeconomics.

Paul's attention should have seized upon this oddity a long time ago, but he'd been concerned with other things.

(The letter from De Lesseps, for instance.)

As a matter of fact, he already knew what Maria was going to tell him. The planet was going through a historical tipping point, perhaps even an anthropological mutation. The endless extension of economic logic to every aspect of human life could only happen at the expense of all competing systems, including those of state entities. The process had been underway for years.

Financially ruined and deprived of their ancient prerogatives by the rise of private Powers, traditional political entities had prolonged their own agony by coming up with cute names—such as the "entrepreneurial state"—for the stages of their decay, lending themselves to the empty symbolism of media-worthy rituals or taking on the role of unconvincing backdrops for television serials. Decline was unstable by definition, however. Within a few years, a few decades at most, their role in the collective arrangement of human affairs would fade until states winked out of view, like outdated mirages.

"That's where the Board will come in," Marianna explained. "At first, it will sell itself as an advisory council including delegates from the major Powers. They will deliberate in parallel with the UN and set out the guidelines for a perfectly rational world economy. Things will happen softly. At first, they'll speak of a superministry for the economy, a global pact for development, and so on. The medium-term goal will remain: turning the Board into a world government."

"Maria! Maria!" Paul made placatory gestures as he might have done to soothe a madwoman. "What's the connection with me? I'm a historian, not a futurologist."

"Your research for the Foundation . . ."

"I don't work for the Foundation. It pays my way, nothing more. I hold the full title to whatever I come up with. It's spelled out in the sponsorship agreement."

"Do you still believe Jonahsen is funding your research out of a philanthropic urge? Wake up, Paul! Your investigations are part of her project!"

He should have gotten up, taken her in his arms, and told her not to worry so much. Or suggest that they make love, since they both needed it. But she was unstoppable. Overcome by rage, she laid out a prophecy of her own devising, leaving him to nod along and hope to forestall the worst.

"Once the Board gathers the authority it needs, a new era will begin. On that day, all former borders will be erased forever, *pfft!*" She blew on her fingers. "The only collective based on a political reality deserving of the name will be the Village. Everything else will be subject to private law, competition, and property rights. Including human beings."

"No, my love. You're coming up with a nightmare that cannot happen as such. The Village is about two billion people, just a fifth of the world's population. About ten percent of the world's landmasses. The rest of the world will not tolerate that—"

She cut him off. "The Powers have been buying up land for decades. Entire regions! Haven't you been listening to what I've been telling you for weeks now? In the records I've seen at the Foundation, their holdings amount to nearly two-thirds of the world's landmasses. The whole planet is becoming *private property!*"

The idea staggered him, but he could not figure out what to do aside from turning it down a notch.

"So what? Civil law will still apply. Owning land does not mean—"
He stopped himself.

Maria was grinning, but it was the wrong smile. The one she allowed herself when she won a victory that she did not enjoy.

"Yes, it does mean *that*. You of all people know it."

♦ ♦ ♦

When he was asked what he was working on, Paul selected an answer based on the person asking him. Rome was the perfect mirror for most people's private obsessions and fantasies, and it was even more interesting to wait for people's reactions when he spoke of past Popes. Still, he was a historian, and his work on Stephen II and the Donation of Constantine was intended to tackle an entirely secular quandary.

*Who rules, and on what legal basis?*

Marianna saw that he'd understood, but she wanted to have the last word. Leaning over, she stared into his eyes.

"If the Board takes over one day, it'll be on you."

◆ ◆ ◆

He gulped down two caplets of D-late and slept fifteen hours. When he got up, his head was heavy, and he faintly recalled dreaming... It took him a moment to realize Maria was gone. In her place, a maintenance drone was checking the air conditioning.

Utterly depressed, he locked himself inside the bathroom, took a cold shower, and brushed his teeth several times in a row without getting rid of the bad taste in his mouth.

*Your fault. It will be your fault.*

He went out for a walk, but he'd been wrong to think that the air would be cooler outside. In the Campo de Fiore, he drank a coffee and leafed through the *L'Osservatore Romano*, the Vatican's daily newspaper, an old habit dating back to his early work in Paris on his dissertation. He recalled a professor who was so impressed with his astute deciphering of the newspaper's convoluted prose that he liked to tease him about it. "You missed your calling in life. Forget about research, Paul. You're too good at this. The Vatican is partnering with Primus to offer training. You should have a look. It's gratifying and very well paid!"

From a professional historian, such advice was troubling. *Or merely practical*, Paul told himself, as he thought of the previous day's discussion. Not that he wanted to keep thinking about it! His mind, like an obedient machine, changed course and the name of Barthélémy De Lesseps came to him spontaneously, like a foretaste of a long-promised vacation.

Yet he rejected the prospect. Now wasn't the time!

(It's never the right time.)

He could feel the Campo de Fiore vibrate under his feet, like a stone drum pounded by tourists. He headed for the big top on the other side of the plaza. Inside, he discovered a holographic terrestrial globe, about ten meters in diameter, slowly revolving on its axis. Above the simulacrum, an appeal blinked stroboscopically:

\* FIRST PUBLIC SUBSCRIPTION \*
became a shareholder today of
RUNNIN' FOR DARWIN
*An offer guaranteed by Braunen Corp.*

Along the tent's periphery, hostesses were redirecting gawkers toward the company's sales desks. The selling job seemed to be working. On the holographic globe, a continuous red line went through most of the world's metropolitan areas, striding around seas and oceans.

WITH YOU ON OUR SIDE, WE'LL BUILD
**DARWIN ALLEY**
AROUND THE ENTIRE WORLD
* SUBSCRIBE NOW *

He'd heard of it, naturally. Braunen Corp, the world's top-ranked construction Powers, was going to build a street around the Earth.

It made no sense from a financial point of view, but the symbol was striking. If Maria had been there, she would have said that this road erased all of the world's borders, save one—the only one that still mattered—the one that isolated the complex of hypertechnological metropolises, wealthy and Anglophone, making up the Village from everything else.

It was sick. *Everything else.* Three-quarters of humanity were stranded in a jurisdictional no-man's-land and left unprotected to the whims of the Powers while the system's elite was going to party on Darwin Alley.

*It'll be on you.*

He left the big top, heading for St. Peter's Square. A few steps reduced his anxiety to bearable levels. The basilica's dome shone with a coppery gleam in the sun, draping its peaked shadow over Nero's obelisk.

A small group of men, their every motion in perfect sync, exited the belvedere and crossed the St. Damasus Courtyard. They bore weapons and wore red, yellow, and blue. The Pope's private guard.

Ever since Paul had moved to Rome with Maria, he returned to this spot at least once a week. She could work anywhere in the Village, but he needed this place. He knew practically every square meter of the Vatican, not only because of his research. He was fascinated by its origins, by the sheer fiction upon which rested its whole existence.

Back in the eighth century, Pope Stephen II, threatened by the Lombards, had sought the aid of Pepin the Short. Three years earlier,

Pepin had become king of the Franks with the support of another Pope, Zachary, who had sanctioned his accession because he was the only real force in the West, and because the pontiff believed that kingship primarily lay in the "ability to exercise real power." Pepin had beaten the Lombards and yielded his conquests to Stephen II. But the Byzantine emperor, at odds with Rome, had claimed them for himself. Stephen II then invoked a donation made by Constantine to the bishop of Rome after his conversion to Christianity, four centuries earlier, in order to keep the lands retaken from the Lombards and convert them into the basis of the Papal States, the predecessor of the contemporary Vatican.

Yet, the Donation of Constantine was a fake.

The first time Paul had come across this story, he'd struggled with the idea it was both true and so little known. The internationally recognized existence of the Vatican was built on a forgery twelve centuries old that nobody denied! One deep dive into the original documents later—plus months of additional reading—he'd decided to turn the object of his fascination into a thesis topic.

His supervisor's reaction had startled him.

"How old are you?"

"Twenty-six."

"And your degree is in political science, right? Do you know that we think of you here as a promising medievalist?"

Some questions aren't meant to be answered. He understood as much and took in the compliment while waiting for the other shoe.

"The Vatican. Stephen II. Think again. That won't get you anywhere. Professionally, I mean. Please trust my experience; you won't dazzle anybody with such a topic. And you deserve a chance to dazzle. To put it bluntly, the legal basis of medieval land ownership has been done to death. And don't forget the problem of sources. The Holy See rarely grants full access to its archives."

Other objections, just as reasonable, had been raised. However, Paul had thought it through, and his choice was made. If his supervisor refused, he'd submit the topic to somebody else.

The old silverback let himself be swayed in the end. Yet, Paul was never able to convince him of his work's value, even after defending his thesis. The Merovingian sources about the Donation of

Constantine were so well-known that they harbored not even a last remaining enigma requiring elucidation.

Such was the doxa.

Yet, he was positive that he was onto something. It was irrational, hard to justify in purely academic terms. He had a hunch that the way Stephen II had converted a fiction into hard fact held unacknowledged relevance for the twenty-first century. *"He is truly king who is able to exercise real power."* Behind the historical riddle, he suspected the presence of an unnoticed kernel, the germ of an original theory, even though he was still unable to guess what new thinking it embodied. Even after finishing his thesis, he wanted to keep exploring the topic and devote an essay to it. *"Yes, Mr. Coray, the Fuller Foundation is open to supporting this line of investigation."*

Who gets to rule, and on what legal basis?

Transitioning from de facto dominance over a given territory to full, unquestionable sovereignty de jure, Stephen II had buried the recipe for this alchemical transmutation in the Vatican archives. Now, Paul Coray was bringing it to light for the Fuller Foundation.

Jonahsen had turned him into the unwitting theorizer of the Board's future legitimacy.

# 3

Once his self-loathing had aged into a hard and blackened husk, he went home and sat at his desk. The maintenance drone was gone. He was relieved; an outside witness would have made it tougher for him to proceed.

Using his voice, he called up his first work file and ordered its erasure.

"Are you sure?" his computer asked. "These are your notes for the paper on Lombard law."

"Destroy them all."

The percentage climbed gradually as the histogram reflected the disappearance of his notes. His heart was beating so fast he had to grip the armrests to keep himself from fainting. Part of him sniggered as he thought of the disappointment in store for the Fuller Foundation, but another part was screaming at him, *Stop!* If he acted fast enough, he could still ask the computer to recover the data. They remained in a cache for a few seconds after deletion.

But he'd foreseen the temptation and he withstood it, calling up another file. The first draft of a short, very technical essay on real estate law in the Holy Roman Empire that he was supposed to submit by year's end.

*Now what?* He watched months of work vanish into digital limbo. *Once it's all gone, what do I do next?*

He had no idea. Burning his paper notes and destroying his hard drives seemed logical enough, after which he would gobble down enough D-late to forget it all. It would be a long sleep. Little by little, he would curl up on his bed, deep inside the deserted apartment. Maintenance would give up on him. A thin layer of dust would coat the windows, and the subdued light would transform the lifeless rooms into a dimly lit tomb.

Whenever Jonahsen planned to stop by and gloat that a new world was born, in spite of his defection, there would be nothing left of him.

He was on the verge of selecting a third file when the computer spoke. "Your request for information about De Lesseps has been answered."

*Delete it like all the rest,* he replied immediately.

Or he thought he did. Something was wrong. The words coming out of his mouth were not the ones he had in mind.

"Does the message mention Liverion?"

"Yes."

It was unhoped for. So much so that he believed for an instant that he had died without realizing it and that his brain was producing a meaningful hallucination to let him know.

"Let's see the message," he breathed.

Onscreen, a golden circle irised open. The face of a fortyish man, blond, bearded, and smiling, came to life.

"Mr. Coray, I came across your data seekers on the telmat network. I'm wondering if you've found what you were looking for. Nobody else is interested in Barthélémy De Lesseps these days. And Liverion . . . is something else. I'd like to discuss it with you. My name is Jonathan Wishman."

"End of message," the computer added. "The sender left an address. Do you wish to respond?"

The icon of a crenellated tower was winking at the bottom of the screen, showing that the strongest encryption standard had been used for maximum security. Such wariness was rare. Wishman would have paid at least five hundred marks for the option.

Paul briefly tried to resume his self-immolation. He revived in his mind's eye the image of Marianna—the Maria he'd known and loved in Paris—to feel anew the burn of her absence. He reminded himself of the Foundation's hijacking of his research and the two destroyed files. Of Darwin Alley's globe-girdling red line. Yet, whenever he opened his eyes, he was faced with Jonathan Wishman's crenellated icon as the names of De Lesseps and Liverion whirled once more inside his head, like the wind-scattered pieces of an inexplicable puzzle, and his heart raced.

He still wanted to know. (He wanted to live.)

His prolonged sigh was like a return to ordinary existence.

"Call him back. Check his agenda to see where and when we can meet. Make it as soon as possible."

# 4

". . . I don't know why I'm telling you this. I haven't spoken to anyone in days, aside from my computer. I don't know where my wife is. I don't know if I still have a job. I'm rather lost, in fact. I got your message in the nick of time."

"The spleen of Old Europe," Wishman muttered as he tried to light his cigarette. "Still, I'm glad I came."

The old port in Hamburg was windy, extremely windy, and the seagulls wheeling above the basins screeched angrily. A waiter brought their beers, and they clinked their pints.

"You would have come anyway, right?"

"I'm here on business, but that's why I wrote. I figured I would take the opportunity to get in touch. Tomorrow, I'll be in Abidjan."

A supertanker from the century's early years—the *Jordania*—was moored inside the nearest basin. Its overwhelming bulk loomed over the port. Passing by the ship to find Wishman, Paul had read on a plaque that it was a municipal asset. Purchased and stabilized with a hypercarbon layer three microns thick, it served as a museum, a destination for school groups, and a sandbox for students of industrial history. Today, tourists were in short supply and children were entirely absent. Was it a school holiday in Germany? Not that the weather helped. It was twenty degrees colder than in Rome.

"I'm American, with Irish and Hungarian roots," Wishman had said as they shook hands. "I've always felt connected to Europe. I come often. That being said, I couldn't live here. Everything is too small."

He towered above Paul like a professional basketball player, but there was no blaming him for his size. Paul had taken an instant liking to the man, as soon as he'd met him in person. He knew he was overcompensating, but he needed to connect after days alone. Avoiding the topic of Jonahsen and the Board, he talked about his breakup.

"It's always the same story," Wishman observed neutrally.

"It is. And that's why Liverion . . ."

The American shuddered. He'd finally managed to light his cigarette. He blew out a long smoke trail, instantly scattered by a gust of wind, and he lowered his voice. "I'd rather you did not pronounce that name."

He raised his gaze and Paul did likewise. Above them, perhaps half a kilometer up, a recreational airship belonging to the Orion Lion was drifting lazily through the pale sky. Village hedonism floating above the old industrial world, forever soiled. A banal image. Paul queried Wishman with a look to find out what the American feared, but the other man gestured with unconcern, as if he'd just expressed a personal preference.

"There's something bothering me," he said. "Why are you so interested in De Lesseps? He was a man of the Enlightenment and you're a medievalist."

It was such a good question that Paul felt trapped.

"We've been sitting at this table for almost twenty minutes, and I still know nothing about you. That's what I find odd."

"Touché." Wishman stroked his beard. "What do you know of DATEX?"

"The usual. A telecom Power. The largest shareholder of the telmat network."

"Good enough. DATEX is rich . . . I suspect neither you nor I can truly imagine how rich. These last few years, it's been buying land. It has over thirty property management companies working for it on five continents. I head one in Portland."

The world of the Board and Darwin Alley was becoming tangible, bit by bit. For now, it was still an epiphenomenon, a mere detail in the professional life of an American business lawyer. But it was coming. Paul strove to remain inexpressive.

"I read your thesis last year," Wishman continued. "It may surprise you, but I love legal history and theory. It keeps me from drowning in my own cynicism. Online, you're linked with land ownership issues, even though I fully understand that it's not your main topic. I said I'd read you, but as a matter of fact, I just looked through your introduction, conclusion, and table of contents. Isn't that standard operating procedure in academia?" Wishman's grin was disarmingly candid. "The case of the forged Donation of Constantine struck me. Hence my surprise when I came across your data seekers. De Lesseps has nothing to do with the Early Middle Ages or the Vatican."

"No."

"But he has everything to do with land acquisition on the grandest of scales."

Paul breathed in. Either he could trust Wishman, speak with him, and find out what he knew about Liverion or he could go back to Rome and resumed deleting his research notes.

"I got hooked on De Lesseps for the same reason you took an interest in my thesis," he said at last. "Because it's my job. Except that it soon turned into an obsession."

Three months earlier, as he kept floundering with Stephen II and Constantine, he'd taken a chance. The data seekers he was using to trawl telmat and other networks were retrieving the same documents and the same references. Merovingian sources and their commentators had nothing to add to the owner vs. ruler question, vindicating his supervisor's misgivings. Paul had opted to extend his research beyond the eighth century.

"A professional historian shouldn't be doing this. It's a dangerous game. When you try to figure out a historical situation by looking at later events, you run the risk of producing mirages. Causes and effects get confused. You're easy prey for anachronisms and teleological fallacies . . ."

"I see," Wishman said politely.

"I spent an entire term reading the Scholastics and later legal theorists. That's how I came across a letter by De Lesseps."

It was held by an archival fonds of the French Academy of Sciences in Paris. He'd discovered it as he was going through documents ranked quite low by his data seekers due to a lack of congruence with his topic.

Now, he knew it by heart.

*21ˢᵗ Brumaire, Year II, St. Petersburg[1]*

*Monsieur & dearest friend,*

*Your latest letter was just vouchsafed to me by Monsieur De Lesquielles, our young attaché, recently back from Paris. The press of current affairs deprives me of the pleasure I would find in answering as completely as desired & with all due subtlety. Such an abhorrent neglect of the mind's faculties, since subtlety & completeness are the truest hallmarks of yours! However, I have nothing to teach you about the obligations of public affairs, on this or that side of the borders of France.*

*Nonetheless, I will respond to your latter question, as it seems the most urgent, while retaining the hope that I can produce, as soon as I am given the opportunity, a more appropriate expatiation.*

*You referred to the deception practiced by Stephen II. It is an excellent thought & it requires all my affection for you to stifle my resentment that I should have remembered it first. Indeed, the manner in which the Pope used the forged Donation of Constantine might serve as a model for our own designs.*

*However, think on this: if we reproduce this maneuver, Liverion will also rest on a fraud, which I reprove for two reasons. Firstly, we will never have, even in the best of cases, the ability of the Holy See to muzzle its critics. Secondly, it appears to me that we would compromise the tree by poisoning the seed. Our city would necessarily suffer from basing its constitution on the moral law of Monsieur Kant while plunging its roots in the fetid loam of an ancient swindle.*

---

1 The French Revolutionary calendar's equivalent of November 11, 1793.

*Moreover, do not overlook the time & monies that I am devoting here to buying the lands we discussed previously, such that we are becoming the legitimate landlords of our demesne. What need do we have to imagine such a despicable trick to establish our rights? If everything happens as planned, nobody will ever be in a position to dispute them.*

*I believe such objections cannot be dismissed lightly. After all, wasn't it our goal to overcome such contradictions & more complex ones besides that we dreamed of Liverion?*

*Your faithful and devoted servant,*

*Jean-Baptiste Barthélémy De Lesseps*

Wishman kept nodding as he listened to Paul's tale.

"I came across that letter about ten years ago," he said. "I was working on ancient rules of land ownership in Denmark. I'm not a historian, but I must admit this letter fascinated me. I did some research of my own . . . When he wrote it, De Lesseps was the French consul in St. Petersburg. Do you know to whom he was writing?"

"Yes. Mathematician and geographer Jean Maleterre."

The American smiled, and Paul gathered that the other knew as much as he did. In 1785, Barthélémy De Lesseps, the freshly appointed French vice-consul in Kronstadt at just nineteen years old, had sailed with the French explorer La Pérouse on a lengthy scientific expedition destined for Japan. Two years on, he had been ordered to leave ship in Kamchatka to travel overland back to France, with the observations collected up to that point, while La Pérouse continued by sea. It was likely upon his return to Paris that De Lesseps met Maleterre, who was attached to the Royal Observatory.

"In this letter," Paul concluded, carefully picking his words, "it is easily understood that De Lesseps and Maleterre shared a common goal . . ."

The time had come to speak of Liverion.

"Yes," Wishman concurred. "And I don't believe they were alone. They were contemplating the construction of a city, no less! I've pondered this many times . . . They must have had collaborators."

Paul had come to the same conclusion, many times over.

"It's only logical. Still, I've done extensive research, and I've used the best data-seeking agents on the market. I've found no other reference to the project outside of this letter. I've examined all of the available sources on De Lesseps and Maleterre, starting with their correspondence. I've noted about two dozen letters where they allude to their enterprise, using various circumlocutions. But nothing more."

"And you don't find that intriguing? I mean, we have a group of thinkers from the Enlightenment who are plotting to create an ideal city and—"

"There is no proof that such a group existed."

"Indeed," Wishman yielded with a smile. "Still, it would make sense that the project be mentioned in more letters from the same period, wouldn't it?"

"As long as there was a group, which cannot be inferred from this letter," Paul insisted, though he didn't like playing the hairsplitting academic.

Wishman sighed and finished his beer.

"All those ancient documents we're talking about . . . they didn't appear online by mere chance. They were scanned and indexed. Think about the work involved in scanning and indexing all of the world's archival fonds. Do you know who took it on?"

Paul had never wondered.

"Their owners, I assume. Universities, inst—"

"DATEX. That's its strong suit and how it became a Power: by digitizing 80 percent of the world's archives and offering them online. You know what that means . . . The documents we're discussing were selected. Not everything is online."

Wishman fussed with his glass while giving Paul time to assimilate the idea and its implications. "That letter from De Lesseps probably went unnoticed by the digitization teams," he added. "The process was so massive there had to be mistakes. Most everything else was caught in the net. That's why you're not finding anything more."

It sounded like a conspiracy theory, but Paul's anxiety surged as he considered that it might be accurate. He tried to recall the letter by De Lesseps—not the digital facsimile he had examined over and over but the physical object made of eighteenth-century paper, yellowed and coarsened by the years, inscribed with the author's beautifully expressive handwriting, faded but legible— as he'd found it in an archival box at the Academy of Sciences. If he traveled to Paris, he could ask to see it and handle it. Yet, he would know DATEX had been there before him and that, for every document it had digitized, another might have been willfully ignored. Or destroyed. Same difference. If it wasn't online, it did not really exist.

"Why would DATEX censor the Liverion story?" he whispered.

Wishman looked up. The Lion of Orion airship was losing altitude, yet it was still drifting above them, as if it was moored to a fixed point. Paul no longer felt like playing the man's game.

"Well, *I* know why I find it interesting," he insisted. "Recently, it's been the only thing still getting me out of bed in the morning. My last line of defense against the spleen you mentioned. But it's more than that. De Lesseps and Maleterre are historical characters. There's something to dig up."

"An invisible city! We can guess why DATEX is after it, right?" Wishman checked his watch. "Anyway... online, the letter dated 21st Brumaire has the only overt reference to the project that wasn't suppressed, okay? However, I've discovered another text, more or less credible, where it emerges under another name. That's why I wrote you. I'm not a historian, so I have no idea how to take advantage of such a document, and I don't have the time, frankly. Still, it should be possible to use it to locate the city."

Paul couldn't believe his ears. "Seriously?"

"Absolutely. An essay from early this century available online. Since the city's name isn't used, the DATEX team didn't notice anything. The author relied on a code. A very simple trick, childish even."

"What is it? Who's the author?"

Wishman bit his lower lip, as if he drew as much pleasure as embarrassment from what he was about to say. "You are going to hate me, but I believe you need to find out by yourself."

*What?*

"Before you start shouting at me, listen. The code is *really* simple. If I give it to you, you'll hate yourself forever because you didn't crack it on your own. Furthermore, you have all you need to identify the author. You know what documents I used. You have the same ones. You only need to ask the right question, and that's your job. Compared to you, I'm just an amateur. You're going to find it."

"Wishman—"

"No, let me finish. Those are details, mere logistical issues. What matters is what happens during your investigation. Let us suppose I tell you the author's name... you'll save time, but you'll lose something else: the transformation that happens inside when you solve the mystery. If I deny you that experience, you'll be mad. And you'll be right."

Everything was silence. Even the seagulls above were quiet. Paul searched for an argument that might get Wishman to change his mind, but he came up empty-handed.

"We're different," the American added. "The world agrees with me. I enjoy my life, and I don't need to brood over the lost city of the Enlightenment to get out of bed every morning. There's pleasure involved, but I get the same kick out of tackling a crossword puzzle or a chess problem. It isn't existential. And, fundamentally, it's a European story. Even if I wanted to pursue it, I'd lack a certain something... The last step is up to you."

# 5

He traveled back to Rome. The maintenance drone had failed to fix the air conditioning and the apartment was like a greenhouse. After enduring Hamburg's chilly weather, he almost welcomed the heat. He turned on his machine and sat down in front of the screen. Silence gathered. Nobody had called. Nobody had come. Not even Maria.

Well, too bad.

*I'm going to Liverion.*

He got to work, without a plan or a method. He read the letter De Lesseps had sent to Maleterre time and time again, as if it were some three-dimensional object he could rotate mentally to examine it from all angles.

"*I believe such objections cannot be dismissed lightly. After all, wasn't it our goal to overcome such contradictions & more complex ones besides that we dreamed of Liverion?*"

Who was De Lesseps? A young aristocrat, clever and liberal-minded, in his twenties when the French Revolution had begun. A man of the Enlightenment. After traveling to the South Seas with La Pérouse and returning to Europe overland all the way from Kamchatka, he had manned a consulate in St. Petersburg, before rising to be a *chargé d'affaires* in Constantinople.

During his stay in Russia, he'd corresponded at length with Jean Maleterre—and others, most likely. The letters released by DATEX expressed, by 1793, real anguish. What was the Revolution turning into? Was it losing its original ideals? Where was the dividing line between democracy and tyranny? War abroad and repression within?

De Lesseps and Maleterre had finally found an answer. Paul guessed as much from a letter dated January 1793, even if Liverion's name did not appear as such.

*"If we cannot gain & sustain liberty inside our borders without making war on the entire world because liberty terrifies them, all is lost. We are doomed to live forever in the dark city our fathers knew, devouring each other & our laws that command in name only. As for that other city, the one we have dreamed of so many times, it would need to be at once so near & so far, so mighty & so little in sight that it may be doubted that we will ever find it. Easier by far would it be to build it with our own hands, beyond all borders. Better by far would it be for it not to exist, or more precisely, to exist nowhere at all. That would solve everything."*

In the course of his research, Paul had found a dozen papers devoted to Barthélémy De Lesseps. Two of them mentioned this letter, but of course, they considered the "other city" to be a metaphor, an allusion to the utopias beloved of the Enlightenment. The idealistic basis of the Revolution's beginnings.

Yet, the other city had a name: Liverion. And it was not the common dream of two men of letters: neither De Lesseps nor Maleterre qualified. It was clearly a political project. Just as Stephen II had created the Vatican using a fake imperial donation, De Lesseps and his group had founded an ideal city in a historical and geographical blind spot.

Utopia: the non-place. Liverion could only be nowhere.

Yet, it *existed*. In his letter from the twenty-first Brumaire, De Lesseps reported that he was purchasing extensive landholdings. Why, if not to build a city?

As night fell across Rome, it crept inside his apartment. The memory of his meeting with Wishman was flickering and fading to black, even though it had happened mere hours ago. All was dark, nothing moved. The screen seemed to be the only living thing.

"Where is Liverion?" Paul asked aloud.

(It was not intended as a query, more as an attempt to make the city exist by speaking its name. However, the workstation was unable to deal with human subtleties.)

"I have discovered nothing new since our last work session."

"Sorry. I'm speaking to myself."

He tried to recall the exact words used by Wishman. Somewhere online, there was an essay from the turn of the century that discussed Liverion under another name. How had he put it?

"*The author relied on a code. A very simple trick, childish even.*"

What kind of code was he referring to? Did "very simple" mean "obvious"? No doubt. Otherwise, Wishman would have thrown him another scrap, anything to set him on the right track . . . Since he hadn't done so, Paul should be able to locate the essay using the elements he'd gathered.

The letters of De Lesseps?

He stopped. *The letters.* Yes, it could be. Not the letter that mentioned Liverion: he'd mined it for all it had to offer. But the rest, the mundane correspondence haunted by the cities like an allusive private joke, baffling for the uninitiated yet crystal clear for those who knew of the project underway.

How had De Lesseps managed it? This was a problem, rooted in syntax and vocabulary use, that his workstation could tackle; it was programmed to deal even with the language of medieval cartularies.

Galvanized, Paul created a new database incorporating all the letters with at least one reference to Liverion. The computer produced in a couple of seconds the list of typical phrases used by De Lesseps to allude to the city:

| | |
|---|---|
| *the other city* | *42 hits* |
| *our city* | *41 hits* |
| *the city we're dreaming of [we dreamt of]* | *26 hits* |
| *this very city* | *15 hits* |
| *the city of our dreams* | *11 hits* |
| *the city* | *9 hits* |
| *the city that you know about* | *8 hits* |
| *the city we [will] need to build* | *3 hits* |
| *the inverted city* | *2 hits* |

Paul glanced at his screen's clock: 22:08. Back when he still enjoyed a normal life, when Maria was there, working in her own half of the office on her own research and looking up sometimes to watch him, that was approximately when they decided to go for an all-nighter or stop for the day.

Tonight, he was alone. The lost city of Barthélémy De Lesseps was the last mooring point still connecting him to reality.

He rose, shivering as his shirt stuck to his back drenched in sweat. He made himself a coffee in the kitchen before returning to sit at his desk and roused his program. "Make me a list of all the works with a title matching one of these phrases."

"Typology?"

"Nonfiction. All lengths."

"Time period?"

"From 2001 to, well, 2040."

The results appeared onscreen.

| | |
|---|---|
| *the city* | *2046 hits* |
| *our city* | *1029 hits* |
| *the city we're dreaming of [we dreamt of]* | *541 hits* |
| *the city of our dreams* | *361 hits* |
| *the city we [will] need to build* | *154 hits* |
| *the inverted city* | *42 hits* |
| *the other city* | *14 hits* |
| *this very city* | *11 hits* |
| *The city that you know about* | *3 hits* |

Paul had been working on Merovingian sources for so long that he'd forgotten that he might have to go through thousands of documents! He fought discouragement. "Keep only the works matching one of the following keywords: Barthélémy De Lesseps, Russia, utopia, revolution, real estate."

He knew adding Liverion to the keywords would be useless.

The computer's report identified over thirty documents, mostly articles. Paul skimmed through them. As he suspected, not one was the essay mentioned by Wishman.

"And now?" the computer asked.

"I don't know... I may be on the wrong track, and from the very start."

"What are we looking for exactly?"

"A source referring to Liverion under an assumed name."

"Produced between 2001 and 2040?"

"Yes."

"There's no evidence the author would have reused one of the circumlocutions of De Lesseps."

*No. However, Wishman said—*

Paul did not pursue that thought and grabbed another idea flitting by. "Are there other recurring phrases in the letters besides those you've already found? Something with an actual connection to Liverion?"

"Please specify."

"I need a count. What is the most common phrase used by De Lesseps in his correspondence when he is not referring to Liverion?"

*the dark city [the darkest city]*                           *23 hits*

"Presumably a metaphor for Ancien Régime France," the computer suggested.

"For instance?"

"In the letter from January 11, 1793, that you were reading earlier, '*If we cannot gain & sustain liberty inside our borders without making war on the entire world ( . . . ) [we] are doomed to live forever in the dark city our fathers knew, devouring each other.*'"

"I see." Paul was now fully committed to the game. "Would you say that De Lesseps is opposing the dark city to Liverion? That he uses one to designate the opposite of the other?"

"Yes."

"All the time?"

"Every time the phrase is used."

"So, it could be that the essay's author did not reuse it verbatim."

"He could have reversed it. The white city? The white town?"

It was a good idea.

"Search for all essays with a title of that sort. Same typology, same time period, same keywords as earlier."

The computer found sixteen works, but none that made sense. Paul smothered his rising anxiety and checked alternative keywords. *City* was replaced by *region, country, nation, state . . .* He next tackled *white*, substituting every synonym used in the early twenty-first century to signify what was pure, clear, and luminous.

It was 01:55 when the computer offered its final verdict. There was nothing. Paul went back to the kitchen. This was a two-coffeepot problem. At least. The water was heating up when he noticed an old cigarette pack by the sink. *Standards*. Maria's favorite brand.

He took one as he thought of Wishman, placing it between his lips and pulling. The end turned on with a spark. He'd stopped smoking after prohibition, but an all-nighter was as good a time as any to give in.

It took only a few moments, though, for his head to start spinning and he was forced to sit. Elbows on the kitchen table, he watched the coffee drip into the pot. His mind was elsewhere. He hovered above a mountain covered in virginal snow. Liverion. The white city. Undiscoverable by men outside it. Invisible. Inverted. And yet, it was there.

He frowned. Inverted? How had he come up with that?

Right. The "inverted city" was one of the phrases used by De Lesseps. The white city or town. The opposite of the dark city of old. Which was perfectly normal. Unless . . .

Suddenly agitated, he grabbed a pen and wrote on the wrapping of the pack of *Standards*, carefully tracing each letter:

# LIVERION

That was the code. He only needed to read the word the wrong way, from right to left. The *boustrophedon* way, the Ancient Greeks would have said. The answer appeared, starting with the feminine form of the French word for "dark" or "black."

## NOIRE(-)VIL

He rushed back inside his office.

"Let's start again!" he told his machine. "Every piece of nonfiction between 2001 and 2040 with a title using the word 'Noirevil' with the same keywords to refine the search."

"As simple as that?" the computer replied, managing a slightly supercilious tone.

"Get going!"

It was precisely 02:25 when the software offered its verdict. "No matching document was found."

Gripped by an icy hand, Paul protested, "Impossible. There must be something."

"Nothing as such, but I do have a hit with a partial match, as the word has two additional characters: 'Noireville.'"

Funny how the system could be so rigidly precise. Paul still flinched as if shocked with a current of pure joy.

"Well," the program said, "is that it?"

The screen spelled out a title. *Noireville, the dark city*, by M. Hassberg. Yes, that was it. Barely tamping down his euphoria, Paul asked for more details about the author, and the computer summarized the available records.

"Hassberg, Markus. Born in Paris in May 1943. Died in London in January 2038. Nothing out of the ordinary until 1966. Then, a qualification in mathematics, doctorate, and leadership of a CNRS[2] research team. He was a respected specialist in the theory of dynamical systems."

---

2   The *Centre National de Recherche Scientifique*. This is a real French research organization composed of national institutes in areas such as physics, ecology, and social sciences.

"Go on."

"Starting in 1990, Hassberg shifted to the official sphere in a big way. He became one of the scientific advisors of the president of the French Republic and was named a *chargé de mission* to the European Parliament, several times, until the adoption of a federal constitution. Fought the privatization of universities. Gathered a small group of researchers from the social sciences, including one who might be considered a disciple, a certain Dirac. Created an important database on the long-term strategies of megacorps in the sciences, the arts, and general culture."

"Would have hated Darwin Alley," Paul said, aping the system's telegraphic style. "Anything else?"

"He was also a respected amateur archaeologist. He penned a number of pieces on the first Celtic settlements in the Paris region."

Paul nodded absentmindedly. He was no longer listening. His hands stuck to his cheeks, he was seeing the invisible Noireville.

*Liverion.*

Hassberg's short essay had been written in 2029, as part of a study sponsored by the European Parliament on satellite cartography. In his introduction, Hassberg set out his views of the field. "*The age of the great public space agencies is over. Today, Earth's orbit belongs to private interests. We may assume this new reality will profoundly change our representations, even though we had seen it coming for at least two decades. We will no longer view the planet's surface in the same way since our maps will no longer be scientific documents, but mere consumer items.*"

To support his reasoning, Hassberg pointed to the intriguing case of bus and subway maps transforming cities into two-dimensional schematics. "*You are moving from one point to the next, along lines of this or that color. You descend below ground here. You return above ground there. In between, there is nothing. Miss a subway stop and the city where you've lived since you were born turns into an alien landscape. The same applies to road maps, sea lanes, or mountain paths. A map needs to be, it is true, both useful and intelligible. So, what will happen to our maps when publishers realize that keeping track of a hill's contours, a seashore's indentations, and a river's twists and turns is expensive, and that such details are hard to render and hamper the map's readability?*"

*What will happen when private companies end up controlling our grasp of the world's geography?"*

Hassberg's answer was surprising. For the first time in over a century, blanks might show up on the world's maps. Such a shift might not be entirely negative. *"We must ensure that the scientific heritage left to us by yesterday's geographers is not squandered. Multiple institutions have hired technology companies such as DATEX to digitize their archives; we should fear the worst. However, we may also imagine a metageography, a place where history might resume its progress. A new Earth will slowly emerge. An Earth that is open in the same way nineteenth-century explorers imagined an open sea around the pole. Most of us will not see it, or will walk on by without even noticing its presence, but . . ."*

Twenty-five years or so later, Paul understood perfectly what Hassberg was trying to say. Another Earth, unmapped, a true European utopia. Wishman had been right.

*"This other Earth exists where the roads don't go because the maps are no longer true. I glimpsed it once. Mr. Dirac, who worked with me, even spent years surveying it. His quest turned into a compulsion. He rejected our transparent cities, their clinical coldness, and he would answer, when asked what he was looking for instead of our megalopolises, Noireville. For him, that was explanation enough.*

*The last time I saw him, he was following the Kura valley to leave Tbilisi, going east. I do not know if he found that town. I doubt it exists, actually. However, one day, I know that we will share his passion and follow in his footsteps. We will look for the city that is nowhere, unmarked on the world's maps, because that world will no longer belong to us. The Earth and the heavens may become the property of a few, but Noireville belongs to all of us."*

A half-shaped idea scampered through Paul's thoughts. A reminiscence of a time when he'd registered for a seminar in physical geography for historians at the Sorbonne. He struggled to collect his memories. There was something about algorithms . . .

He fetched Marianna's cigarettes with a shiver of transgressive pleasure.

As he smoked, he looked over the online atlas of the Tbilisi area. If Hassberg was telling the truth and his disciple had really vanished in this part of the world, it meant Liverion was located somewhere in Georgia, not far from the Russian border, in the heart of the Caucasus.

Was this deduction compatible with the real estate transactions carried out by De Lesseps while he was in St. Petersburg? By the end of the eighteenth century, Georgia had willingly become a Russian protectorate to stave off the Persian threat. In 1783, a Russian garrison was quartered in Tbilisi, an obvious prelude to outright annexation. De Lesseps must have played his cards right, moving to Constantinople as a *chargé d'affaires*, ending up far closer to the area that Paul was eyeing on the map.

Liverion. The city was there, somewhere. Nowhere. It had to be. Paul had no trouble understanding that disciple of Hassberg surrendering to temptation and hitting the road for Liverion. All his life, he'd longed for a flight of this sort. His obsession with the Donation of Constantine had been—it was clear, now—just a waiting game, delaying the inevitable.

He called the Fuller Foundation, but Maria wasn't there. He left her a message. *I'm going to Liverion.*

Of course not. "I'm going away for a few days. I miss you terribly, and the 2051 Carnival as well." That's what he wrote.

He wondered if he should call Wishman and tell him what he'd discovered; after all, he owed him. He kept quiet in the end, recalling Wishman's words: "*I don't need to brood over this story to get out of bed every morning.*"

For Wishman, Markus Hassberg's essay was a mere puzzle. For Paul, it was an unmistakable signpost. Liverion was no longer a name preserved by chance in dusty archives, a reminder of undefined Eastern European daydreams, but a real point to be found on maps through careful deduction.

And he knew what to do to locate it.

# 6

Outside the Paris-Sud terminus of the Very High Speed Train, he took a cab for the Sainte-Geneviève district. As in Rome, imposing holo-ads cluttered the overcast yet light-filled sky. A warm breeze swept through the streets. The taxi driver followed the river bank, pacing for a few minutes a drifting tourist island of the Reed Guild.

"They're taking advantage," the driver complained in English. "I give it another couple of years and Braunen Corps will pave over everything. Did you know they're planning to have Darwin Alley run over the Seine?"

The driver pointed out the huge building site sprawling along the river's north bank. Braunen, rolling in money after the success of the *Runnin' for Darwin* public subscription, had purchased about 80 percent of the residential area on the water's edge. Over a full kilometer, a swarm of robotic cranes were taking apart the historic buildings, one stone at a time. The concept for the new city neighborhood involved creating gardens at ground level and reconstituting the ancient buildings ten meters above them, on stilts. With an unsurpassed view of the Notre Dame bubble to the west and, even farther along, the one-to-one-scale facsimile of the Eiffel Tower.

Paul had to admit nothing seemed familiar anymore.

"You don't say?" The driver glanced at him in the rearview mirror and smiled. "It hasn't changed that much."

"Are you from here?"

"Chandernagor."

"India?"

"Where else?"

"So, you've been living in Paris for a while?"

"No, but that doesn't matter." The driver's smile widened. "It's all the same, right here or over there. The same Village."

The taxi went up Saint -Jacques Street and stopped at the intersection with Gay-Lussac Street, in front of the Geographical Institute. Here, at least, nothing had changed. Same old stone pile, same old façade overloaded with columns, same old monumental gateway open to all yet forbidden to visitors.

"No, *monsieur*. You must go in through that small door, by the side."

He took the elevator to the fourth floor and looked for the cartography laboratory. In a hallway, he came across a former fellow student, who identified him at once.

"Coray! Hello, how are you doing? Do you still have that Kuhn book I loaned you?"

Three years later, as if they'd last met yesterday!

Paul smiled and confessed. Thomas Kuhn's *The Structure of Scientific Revolutions* was still in a bookcase at home, but he'd forgotten its owner's name.

"Understandable. We just saw each other a couple of times in the lecture hall. I'll lend my books to anybody. An expensive habit." The man smiled in turn and stretched out his hand. "Lamine Keita."

"It's good to see you again."

"I read some of your papers online. Good work. I like your style. And I like the way you tackle problems from the ground up. Too many historians forget there's a real world out there."

Paul savored the praise. "It's true, I try. I don't remember . . . Didn't you write a geography thesis?"

"Yes. *The Geomorphological Approach in the Analysis of Natural Environments of the Humid Tropical Zone.* I had this crazy idea . . ."

"Any idea is better than none."

They tittered like superannuated students and Paul asked for the cartography lab.

"It's just upstairs. They moved it last year. I'm working there as an assistant. As long as DATEX doesn't cut us off, of course. Do you need anything specific?"

"Specific may not be the right word. But I've had an odd brainwave, and I need to check if it makes any sense."

Lamine Keita led Paul to the end of the floor and opened the door to a winding staircase. "What kind of brainwave?"

"Is it conceivable that a major morphological element, such as a valley or a mountain, might have been overlooked for centuries by travelers and cartographers? And might even go unnoticed by today's satellites?"

Keita froze, his hand on the staircase handrail.

"Do you have a particular area in mind?"

"In the Caucasus. Somewhere between Tbilisi and Baku."

"Seems unlikely. That area has been subjected to nonstop scrutiny for years because of the Caspian oil fields. Ten times more extensive than expected. Not to mention the Armenian problem. There are never fewer than two satellites overhead."

"I wasn't thinking of an unobserved location. Is there a way not to be seen from space?"

"In the case of a valley or mountain?"

"Yes."

Keita frowned. "You'd have to create some sort of topographical distortion . . . That would be interesting. Follow me."

They ended up in the lab, a large room whose walls were covered with HD screens. Keita performed a few manipulations to bring up a one-to-five-thousand ratio map of Tbilisi's surroundings. A series of numerical parameters, enclosed within a blue-green box, tagged the image.

"There are two satellites with eyes on the area," the geographer confirmed. "A Saxxon *Hawkeye* and an ELIXIR sentinel. Now, look at this."

He pressed a button. Onscreen, the image scale climbed brutally as if the camera was dropping from orbit and plunging to the ground. When the zoom steadied, Paul could have counted the individual cobblestones paving the Tbilisi streets.

"It's the same for the entire geographical area, generally speaking, for most landmasses, aside from deserts and oceans. Happy?"

The existence of Liverion was a historical and literary enigma, but Paul had always been scientifically minded. He needed to understand. "How do optical systems process the imagery?"

"Depends on the terrain. Most of the time, we don't work with the raw data. What you see here is a representation of reality. Extremely faithful, down to the centimeter level, I'd say, but still a representation. Between the ground-level reality and the picture that is delivered, there are significant alterations. By the time we get an image, it's been processed algorithmically."

"By what kind of algorithm? Do you use the same algorithm to build your images regardless of the terrain?"

"Of course not. A single calculation scheme to handle both the Sahara and the Himalayas? Come on!" Keita gave him a chiding look. "Can you imagine using a flamethrower to light a cigarette?"

Paul was definitely taking a liking to Lamine Keita's sense of humor.

"Very well, I get it. There will be one algorithm by geomorphology type. How do you come up with them?"

"We start with the physical data."

Keita cited the case of a famous method from the history of mathematics for the calculation of pi. To establish the ratio of the circumference of a circle to its diameter, Archimedes had begun with physical measurements, like his predecessors.

"Every time, he would get a value close to three, whatever the actual size of the diameter. So, the ratio was constant. However, to determine whether pi could be calculated, he needed to connect a series of operations, thus creating an algorithm. Archimedes used polygons inscribed within a circle. He doubled the number of sides of successive polygons to get closer and closer approximation of a circle."

"He would've had to do so an infinite number of times. Pi cannot be calculated. But what's the connection with the Caucasus?"

"The problem is a bit different. We're not trying to *calculate* mountains. What we're looking for is the best possible representation. So, we use a custom-made algorithm, based on the available approximate values."

"Meaning?"

"Those taken from field surveys. The amusing thing is that we're sometimes forced to rely on nineteenth-century surveying reports when there's nothing more recent. Which happens often enough. DATEX won't fund new ground surveys except in truly strategic zones."

"What about the Caucasus, then?"

Keita opened a file onscreen and uttered a surprised squawk. "Now, that's a record. 1790!"

Paul smiled as the geographer rocked his chair. "Do you realize what that means? The *live* satellite image of Tbilisi we're looking at is being processed with an algorithm based on surveys from the tail end of the eighteenth century."

"Do we know who the surveyor was?"

"It's written right here. Jean Maleterre, a cartographer and mathematician from the Paris Observatory. There's even a copy of his mission order, signed by the French consul in St. Petersburg."

Keita printed the page. Paul looked it over. Mostly words and more words. Recommendations. Clarifications. Elaborate salutations. And two numbers.

42°21' N, 45°30' E

He folded the sheet neatly before pocketing it, thanked Lamine Keita, and left.

♦ ♦ ♦

He spent the rest of the day wandering through Paris and thinking about his next steps. As evening fell, he walked back to the Sorbonne and rented a room at the *Géomètre*, on Victor Cousin Street. Reading his name on the screen before him, the receptionist raised his eyebrows.

"Mr. Coray, from Rome? A telmat message for you came in this afternoon. I'll transfer it to your room's workstation."

It was Maria. She'd called him from a public booth on *via* Andrea, making sure the call was encrypted. A small, crenellated tower icon shone at the bottom of the screen, like Wishman's.

She was anxious. Every ten seconds, she swept aside the fringe of blond hair falling back across her forehead and stole quick glances to the left and right of her, as if afraid of being watched.

"There's so much I want to tell you that I don't know how to begin! I got your message, and I hope mine will reach you. I was sure of the hotel's name: the *Géomètre*. We spent our first night together there during the Carnival. But I have no idea whether you're there right now."

She was speaking faster and faster, in a fever.

"Whatever. It doesn't matter anymore . . . Paul, the Foundation has been manipulating both of us! Three months ago, Jonahsen came to me and asked me to draw up your psychological profile. She told me the Foundation was considering you for a research mission to an exceptional site. Obviously, I was not allowed to tell you about it before they made a decision . . . All right, I'm an idiot. I accept it. Your work on Stephen II and Constantine was leading nowhere. We were starting to fight, we didn't go out anymore, you didn't want to see anybody, and you were growing bitter! Remember how we swore, back in Paris, never to be bitter? I told myself we needed this. Leave Rome, start something new somewhere else . . . I delivered the profile and Jonahsen used it to shape your perceptions. She knew about your escape behavior, your avoidant tendencies . . . She relied on that and got you to come across a document about this place I know nothing about. You needed to think you'd discovered it yourself! She emphasized that, said that it was a psychoactive key. I didn't show it, but I was impressed she knew the term. Not that many people are familiar with the concept . . . Jonahsen was positive you'd throw yourself at any bone if the pressure became too much for you. That's why I kept nagging you about the Board, those nights at our place. Not that I had to force myself. I'm really worried about where it's going! But it worked, you took the bait."

Right then, she dropped something (her bag?) on the floor of the booth, and she bent down to pick it up. Her face left the screen for a couple of seconds. When her head popped up again, her hair was mussed, and she smoothed it absentmindedly as she resumed, her voice steadier.

"After our dispute, Jonahsen sent you one of her men. I'm not sure of the name, it could be Fishman. I was mad, I didn't think she'd go that far. So, I went back to the Foundation, and I did some eavesdropping . . . Paul, they never meant to entrust you with a research mission. *They've been using you as their hound dog.* They want to reach this site you're obsessed with, but they can't pin it down! I fail to understand how that's even possible nowadays, but it's the truth. They're getting you to look for it because they're unable to find it themselves."

Paul was listening, perched on the edge of the bed, elbows on his knees and hands cupping his chin. He remained without moving so long that he felt encased in a block of ice. Onscreen, Maria glanced up.

"You have to know they're following you. With satellites. They're hoping you'll lead them to this place. That you'll find it for them. They don't understand how you think, so they need to watch you every step of the way. I don't know what you can do to shake them, if it's even possible. I'd like to help, but all I have are dribs and drabs, bits of a larger story. And I'm guessing that I, too, may not know how you really think." She flashed a hurt smile. "I hope you'll get where you're going. Really. I sincerely wish for you to find the unfindable place. That would be right up your alley . . . If it ends well, let me know and I'll join you in Rome. Gotta go now. I love you, I'm with you."

The screen went dark.

"Do you wish to watch the message again or download a transcript?" the terminal asked.

Paul fell back onto the bed, holding his head. Scrolling crazy fast through ideas and images as he shook with bursts of raw emotion. He felt like a battlefield in a proxy war, as if two enemy forces, remote and mysterious, were clashing over him, vying for his loyalty or submission. Barthélémy De Lesseps against Virtù Jonahsen. Liverion against the Board. He couldn't side with one without defying or betraying the other. And how could he tell whether the succession of nested manipulations was over? How could he be sure Maria was sincere? She might have been threatened into recording that message. Then again, it might the final phase of a plan—the ultimate *psychoactive key* fashioned by Jonahsen.

Not that it changed the fact that he had a choice to make.

"Do you wish to watch the message again or download a transcript?" the terminal repeated politely.

# 7

The next morning, he paid for a cab ride to Roissy II, where he bought a Saxxon flight to Tbilisi, with stops in Belgrade and Odessa.

The Georgian capital was a small town compared to the conurbations of China, India, or the United States. Yet, it was still part of the Village. The first thing he saw inside the city walls was a team from Braunen Corp, wrapping the old Metekhi Church in clear plastic. Ever since the 2034 earthquake, it had been on the brink of collapse. Paul watched the worksite. An informative holo claimed that, within a year and a half, St. David and the Armenian temple of Vank would also be fully restored as part of the new tourist zone.

The Village was evolving and changing. As it became aware of its own existence, it neutered the past by encasing it in plastic or hypercarbon to subject to its own rules.

Paul wandered through the older neighborhoods north of town, taking his time. Come noon, he picked a Vietnamese restaurant— more of a cart parked under an arcade—and lunched with an Austrian industrial entrepreneur and a Turkish newswoman. Both wanted his take on the future routing of Darwin Alley. The newswoman thought the idea of a circumterrestrial street was extraordinary. The entrepreneur thought it was mad.

Across from Paul's narrow banquette, a screen set to the channel of the United Nations Senate was showing a debate over the prospects of political independence within the cislunar perimeter. Several orbiting habitats had already signed up to a preliminary chart. The broadcast cut away at times to feature reports on the settlement of the Lagrangian points.

Yet, Paul's attention was on the screen itself: a technological gadget produced by DATEX and plastered over a thousand-year-old stone wall to sate the curiosity of tourists.

Why not, as a matter of fact? It was no great evil, this slow replacement of an old world by a new, anesthetized one. Byzantine engineering and pillars, walls of unfired clay bricks, the curved eaves of pagodas, mirrored glass façades. Given time, all of these specific forms would vanish, subsumed by the one thing uniting them: the pictures of the Village in the screen.

He found a shopping center where he bought an optical relay linked to the *Hawkeye* satellite network. The sales clerk checked the tuning and the image quality, but Paul insisted on a final verification. He went outside, lowered the relay's eyepiece over his left eye, and saw himself through the satellite's optics, with one-centimeter resolution: a brown-haired man standing in the middle of a pedestrian street. Around him, tourists were coming and going, without paying any attention to him. It was rather intoxicating.

With his left eye, he saw them from above, like a spirit floating above the crowd.

With his right, he saw them face-to-face.

He went back inside the shopping center and added to his gear. Good hiking shoes, warm clothes, a backpack, a stock of freeze-dried protein, a ten-liter water container, and an emergency kit. Plus some one-to-five-thousand ratio paper maps and a compass, obviously. He rented a car from the nearest Hertz agency.

Leaving Tbilisi by night, using the eastern road, seemed like the wisest course. The car took forever to accelerate, even for an electric Ford, but he intended to ditch it as soon as possible, so he kept going for two hours. Darkness gathered. To his left, below the road, the Kura's dark waters flowed towards Baku and the Caspian Sea.

From time to time, he watched the road behind, but other cars were rare and mostly driving the other way. Nobody was following him. In any case, Marianna had said the Foundation would use a satellite.

That was the only important question, really; why were Jonahsen and the Foundation unable to locate Liverion? Rather, to his surprise, Paul found that he was willing to accept a mystical explanation: *because they want to find it for the wrong reasons. Because it's a blank on their maps and there is no room for such a thing in a Darwin Alley world.* However, his mind's rational armature demanded a logical explanation.

The Maleterre algorithm was one. If all of the available maps and images of the Tbilisi area were based on his 1790 mapmaking, then Liverion did not exist. The *Hawkeye* sats could not see it. It would even go unseen by random overflights as long as pilots and observers interfaced with a screen—as they surely did. Even hikers used maps and would be compelled to detour around the mathematical distortion created by Maleterre to protect the city.

◆ ◆ ◆

A hundred and thirty kilometers away from Tbilisi, he stopped the Ford on the shoulder to stretch his legs. Beyond the bluish lighting of the road, there was nothing but darkness and silence. He inhaled deeply. The air was damp and cold, but it was not the cause of his shivering. He'd reached the point of no return, and he was afraid. He gathered his things, fastened his backpack. He climbed over the crash barrier, almost stumbling, and plunged into the night.

He walked blindly for a hundred steps. The bank sloped down from the shoulder to the course of the Kura River. He reached the water's edge by tripping over the large rocks strewn over the ground. He was struck by the force of the nearby stream's burbling and squatted to catch his breath. This was a new experience, venturing into the wild. A long time passed before he got underway again. The bag weighed him down and his calves burned already. He stuck it out until he found what he was looking for: a bridge. An aluminum footbridge, to be more precise, connecting the river's banks. There were no railings, but it allowed him to head north and finally get away from the road.

Relieved, he crossed the river. On the other side, he turned back to contemplate one last time the lights of the Village. The thin blue line tracing the crash barrier followed the dips and rises of the road before fading in the distance.

He lowered the eyepiece of the *Hawkeye* system over his left eye, half-filling his visual field with a greenish world. Pressing with his forefinger, he increased the picture's scale and tried to locate himself inside an area spanning thirty square kilometers. The Kura snaked among high grassy hills, its base wreathed with black fir and rocks. To the north, these hills rose steadily until they joined with the foothills of the Caucasus Mountains.

He decided to walk as long as he could, his eyes on the horizon's darkened outline. He managed two hours of progress, covering a distance of four kilometers, before collapsing to the ground. His remaining strength allowed him to spread out the insulating blanket on the frost-stiffened grass. He went to sleep instantly.

◆  ◆  ◆

When dawn came, a stubborn fog was hiding the sun and all his gear was wet. Munching on a protein bar from his stock was still new and awkward. He drank straight from the water pack, too tired to empty the whole bag just to get the cup he'd left at the bottom. He stowed the rest as best he could, then headed north again.

The land rose steadily. Far ahead, a dark and ragged mass weighed on the horizon. The Caucasus. After an hour's walk, he checked his map and took sightings on the most recognizable peaks. The overlay of his visual field provided him with his geographical position in a box:

LATITUDE: 41°89' NORTH.
LONGITUDE: 45°49' EAST.

Another forty kilometers to go, northwards, as the crow flies.

He was starting to enjoy the journey, and not only because he was going to Liverion. The simple act of walking without speaking was a relief. He felt unburdened beyond belief.

Zooming in playfully with *Hawkeye*, he saw himself sitting on his bag, the map unfolded at his feet. The satellite image was so precise he could almost read his handwritten annotations along the edge of the sheet.

He ate and drank, without having to force himself to do so. He retrieved his cup from the bottom of his bag and carefully put it back before heading out. He was in no hurry. When he was hungry or thirsty, he attended to his needs. If he grew tired, he rested. He compared his observations with the map and checked his route. When night fell, he listened to the noises in the hills. More than once, he heard animal sounds. Human voices, a couple of times, though happily far-off.

He crossed a pine forest so dark it might have been carved out of solid coal. The forest floor crunched with deadwood. He gathered enough to light a fire in front of a rock shelter. When he stretched out on his sleeping mat, the day was tipping into dusk. As he yawned, he noted that his circadian rhythm was shifting. He was going to sleep earlier each day.

◆ ◆ ◆

Human voices awakened him in the early hours of the morning. Very close, this time. Checking that his fire was out, he crawled among the rocks to the edge of the forest. Three men bundled in military parkas were coming down the hill. Paul lay flatter on the ground. The men spoke a tongue he did not know, and they carried guns.

His heart beating faster, he watched them go by, then move away. Soon, their voices dwindled into a distant rumble, merging with the wind. He realized that he'd briefly slipped into outright fantasy. No, these men did not speak the tongue of Liverion! They were Georgians, nothing more. However, he'd caught one word, used more than once. A term Paul had no trouble understanding.

*B-men*.

Returning to his campsite, he began to pack. Jonahsen's agents were now hunting him. Which might not be bad news as such. If Maria's message to the *Géomètre* was right, he had nothing to fear as he was doing exactly what was expected of him. Discovering the location of Liverion.

To betray it to the Fuller Foundation and the Powers.

He nearly stopped to think it over once more, but he reminded himself he'd already done so and made his choice. There was no rational answer to his conundrum. He would keep moving forward and have faith in De Lesseps and Maleterre. After all, they'd managed to preserve the secrecy of their city for over two centuries.

The thought soothed his panic. He ate, drank, scattered the ashes of his fire, and left the woods.

◆ ◆ ◆

The next three days, he walked in solitude. The sky lowered. It was no longer quite so cold, but rain threatened. The first drops fell as he was tackling the foothills of the Caucasus. Ahead, large, curved rocks thrust out of the plateau like the curling claws of a forgotten giant, turned into rock millennia earlier.

He ran to the closest one to get out of the rain.

His gait was improving day by day, he noticed when he watched himself with the eyepiece of the optical relay. His stride covered more ground, more smoothly. The bag no longer bounced up and down like a toy on springs. He'd lost weight, and it suited him. Looking up, he smiled at the spycam. Within the greenish world he watched with his left eye, his face was pale and sported a growing beard.

He let the storm pass, snacked, and slept a full hour before resuming his trek. He had yet to come across a real road in the area, though small cairns raised every so often signaled an ancient human presence. Of what sort? There was no way of knowing. Night was falling already. He moved inside a cave whose fireplace still held enough charcoal to set fire to. Later, the wind rose and the rain resumed. Curled up near the last embers, he slept and dreamt of Rome.

◆ ◆ ◆

The next two days should have exhausted him. They only served to harden his resolve. He climbed through fields of scree tumbling down eroded slopes. Twice, a misstep set the ground into motion and he slipped down a hundred meters on a rocky avalanche. He swore and started climbing again. On the morning of the third day, he reached a plateau crowned with a massive oak tree. Yielding to temptation, he clambered to the very top and surveyed his surroundings. Snow-laden peaks clawed at the sky all around. He smiled at the satellite, like every other day, and zoomed out. The oak's silvery foliage, filling the visual field, shrank and vanished, as if swallowed by the ground, while his left eye saw the mountains cluster together. Broad lines appeared, dotted with white, merging with other lines until they sketched the craggy wall of the Caucasus Mountains. Two blue curves encroached upon the edges of the image. The Black Sea to the west and the Caspian Sea to the east. The whole world was spreading itself out for him, and he could even discern the line of the terminator receding westward.

He walked north once more. The far rim of the plateau turned into a natural staircase, leading down into a mist-filled valley. He located the visible mountain massifs and circled them in red on the map. Halfway down, the staircase split into a series of small canyons. Paul picked one and followed it all the way down. There, he ate before spreading out his insulating mat to rest a while.

Paul was starting to doze off when a strange rolling sound broke the silence. He got up, ready to pick up his pack and head back inside the maze.

A rider appeared from behind a massive granite boulder, glass-smooth. The noise was produced by his mount's hooves, multiplied and distorted by the echo. The man pulled up as soon as he saw Paul, observing him a long moment, his curiosity clear. At last, he spoke.

"May I trouble you for a sip of water? I am parched."

His voice was soft, and his old-fashioned English tinged with a touch of a French accent. Paul shivered. He hadn't spoken to anyone in ten days. He filled his cup and passed it to the rider, who thanked him with a nod before drinking.

"My name is Paul Coray."

"Martin Dirac."

There was a long silence. Paul held his breath, afraid a word would break the spell. He glanced at the eyepiece.

LATITUDE: 42°21' NORTH.
LONGITUDE: 45°30' EAST.

He'd made it.

Dirac stopped drinking with a contented sigh. He was elderly, at least eighty-years-old. Yet, he sat erect on his saddle and his thick-set frame exuded an unmistakable impression of strength. He wore age-old clothing: a leather jacket, a thick shirt of an indeterminate color, cotton pants, and boots. His hands were gloved and curls of snow-white hair sneaked out from under a bizarre felt cap. He was close-shaven.

"Is that water from the Korach Spring?"

"I wouldn't know."

"It's a natural spring about two hours heading that way," Dirac said, pointing south. "Below a rock shaped like an elephant's head. The water has a taste all its own."

Paul nodded. The description matched the location of his last refill.

"Are you going there?"

"Actually, no. I'm just taking this old lady out for a stroll to keep her happy." Dirac patted the mare's neck and his mount snorted, shaking its head. "Still, she tires easily, and we've gone out too far. We were heading home."

Paul's brain felt paralyzed. He could not think straight.

"Would you mind if . . . I came along, for a bit?"

"That is very kind of you, but I do not need anything more. Thanks for the water. I was truly thirsty."

Dirac threw back the cup to Paul, who caught it without thinking. The suddenness of the motion was surprisingly prankish.

*Say something.*

"I'm glad I was able to help you."

The rider used his legs to turn the mare around. Paul was petrified as he watched him move away, skirt a large rocky outcrop shaped like a raised fist, and vanish inside the maze. The cup was still in his hand. He dropped it and ran to the outcrop. Dirac entered another gorge, the slap of his mare's ironshod hooves on the bare rock echoing between the canyon walls.

Paul glanced at the satellite image. His silhouette, seen from above, was still visible. Around him, the tangled canyons crisscrossing a couple of acres resembled the close-up of a brain. Yet, Dirac was nowhere to be seen.

Paul picked up the mare's trail on the gravel bed of a canyon bottom, and he could still hear the ring of its horseshoes. He followed cautiously, keeping an eye on the image that showed his double's progression inside the brain's grooves. Both of them crossed a kind of natural bridge, beyond which the trail swerved to his left.

His double disappeared.

Paul stopped, as if he'd heard the *click* of an armed mine beneath his foot. He remained motionless a second or two, then took a very slow step back.

His double appeared again in the center of the satellite image.

The border defined by Maleterre's algorithm ran through here. Precisely here.

He crossed it again and pocketed the now useless optical relay.

He was *below the map.*

Inside him, some nameless thing trembled in awe. Did the idea frighten him or fill him with joy? Both, probably. He'd been living for ten days with a satellite image as his traveling companion, but his dependence on a world of maps was far older, and not only because of his work. Like everybody else, he was coming and going within a space that he assumed to be entirely known and internalized. Not once had he really wondered *where he was.* There was always a screen, a sign, a name to tell him, before he even needed to think about it.

That sense of security no longer applied here. Universal surveillance ceased. He was nowhere.

He looked around him and the landscape seemed slightly different. That was absurd, of course. Geologically, there could be no break. The change only existed in his head.

He followed the track of the mare, but within a hundred meters, large rocky slabs replaced the gravel, and the tracks were no longer visible. He still heard the echo of the mare's shod hooves, but it grew weaker, muffled by distance. He was losing Dirac.

Somehow, it felt like the universe was unfolding as it should. He clambered to the top of a granite mass and gazed upon the landscape.

The maze of crisscrossing canyons extended as far as the eye could see.

He considered crossing the area in a straight line, guided by his compass. When his double popped up again on the satellite image—in the very same spot where he'd disappeared, as the world created by De Lesseps was a space compressed inside a dot—he would know one of the dimensions of Liverion. If he repeated his traverse several times while shifting his starting point, he would end up with a rough map and might be able to locate its center. How large a surface area was it possible to pack inside a geometrical point without generating insuperable topographic discrepancies? Lamine Keita might have been able to answer that question by considering the effects of the distortion created by Maleterre. A few dozen square kilometers, Paul guessed. Up to a hundred, maybe. He had nothing to back his hunch, but it helped him to think.

Paris covered a hundred square kilometers. He could extend his knowledge of the French capital to the landscape around him, suppose that the granite rock he was balancing matched the location of Vincennes and that he would have to walk in a straight line all the way to Boulogne.

A leaper with markings of the Georgian military arrowed through the sky, far above him. He looked up and watched it as long as it took to see it vanish over the horizon.

The Fuller Foundation knew where he was, *but it could not see him.* How was it keeping track of his every action?

Paul dug out the optical relay once more and looked into the eyepiece: a greenish world materialized. It was unchanged. He was still absent, hiding inside the anomaly at 42°21' NORTH., 45°30' EAST.; however, he was not looking for his own image. He zoomed in to explore the surrounding area and finally spotted three groups of B-men, on the edge of the algorithm.

They were hardly more than a handful. Over a dozen men, Paul wondered, until he remembered the Georgian soldiers he'd glimpsed. Thinking of the Russian border nearby, he understood that any larger force of B-men was out of the question. The area was a sensitive one for both countries. Incursions would not be tolerated. Nor would overflights with camera-equipped drones or anything of that sort. The Fuller Foundation was blind, and powerless to even grope at random in the borderlands. The B-men surely hated a mission that forced them to take off their LCD glasses—cutting themselves off from the uninterrupted flow of data and information they soaked in.

They were using binoculars to watch him, like kids. Recording his every move in a *paper* notebook, perhaps.

That was when he decided to return to Rome. He'd made his choice a long time ago, in fact; Marianna's message left at the *Géomètre* had produced results, but he'd only realized it then. He surveyed one last time the canyons carving the land, thinking of De Lesseps and Maleterre. Two and a half centuries earlier, they had done so as well, maybe from the very same location. The city was there ... he might as well imagine it.

There would be a lake, necessarily, and a river. Both would be relatively shallow. If any boats sailed them, they would be barges, tying up at a dock, in a small port maybe. A city consumed large quantities of goods and supplies. Pastures for cattle and cultivated fields would be required, with the help perhaps of amazing steam-powered machines. It seemed likely the town's citizens might be troglodytes: the most rational solution to life in a landscape of deep canyons. He granted them hanging booths and covered terraces, linked by passageways and intertwined staircases.

He imagined pods shuttling to every level of this vertical world. If he concentrated fully on this vision, immersing himself, he could even glimpse figures strolling down the passageways, hailing each other between one cliff and the next. Lower down, all the way down, he had no trouble recognizing Martin Dirac when he showed up on his mare, with that weird felt cap and a story on his lips about his outing to the Korach Spring.

He could imagine anything he wanted. He was nowhere.

◆ ◆ ◆

He headed back an hour later and reached his campsite. When his double emerged from the point at 42°21' NORTH. and 45°30' EAST., occupying once more the center of the satellite image, he shivered slightly. Right afterward, though, he felt strangely satisfied, as if each of his selves had missed the other.

What mattered was knowing there was on Earth a place where his image did not exist.

He rolled up his insulation pad, recovered his cup, and took his time before he left to pack everything in his bag as neat as can be.

He walked for another ten days, stopping for the night in places he'd bypassed previously. Twice, he met small groups of B-men, all of whom wore LCD glasses and paid not the slightest attention to him when he walked by, as if he weren't there.

As a matter of fact, perhaps he wasn't.

## 8

So ended his story. While he waited in his *via* Andrea apartment, he'd thought long and hard about sharing it with Virtù Jonahsen. Not that he feared putting her on the path. Quite the reverse; now that he knew the truth, he was sure she would grasp none of it. For her and for anybody committed to the Board's overarching agenda, it was a leap too far.

Learning how to exit the map.

He chose to say nothing, and the B-men brought him back to his place.

He took a scalding-hot shower before letting himself slip into sleep. The next morning, as he sat in front of his computer for the first time in a long while, he felt a new energy grow inside him. During his long walk back, he'd started thinking again about the Donation of Constantine. The problem had been a game to keep his mind busy, but now that he was home, his involuntary mulling was paying off and a daring hypothesis was emerging, apt to shed unexpected light on the whole affair.

He knew he could not resume his original work without hastening the rise of the Board. Yet, the idea suddenly felt like an abstract conceit. As if something essential was now safe.

Months passed. Over the summer, he wrote an account of his trip to Liverion and he published it online. *Far from the Village: A Season in the Dark City.* The title was surely overlong, but its main selling point was that it echoed Hassberg's essay. What Paul had done, anybody would be able to do again.

He wrote Wishman a scornful letter.

He mailed the Kuhn book back to Lamine Keita.

Finally, he left a message waiting for Marianna at the Hôtel du Géomètre. "*I've been to Liverion.*"

Yes, he had written those words.

Nowhere at all, in Liverion.

# EXPANSION

Serge Lehman: "Nowhere in Liverion"

French title: "Nulle part à Liverion"

First published in the collection *Genèses*, with texts chosen by
Ayerdhal, by J'ai lu, collection Science-Fiction, in 1996. Then, it
appears in several anthologies in the years 2000.

*Translated by* Jean-Louis Trudeau

Serge Lehman is a major and versatile author of French science fiction
who has published novels and short stories mostly in the 1990s, and,
more recently, turned to comics for which he writes scenarios. You
can read his comic series, *The Chimera Brigade*, created with Fabrice
Colin in English translation. It is a creative mix of fiction and history
with superheroes and villains that starts in WWI. Lehman has also
edited several anthologies and written essays.

"Nowhere in Liverion" (1996) appeared in several anthologies, yet
most notably in Lehman's short story collection *Le Livre des ombres*
(*The Book of Shadows*, 2005). It encompasses several themes, tropes,
and types of characters found in his other works: a detective-type
story, a lone male hero, a dystopic future dominated by *l'Instance*
(an upcoming or established—depending on the stories—oligarchy
dominated by corporations that replaced nation-states with a uni-
form territory, the *Village*). Also, major cities are connected through
*Darwin Alley*, a concept picked up by another author, Jean-Marc
Ligny in his post-apocalyptic novel *Exodes* (2012). In Lehman's great
trilogy *F.A.U.S.T* (that won the Prix Rosny-Aîné and the Grand Prix
de l'Imaginaire in 1998), readers could already feel the imagined
impact of this new order based on virtual entertainment, accessible
only to the privileged, leaving many in a no-man's-land. However,
in "Nowhere in Liverion," the anarchic and marginal no-man's-land
turns into a positive and hopeful alternative, returning the concept
of utopia to its original optimistic flair when most science fiction, for
a while now, has been delivering decaying cities and dystopic regimes.
The tension between these two sides of a potential future for our
society is what distinguishes this short story from many other texts.

Lehman's fluid text creates in a few pages an estranging world, yet easy to visualize in our contemporary, media-saturated society, and keeps us hanging until the end, back to a future-past that proves quite powerful.

## DISCUSSION QUESTIONS

What drives Paul in this story?

How is this science fiction short story also a detective story?

How does Lehman conjure up past ideas to form his futuristic ideas? What do you think of this connection to the past? Can you see the past in the future?

Can you think of other authors who write science fiction set in the past—a realistic or imaginary one?

In the story, people manipulate virtual information to create a new reality—is that for better or for worse?

Utopia, even if it has cities, is often understood as closer to nature, closer to traditional values. Can utopia, or the idea of peaceful harmony between humans and nature, ever be compatible with our contemporary way of life? Why doesn't Paul opt to go live in Liverion?

# Inside, Outside

*by* Sylvie Denis

*translated by* Aishwarya Marathe with Annabelle Dolidon

"WE, FREE AND UNIQUE MEN, *declare that man can live freely and responsibly in a self-organized community, without hierarchy or State.*
*We believe that the purpose of all socioeconomic organization is to serve people, not to serve itself or those who have created it. We believe that the community must not alienate the individual, that the individual must not endanger the community. We say that the community must serve the individual must serve the community must serve the individual.*

*We, Free and Unique Men, commit ourselves to never using the discoveries of genetics and biotechnologies to create a supposedly unique, definitive, and perfect model of human being.*

*We, Free and Unique Men, commit ourselves to never conflating description and prescription, observation and injunction.*
*We commit ourselves to never using the discoveries of history, psychology, psychiatry, neurology, sociology, sociobiology, anthropology, ethnography, and other human sciences to reduce and imprison humans within any definitive model of humanity, or to alienate any branch of humankind in a role or status they would not have chosen.*

*We, Free and Unique Men, refuse to create and use machines that imprison humans in the machine-verse of transcorporations we condemn. We commit ourselves to never creating other machines or intelligences than those that serve humankind and one's liberty to invent themself.*

*We, Free and Unique Men, refuse to hurt and use animals, save for the cases in which our immediate physical survival is concerned.*

*All of humankind is born in a socio-historico-economico-cultural context. We, Free and Unique Men, believe that there is nothing more difficult than finding a middle ground, a place where humans can live in complete accordance with themselves and their identities. Nevertheless, we commit ourselves to ensure that all human cultures on the planet are cherished and preserved, so long as they do not carry within themselves the germs of destruction and intolerance that have harmed us so much in the past.*
*That which differentiates us does not separate, but rather, enriches us.*
*That which unites us, unites us; it does not elevate us above those who have chosen other ways of existence.*

*We, Free and Unique Men, declare that no other humanity exists apart from the one we create day after day, no other destiny than the one we forge day after day. No other future than the one we build."*

*(Excerpts from the Declaration of Rights of Free and Unique Men)*

No need to explain it to me: I *know* that the outside world is dangerous.

Otherwise, why live in the shelter of our Enclave, behind walls laden with barbed electric wire and heat detectors? Why code and card readers at the gates? Why guards armed with missile launchers? Why, huh, if not to protect us?

Because outside, it's hell.

I know this because at school I am always the first to finish my exercises. I could call for Aunt Simona, ask her to give me something else to do, but I prefer to exit the program and go explore. I visit. I managed to get a small Ferret, not very high-performance but enough for me to get into an Agora, a museum, a few Discussion Forums. It's a blessing that our world extends into virtuality. With a bit of common sense, we can force the Control System of our Enclave to connect to the global network. Of course, I don't get to choose; there's no time. But I am learning all the same. I am learning that there is always something to learn. That's something.

For example, I know that in Paris and Brazzaville, in Madrid and Tokyo, executive partners at transcorporations send their companies the genetic card and educational program they have chosen for their kids, to increase their chances of being on the waiting list for position vacancies.

I know that Russian pimps go to Asia to look for little girls who they fit with monitoring implants and imprison in brothels from which they don't come out until their death.

I know there are nearly no cows left.

In short, I know that here, it is better than outside: no hordes of jobless people ready to skin you alive to nab your identity chip, no cyborg cops whose neurotransmitters sweep along more synthetic products than natural molecules, no kids left to themselves while their parents get laid on global virtuBangs. Here, the air is breathable. We have grass and cows—just a few, that we try to breed, in the hopes of reselling their genetic material to the government. We even have trees, and everyone who lives in the New City, the Jerusalem of the White Knights of Europe, is convinced that it's paradise. The proof? It's that they never leave, except to go spread the Good Word once every two or three months. But it's reserved for those older than eighteen. The others remain inside, sentenced to paradise, so to speak. Some of them impatiently await the day they can bring the word of God and John Paul Sambara to the faithless. I'm waiting too: for the day I'll be able to get away from here.

◆ ◆ ◆

Life is monotonous in the celestial city. Sadly, I'm apparently the only one who notices.

In the morning, the alarm clock rings and projects the hologram of a trumpet-playing angel on the ceiling. I get up. My *mother* is already in the kitchen. She has already made breakfast for my *father* and me. I just say good morning—I don't like it, kissing them is an effort, every day, regardless of their attitude, regardless of my mood— sit down at the table and eat. In general, it's good. She can cook, that's for sure. Toast, pancakes, porridge, fruit salad, homemade yogurt, muesli—anything you want, when you want it.

Little Brother is already up and dressed. In general, she has him eat before us. He's on his feet in the AutoPark. Head thrown back, he sways and stares at the ceiling. When he's had enough, he lets himself fall and the AutoPark catches him. This AutoPark is a brilliant thing. A park, like the name indicates, but in the shape of a geodesic dome equipped with padded and jointed arms, on the sides and up high, to catch Little Brother no matter what.

The AutoPark isn't very smart. It nevertheless knows how to perform a certain number of useful tasks: feeding, dressing, undressing, changing, offering and shaking toys, and putting on music.

I almost forgot to mention. Little Brother is ten-years-old and has never spoken.

After breakfast, I wash up (sometimes I pretend to), I get dressed, and I leave for school.

My mother and father stand at the doorstep: her with her blonde, well-brushed hair framing a perfect oval face, him in a suit and white shirt, his hair still damp from his morning shower. Happiness shines in their eyes and trickles from their smiles. They're so chock-full of it that it always seems ready to overflow. They wave and smile. Like in a movie.

On the way to school, I always run into the same people. There's the neighbors' daughter Francie, and Pierre and Fabrice, the twins from across the street. They're idiots. The girl, Francie, stops three or four times on the way to brush her brown curls and check her makeup. The second I arrive, the boys cut off their conversation. They make signals to one another they believe to be discreet, as if they shared a big secret, then resume their account of the latest episode in the series produced by the society of John Paul.

I think they're totally incapable of hiding anything from anyone at all, and I stopped listening to them ages ago. In winter, I take every opportunity to think about the manipulations I'll have to perform to find a decent place in the network. In the spring and summer, I observe the piece of land that prospers within our walls. Between the groups of houses, we have grass, trees, horses, and cows. I don't like horses, those stupid animals that let themselves be climbed on, but cows seem pretty nice to me. They make milk: I love milk. We didn't have it in the city, just some kind of semi-transparent liquid supposedly full of everything that is necessary for growth, vitality, and development.

Seeing my size, you'd doubt it!

So, every morning I look at the real cows, the big white livestock with flat snouts that you just want to kiss.

I don't know what the twins and Francie think about cows.

They believe in God and his prophet John Paul Sambara. They never talk about anything but the books of John Paul and the great Knights who are building the Celestial City. And it's impossible to communicate with them, other than through stereotypical sentences. There are some on respecting life, against abortion, against the mixed-race hordes, against working women, and sex outside the bonds of marriage. Nothing on loving cows, who we saved from extinction only to resell them to the dairy product branch of some or other transcorp.

I think that the twins and Francie are the worthy children of their parents. They don't care about cows, and they believe in God and in Sambara.

Me, I don't believe in them.

I'm no one's worthy child.

I read somewhere, I don't know where anymore, that it's a childish thing. A fantasy or something. Possible. For others, not for me.

My *parents* aren't my parents. My *mother* didn't carry me in her belly, my *father* did not ejaculate the sperm that presided over the mix of genes that made me who I am.

So, you're saying to yourself, I'm an adopted child.

And it's right. It's about right.

Except that they were conned.

My mother—my real mother—lied to them. I know it: she told me everything, before they came. Then, while they were talking, I was supposed to play in my room. In reality, I was hiding behind the door and listening to them.

My mother's name was Alisson. She was seventeen years old when she met them for the first time, at the shelter they ran. She told them she was fifteen. She already had a daughter: me. I was five and a half, but I was small, rather puny. She told them I was three. Okay, it's not good to lie, but you know how it is: if you tell the well-dressed gentleman and lady that the poor little pregnant girl is fifteen years old, and that it's happened to her before, at an even more tender age, it moves them, it stirs their imagination in the most incredible way. All of a sudden, the gentleman and lady in suits see the future: the difficult pregnancy, alone, in dreadful sanitary conditions. Next, finding work. My mother knew how to read and write and use a console, but to get up every morning at the same time to go help a transcorp rake in billions, that is another matter. The gentleman and lady see all this, their hearts bleed, they feel a great rush of compassion, and they bent over backwards to help her.

They worked—still work—for *Save All Lives*, a neat little organization that looks after girls like my mother.

*Save All Lives* is a model association whose aim is to ensure that the babies of girls who don't want them are born anyway and are adopted by resident couples of the Jerusalem of the White Knights.

They have the status of a nonprofit organization and what remains of the State pays them subsidies.

They didn't adopt me right off the bat. First, they placed my mother in what they called a therapeutic apartment. She took courses. We had a console, a headset, and gloves, and programs for the gym. I believe she also did stuff in swimming pools, with bubbles and all.

So, there you have it: I was six years old and when they came, I pretended to be three and a half. It was easy. Like I said already, I'm small, with a slender figure, a face with fine features. With the right clothes, you couldn't notice a thing.

I liked this time, when we were in the apartment, while we waited for Little Brother. Of course, sometimes my mother cried because of Dimithri, the guy who had made the baby and left, like the one who had conceived me (I don't know his name), but for the most part we weren't unhappy. We had comfort, the block of buildings didn't have too bad a reputation, my mother would meet girls and guys she had known in the past, and that cheered her up. I was young, but I was aware. But most importantly, I remember . . .

Where things began to go wrong was after the delivery, when they started telling her that she had to get ready to part with me and the baby.

She didn't want to anymore. She no longer wanted us to go live in the paradise of the cows, she didn't want her kids to know Eternal Salvation and the glory behind the walls of the Jerusalem of the White Knights. My mother believed in the real world, the one that wasn't behind the walls.

So, it didn't go well, but I'm not supposed to remember it. It was ten years ago, and I was so little: at three and a half, you don't see anything, you don't hear anything, you don't pay attention to anything. But I was six.

My adoptive parents came at dawn to try to convince her. For hours. She still didn't want to. They left again. Came back again the next day. This went on for days. She held steady. She wanted to keep us. Me, the first, she had wanted me, for a guy who was as handsome as a god but who, no luck, made his dough as a gangster. The second, it was an accident; she would have aborted it for sure if she hadn't met my parents and their group. If they hadn't given her free meals, if she hadn't preferred their homeless shelter to the street . . . she would have found a way, and boom, he'd be gone, the kid. He would never have been here.

But now we were here, both of us, and she didn't want us to stay in the hands of Sambara and the buddies of God.

She would say it at the kitchen table, in front of the coffee no one was drinking.

"But you can't raise them!" my *mother* would retort. "You don't have a job, you hardly know how to read and write, and you don't have a sound knowledge of any iconic language. Not to mention that with your background, no one will want to give you work! Whereas if you enter one of our centers, you'll get professional training there, a future. You'll learn in better conditions if you know your children are in good hands . . ."

She didn't know what to do. I saw it on her face, in her hands which she was wringing, in the glances she was casting everywhere in the room so as not to meet my gaze. I vaguely sensed that she didn't want to abandon us, that she didn't want to go into their center either. That she was stuck, done for, obliged to hand us over to people who had helped her but whom she didn't like.

"Couldn't I go into your Enclave to follow your program? That way I could see my kids."

"No. It doesn't work that way. And you know it, you signed the contract."

He showed her the sheaf, on the polished, self-cleaning table-cloth—even though, two minutes earlier, his wife had told her that she didn't know how to read. They were rather on edge.

"No point in discussing it," my future *mother* finally said. "The kids are ours. *She* is going to the center, that's it."

What happened next is more blurred in my memory. I believe there was a scene. Screaming. I found myself in a corridor with my mother. We were alone. She clutched me in her arms, and she said to me, in my ear, in a voice filled with sobs which caused me pain:

"It's not my fault, I thought it was the best solution. You can trust them on one thing, only one: they'll take good care of you. But don't believe them when they tell you about the world, or about God. On all of that, they're liars, you hear me? Liars."

I've forgotten what happened next: I guess they caught us, separated us. I don't remember my mother's face at the moment she saw me for the last time.

In fact, I'm not meant to remember anything: neither the years before the Enclave nor the contract nor my mother: zilch, nada, nothing at all. I'm their daughter, and my Little Brother is their son. Save for one detail: I am two and a half years older than they think, and I know they lie. That they never stop lying.

◆ ◆ ◆

The best part of the day ends at the entrance of the school. Because at the school entrance, there is the Door, and in the Door, there is the prisoner, and every time I see him, I say to myself that the outside world can only be Hell, and that, at the end of the day, maybe I'd better stay here.

I've heard that somewhere, underground in certain cities, some guys still believe themselves to be the government of Europe and attempt to organize the existence of people who have asked nothing of them.

For example, if the bastards that work for them (and who have the gall to call themselves the police) catch modified seed dealers "without the authorities' approval," or people who use Free Money, or who consume things they don't like, well, bingo! They bring them in. Since the transcorps refuse to fund prisons, they contract with communities like ours, entrusting them with the prisoners, and we use them as we see fit.

So then, I don't know what the guy from the Door did in the real world, but he's here, among us. The school is a circular building. You go into the schoolyard, passing under a Door whose lintel is a transparent sarcophagus. The guy is there, lying in a harness, his body and head covered with wires and tubes. They've connected his brain to the building's internal system (apparently, it's simpler and less expensive than training an AI), and he does this all day: opening and closing doors, monitoring the kids, and directing the maintenance robots.

At night, they inject him with something to sleep, and he sleeps. I don't know if he dreams. All I see, when I pass by, is his body stretched out on a green foam berth, in the transparent plastic aquarium, with the tubes and needles, and the headset on his head. I guess it's lucky that we can't see his eyes.

Once we've passed the Door, we go into the schoolyard, where weeder, shearer, and sprinkler robots come and go. The children of the Enclave are split up into groups, and to each group is attributed a class and an educator, whom we call Uncle or Aunt.

We sit down at our consoles and prepare ourselves to endure the torrent of inanities that make up the day's schedule. Except when, like me, you've found a way to get out. Well, getting out, it's easier said than done. My poor little Ferret is getting out of juice faster and faster. I'd really like to access a place led by the Free and Unique Men, but how? They move all the time to elude their enemies, who have apparently never heard about the Declaration of Rights of Free and Unique Men.

So, here I am, the others are struggling on a history test—it's a matter of responding to questions such as, "Why did God allow for several sorts of primitive peoples to evolve before choosing the white man to populate the universe?"—when I see an icon shining in the grayish fog I'm stuck in.

The icon depicts a door, and God knows why, I understand immediately that it's the guy from the entrance.

"Hey," I say to him, "do you hear me?"

"Of course," he says. "I see you as well. You should be helping your friends answer their questions, but you're trying to go elsewhere. And it's not the first time."

I have a moment of doubt. What if he reported me to Aunt Simona, who is fussing on her console instead of working with us?

"I don't give a damn," he says. "If you don't want to work, don't work. As for me, all that interests me is that the building functions."

I find him very alert, for a guy whose brain is supposed to be permanently immersed in a flood of inhibitors.

"You get used to it," he says. "It depends on what you've taken beforehand. Some products reinforce synaptic connections. It prevents the brain from getting reconstructed by any crap."

Now, I wonder if the guy from the Door wasn't imprisoned for mental babbling. Nano-concoctions that maintain synaptic circuits? It's too complicated, even for the best bioengineers. If such a thing existed, my *father* and my *mother* would already sell God in a bottle: but the product isn't yet available in stores. I'm on the verge of asking the Door to explain to me what he means, but Aunt Simona has come out of her trance and has connected with me. I return to my exercise, pronto, and we leave it at that.

◆ ◆ ◆

I think of my mother often. I remember word for word what she would say to me. Does she still think of me a little from time to time, at night, in her room? Or have they made her take so many drugs and so much crap that she's forgotten us? Wouldn't it be better for her to have blotted us out from her memory after all?

Me, I've erased nothing.

My mother believed, among other things, that fertility is power.

"To give life," she would say, "it's the best and the worst. The moment before, there is nothing, and the moment after, there's you: like a flower whose petals open. Inside, there is an eye. That's what you are," she would say, "a gaze upon the universe."

"It's for this reason," she used to say, "that we have the power, us women: because you don't know who's going to be born, you don't know what new consciousness you're going to give to the universe. It could be the best and it could be the worst. You can never know."

So, there you have it, I'm a gaze, a fragment of the universe that has had access to consciousness. The day I die, the universe will no longer see itself the same way.

It's possible. Right at this very moment, what's hard is to live, day after day after day. Until now, I've always managed to pretend, to pull the wool over their eyes, but now I think I'm going to crack.

Let me explain.

They're not against science. On the contrary. They believe that progress and knowledge were given to mankind to carry out the word of God and Sambara.

Consequently, they establish for each of us a profile—like the people on the outside construct a Blazon that they use on the net, except that we can't choose what we put on the icon, and we don't have access to the file. It contains all the results of our tests, our psychological profile, plus information about our tastes, our behavior, our plans. They stick this in the Grand Computer, and poof! Guess what? A husband.

I don't know all the details of what happens next—it's a Divine Mystery, reserved for adults. I know that the series of rituals ends with a collective wedding, after which the couple goes away to live their "life" somewhere in the world, in the community chosen by Sambara.

A magnificent fate. A radiant future.

◆ ◆ ◆

They don't have any trouble with Little Brother. His existence doesn't pose the least problem to them: God wanted him to be born, and everything that God wants is good, including living in an AutoPark and not being able to walk nor speak nor show the least bit of perception of oneself or the surrounding world.

Me, I have trouble. I tell myself that spending time swinging, without playing, without running, without messing around with other kids, that's not a life. If God, or Nature, or the Universe, or whatever it is that made and desired us, also wanted Little Brother, then the Universe doesn't know what it wants.

And *I* think of what the Door told me about the nanos that reinforce synaptic circuits. I think that on the outside, they must have invented lots of substances that I've never heard of. That can possibly put right what isn't working in Little Brother's brain.

But for that I'd need to get out. I think about it nonstop, but I don't see how; the outer wall is riddled with sensors, the main gate is guarded day and night by implant-controlled dogs, everything that enters and exits is x-rayed. For me to pass would be a miracle; for me to pass with Little Brother would mean God exists—and I don't believe He does. No, what I need are contacts, connections with the Free and Unique Men. But those people are in hiding. They're nomads, just as much in the real world as in the virtual one. Apart from some towns, up in the mountains, which have seceded from Great Europe, they don't have a fixed position, no place where one would know to find them. They say that they move under the cloak of circuses, theatrical troupes. How to know whether one of them could come around in the vicinity?

◆ ◆ ◆

In class, I regularly search the library. Not ours—it only has writings by Sambara, his disciples, and the leaders of the major communities—but the one in the neighboring city, which, in certain circumstances, is relatively easy to access. It doesn't get me very far. Ah, if only I had a good Fox Terrier, instead of this anemic Ferret.

A few days ago, I finished my exercises before everyone, as usual. I was just about to launch my Ferret when the Door appeared.

"What are you looking for?"

The moron scared me. I am worried that someone saw me jump. With a finger, I raise my headset to make sure. No, they all have theirs on their heads, and they are typing away like crazy, except for Francie and the twins, who are whispering in a corner. Aunt Simona, tied up in checking I don't know what, didn't see anything.

"A Fox-Terrier. I want to find information about the Free and Unique Men, but my Ferret is daft and the ones at the public library aren't powerful enough."

"I see," he said. And he disappears.

I continued to look, but in the Enclave's database. I've heard my parents talking several times about compilations of infidel places and forums—whose coordinates, protected by first-class Cerberuses, are only accessible to those whose mission is to keep them under surveillance.

Meanwhile, the others had finished their work. The twins took advantage of the opportunity to fling pieces of foam upholstery from the microdisk cases at each other. Francie tried to access a game that's reserved for adults, triggering an alarm that made Aunt Simona jump. In a single movement, she tore off her headset and her bun and started shrieking.

"End of the lesson! Turn off your consoles and get out of here!"

Furious, I grit my teeth. Because of these idiots, I may have to wait weeks for the Door's next visit.

Aunt Simona had stood up. I moved my hand towards the keyboard. She was walking through the rows to make sure we hadn't damaged anything. Just as she was coming over towards me, the Door threw me a Fox Terrier—right into the microdisk I'd surreptitiously slipped into the drive. Clever, this Door.

I turned everything off, took the microdisk, and went back to my parents' house with the twins.

♦ ♦ ♦

It's crazy what you can do when you have the right tools.

At the public library, I launched my new Fox Terrier on the word "autism," and I found a ton of references I had never come across before.

I found out some surprising stuff.

All autistic people aren't alike. Despite their disability, many develop a personality—an internal life that can't be expressed due to their neurological problems.

But there is a way. They've gotten them to talk: if someone holds their wrist and helps them type, they're capable of using a keyboard.

It only works in certain cases, but it works. In others, more rare ones, they use a robotic arm that's adapted to fit a wheelchair. They've been able to make them use the same optical commands as tetraplegics. In short, regardless of the techniques used, we can communicate with them.

And so, when the parents aren't here, I take the cellphone they gave me as a birthday gift two or three years ago, and I show letters to Little Brother.

I have to admit that, so far, he hasn't shown the slightest sign of interest, but it doesn't matter: I try all the same. I don't believe it's forbidden to meddle with the work of God.

◆ ◆ ◆

This is it. I knew it. In two weeks, they're sending me to Spain, to a Sister Community. I'm going to ride horses, listen to conferences in the company of other Young Elects, and—it's supposed to be the highlight of the trip—spend an hour in a tête-à-tête with my betrothed!

How, but how am I going to be able to escape this without causing a scandal whose first victim would be me? How?

I think about it during the day, and I don't sleep at night, without getting a glimpse of the slightest solution. And, to make matters worse, I can't find the Door anymore. He's always there, in his box, when I enter the school in the morning and leave in the evening, but it's impossible for me to get in touch with him. Did they, by any chance, catch him? What punishment can you inflict on a guy who's already locked up?

I'm so preoccupied by all of this that on the way to school I listen to even less of the twins' conversation than usual—that is, until the moment something in the tone of their voices spurs me to prick up my ears.

"I'm telling you we shouldn't talk to them about it," says Fabrice. "It's the best way to ruin everything."

"Ruin what? They're incapable of organizing anything! *I* think that we're not risking anything by giving it a try."

"Nonsense! If we talk to them, all we'll get is a sermon. Nothing more."

We're nearly under the porch. It's no longer the tone of their voice that compels me to listen, but—strange, exceptional situation!—the content of their conversation. I'm convinced they haven't changed the subject since we left, but I don't know what they're talking about.

"Hey, you two, why are you arguing?"

I try to look as innocent as possible. It must work, because they cut off immediately to shoot me a look of pity mingled with exasperation.

"It's none of your business," says Pierre.

The pity has disappeared from his expression. Replaced by something that strongly resembles disdain.

"Why?" Fabrice asks. "She must have seen it anyhow."

I have a weird feeling. I see that he's having doubts. That he's wondering whether or not they should let me in on this. It's like my twins have been transformed. Replaced by imposters. As if all of a sudden, they just pulled off their syntheskin masks. An instant before, they were robots programmed by Sambara, now they might be real people who, like me, are playing a part. I can't get over it. I stay stupefied, speechless. I look at them one after the other, wondering what mind-blowing conspiracy they could be talking about.

Then, Fabrice points her finger to our right, towards the city.

"That," she says. "You know what that is?"

It's humiliating. They're really taking me for an idiot! That'll teach me, I suppose, to play my part too well.

What Fabrice is showing me is a Ferris wheel. I've never seen one in real life before, but I must have read stories in which there were some, or ended up in a place established in a virtual fair. I don't know anymore.

"It's a Ferris wheel," I fling back. "There's a fair in town? Well, that's a first."

They don't deign to nod their heads in agreement, but I sense that I just went up a notch in their respect.

"Has it been there a long time?"

"A day and a half. Everyone's seen it, except for you—and the parents, of course."

And suddenly I understand: someone among the kids saw the wheel and described the wonders of the fair to the others. No doubt based on memories of a past life because I can't believe that one of them was able to secretly access the network without me noticing. Be that as it may, a fun fair's Ferris wheel is turning in our sky, and the children of God are tempted.

"We'd like to see," explains Fabrice while we cross the porch. "There are two camps: those who think that we must ask Aunt Simona for permission to organize a picnic on the observation deck and those who think we should organize one at night—without permission."

◆ ◆ ◆

I'm sitting in my seat, and I think about it—about the idea that some kids of the Enclave could not only be curious about the outside, but get organized to assuage this curiosity—when I come across, as it were by chance, a message the Door has left me.

He says this, "Serotonin inhibitor levels increased, difficult to reach network. Fair Free Men cover: contact Zirah the Truth Teller."

While I delete it, Francie throws foam at two girls in the last row. I'm about to tell her to cut it off when I catch on to her movement: she's stuffing something into the ball of foam before throwing it. It's a ruse! A trick to pass messages to people we only encounter at this time of the day. Having seen Fabrice and Pierre behave like normal human beings was enough to change my viewpoint. All at once, the twins and the others appear to me in an entirely different light. I wonder how I could have been foolish enough to have believed that, of all the kids that live here, I was the only one to resist!

They meet in the evenings, at the foot of the main wall, behind a garden shed that serves as a cemetery for broken or unusable tools. No one ever comes here.

The twins slipped me the meeting time on the way out of class. Like every evening, I went to bed, and then I went out through the window while thinking that, despite all of my dreams of the Great Departure, it was the first time I'd dared a getaway like this.

I creep stealthily between the houses, cross the lawns with the—absurd—temptation to take off my shoes and run until I am out of breath.

Behind the shed I find the twins and Francie. They are already deep in discussion, and I don't think it useful to interrupt them. I take advantage of the opportunity to listen and observe.

"No, no," said Francie, shaking her brown curls as if to detach them from her head, "I don't agree, if we present things to them like that, it's not going to work. We shouldn't tell them we want to see the fair."

"Excuse me? We're not going to tell them we want to *go* there, not really!"

An expression of absolute certainty sweeps over the face of this girl who I've always considered a featherbrain of the first order, even though she's fifteen. "Yes. We're not going to do it ourselves. It's too risky."

"So, then who?"

"The zombies," she said.

That's what they call the kids whose brains have been permanently colonized by the word of God and Jean Paul Sambara.

"We're going to talk to them, and we're going to get them to understand that it would be good to go to the fair—not to see the attractions, of course!"

She pauses, prolonging the suspense.

"To carry the Good Word. Believe me, it's going to work!"

We are sitting in the grass, in the dark, but even so I see the twins' eyes widen.

"Now that's an idea!"

"What did you think, loser."

And she explains to them that it would be convenient to whisper to the zombies, in the days that follow, so that they pass on the right message to the Uncles and the Aunts.

"At any rate," Francie concluded, "it's not because they aren't aware of it that they don't want to leave too. It can't fail."

I sense then that the silence that sets in is for me. They are waiting for a reaction, an opinion, a comment.

"It can work," I say, trying to be neither too enthusiastic nor too skeptical. "But how do you plan to make the most of the attractions?"

"Good question," said Fabrice. "We haven't had the time to think about it yet."

Which means I probably need to come up with an idea.

"We'll talk about this again," Francie said, consulting her watch. "Tomorrow night, same time?"

The twins nod. Francie gets up and quickly disappears from our view. We stay sitting in the grass. The fair warms the night with a pale green, violet, and orange glow, the Ferris wheel stands out in the sky like a giant Christmas ornament. And we hear music. Not the songs they are playing, no, but like a massive pulsation, the rhythmic beat of an artificial, synthetic heart.

I must look surprised because Fabrice says to me, pointing in the direction Francie disappeared, "Her dad checks if she's in bed every night at the same time."

"It doesn't stop her from going back out," says Pierre. "But not tonight. Should we go home?"

I stood up.

"Let's go."

The day has been full of emotion and revelations. It would be good to go digest all of this under the quilt.

The twins seem to agree with me. We walk in silence to the spot where, in the morning, we meet to go to school. It is here that Fabrice turns to me and says, "You didn't suspect a thing, huh?"

I must admit I didn't.

They don't press further, but in the dark I see them exchange broad smiles.

"But we did. We know about you."

Now I was starting to get it, that they knew. But what, exactly?

"Yeah," Pierre concludes. "And we think that being able to fool everyone about your age, it's not bad. But to be so old and not see what we're up to, that sucks!"

"*You* suck," I say to myself as I slide into my bed. It's just because I'm too old that I saw nothing: you and I, we don't belong to the same world anymore. In relation to you, I'm like the parents, who live in a parallel dimension. But here's the thing: if your crazy plan works, me, I'm not going to settle for a ride on the merry-go-round. I'm going to get out of here.

◆ ◆ ◆

The next morning, I realize the second I wake up that something's wrong. Normally, a chaotic melody emerges from the kitchen, an ensemble of disorganized yet harmonious sounds that remind me of an orchestra preparing for a concert.

But now, from my bed, I hear cupboard doors closed harshly, glasses set down carelessly on the table, piles of plates that clatter because they're being carried unceremoniously.

A series of rapid footsteps to my door, which opens with full force and rebounds on the wall.

"Get up! It's time! And hurry up!"

So, it's my *mother* who's in a bad mood. It happens to them, to one or the other, from time to time. It's rare that they tell me why, but it generally has something to do with what they call their "work" and which always consists, for him and for her, of identifying and saving from death the poor little souls condemned by their unworthy mothers, then finding them a new home.

I understand what's wrong when I enter the kitchen. The AutoPark is out of order. Two of its arms stretch towards the sky, toys jammed in their claws, and a third jerkily shakes a completely tangled mobile. Little Brother has taken refuge in a corner, away from this strange noise. He conscientiously knocks his forehead against one of the bars. I slip my hand between his head and the plastic to prevent him from hurting himself, and I return him to the middle of the AutoPark, wedging him in place with cushions. Then I say good morning to my *father*, who is polishing off his breakfast.

"Sit down," he says to me. "I need to talk to you."

Whoa. Is it the morning of catastrophes or something?

I sit down and serve myself cereal. My brain runs at full speed. I can't believe that he's found out about my little outing last night.

"It's about the fair. Your teachers got wind of the fact that some of your classmates had decided to organize a secret picnic. They intended to punish them, but others suggested inviting them to join the group that is going to bring the word of God and of our Prophet to the very heart of this den of iniquity. The proposal is going to be debated during the general meeting this morning. If it's accepted, and I believe that it will be, the leadership of certain groups will be entrusted to students of your section. Your mother and I intend to reward your good behavior by nominating you."

I search for the right response, but fortunately, my *mother* comes back from the bathroom and says, "If the repairman doesn't get here, I won't be able to attend!"

"He's going to come," says my *father*.

The broken AutoPark doesn't concern him. It's my *mother's* domain. It's then that I hear myself say, without really having thought about it, "I can stay, if you want."

"Sorry?"

"I can keep an eye on my brother. That way, *mother* will be able to go to the meeting."

They look at each other. If they can entrust the word of God to me, they can also trust me to supervise Little Brother. They accept.

Once the door closes on them, I find myself alone and I finally realize that if I offered to do this, it's not only to be alone with Little Brother. It's also because I have a feeling that I'll have to leave him soon.

• • •

I should have consulted the public library before we left. But, from the moment when they confirmed to me that I would lead one of the missionary groups, I haven't had a minute to myself. I haven't had time, neither to inform myself about fairs nor to contact the Door. I stayed a whole five minutes looking up under his sarcophagus, but I didn't see him move a limb. I imagine he's joined the kingdom of molecular dreams, the coma of Divine druggies.

Be that as it may, if I'd had the time to gather information, I wouldn't have, like the others, opened my eyes wide and nearly unhinged my jaw while entering the fair, which is a village.

A village, what am I saying, a city! A small city of stretched canvas and steel ropes, of bioplastic lines and guy wire, of sails and bubbles. All of it bursts with vivid and fruity colors, and gives the impression that, if the ropes and cables weren't firmly anchored to the ground, the rides, the houses of horror, the cafés, the arbors, the pistola-ser shooting booths, and the virtual labyrinths would take off into the skies.

The adults who organized the entire operation have placed us at supposedly strategic intersections, which we're not meant to move from. Our mission is to distribute leaflets, mini video bulls, and T-shirts with the holographic image of John Paul. Whether or not the location is strategic, a wave of kids and teenagers circulates between the rides and passes in front of us without showing anything other than a cosmic indifference. My group—which they let me put together as I wished—is composed of Francie, the twins, and two other girls whose names slipped my mind as soon as they said them. We came to an agreement with Francie and the twins: they're enjoying one of the rides while we keep watch and distribute leaflets, badges, and mini bulls. To the two zombies, we said that they were in the bathroom, and they ate it up.

We're at a crossroads, or rather a small, open space where six paths converge. Since we arrived, I keep watching the rides in the hope of coming across a sign of Madam Zirah's presence.

To my left, kids between four- and eight-years-old ride pale blue dolphins, pink unicorns, white whales, and silver elephants on a carousel. Their parents wait for their turn to end while casting sideways glances at the Octopus Kingdom, where, if I've understood correctly, you put on a costume to hunt treasure in the glaucous depths of the virtual tropics. I've heard several people recount their combat against the octopus with the very convincing intonations of seasoned sailors . . . The teens seem to prefer the Jungle, a labyrinth of moss, gelatin, and plastic, painted in green tones, at the heart of which they pelt each other with balls full of orange or bright pink gel. They come out of it looking wild, with colored hair and laughing expressions, holding in their suddenly too-small arms stuffed toys that represent lions or giraffes . . .

Fabrice and Pierre are across the way. They're going in circles under the stretched-canvas roof of the Insect Kingdom. I recommended to them to choose a car that's well-visible: for twenty minutes, they've occupied the same bright-red ladybug.

The twins, I must clarify, solved the delicate problem of money for us by bumping into some kids dressed in the uniforms of schools sponsored by the food-processing branch of the third European transcorp.

Which in no way gives them the right to break our contract and enjoy the carousel for twenty minutes, when we agreed on ten. I lean toward my neighbor.

"Francie, do you want to go tell these two idiots that their turn has ended?"

She doesn't need to be told twice. I follow her with my eyes while she crosses the small space; so well that I nearly miss the advertising robot that is coming towards me. These machines are so primitive that they're funny: a cart with remote-controlled wheels, on which is an animatronic marionette. It holds a television that broadcasts a video ad. I've already caught sight of several, but they passed by too far away for me to see their message. This one takes around a Pierrot that holds a white and gold television set. On the screen, a woman of a certain age explains that she can tell you if your boyfriend really loves you, by examining your brain. Madam Zirah is a clairvoyant psychic!

Madam Zirah!

The cart hasn't stopped moving. I jump in front of it to see if the screen shows the place where Madam Zirah works. My motion triggers the mechanism of the Pierrot, which hands me a flyer. On the front, Madam Zirah smiles at me; on the back, a map shows me which aisle her consultation room is in.

My heart beats at full speed.

Luckily, the twins are back from their ride on the carousel. I dump my bundle of leaflets and T-shirts into their arms.

"You two, stay here. Watch Francie and the two zombies. And if anyone asks, say I'm with our leaders."

"But you had said . . ."

"This is a case of extreme emergency."

And I ditch them.

◆ ◆ ◆

Madam Zirah runs her boutique in a fake pumpkin.

I enter a waiting room hung with almond green velvet and full of cushions made to look like red fruits: strawberries, raspberries, cherries, and red currants. Madam Zirah doesn't have many clients at this hour of the day; I wait by myself for her to lift the plastic flower-printed curtain, concealing what must be the entrance to her consultation room.

I'm starting to feel like time is dragging when she appears. A plump figure but, how can I put it, energetic. She has blossomed in width without any complex, or the least amount of fuss. Shorter than I am, yet imposing. A more warm and real presence than all the Aunts who pride themselves on the love of God. She studies me for a couple of seconds and says:

"All alone? Or is the lucky guy not going to be long?"

I take a few seconds to understand.

"Alone. It's the Door who told me to come see you."

"The door?"

"In the Enclave. He's a prisoner."

Her face lights up. She raises the curtain.

"Come in! Quick. How much time do you have?"

How much time? But I'm not leaving again. I have all the time I need.

We go down a step to go into a room without windows. The walls are hung with black velvet, the floor covered with a carpet of the same color. Lighting is provided by optic fibers running on the ground. They give off a red light from which arises an atmosphere at once mysterious and cozy. Nothing trashy or fake. When my eyes adjust to the lack of light, I make out two semi-circular sofas that encircle a table with a set of consoles. Two headsets are set on it. The final decor element I become aware of is the screen inserted in the wall, facing me.

"Sit down," says Madam Zirah, pointing out the sofa facing the screen and sitting in the other with her back turned to it. I obey. Because I don't know what to do with my hands, I pick up one of the headsets and examine it.

"We use them to obtain an image of the brain's electrical activity. The client focuses on a word, and I interpret the image projected on the screen. But you're not here for that. What did Michael tell you, exactly?"

"His name is Michael?"

"Michael Bontemps."

"He didn't say anything to me. If I've understood correctly, they became aware of his activity and adjusted his inhibitors. We haven't communicated for days."

"I see."

She settles comfortably into the black velvet of the sofa and observes me.

"You can't stay here."

"Sorry?"

"Don't worry, no one knows anything. Just one look at you is enough to guess your intentions, young lady. But what you want to do isn't possible."

I try to meet the gaze of this woman whom I find infinitely kind and reassuring, and a big black thing explodes under my skull. A dark nebula. A black hole.

"There are two reasons for that. On one hand, the Free and Unique Men don't have the means to take in and protect whoever appears at their door. What's more, we've had quite enough of the White Knights. We'd like to rid the world of these people."

"You mean . . . destroy the Enclaves?"

"Perhaps. Not right away. Even with the latest deconstructors of synaptic networks, it's extremely difficult to deprogram adults, but children . . . we'd like them to stop attacking children. For that, we need agents who can act from the inside."

I'm starting to understand. But Madam Zirah hasn't finished.

"The second reason," she says, "is that Alisson Mollet is dead."

"Pardon?"

"Your mother is dead. Michael did some research, which we completed by looking up files from the rehabilitation center where they had sent her. She committed suicide after a year in their re-education program."

I don't say anything. Shrink a bit into the sofa. The black hole in my head fully engulfs me. My mother is dead. Even if I don't return to the Enclave, I will never see her again. All that I have left of her are the images of our last moments together, and everything she used to say to me.

"What do . . . what will I need to do?"

"Not much more than what you've always done."

"They want to marry me off. How am I going to be able to help you with a zombie on my back?"

She furrows her brow.

"That's true. We'll deal with it. We'll find a way: either by finding you a 'husband' who'll be a part of our troops or by tampering with their tests so that they're convinced it's better that you don't marry. We've done it before."

For a few seconds, she seems lost in thought, then she resumes, "Michael told me that a number of other kids in the Enclave are quite street-smart."

"It's because of them that I'm here."

"That's what I understood. But they've only come here to have fun. It's going to be necessary to keep a close eye on them, study them, bring them in little by little to consider the possibility that they can get out. I mean in a concrete and permanent way, not only with temporary distractions. You see what I'm saying?"

I understand, but I feel like crying, and I respond with only a nod. She leans over, opens one of the table's compartments, and hands me a black, plastic box.

"Michael is in trouble. For him to survive, you would need to inject the contents of this syringe into his nutritional system. It's a virus that will permanently protect him from the inhibitors."

I take the box and hide it in my underpants. Then I stand up. Madam Zirah gives me a kiss—I don't have the time to stop her from doing it.

She sees me out to the entrance of the pumpkin. As I'm leaving, I turn to her.

"By the way," I say, "your business of interpreting images of brain activity, is that bullshit?"

She smiles wide and gives me a whack on my behind that propels me outside.

"Yes," she says. "But that doesn't matter. What counts, it's not what we look at, it's the way we look at it."

◆ ◆ ◆

A few minutes later, I have caught up with the others. Francie and the twins, in the joy of having deceived our wardens, didn't notice that I wasn't really in my usual state anymore. We returned to the fold, and they congratulated us on our good behavior.

Since then, we meet every evening behind the tool shed, and I listen to them recount their exploits. I think Zirah is right: it's pointless to talk to them about anything as long as they haven't demonstrated a desire other than to treat themselves to a ride on the merry-go-round.

The carnies haven't left yet, and when the wind blows in the right direction, you hear the shrieks of the girls that the Giant Octopus carries toward the sky.

I suppose that one day we, too, will go to the fair. First, we have a lot on our plate. It's time that the Uncles and the Aunts, the Fathers and the Mothers stop believing that they can impose their warped vision of the world without encountering resistance. Time to show them that they don't have the right to take possession of other people's lives—even if they're poor, uneducated girls.

There is no God and life is nothing without the freedom to choose it. The followers of John Paul aren't free. They believe that to live this life they must find an answer, an interpretative framework that will enable them to understand the world at last. But it's not a grid that they're making: it's a cage, and they want to put all of us inside. They don't want to understand that our only freedom is knowing how and why we aren't free.

Because there is nothing to find. There is just being, making, and creating. There is no other God than the ones we imagine. There is no other humanity than the one we invent, day after day.

In the meantime, I've gotten permission to look after Little Brother one morning a week. When they leave, I unplug the AutoPark and we go for a walk. Little Brother is incapable of walking by himself. The second you let go of his hand, he's terrified. He stays on his feet, paralyzed, shaking all over, unable to move forward. The second I put his hand back in mine, he starts moving forward again.

◆ ◆ ◆

The package that Madam Zirah gave me contained the syringe and microdisks to use on the school's consoles. I now have a Fox Terrier and Ferrets that enable me to go where I want, when I want. And even a Cerberus, which guards my pocket of personal data. I had to wait before making use of the syringe. I needed to procure some tools. For that, I deliberately sabotaged the AutoPark. The repairman came; while he talked with my mother, and fiercely defended the work he'd done during his last visit, I borrowed two or three little things from him.

Tonight, I leave through the window of my room and run in small strides toward the school's door. A ladder awaits me, hidden behind a flower bed. I put it up against the wall and climb to the height of the sarcophagus in which lies Michael Bontemps. I've chosen a clear and starry night, close to the full moon. It's dangerous, but if I have a halogen microlamp that fits in the palm of my hand for finicky tasks, I also need a minimum amount of brightness to not mess up.

He's here, behind a good two centimeters of polycarbonate. Nothing separates us but the somewhat yellow thickness of an assembly of macromolecules. I see the straps that hold him in place, the needles that go into his wrists. His face and his skull are entirely confined in the headset. We are a few centimeters apart, and it's absolutely impossible for us to communicate.

It's not the moment to let myself be overwhelmed by this type of thought. It's what they've done to this guy that repulses me—not him. I take the laser blade I've borrowed from the repairman and cut out a polycarbonate disk next to the base of his neck. There passes a thin pipe that transports the nanos they use to control his cerebral activity and his mood. I pick up the syringe from its foam-upholstered box and carefully put my arm into the sarcophagus. The other hand aims the microlamp at the pipe. An advantage of my small size: I didn't have to cut out too big a piece of the plastic to carry out this exploit. I push down on the plunger, and a diode indicates that the contents of the syringe have been injected.

I pull my hand out. Then I slather the edges of the polycarbonate disk with glue and put it back in place. Next, all I have to do is put away the ladder and go back home.

Tomorrow, at school, I'll be able to judge if my little expedition was useful for something.

While walking, I think, yes, it has helped. And there will be others, many others. And, one day, we'll get out of here.

# EXPANSION

Sylvie Denis: "Inside, Outside"

French title: "Dedans, dehors"

First published in the magazine *Galaxies*, No. 12 1999, then in other volumes, notably Denis' collection *Jardins virtuels* (two editions, 2003 and 2006) with Gallimard.

*Translated by* Aishwarya Marathe with Annabelle Dolidon

Sylvie Denis is an author, a translator, and an editor of science fiction who has greatly contributed to the genre in France. In July 2021, the quarterly French publication *Bifrost* dedicated an issue (No. 103) to her long and prolific career that included an interview, a short story, and a rich bibliography. She has published six novels, including two for young adults, and about fifty short stories. In a meeting with students at Portland State University in 2018, she talked about "Inside, Outside"—for which she received the Prix Rosny-Aîné in 2000—and, when asked if she was pessimistic or optimistic about the future, she answered that she was the former for the near future, but the latter in the long run. Perhaps, this shows in the short story that you have just read, and others in the collection *Jardins virtuels* (*Virtual Gardens*) from 2003. This story is also representative of her approach to writing. In the interview with *Bifrost*, she declared that she liked to put her readers in new situations and for this, she liked to mix the biological and the technical.[1] In "Inside, Outside," the character Michael Bontemps embodies this tension at work in the text between the body and the technology used to (ab)use him. This raises ethical questions about institutionalized methods of punishment, additionally complexified by corporate interests. But the story's characters also explore the possibilities that technology offers to free the body, notably through mechanical and chemical enhancements. Ultimately, the reader will decide what position to take. In other stories in the collection *Jardins virtuels*, characters use technology to transform their bodies. As stated in the "Declaration of Rights of Free and Unique

---

1  *Bifrost* No. 103, July 2021, p. 154.

Men," committing oneself to create machines or intelligences is fine as long as it is to serve people, not imprison them.

Another aspect of the story one might note, besides technoscience, is the role of knowledge in the main character's journey. What she knows (or remembers) and what she seeks are the motors of the narration. In her diptyque *La Saison des singes* (*The Monkey Season*, 2007) and *L'Empire du sommeil* (*The Empire of Sleep*, 2012), this also drives characters who are preparing for a major climate change that many refuse to acknowledge. Knowledge is definitely power, but for some, holding knowledge, not disseminating it, is how they exert control over others.

## DISCUSSION QUESTIONS

Do you think the Enclave is a utopia? Why or why not? Try to explore both options.

What is the position of the Free and Unique Men on technology? On human knowledge and its applications?

How do you see the young woman who narrates the story? What can we learn about her from her tone of voice? What is her story?

What is the role of technosciences in this story? Is it a good tool, evil technology, both, or something else?

How does Sylvie Denis use the concept (the *novum*) of the "Door"—a person in a sarcophagus—to build the world in which her characters live? In other words, this Door is at the intersection of which institutions, laws, and social practices that we can imagine when we read the story?

How does this story help us extrapolate about posthumanism?

# The Swing of Your Gait

*by* Sylvie Lainé

*translated by* Aurélie Brémont and Jean-Louis Trudel

"ISN'T IT A COMFORT, at least? That all her recordings are available... I know you were opposed and that you didn't like her doing them, but still... now, you'll always have those, right?"

Fred is sitting in front of me, almost tongue-tied by an excess of good intentions. He fumbles with the bread and gropes for the knife, as clumsy as the pimply teenager who was already a pal ten years ago. He's really trying. He knows he can't tell me to let go and move on.

But me, I can't get a word out. My brain seizes up whenever I want to come up with an appropriate response, let alone a coherent one. When Lou left me three weeks ago, she turned me into a robot. I'm unplugged. Unrebooted. Holding up my end of anything like a conversation demands immense effort on my part.

"Comfort?"

I'm clinging to that word, trying to taste it after uttering it, to see if it raises an echo somewhere.

There's nothing, nothing but Lou in our hotel room by the sea telling me that she never wants anything anymore from me, Lou leaving, and I didn't even hear the door slam. Fred tries to help once more.

"You've *played* the recordings, right? She has such an incredible talent for making you feel—what it is to be her. That unique way she has of looking at things. Those quick, stealthy glances, left, right, never staring at anything that isn't already motionless. That thing she does with her shoulders. The way her hair sweeps over her eyes whenever there's a breath of wind. That series, *Street Scenes*, I keep going back to it. They're a wonder."

"Yeah, everybody said so. She sold a few thousand anyway. And the competition is tough on the open market."

I can get back on track, speak normally, because it doesn't really concern me. That's the other Lou, the one other people knew, not mine. She was sharing her essential self with strangers, but she shared a different one with me.

"You know she has her own fandom?" Fred insists. "Real online forums, all about her. You've never had a look?"

◆ ◆ ◆

There are many things I've never seen—or not nearly often enough. I don't even own the complete collection of the *Street Scenes* by Virginia 42—that was her name for the immersion video captures. And even my access rights to the few I downloaded have expired.

So, I start by recreating a collection, but a complete one, full length, with three months of unlimited access. I had no idea she had done so many—thirty-three in total. They last from three to ten minutes, and the complete set costs me one week's income.

I put off looking for jobs. I've already taken on four contracts of three days each to finish the month, I should be fine. I take the day off to dive into Lou's reality—her own reality, though it's just a virtual one for me, now. I put on the gloves, position the electrodes, and the headset. And I find myself in the street. A street I know.

But the real body blow is delivered by the flow of her gait—that unique way she has of slightly dragging her feet to strike the pavement heels first, the knees following lazily and the shoulders straight. The set of her shoulders propelling her forward. We often strolled together arm in arm. I was trying to match both her stride and her inner harmony. Now, I'm part of it, effortlessly. She/I raises her/my left shoulder, and I feel the pleasure of my long hair streaming away. An easy shrug, like a spring uncoiling. A secret caress tickling my neck.

She keeps walking, her back feels warm, she sucks in her belly slightly, her shoulders held even straighter, her elbows loose, one hand on her bag—easier to grasp than her hip and swinging just as freely. I close my eyes to focus on feeling all of it, but it's too much, all at once—the vid only lasts a few minutes, but when it stops, I'm crushed, gasping for air, how could she ever leave me when she walks that way? How can you abandon someone who loves you when you have all of this inside you? Me, when I walk, I just feel empty. Lou was filled with light, filled with herself. And I will never love anyone else but her—or she would have to be just like Lou, as tender and luminous as she is.

I gather up my courage and play almost all the recordings—over twenty in one go. In some, she eyes her reflection in shopwindows, furtively, as if she were coming across a stranger. Someone talks to her in the street sometimes and she laughs—when she laughs, it's like being tickled from the inside. And she keeps doing that thing with her shoulders to set her hair swinging, a deeply private pleasure.

I steep myself in her, the way I'd swallow down a cool drink, the way I'd fill my lungs to bursting with the smell of roses.

Now I need to visit the forums. I need to know if everyone feels the same way when we experience Lou's clips, or if it is different with each person. I need to know how Lou inhabits others. I need to know . . . if there are more Lous now. Newly minted little sisters with swinging hips and flying hair.

◆  ◆  ◆

I search through the Real Life forums for Virginia 42 references, but there's so much that I'm drowning. I narrow it down to "street scenes" and I find the right one at last. From January to March they posted over six hundred times on the subject. So many people are speaking of Lou among themselves! I'm afraid to read what they have to say about her.

But I was wrong to be scared, they're only doing what everyone does in forums about a common hobby: talk about themselves, curate an ego-boosting facade, and work hard to convince each other that they're all a great gang of great friends, each one ready to find the other guy fantastic as long as he or she is saying nice things about them. All of which has very little to do with Lou. I did manage to find a girl, Barbarever, who said that she'd played the video "Welcome to Montparnasse" twenty-five times; it takes place in the street where she lives, and she recognized the restaurant and loved the scene.

I have to meet her. I message her to say I'm Lou's boyfriend. It makes her very curious, and we decide to meet in two days.

I hope she's really a girl, by the way. Barbarever. What a stupid handle.

Two more days go by, they're shaped by Lou's absence, by my missing Lou, by the emptiness, by the questions I can't answer and I'll never be able to. What's the point of meeting? And if something of Lou's lives on inside her, and if I fall madly in love with her, would I be betraying Lou?

We finally find each other on a bench near Place Saint-Sulpice. She's a nice girl, the kind that you'll run across on any street or subway platform, and she tells me everything about herself: Her name is Mazarine, and she hates it (I like it better than Barbarever, but it's on her). She's twenty-four, no boyfriends except losers, works as a salesgirl most of the time, has an aquarium, loves manga... I don't give a damn about any of it, I'm waiting for a spark that never comes. She stoops, drags her feet, her hair is tied up, and she talks, talks, talks, talks, and talks some more. She asks me why Lou never did a clip in a clothing store.

I leave her feeling frustrated, as if I had missed an appointment. Lou wasn't here, nor her ghost, not even the slightest hint of her presence.

And then I watch, over and over and over again, the scene where Lou is just walking with that swinging stride of hers, stealing a single glance at a shopwindow to let us see her golden hair dancing on her shoulders, a scene that is like a bright and quiet dance, poised between fragility and balance, performed on mid heels ticking to a soft tempo.

◆ ◆ ◆

I've decided to let my hair down when I go out now. I like feeling it brushing my neck. I shampoo every morning so it's really light and airy, and the strands tickle my skin when I move my head.

I think I'm also starting to get it, how she walks. The trick is to have heels, but tapered ones, and not too high—I've found shoes that are almost perfect. The heel is narrow, just enough to allow a side-to-side swing. My ankles have gained an extra degree of freedom.

Next, I have to swell my chest out, breathe deeply, and keep my chin up. One arm swings back and forth, but the other needs a support point: I hang my phone on my belt and place my hand on it with my elbow relaxed and held outwards.

◆ ◆ ◆

Fred will be here soon, we're going out for dinner tonight, he's got something to tell me. Let's see if he notices anything. I wash my hair, I slip on my new, softer shoes, and I hang my phone at the right height.

Here he is. We exit onto the street, noisy and energized by the afternoon rain, the pavement still wet and shiny. He's wearing a gorgeous afghan embroidered shirt and I congratulate him. He's looking excited, in fact—clean-shaven and smelling good. We exchange kind words—he's delighted to see me looking human again.

Right then, I ask if I can take his arm. Why not? We lock arms and I try out my new gait. It's harder to keep track of my strides and their rhythm when I'm holding someone's arm—Lou must have been so much more experienced. She managed to share her lightness with me, while I marched to my own beat naturally attuned to hers. I'm struggling a bit with Fred because I can't hold him too tight, so I hold his hand. It's more and more common nowadays, especially among young people when they are friends, even straight guys—Fred and I are only twenty-five, we're not that old yet. He lets me, it comes easily to him.

In Montparnasse, I glance surreptitiously at the storefronts; I'm happy with what I see, I look buoyant. A group of girls give us approving looks and I wink at them.

Once we're at the restaurant, we sit down opposite each other on the terrace under a canopy.

"So, what do you think?" I ask Fred. "Notice anything?"

"You look in super shape, I told you earlier. What am I supposed to notice?"

"I learned to walk just like Lou. I watched her vids so many times I think I'm almost there. But it was my first time doing it while holding somebody's hand. What did you think?"

"I thought you'd moved on," he says, taken aback. "You looked so happy I thought you'd found another girl, actually."

How can I explain?

"No, I'm still with Lou. It's like I was making love to her. I'm just soaking in her."

Fred laughs. "You're even using her perfume . . . Anyway, it seems to agree with you."

About the perfume, he's right, but it doesn't work—once I have it on me, I don't smell it anymore. It's one of my rituals when I play Lou's clips, but it's purely pro forma.

"And you," I ask Fred, "what was it you wanted to tell me?"

He orders cocktails, never taking his eyes off me, already savouring what he's about to tell me.

"The recordings, do you know how they're made? Lou must have told you."

"Not really, no. She knew I didn't like them. She ordered the gear online, it took about an hour to get ready because the synching had to be fine-tuned, but I don't think it was that complicated."

Fred leans towards me as if he had groundbreaking news.

"They've issued a new model—now you can vidcapt animals."

The funny thing is, I know right away where he's going with this.

"You're gonna make a vid of Vadrouille?"

"Nailed it."

Fred is beaming. Vadrouille is a big striped tomcat—Fred is crazy about him. A big moody, independent, and possessive tomcat. Highly intelligent, too, according to Fred. A rover, but with an instinct for creature comforts, that's for sure. They're an odd couple. More than once, Fred has gotten up, while we were having fun, and left, saying, "I have to go and see Vadrouille, he must be bored." He did exactly that in the middle of a kayaking weekend in Ardèche—he hitchhiked all the way home.

"Actually, I've ALREADY done it! It works super well. Would you like to try?"

"How is it?"

The waiter stops by to take our orders, but we haven't even looked at the menu yet.

We tell him we're not ready and Fred tries to explain.

"As a matter of fact, from the inside, a cat is all about complete relaxation and absolute readiness to explode. They accumulate energy. You feel like you could jump two yards in any direction if you were just tickled unawares."

I'm laughing my head off.

"Really? So, when he's snoring on the couch, he's actually storing up power, that's it? Then you should do as I do. Play them over and over and try to learn. One day, Vadrouille won't be there anymore."

Lou's invisible presence passes between us like an icy wind—the waiter takes advantage of the pause to come and see if we're ready to order. We improvise, going for the easiest choices, an omelette for Fred and tagliatelle pasta for myself.

It's a strange and pleasant evening, where I shift in a single second from happiness to sadness, while Fred seems to be discovering broader horizons all at once. We're dining on a terrace, on the city's edge, on a continent—Lou is somewhere on the same continent, and when we're done it's time to remember that Vadrouille might be bored.

◆ ◆ ◆

Come to think of it, I need breasts—otherwise there's no reason for me to stick out my chest when I straighten my shoulders.

I'd love to have big, pointy breasts—like torpedoes.

I'm not going to do hormones, I'd lose my manhood—and that's out of the question. There's also plastic surgery, but that's a frightening idea. I want to think it over first. For now, I'll start with building up my pecs by going to the gym.

◆ ◆ ◆

I've met a girl at the club, a well-built, athletic girl named Clara.

She tells me about her job: she's a knife-thrower. No, it's not a joke. I went to see her show, it's a new thing they created to make the zoo more profitable: circus acts with the animals, twice a week. Carla has this weird one where her throws avoid the snakes crawling across a target, but in the end, she nails a mouse for them. The mouse is in a small cage below, there are snakes all around, and when the mouse is killed, a cable raises the cage that has no floor nor roof, and Carla goes to fetch the bloody mouse, still moving, and feeds it to a boa. It's damn bizarre.

Yesterday, something odd happened. I was telling Fred about this, and of course he asks if snakes can be recorded, though frankly I'd be surprised. We look it up and it turns out some people actually tried, but it's static and very boring. Anyway, we were in his living room drinking something nice and cool, and I was watching Fred who didn't really seem to be all there. I mean I would've thought he was dozing off if I hadn't seen his eyebrow quiver. Believe me, when someone's eyebrow twitches unexpectedly, they don't seem asleep at all—but Fred was ignoring me. And Vadrouille, too, was no longer moving—though I think he was truly asleep, his nose buried deep in his fur.

I could hear a big fly buzzing in the curtain folds. And Fred couldn't stop watching it. So, I went silent and waited too. I felt something was about to happen.

Fred began by sliding very smoothly from the couch until he was crouching a yard from the window. Heedless, the fly stuck to its big noisy fly's lifework, bumping into the window every time it left the curtain, its loud drone interspersed with puzzling pauses.

A funny snore, like a shallow hum, suddenly issued from Fred's mouth—a sort of breathy, almost sibilant vibrato, like nothing I'd ever heard come out of a human throat. Vadrouille looked up and stared at Fred in utter fascination. Me, I couldn't breathe. It was so quiet. All we could hear was the fly buzzing.

And then Fred sprang, his hand loudly striking the window, and the curtain sporting a big black stain.

Fred casually made his way back to the sofa and sat down again. Looking very satisfied with himself, he told me that he just couldn't eat them, that would be far too disgusting.

◆ ◆ ◆

I've noticed something else in Lou's clips. I hadn't paid enough attention.

The way she watches.

She opens her eyes wide. Very, very wide, eyelids pulled back as far as they can go. And her gaze aims high—most of the time, she gazes above people's faces. That's why she straightens her shoulders. And why her knees aren't really involved when she walks—and why her rhythm is softer than mine. She reaches for the sky. Her upper body is straight as an arrow, her lower body coils and uncoils peacefully. The boundary between the two runs through her solar plexus. Her gaze overlooks the street, as if she were far taller than she really is—and she sees a lot more than I do. Her horizon is vaster.

It's hard. I have to raise my chin, without losing the elbow's carefree bend. I must open my eyes wide, without forgetting the easygoing, casual swing of the hips. Shake my foundations loose, let them move fluidly and on their own, unfold my face like a flower—and then I have no choice but to put on sunglasses, like she does, and I know I'm on the right track.

◆ ◆ ◆

Carla is a healthy, funny, and positive girl. My temping as a site referencer and indexer leaves me with ample free time, and I'm not going to spend it in front of a computer—so I become a regular at the zoo, Carla showing it to me from the inside. I follow her to the feedings of cormorants and lions; I watch helpers play with baby gorillas as they nurse them with bottles. As of last week, I'm registered as a volunteer. I get to clean the enclosures of the bears and penguins. I have unlimited access to the zoo, and I can take in the animal care or watch rehearsals.

I've given up trying to get a bigger apartment, mine is awfully cramped, but I'm spending less and less time there, since I'm putting less effort into hunting contracts. I've thought it through. To afford roomier digs, I'd need more money, and so more contracts. In my field, they require about twenty hours of work, and eight hours on average of running down prospects. I'd need to spend a lot more time at home to earn the money I need to move out. In fact, sleep hours aside, I'd be spending twice as much time at home. And to do that, I'd need a much bigger and comfortable studio. One where I could cook and relax more. That would mean twice the rent, and a lot of extra work.

I'd rather spend more time outside. I return to my studio to work and sleep, usually from six in the morning until noon, sometimes a bit more. There's no money to waste, but I don't want to go out or travel. Lou's immersion vids let me do both, and so much more. My one luxury is the gym club.

◆ ◆ ◆

Carla and I meet there at least twice a week, and we often spend the afternoon or the evening at the zoo. Some evenings, we meet up with Fred and make an outing of it, sometimes with a fourth person when Fred shows up with a girlfriend—picnicking in a park or public garden and going for a walk. Carla is fascinated by the animal vidcapts, both her and Fred are obsessed with producing some or buying them dirt cheap.

Later, I walk Carla home, holding her arm as I resume Lou's loping gait—it's easier with her than with Fred. She matches the swing of my hips immediately—even if she is way more feline and springy than Lou. Ever more limber, but jumpier too. She's a touch sturdier, as well. More powerful.

One night, she's the one walking me home. We sit down on the bed, since I only have one chair. I kiss her, then take off her clothes delicately—I knew her body already, from having seen her in a swimsuit so often, but I didn't know the broad, dark circles of the areolas of her heavy breasts nor the thick and black fleece of her pubis. We make love simply and tenderly, she tells me she'd wanted it for a long time. Her skin is cool and soft. She's become a close and intimate friend. Now that we are lovers too, I hope nothing will change as far as she is concerned. For me she's a dear friend, a fount of gladness, a strong and flexible body into which I love to dive, but nothing has really changed. I think she knows it.

Some nights, actually, she goes home with Fred—Carla is a curious and greedy girl. She's adamant that she goes there to see Vadrouille, and I pretend to believe her.

◆ ◆ ◆

I miss Lou terribly.

◆ ◆ ◆

This morning there's an ad in the volunteers' locker-room at the zoo: they're looking for an assistant caretaker from 6:00 to 9:00 a.m. The pay isn't much, nothing like what Carla makes, and I would need to organize my work schedule differently, but I'm tempted; I'll find out more.

The job is to clean three elephants with a power washer and scrub brush. I try it out one morning. It's very physical work, and I'm glad I got back in shape at the gym. The hose has to be held very high to wash the skin from top to bottom. Next, I scrub the flanks while the animal's ears and tail flap from side to side, spraying me—it's showing its appreciation, but within ten minutes I'm soaked, and my shoulders are hurting. Since I also have to clean the holding area, I rest my arms by moving out their massive droppings with a shovel once I'm done scrubbing the massive flanks. When I hose down the stony floor afterward, they approach softly from behind and check with their trunk tip the spot I've just scrubbed. They're quiet and inquisitive.

It only takes a few mornings for them to accept me and greet me as a friend. Now, when I show up, they sidle up to the power washer even before I turn on the tap—and I'm getting to know them better as well. I'm figuring out their little pleasures and individual preferences. Basalt, the big one, loves it when I send the water directly in his mouth as he opens it wide while lifting his trunk—it looks like he's laughing.

Basalt watches me out of the corner of his eye. Suddenly, he sits down on his gigantic haunches. Quite placidly. And then he stretches out his forelegs and leans on his elbows. He's closer to my height, almost lying on his belly. Great. Now I can scrub his ears with the brush, even underneath, and I can also clean the top of his back. Basalt seems ecstatic. I scrub down his rear, and then, on sheer impulse, I grab his massive neck and scramble up—my exposed thighs rub against the rough and raspy leather of the elephant's skin, until I climb on his back and settle down triumphantly, with the water jet angled across my legs.

I have a different view of the neck's folds, of the stray hairs jutting out the top of his head, the dripping wet ears—the huge cartilaginous spans dripping with soap water and flapping like sails.

Basalt is the only one to sit down for the morning wash—it's turned into a little private ritual. Every day, after I rinse out his mouth, he lies on his belly so that I can clamber up and find a comfortable perch to clean behind the ears.

But still, I wonder. Did Basalt come up with that trick on his own?

"You should ask Martial," Carla recommends.

Martial is the zoo director. Now that she's officially part of the circus troupe, Carla gets to see him sometimes. I'm starting to realize how stratified the place is. The managers, the veterinary staff, and the permanent employees of the zoo occupy the top rung. Down the ladder, there are the artists with long-term contracts who put on the public shows. Lower down still, the mixed horde of temp workers I'm a part of. We don't know each other very well, a familiar face can vanish from one day to the next, and there are always new ones. Many of them work guest reception and cash registers. You can tell the volunteers by their green cap, but ours is yellow. And I'm sure there are lots of people that I haven't met yet, we don't all have the same work schedule; the aquarium is a world unto itself and so is the aviary. Not to mention the kitchen staff that we hardly ever see.

All this to say that I've never gotten to talk with Martial. I visit human resources to sign my weekly contracts, so I don't even know what he looks like.

As a matter of fact, Carla doesn't know Martial that well either, but she manages to ask the art director a few questions, and she shares what she's learned.

Years ago, Basalt was in a big circus act. He'd been trained in his youth to perform various spectacular stunts, until one day, he put down his foot too heavily on the small of his trainer's back during a show, unintentionally crushing his spine. The trainer survived, but he spent months in rehab and remains paralyzed to this day—he never came back.

They say Basalt's sorrow was terrible to behold. Other trainers tried to take over, but he'd trumpet like mad and recoil whenever someone tried to make him raise a leg or get on a stool. They decided to leave him be. He's too old now for a new try—but I also learn that the two younger elephants, Gypsum and Crystal, are trained every afternoon by a professional who is preparing a new act with them.

♦ ♦ ♦

Poor Basalt. He must feel so lost, so forsaken. He must feel useless when he sees his younger comrades leaving for the training grounds with their trainer while he remains alone.

He felt as much pride, dignity, and personal triumph as an elephant can feel when he understood the most difficult and complex orders and was able to execute them with elegance and utter precision. He must have loved his trainer like you love a friend whose praise you seek, and he waited for him every day to share in the joy of the show. Now, he has nothing. What can I do for him?

The next morning, before getting up on Basalt's back, I talk into his ear for a long time. I rub his cheeks and the top of his trunk. I give him some friendly slaps on the ass. Once I've reached my perch, I do something I've always dreamt of doing, a horseman's move. I give a big kick with both heels—and then another, and another, and another.

Basalt unbends and straightens one foreleg, then the other. I tilt forward steeply, grab his ears to not fall backward, and keep kicking with my heels. Basalt gets up completely: everything is in upheaval, and I hold on as best I can, but once he's completely up, I find my balance again. I'm very high up. But his back is so broad that I should be able to manage.

I let my hair down. Next, very slowly, I squat, and then I rise, inch by inch—Basalt remains perfectly still. There, I'm standing now atop Basalt's body, my bare feet spread apart, sinking a bit in the leathery yet pliable skin. I'm stable. I stop moving and close my eyes a little. My toes clench.

Basalt shivers slightly from the inside, then moves a leg forward. He takes one step. Then another. Under my feet, he starts to roll. His muscles unwind, supple and strong. He finds his rhythm, achieves a smooth and regular stride.

I open my eyes and arms wide, I'm on top of the world, and my hair streams out. I am light and aerial, I'm gliding, I'm flying. The world beneath my feet sways and stomps, its motion periodic and tranquil. Strength and power below my feet. I'm walking, my four feet perfectly balanced, in harmony with the earth and sky. I haven't turned over a new leaf—I'll let the wind scatter the leaves. Look at me, Lou! Look at everything I've learned. Eyes wide open, knees flexing loosely, shoulders straight—I'm not looking at anything in particular, but I see it all. Look at me, Lou! Look how I've grown!

And I'm still faithful to the swing of your gait.

# EXPANSION

Sylvie Lainé: "The Swing of Your Gait"

French title: "Fidèle à ton pas balancé"

First published in Lainé's collection *Marouflages* in ActuSF, collection *Les Trois souhaits* (2009).

*Translated by* Jean-Louis Trudel

Born in 1957, Sylvie Lainé lives a double life: professor of information science at the University of Lyon (now Emerita) and science fiction writer. The two intermingle at times in the epistemological quest of self and other: how do we know ourselves? How do we know others? Through what medium—by which we often mean, in science fiction, through what mediating technology or device? In "The Swing of Your Gait," technology opens the door for people to experience the life of others from the inside out. In return, what do characters learn about themselves?

Sylvie Lainé writes short stories and novellas and has published several collections with the French publisher ActuSF including *L'Opéra de Shaya* (2016) for which she won her second Grand Prix de l'Imaginaire. She won several prizes, among which the Prix Septième Continent in 1986 for "Carte blanche," and her first Grand Prix de l'Imaginaire in 2007 for "Les Yeux d'Elsa," also published in *Marouflages* (2009). It tells a love story between a female dolphin and a man who is incapable of treating the dolphin as an equal and uses her as free labor on construction sites (dolphins are modified beings in the story). The author explained in a class visit that she wrote "The Swing of Your Gait" as a mirror text to "Les Yeux d'Elsa" with a male character who, this time, seeks understanding and finds liberation.

In Sylvie Lainé's stories, as another French science fiction writer (Catherine Dufour) puts it, you don't find laser weapons and exhilarating adventures; her texts are subtle, but they raise many questions. In "The Swing of Your Gait," there is no galactical battle, no apocalyptic upheaval, just the disquieting weighing of the fabric that makes us who we are.

## DISCUSSION QUESTIONS

What do you think of the possibility of embodying someone else—or an animal? Who/Which animal would you like to *know* this way if you could? What could be the negative consequences of doing so?

Do you need to know someone completely to love them?

What pushes us to want to *know* people?

There are always limits to what we can know about others, about what it means to *be* them. Take the expression "to walk a mile in someone's shoes." Is a futuristic world in which people can *vidcapt* other people a better world?

Have you ever done something extreme for love?

At the end of the story, what does the main character learn about himself? How do you understand the ending?

# Beyond the Terminator

*by* Laurence Suhner

*translated by* Sheryl Curtis

LOG OF THE SKIMMER, *ship-bathyscaph operated by Dr. Laura Jain Fall, marine exobiologist, Maline Island, Nuwa, fourth planet in the Cinnabar system.*

When I was a child, I had an imaginary friend.

At least, that's what I believed for many years, even if, deep down, I knew it was something else, that it had nothing to do with my imagination, but rather perception, sensation, intuition, or even some phenomenon that I knew nothing of at that time. Except I don't really understand it any better now.

There's no word for it.

No human word.

My mother, Elisabeth Fall, who landed with the first wave of settlers, worked for NOEE, the company responsible for exploring the planetary ocean on Nuwa, one of the three temperate worlds in the Cinnabar system, looking for extraterrestrial life-forms. She belonged to the group of scientists that proposed changing the star's name. No one today refers to Cinnabar by the name given to it at the beginning of the twenty-first century, by the first international team of astrophysicists that observed it: TRAPPIST-1.

I was quite young at the time, just eight years old. It was three years after my mother and I arrived in that star system, forty light years from the cradle of our birth, Earth. Yet, I clearly remember the party organized in my mother's lab located at the edge of the terminator, on Maline Island, when they renamed the star. The cafeteria, normally a cold, austere place, had been transformed into a ballroom, and the researchers had danced and sung in the sea air for the entire time of what we commonly refer to here, purely for the sake of convenience or out of physiological convention, as the "night phase"—even if night has a completely different meaning on Nuwa and her six sister planets. My recollection is clear since that celebration took place in the hours before I met my imaginary friend, the significant event of my existence, all the more so since it surpasses that day, twelve years later, when I saw the Shennong artifact.

"Laura! It's starting!"

A brief wave of panic washes over me.

"The eruption?"

"No, the Knights! They're arriving."

I rush over to join Annika and Manuel, my two scientific colleagues, on the deck of the *Skimmer*. Our other boats keep a constant watch on the various banks of the Sea Knights located in this region of the globe. I've been waiting for this moment for months. My instruments are ready, and I feel unusually tense, no doubt also a result of the imminent eruption of Cinnabar. A magnetic string has formed, an indication of an increase in solar activity over the coming hours. I admit the coincidence is unfortunate. I pray that Cinnabar will control its enthusiastic outbursts until the Knights have completed their migration. Ultra-cool dwarves, like Cinnabar, consume their fuel slowly. But, from time to time, in an effort to catch up, they blaze suddenly, generating a violent storm of hard radiation.

To overcome my anxiety, I think about Michael who is on duty on the *Rowell* station, in a wide orbit around Shennong, the sixth planet in the system and the last one to gravitate in the so-called habitable zone. *Rowell*, assembled a few months ago, is the sole human construction tolerated in the vicinity of Shennong.

I place my hands on the rail. A gentle vibration lets me know the motors have started up, under Annika's orders. The *Skimmer* looks like a real boat. It has a foredeck, an aft-deck, a navigation bridge, a wheelhouse, a wardroom that people reach by means of an old-fashioned metal staircase and that houses cabins, and a kitchen equipped with an oven and a fridge—absolute luxury. In fact, it's both a spacecraft and a bathyscaph I've been using to explore the ocean of Nuwa and its islands for over twenty-five years.

Holding a pair of binoculars in front of my eyes, I examine the dark sea stretching over the dark side of the planet, in the *Skimmer*'s wake. As a result of their proximity to the sun, all of the planets in the system are in synchronous rotation, which means they always show the same face to the star. While one hemisphere is lit, the other remains in shadow, with a clear, fixed boundary between the two called the "terminator," a narrow strip of twilight that provides the best living conditions for us human beings. That's why our colony was established on the archipelagoes that straddle this natural border. As a result, the sun never strictly dawns nor sets on Nuwa, unless you cross the terminator line.

And that is precisely what the Sea Knights, or at least the individuals old enough to undertake such a long journey, are preparing to do. Feverish, I examine the waves, looking for early signs of their arrival. Annika points out to sea. Five hundred meters away, I see a silvery splash at the crest of the waves, then several more. The ocean writhes, undulates, with smooth, shiny backs that appear one after another in the penetrating light of the *Skimmer*'s powerful floodlights. Based on the data, in this sector, there are a good thousand of them.

The Sea Knights look like large marine mammals—whales, belugas, orcas, narwhals—except that's not what they are. They have a hybrid respiratory system, with lungs and gills, that allows them to bask from time to time on the numerous islands that fill the planetary ocean on Nuwa, on the dark side, even if they spend most of their time in the deep waters, more than two thousand meters down, following the currents and the banks of phytoplankton. But occasionally, they undertake a lengthy and enigmatic migration that takes them from the depths of the hidden side to the surface of the exposed side, allowing them to graze on the rays of the sun that endanger their benthic organisms. When they reach the end of their journey, they spend no more than a few hours to a few days in the lit zone before returning to the colder regions from which they came.

No biological, astronomical, or climatic explanation has ever been found for the massive exodus of these pelagic giants measuring more than twenty meters long and weighing thirty tons, whose behavior seems to be random, at least in the minds of common mortals. For my part, I know that's not the case. I know because someone whispered it to me, that famous day when I was eight-years-old.

For now, the Knights are heading quickly toward the terminator, at a depth between two and forty meters, according to the sonar. They barely increase their depth when they dive below the hull of the *Skimmer*, which has just entered the lit zone. The wave they create on their way forces me to grab hold of the rail. We're going to follow them their entire trip.

For a moment, I admire the peaceful, reddish glow of Cinnabar, sitting like a large half orange on the horizon. The weather is mild. Sixteen degrees. Pangu, at a distance of 1.4 million kilometers at the closest point of its orbit, is setting. Higher in the sky, I see the sparkle of our observation and telecommunications satellites. The image of the *Rowell* station flits through my mind. I hope Michael is recording everything that is happening in the thick atmosphere of Shennong, while praying that nothing will be scrambled by its mysterious inhabitants, the designers of the artifact.

The Sea Knights are traveling quickly, but they merely swim along the border of the terminator, as if still hesitating to venture into full light. They are nocturnal creatures, lacking eyes, that obey an echolocation system somewhat similar to that used by dolphins on Earth, as well as other senses still unknown to us.

The *Skimmer*'s engine rumbles. The bow slices through the waves, driven by a medium to strong swell. Annika, Manuel, and I face into the wind, which whips our faces.

"They're beautiful," whispers Annika. "I'd like to be able to get a closer look at them, to touch them. Is their skin as smooth as it looks?"

I'm overcome with emotion.

*Yes, as smooth and soft as a pebble rolled in the surf.*

I think back on that evening, when I was eight years old, about the basins at my mother's marine biology center, on Maline Island. Once again, I see the tips of my small fingers touching the purple skin streaked with scarlet arabesques.

*And as cold as the water on the dark side of Nuwa, Annika!*

But how could she ever understand? I'm the only human who has ever had such an experience.

"I've got something on radar," says Manuel.

He's frowning. I don't like that.

"Could you be more specific?"

"Five small craft, approaching."

I feel my stomach tense. It can't be them? Already? That can only mean one thing: they've pirated our boats' transmissions. I should have been more vigilant. They're growing more and more ingenious when it comes to spying on what we do.

"Make a scan!"

The look Manuel gives me a few minutes later confirms my fears. I force the motors. I want to be as close to the Knights as possible, just in case they come under attack. I had discussed this eventuality with my crew this morning. At one point, we had even considered the possibility of carrying weapons. But I'm a pacifist. In my soul. Just as my mother was. There's no way I can fight against my deepest nature even if, at this very moment, I catch myself cursing my convictions.

"They're fishers," confirms Annika, a pained expression on her face. "I'm picking up their conversations."

Voices flow out of the speakers on the deck. Laughing, gloating, pandering, boasting to work up the courage they need to take action. Expressing their frenzy for killing. Celebrating the blood about to be spilled, the cadavers they can put on display and compare at the markets on Soesbek and Durmansk, the two large islands that border the western coast of Maline Island.

The only time the Knights approach the surface is at the start of their enigmatic migration when they swim along the terminator for dozens of kilometers. They're easy prey then. Hunting started just fifteen years after the first colonists settled on Nuwa. And it has continued since then because, apparently, their flesh is delicious and these giants from the sea are peaceful travelers. They don't defend themselves. For twenty years, I've been fighting this barbaric practice. In vain. Nuwa, and the other inhabitable planets in Cinnabar system, have taken the same path as Earth, with the exception of Shennong. Will we never learn? The Knights are considered to have low-level intelligence. Common animals. Speciesism! That's what it is. It's what finished off my mother, I believe, last year. This heresy, this propensity for killing, hunting, destroying life in all its divergent forms, out of fear or ignorance. This stupidity makes me sick. If all we had to do was bring our worst faults to Cinnabar, we should have stayed on Earth, forty light years away. And died there!

That's why I want so much to prove my argument. To prove it *irrefutably*. To shut them up once and for all. There are ethical laws, implemented in the early days of extrasolar expansion. If organisms presumed to be intelligent are discovered, they must be preserved at any cost. It would even be preferable to prohibit all contact. If my hypothesis is confirmed, we'll be obliged to respect such precepts.

Fifteen kilometers swallowed up by the *Skimmer*'s bow. The Sea Knights have finally started to move away from the terminator. But it's a little late. I can't take my binoculars off the five speedboats racing along in their wake, mechanical harpoons pointing ahead. It will take some time for the fishers to catch up with them. They don't have the leading-edge technology we enjoy. But, sooner or later, they will be on the Knights. On us. The butchery will start, and we won't be able to lift a finger. Each time I find myself in this situation, I watch for the moment when the Knights will be too deep into the exposed side of the planet for the hunters to be able to continue their raid. Yet, despite their persecution, the Knights have never wavered from their habits. Something stronger than fear and death dictates their unchanging behavior.

The *Skimmer* is traveling over the heads of the front-running Knights at close to forty-five knots. I switch from the sonar to the scanner and watch the leader of the herd. A large individual, no doubt very old, its coal-gray livery dotted with purple and scarlet spots. A patriarch. It slices through the waves quickly, obeying instinct or some secret impulse.

I zoom in on its body, immense yet agile, undulating gracefully. I freeze, dumbounded. It's almost as if . . .

"Laura!"

I turn toward Annika, just as the ambient light intensifies incredibly. My goggles darken to protect me from the dazzle. I curse the star's unwelcome coordination. Then I catch myself. It's a windfall, actually!

We leave the outer deck and make our way to the wardroom. The hatch closes behind us. It will protect us from the rays emitted during the various phases of the eruption. First, the energy is liberated in the form of X-rays, which will fortunately be absorbed by the atmosphere, then, as soon as the plasma grows hot enough, a flash of light or radiation, followed by other rays of the electromagnetic spectrum: gamma and radio waves. It's as if we were already in the middle of the bright side, except that the eruption releases far more hard radiation. During solar storms, my mother and I would lock ourselves up in the basement and wait until the energy levels returned to normal. That was one of my worst fears when I was a child. That, and the hypothetical telescoping of the planets; since the system's planets are located in a patch the size of a handkerchief around the star, people had long questioned the stability of their orbits. Like marbles or billiard balls!

"We're pushing on!"

I take the controls of the *Skimmer*. I force the engines until we overtake the herd of Knights.

Annika casts a complicit glance in my direction. She understands.

By diving in front of them, I hope to suggest to these sea travelers that they follow us quickly into the depths. And kill two birds with one stone: get them away from the fishers and the star's jolts. As a bonus, the column of water will protect our scientific equipment from the electromagnetic disturbances caused by the eruption.

The *Skimmer* has initiated a rapid descent. My eyes are glued to the screens. At the outset, the Knights don't react: they continue to swim close to the surface, exposed to the fishers' harpoons. Then, slowly, the leader of the herd turns its nose toward our ship. For a second, I have the impression that it is staring at me, even though I know it's blind. Then, suddenly it dives straight down, just as we'd done. The others follow immediately.

My ship-bathyscaph continues to dive. It is able to withstand both very high and very low pressures. The sea, the depths, a different universe spread out around us. We are moving among the Knights as if the *Skimmer* were one of them, while the large individual with the purple marbling continues to guide the bank. The longer I examine it, the more I'm convinced: it looks like the one I met that fateful night when I was eight years old. I'd bet my life on it. *It's him!*

Just then, a string of sound modulations echoes in my ears—a call, an invitation, a greeting?—as a mental image, a succession of colored shapes, forms in my mind. Like on that day, on Maline Island.

*You trusted me. Today, I'll do the same.*

Emotions wash over me. Am I dreaming again? No, I never dream. It can't just be chance. He understood my intentions, my desire to prove my argument, that very day.

*After all these years, you waited for me?*

Then the truth became obvious to me. He has not waited for me. He was just there. Hidden away in a corner of my being. Except that I didn't see him, I didn't feel him.

Was he what made me what I've become? My will, what I thought was my will ... could it be ... *his?*

Our boat and the Knights are now diving into the deepest part of Nuwa's ocean. The water turns a cranberry shade, then ebony black. Luminous spots coat the waves with living stars, as if reflecting those that stud the planet's nocturnal sky.

That's when the Knights start singing. Their melodies fill the *Skimmer*'s cabin. They will sing for hours, and then head back to the dark side of Nuwa, as usual.

We all hold our breath and remain silent, conscious that we are enjoying a privileged moment.

We start our climb to the surface, the Knights following close behind. We remain connected by an invisible bond, which I see clearly this time.

On the surface, Cinnabar has returned to its reddish clarity. The eruption is no more than a memory.

As soon as we reach open air, we pick up a message.

"Laur ... Laura ... can ... you hear ... m ...?"

"Michael!"

"Laura, can you hear me?"

"Yes, Michael. Everything's fine. Communication has been reestablished."

"Laura, did the Knights complete their migration?"

I detect tension in his voice.

"Yes. The fishers were after them. We dove to encourage them to follow us and escape from the eruption at the same time."

"That's what I thought. But, where are the Knights?"

"We're with them, Michael, we're inside the herd. We're on the bright side," I glance quickly at the data, "at latitude 2°4' Day side, according to the substellar reference point. And we're looking at Shennong!"

In fact, Shennong hangs overhead, high in the sky, like a small moon.

I hear a squeaking sound from the other end of the waves. Is Michael laughing? No, he's crying. For joy.

I hang on his every word.

"On Shennong, the clouds are pulling apart just now," he finally says. "We can see the artifact clearly! I can see it with my own eyes, Laura, just as you predicted. It can't be just by chance. There's a connection, Laura, that's for sure. There is a connection."

Intense happiness fills me, even though I had expected this outcome. The Knights precede each appearance of the artifact in Shennong's atmosphere by a few hours, as if they know when this enigmatic structure is about to appear through the thick cloud coverage, following the emergence of particularly violent winds.

The Knights come to greet the artifact for a few hours.

And they sing for it.

How can they know when to start their migration? We have no idea. I've presumed it's homeostasis on the scale of the entire system: synchronicity, harmony, correspondence, or at the very least, a type of chemical or biological communication that is nothing at all like radio waves. Something connects the planets of the Cinnabar system, beyond a simple exchange of kinetic moment and gravitational energy resulting from their proximity. My research over the past twenty-five years has been based on this postulate. A sort of panspermia, spread by meteorites perhaps, that could have interconnected all of the living creatures in the system millions of years ago.

And the source of this intangible bridge lies on Shennong, the sixth temperate planet in the system.

What exactly is the artifact?

The scientists who discovered it, in the early days of colonization, imagined that it might be some sort of atmospheric processor or a space elevator or, in other words, the expression of a technology developed by an advanced civilization that had been born on Shennong, a world that is still forbidden to us. Since we arrived, almost forty-five years ago, none of our exploratory ships have been authorized to land there.

As for me, I prefer the idea of a living entity, the source of a vast group of organisms gifted with reason that maintain an ongoing dialogue, a close bond, that is beyond our understanding, given our specific human cognitive faculties.

Intelligent life exists in the Cinnabar system. And that intelligence is nestled around us, on Nuwa itself, in the majestic beings that travel the oceans, the Knights, but also no doubt in other creatures on the planet, just like the more elementary forms of life we uncovered on Pangu.

An intelligence I encountered when I was eight-years-old, in my mother's laboratory. The details of that famous day, the starting point of my long career as a biologist, are engraved in my mind forever: the scent of the sea, the gentle, cool trade wind that ruffled my hair, the dark water of the large basins in which my mother and her colleagues had managed to catch three Knights so they could study them. Two of them had not survived captivity. There was only one left. As a result of that fiasco, the scientists had decided to release it the day after the party. My mother was very busy with the preparations for the ceremony that would bring together all the top people in the colony. A congregation of researchers from Pangu had even planned to attend. The Cinnabar system planets are so close to one another . . . A short week's travel separates us.

So, I was alone, sitting on the damp ground, my pants wet, under the reassuring brightness of the spotlights that lit up the infrastructures.

And I was listening.

I was listening to the sound that rose from the basins, deep respiration with a counterpoint of whistles and gurgles in which I was trying in vain to perceive words.

I remained still, so long that my buttocks hurt, until the creature emerged from the waves. Its supple body brushed against the surface, and it floated over to the steps carved in the concrete, a meter away from my bare feet. I didn't move.

I wasn't afraid, simply curious. Deep down, I felt happy, for some mysterious reason.

The Knight lifted its large head out of the water and laid it down in front of me. I stood up and placed my hand on its skull. I caressed its cool, smooth skin. Taking my time.

*My imaginary friend.*

During the weeks that followed, I described the scene to my mother in great detail. She explained to me that it was common for imaginative children, like the eight-year-old girl I was, to invent friends to overcome their solitude and respond to their dawning questions. There was nothing more natural than this need to create, imagine, talk with another being, even if it is only a facet of ourselves. These imaginary characters generally disappear over the years, she added, no doubt in an effort to reassure me.

Except that my imaginary friend never went away. He's still there, in my heart and, at this very moment, beneath the hull of the *Skimmer*. Today, he spoke to me as he did in the past, while the first guests were arriving at the lab, as all of the scientists were preparing for the party.

I know why I'm fighting for the Knights and for all the life-forms that live on Nuwa. But it took me more than twenty-five years to find a way to prove it.

Ever since we arrived, we've been looking for a way to contact those who created the Shennong artifact. And that way stands before us. We will have to learn to communicate with the Sea Knights. But, above all, we have to stop viewing them as inferior beings and massacring them for their flesh.

That's our challenge.

And we have to succeed at any cost.

For now, I have to convince the entire colony. Perhaps, that will sound the death knell for our installation in the Cinnabar system. Perhaps we'll have to withdraw to our spacecraft and our orbital stations. Perhaps, we'll even have to leave, head for a new land of exile.

Deep down, that would please me.

For we will have finally learned.

Respect for others.

But we've still got a long road ahead of us.

Despite everything, I feel positive. I've always been a positive person.

They will understand.

I'm convinced they will understand now.

# EXPANSION

Laurence Suhner: "Beyond the Terminator"

French title: "Au-delà du terminateur"

First publication in Suhner's short story collection *Le Terminateur*
(L'Atalante, 2017). Sequel based on the short story "The Terminator",
published in *Nature*, February 22, 2017.

*Translated by* Sheryl Curtis

Laurence Suhner (1966–) is a science fiction author and graphic nov-
elist from Geneva, Switzerland. She started to write stories about
aliens, the future, and physics when she was very young. Suhner, who
studied English literature and archeology, has always shown an interest in physics, and her novel *Vestiges*[1] shows how she combines these
different fields in her fiction. *Vestiges* won the Bob Morane and the
*Futuriales* Awards in 2013 and is the first volume of her *QuanTika* trilogy. In the novel, humans found extraterrestrial artifacts as they were
colonizing the planet, Gemma; and there's more, not only are there
places around the planet that defy laws of physics, but the discovery
of more alien ruins disrupts the colony's life.

Her short story, "Beyond the Terminator" was first published in
2017 in the English magazine *Nature*—a scientific magazine destined
to the general public. Despite taking place in a faraway galaxy, the
story is a tale about human-animal, or human-alien, relations. The
story catches up with Laura, an exobiologist, on a scientific mission to study the Sea Knights, beluga-like creatures whose peculiar
seasonal migration remains a mystery. While following the Knights,
Laura remembers an event from her childhood, and her first encounter with someone who might not have been an imaginary friend after
all . . .

---

1    *Vestiges* (ASIN: B07YQ6VZKY) is available in English translation in Kindle format on
Amazon.ca.

## DISCUSSION QUESTIONS

What do the Sea Knights look like? How do you imagine them?

What is unsettling about their mass transhumance, or seasonal migration?

What is happening with the fishermen and the Sea Knights? Can you think of similar situations in our world?

What does "speciesism" mean and why is this term used in this context?

Did you ever have an imaginary friend? Why did no one believe that what Laura had seen was real?

What does Laura discover about the Knights' migration? What are the implications of this discovery?

Do you think there is sentient life out there? Does it or does it not matter to appreciate this story and science fiction stories in general?

In the general introduction of this anthology, we state that this story is about "beauty." Do you agree with us? Why or why not?

# The City, That Night

*by* Jean-Claude Dunyach

*translated by* Tessa Sermet

THE CITY, THAT NIGHT, belongs to the dead. Wisps of fog cling to the lights; the streets' brouhaha is oddly smothered. Under the grayish halo of lights suspended three meters above ground, the rare passersby resemble ghost ships muffled in their long winter coats. From his window, Daniel feels like a lighthouse guardian who has been denied access to the sea.

Once more, he is not allowed to go outside. His mother warned him in her soft and never troubled voice; his father repeated it in his usual brusque tone. After tonight's meal, leaving the house is not an option. He is cooped up in his room just like a baby.

He does not understand. He will be killed in a week, maybe two. He would already be dead without this stupid flu that forced him to stay in bed, pushing back the planned date of his passing.

"It's better to avoid dying when we're sick," explained the doctor. "The organism requires longer to recover. You do not want to be out of school for too long, right?"

Daniel had blushed under the practitioner's gaze. Missing classes wasn't a big deal, but the idea of not seeing Jacqueline and the rest of the group all this time . . . Maybe, despite it all, she will visit him at the hospice. He imagines himself buried under the black sheets, holding his breath to prank her. *It won't work*, he suddenly realizes, *she died the day before today, while I was sick. She knows.*

The idea that she would be allowed to go out tonight, and not him, brings him down. For the first time, he dared go up against his parents and contest their decision. His voice was in turns pleading or indignant; he used all the tricks discovered during the twelve years of his childhood. It was a wasted effort; the wall didn't breach.

"Don't throw a tantrum, darling! You cannot come with us tonight. We will have other things to do than take care of you. Believe me, you will have plenty of time to get tired of this sort of outing when you're dead."

Big boys don't cry. Daniel thus retained his tears; but his mother noticed his trembling voice:

"Be reasonable and dad will take you to the movies next week. What do you think, Marc?"

"Let's say Tuesday."

His dad skimmed over the calendar hung on the entrance wall, frowning.

"Yes, Tuesday will be good since I'll probably get stuck in the office the rest of the week. You can choose the movie."

Daniel doesn't care about movies. Children's stories bore him, and the others are still forbidden. He often wished to already be dead so he could walk across the adults' theater entrance and nonchalantly get his ticket at the booth. But one cannot say that to their parents, not on a day like today.

"Be good while you wait for us?"

His dad kept the door slightly open while his mother slipped out the door wearing her Sunday best, then he closed it carefully. The key turned twice: silence fell.

He took another cookie from the metal tin his mother had left on the shelf—an oversight that was unlike her. There is something in the night of the dead that makes adults feel guilty. Daniel is big enough to understand that—he has been pubescent for months and knows what guilt is. However, he hates being left out.

Dragging his feet, he goes upstairs. His bed is waiting for him, as warm and cozy as a cuddly toy. It would be easy enough to open the curtains and seek refuge inside the world that belongs to him. Daniel saw the day go down through his window. He particularly enjoys twilight, the moment when shadows ooze like a greasy liquid, before streetlights switch on and chase them away. He hopes every time that obscurity will reach the edge of his bedroom and that he'll be able to drown in this black tide; a hope shattered by the raw white lights coming from the streets. Tonight's yellow mist is a half-victory, a transgression from an established order.

This haze could hide him, if he dared to wrap himself in it.

The window's panel creaks and gets stuck when he tries to open it. He must push as hard as he can to clear a path through the edge of the roof. The damp air scraping his throat makes him shiver. He returns to his bedroom, grabs a sweater, a windbreaker, and a scarf. Apparently, those who are already dead don't need that sort of protection. The rest of the gang will make fun of him when he finds them. He has a choice: go out almost naked, facing the freezing wind armed only with his bare skin, or bury himself in comfortable childish layers, such as his slippers; they restrain him, but they keep him warm.

*When you're dead, you won't have to worry about such decisions . . .*

The one and only time he tried to kiss Jacqueline—after grabbing her hand in a way that he hoped looked natural—she turned her head at the last moment. The corners of their mouths brushed past each other.

"Wait until we're both dead," she whispered moving aside. "Mom told me that—"

She bit her tongue before saying too much. Today, she knows everything there is to know; meanwhile he remains imprisoned in his room and his fear.

He keeps the sweater but leaves the windbreaker. No scarf, his adult throat remains naked. The flu gives him a rusk and low voice, an adult tone. He will have to find the words to match it.

The house expresses its disapproval behind him when he drops on the lawn. He does not look back.

The cemetery where the festivities are taking place is a few blocks away, at the end of the main road. Daniel walks along the sidewalk looking down, worried at the idea of being seen by his parents; but he looks like a specter within the mist that is wrapping everything around him. Even his slippers' squeaking is muffled by the night. The silhouettes he encounters do not see him, or at least do not have eyes sharp enough to read his own gaze. When a group seems to get too close, he turns towards the windows of still lit up stores. The main grocery shop is closed; the Asian restaurant as well. According to the legends spread by the older children of the group, those who are already dead celebrate by drinking black-lined milk while eating translucent skull-shaped sweets. Nothing actually bloody, compared to the Halloween deserts his mother bakes every year for his friends, the ones that look like cut fingers smeared in ketchup. They are simply hotdogs wrapped in puff pastry, with thin almond slices to imitate nails. Absolutely horrific and delicious, if you're brave enough to take a bite. These are such easy tricks that they're almost suspicious. Knowing too much about it makes magic boring.

There must be something else about death, something more exciting. The rest of the gang knows it. Daniel, therefore, must find out for himself.

He looks in vain for a mirror to go through. The next shop is the animal trader. It is dark, too, but one can hear noises from the cages. Cracks, plaintive whines. Life. The parakeet perches creak; the hamster wheel spins wildly. Eyes shining despite the obscurity. Animals do not die like us, his mother had explained. They disappear when their time comes. They do not know anything.

Daniel turns his back to the street, flattening himself against the glass to escape the line of washed-out figures wordlessly progressing at the same pace. The animals fall silent as they pass. His heartbeat goes wild. Feverish thoughts take over the cage that is his mind. He needs to find his friends, quickly, before the night steals him away.

A hollow cough tears up his chest. He bites his lips to avoid making noise. The dead are never sick. Never worried. He remembers the stories told around the campfire, when the kids are sure no one is listening. *If you stay outside late, the night devours you and spills your bones out.* Children stuff . . . He is twelve, damn it. He has done things with his sex that no one suspects, not even his parents. He is beyond the age of believing in monsters under the bed.

Plus, he should have died a week ago. Whatever that means.

He keeps going in the familiar setting of his childhood, transfigured by the night of the dead. He crosses without dwelling on all the places where he lived, felt, dreamt. These are his traces, his ghosts. Not his ghosts, his father once corrected. Echoes. We don't have ghosts anymore.

He does not need to find his bearings.

"Our city is like any other," his mother told him when he was of age to ask questions. "Diversity is a necessary evil, but it can be controlled. Look . . ."

She had poured a big ink drop in a tissue and let it spread like blood through capillaries.

"Here is our city."

Then she slowly refolded the tissue, once, twice, before unfolding it. New marks stained the tissue, all linked to the first one with blackish strings.

"And here are the others. Not really identical, but very similar to each other, essentially."

"Which one is the first?"

"Does it matter?"

His mother threw the paper away and washed her hands carefully, until the ink darkening her fingers disappeared.

"What matters is that we cannot get lost anymore."

One day, he will leave without turning back. He feels it, he knows it. Jacqueline will come with him, or she will wait. In his dreams there are multiple options. He will go from one city to another without ever stopping. He will explore unknown lands. His steps will connect the world like a spiderweb. Those who will have the courage to accompany him will see unbelievable wonders. If needed, he will make them up.

Keeping his arms at his side, he joins the lines of people getting to the cemetery, pacing himself on their steps. There aren't any stars anymore because of the fog. Only shining light bulbs above his head, looking like human constellations.

It's starting to be damn cold.

The city has been too narrow for him for a while now. She slowly shrunk around him, while he was growing up. Every new street was a challenge before becoming familiar, then boring. He had seen it all. It's only a big village, a handful of numbered streets all like each other, punctuated by the essential buildings: stores, school, gymnasium. Some offices, some storage buildings; the crematorium, whose access is forbidden. The community center.

A cemetery.

The metal gates encircling the rows of tombstones are wide open. Each sepulture is ancient, consumed by the passage of time. The moss erased dates and chronologies. Daniel never entered through here, but he had peaked through the portal. He had even asked his father why it was closed. He didn't really expect an answer, yet he got one. He found himself pulled on large and hard shoulders, uncomfortable, but which let him see better.

"Stop fidgeting!"

He kept still, taking the time to observe. His father held him steadily and approached the metal gate.

"We only come here for the night of the dead. It is a cemetery. We shut away what has been, isn't anymore, what we decided to forget."

He tightened his hold on Daniel's legs and whispered pensively:

"There was a time when people used to die bit by bit. I didn't experience it, neither did my parents, so what I'm telling you comes from a time as distant as the other side of the sea. Humans would wake up one morning to discover that their hands' touch had lost its acuity. They would caress another skin, or theirs, and be surprised not to feel anything anymore. They lived little, and poorly. Each one going at their own pace, breathless. They didn't know how to talk about it, so they didn't.

"We are like them, but we seized the issue with both hands. Thanks to medicine's progress, we cross this unavoidable border very early, turning a blind eye to it all. And the mystery ceases to be one."

"I like mysteries," Daniel replied.

"They end up killing you. Or disappointing you, which amounts to the same thing."

The adult lifted the child, keeping him up in the air for a moment, then put him down. They never broached the topic again. On the way back, his father gave him a cookie and a soda. He didn't get himself anything. As they were leaving the drugstore, Daniel let go of his hand and headed out to the sidewalk, his mouth full. He felt the adult's gaze upon his shoulders but got free of it. With all his strength, he ran up to the next street corner, where they had to cross.

He obediently waited for his dad to join him.

Now, he stands in front of the cemetery's entrance, too heavy to be held on anyone's shoulders. The grids that drew an impassable barrier between here and the beyond have ceased to be an obstacle. He can cross the border; choose knowledge.

But Jacqueline went first. Nothing he can discover here will surprise her.

He thinks about turning back. The humidity is oppressive, so is the dirty-yellow-tinted fog. Exploring is easy when you do it from your bed, a fluffy comforter over your head. You nonchalantly brush monsters away with your hands, blow out to dissipate bad dreams. But the night always ends up winning.

He then moves forward hesitantly. The gravel squeaks under his shoes. Candles have been placed on the granite pavement, tracing paths leading to nowhere. Daniel hears voices resonating on the stone mausoleums. There are also murmurs, brushings. More undefinable noises. Nothing really strange, after all. It's not at all like he had imagined. It doesn't even look like the scary stories that the group used to tell each other in their secret place. It is like a picnic on a plain night. Without anything to eat.

He breathes quickly to avoid being betrayed by his breath's condensation. When a couple brushes past him, he pricks up his ears. Their conversation is banal, a little unreal. Adults' sentences, incomplete, almost as if they each knew in advance what the other one was going to say. They talk to feel alive among the dead surrounding them like terminals. They do not have dreams anymore; only plans.

A few woo each other with detachment.

Daniel hurries up so as to cover his cough with the sound of the gravel. The more he keeps moving, the more crowded the cemetery gets with people who are already dead. They walk slowly, in little shuffling groups. Other silhouettes are simply sitting on the humid lawn or leaning on a statue corroded by time, its visage damaged by scars. In contrast, the dead ones look brand new. Their eyes are wide open, but they are not looking toward anyone. One can distinguish the white of their eyes, the white gash of their teeth.

There aren't any kids his age in this part of the cemetery. Those who meander here are his parents' age, even their parents' age; they left when he was a child. He remembers them, their sweet smell when they leaned toward him to rub his cheeks. The weight of their gaze too.

One day, he worked up the courage to ask why they were not there anymore. It was his dad who answered, a year later, when he had already forgotten the question. They were both walking to the basketball court for his Saturday practice. Daniel was bouncing the ball on the sidewalk, dodging imaginary attackers. His dad was carrying the bag with all his stuff—a change of clothes, a snack prepared by his mother, Band-Aids for the inevitable boo-boo. It was an indecisive time, when the child who he was was beginning to crack. *To grow up is to choose*, said his dad. *And choosing is already to start dying.*

"We will spend Christmas without them."

His dad's voice lacked inflection.

"They decided not to go on."

"Where did they go?"

"To the other side."

"Why don't they want to come to see me?"

"It is a border one can only cross once, son."

Daniel was outraged. Silence had answered him. The basketball's obsessive rhythm on the asphalt had helped him to keep moving.

"It is their choice," his dad had finally said while they entered the locker room. "Eternity never is forever."

He had mechanically brushed Daniel's hair, like he did before each game; but this time his hand lingered on the back of his skull.

"Your death is inscribed in your brain, in the oldest memory area, the one we cannot access. When we delete this information, the body puts itself on hold, in slow motion. But the deleted area never totally disappears and recreates itself somewhere else. You must burn it regularly. Until you cannot stand it anymore."

"Does it hurt?"

His dad had shrugged his shoulders.

"We never remember."

The cemetery's main alley is a gentle slope.

His heart beats differently when thinking about Jacqueline. It thumps, it races. It is like a song belonging only to her. Something primal, joyfully painful, that leaves him sweaty, out of breath in advance.

The freshest dead are assembled next to the oldest mausoleums, in the back of the cemetery. There, the crosses are crooked or completely knocked down, the names unreadable. Large patches of blackish foam hang on top of a wall whose bricks have become cracked. *I could have gone through there,* Daniel thinks. *With a rope ladder, like a magician.* He pictures himself leaping like a tiger between the tombstones, which are pitched on the ground like teeth. Roly-poly, screams, and fury. Miraculously escaping from slow and graceless zombies. That's what he'll tell Jacqueline when he finds her, hoping she believes him.

Tussocks stick out like water drips between the gravel. The legs of his pajama pants are soaked, and so are his socks, but he doesn't care. His friends are close by. Sitting in a circle on a cracked paving stone, they whisper, head against head. Daniel comes closer, making noise. Keeping his shoulders up, he brushed aside the clumsy strand of hair on his forehead. Yet, he hesitates. None of the others are shivering from the humid wind. All seem frozen in collected postures, barely aware of the haze wrapping them up. Their whispers vanish into silence.

"I managed to escape," he lets out approaching them. "Everyone is looking for me everywhere."

Heads turn toward him very slowly.

"We didn't think you'd come."

It was neither a question nor a reproach. Only a fact.

"I'm here."

He fights his way through his friends' circle until he is in front of Jacqueline. She moves to let him sit but turns aside when he tries to catch her eyes. She is wearing her normal school clothes, not the low-cut dress she usually wears when they meet over the weekend.

"What do we do?"

Without waiting for an answer, he raises his voice.

"I saw some tombstones moving. Maybe even some fingers digging through the ground into the open air. We would do better to hide."

"Why?"

It's Do, Jacqueline's brother. A timid boy, to whom Daniel never hid his feelings for his sister. So, he became his trustworthy second. He compensates for his lack of imagination with flawless obedience. But here, he shakes his head, slowly, puzzled.

The others don't say anything. It's embarrassing. Their silence infects him.

He scrapes his feet on the gravel and the noise is weirdly satisfying. When he raises his head again, everything is congealing around him: the alleys' convergence lines, the scaly stump-dark tombstones; the dead prowling over there, ready to act whenever he decides to. He is the conductor. His thoughts combine into a spectacular melody nobody else can hear.

"I have a plan," Daniel answers.

He opens his hands, outlining strategies through the mist. He is improvising, but it usually works.

"First, we get out of here, trying not to be noticed. We will have to avoid the older ones, the ones who are here to prevent us from leaving. We will crawl, until we can stand up and run, so fast that our shadows will never catch us. Then . . ."

His words redraft the world, repel borders beyond the horizon.

"We get ready for a new expedition, further than we've ever been."

His dreams jump over the wall, past the square-patterned streets, past the horizon that is too close. There, everything is to be imagined. And without thinking, without even planning, he takes Jacqueline's hand and leans towards her lips.

She looks away with a pout that makes her look older, and snaps: "Don't be a child!"

◆ ◆ ◆

Daniel is back in his bedroom, the covers assembled all around him. He will soon be pulled out of this cocoon. He's shivering, chattering his teeth. Nothing can warm him up. His friends let him go without looking at him, without even trying to hold him up. They have crossed to the other side, beyond revolt and infinite dreams. Where immortality is just boring.

The night of the dead will end without him, but, in a few hours, they will come for him. When he returns, Jacqueline will be there waiting for him. Or not.

At that point, it won't matter anymore.

# EXPANSION

Jean-Claude Dunyach: "The City, That Night"

French title: "La Ville, ce soir-là"

First published in French in *Frontières*, the anthology of the festival Les Imaginales in Épinal, France by Éditions Mnémos (October 2021).

*Translated by* Tessa Sermet

Jean-Claude Dunyach (1956–) earned a PhD in applied mathematics and worked for the French aeronautic corporation Airbus in Toulouse until his retirement in 2020. In parallel to his professional career, Dunyach has published nine novels and ten anthologies of short stories, becoming one of France's most famous science fiction writers. He also writes lyrics and is involved in music production. His novel *Etoiles mourantes* (*Dying Stars*), written in collaboration with Ayerdhal, won the prestigious Eiffel Tower Award in 1999 and the Ozone Award in 2000. His work usually falls under the category of hard science fiction, and according to science fiction scholar Amy Ransom (2014),[1] his cyberpunk fiction has even earned him comparisons with William Gibson. Ransom also adds that contrary to a lot of French science fiction, many of Dunyach's stories have been published in English thanks to a group of translators lead by Canadians Jean-Louis Trudel and Sheryl Curtis—who also translated a few of the stories found in this anthology!

However, the tone of "The City, That Night" is far from hard science fiction. The main character, Daniel, is a sick young boy who, instead of staying in bed, sneaks out of the house. The reader follows Daniel through the town in a dark and spooky night, not quite sure of what he's looking for, or what is going on at first. He is craving the metamorphosis from childhood to adulthood his friends have undergone without him and finds himself alone, outcast for it. This story comments on what one gives up when becoming an adult, and

---

1 Ransom, Amy J. "The New French SF: The Imaginary Worlds of Jean-Claude Dunyach" in *The New York Review of Science Fiction*, Issue 309 (May 2014).

how monotonous and shallow adulthood can look like through the eyes of a child. And yet, Daniel cannot help but want to be an adult. Dunyach's text takes us to the fringes of science fiction, when the absurd and the *fantastique* join to create a touching and sometimes unsettling coming-of-age story.

## DISCUSSION QUESTIONS

The idea of life after death is presented here in a literal, almost surrealistic way. How are rites of passage to adulthood and death mixed in this story? What is the effect on the reader?

What do you make of the explanation of why the different cities are connected? Why do you think Daniel's mother says, "what matters is that we cannot get lost anymore?"

Daniel's father says that mysteries end up killing you "or disappointing you, which amounts to the same thing." How is adulthood portrayed in this story? How would you describe the adults' behaviors?

At the end of the story, Daniel describes his friends with the following words: "They have crossed to the other side, beyond revolt and infinite dreams. Where immortality is just boring." What does this quote say about growing up? What does it indicate about people's behavior towards life and/or death? Are mysteries worth dying or living for?

Do you think Daniel will choose to "die" anyway or will he resist the transformation to remain in the "country" of childhood? Does this remind you of another famous character?

# ADDITIONAL READINGS

Most of these texts have not been translated into English. Those available in English translation are marked in **bold**. Some authors have an extended bibliography, our selection is based on most famous books, privileging short story collections when appropriate. We also mix famous authors and new, younger writers whose stories have marked us recently. Needless to say, our selection is biased, and we encourage you to do your own research. There are many, many more authors to read than the few mentioned here.

## AUTHORS IN THIS COLLECTION

### Sylvie Denis

This author has also published many short stories in magazines. Her two-volume space opera is mentioned in "Expansion" that follows "Inside, Outside."

*Haute-École* (2004)—novel for young (and older) adults, fantasy
*Pèlerinage* (2009)—short stories
*Phénix futur* (2009)—novel for young (and older) adults
*Étranges enfances* (2014)—short stories

### Jean-Claude Dunyach

**Novel**

*Etoiles mourantes* (1999) in collaboration with Ayerdhal

**Selection of short stories translated in English**

"**Separations,**" in The SFWA European Hall of Fame (2007)
"**Paranamanco,**" in The Big Book of Science Fiction (2016)

**In the sci-fi magazine *Galaxy's Edge***

"**God, Seen from the Inside**" (2014)
"**Love Your Enemy**" (2016)
"**With a Wink of the Heron's Eye**" (2017)

## Colette Fayard

*Les Chasseurs au bord de la nuit* (1989)—short stories
*Le Jeu de l'éventail* (1992)—novel
*Par tous les temps* (1990)—novel

## Sylvie Lainé

Lainé's short stories are either published in the collections already mentioned at the end of "The Swing of Your Gait" or in various magazines, zines, and collective anthologies. More recently, she contributed short stories in multi-author collections published by ActuSF:

"**Nos Futurs**" (2020) on climate change.
"**Nos Futurs solidaires**" (2022) on social inclusion and community building.

## Serge Lehman

### Short stories (collections)

*Le Livre des ombres* (2005)
*Le Haut-Lieu et autres espaces inhabitables* (2011)
*Espion de l'étrange* (2011)

### Novel

*Le Cycle de F.A.U.S.T.* (The whole collection was published in one volume in 2019.)

### Comics

*The Chimera Brigade* (2009–2010, English translation 2014)

### Film

*Immortel, Ad Vitam* (2004)—Serge Lehman worked on the script of this adaptation of Enki Bilal's graphic novels.

## Jacques Sternberg

*Entre deux mondes incertains* (1958)—novel
*Futurs sans avenir* (1971)—short stories
*Mai 86* (1978)—novel

## Laurence Suhner

### Novels

*QuanTika Series* (Gallimard)
**Vestiges** (2017) see Expansion for "Beyond the Terminator" for more
information on the English translation.
*L'Ouvreur des chemins* (2018)
*Origines* (2018)

### Two additional short stories

**"Homéostasie"** (2010)—published in *Dimension Suisse: une anthol-
ogie de science-fiction romande (Anthology of Swiss francophone science
fiction short stories)* 2010.
**"La Chose du lac"** (2012)—published in *Utopiales 12*, ActuSF, 2012

### Two graphic novels

*Le Chaman* (2007)
*Confidences* (2007)

## Julia Verlanger

All her work has been collected and the cycle *Intégrale Julia Verlanger*
by Bragelonne in five volumes in the collection Trésors de la Science-
Fiction. We recommend these two, but you may also be able to find
old editions of singular novels. She also published under the name
Gilles Thomas.

*La Terre sauvage* (2008)—three novels, "Les Bulles" and its sequel
"Le Recommencement," plus a nice dossier about the author.
*Les Parias de l'impossible* (2010)—three novels and over twenty
short stories

## Robert C. Wagner

### Novels

*Les Futurs mystères de Paris* (1999)
*Rêves de gloire* (2012)—a uchronia based on the Algerian Independence War

### Short story collection

*Musique de l'énergie* (2000)

## OTHER AUTHORS

## Ayerdhal

*Demain, une oasis* (1992)—novel
*Cybione series* (1992–2001)—four novels

## Pierre Bordage

One of France's best-selling authors of science fiction, he won many awards. He published over thirty novels—several in cycles—and collections of short stories.

*Les Guerriers du silence* (1993–95)—trilogy gathered in one volume by L'Atalante in 2014)
*Les Derniers hommes* (1990s)—a series of short volumes reedited in one volume in various editions by J'ai Lu (the last one in 2017) and Au Diable Vauvert (2010).
*Wang* (2000)—novel
*Chroniques des ombres* (2013)—novel
*Hier je vous donnerai de mes nouvelles* (2016)—short stories

## Sabrina Calvo

One of the most beautiful and inventive prose in French science fiction. You may find these novels published before 2017 under the name David Calvo.

*Elliot du néant* (2012)—novel
*Sous la colline* (2015)—novel
*Toxoplasma* (2017)—novel

## Alain Damasio

*La Zone du dehors* (1999)—novel
*La Horde du Contrevent* (2004)—novel
*Les Furtifs* (2019)—novel

## Jeanne-A Debats

The artistic director of Les Utopiales, the yearly festival of science fiction that takes place in Nantes, she also writes fantasy for adults and young adults.

*La Vieille Anglaise et le continent* (2008)—novella
*Plaguers* (2010)—novel
**"Chéloïdes"** (2022)—short story available for purchase from Actusf.fr

## Catherine Dufour

*L'Accroissement mathématique du plaisir* (2008)—short stories collections
*Le Goût de l'immortalité* (2005)—novel

## Laurent Genefort

*Colonies* (2019)—short stories collection

## Christian Léourier

*Helstrid* (2019)—novel

## Jean-Marc Ligny

*Aqua*™ (2006)—novel
*Exodes* (2016)—novel

## François Rouiller

*Métaquine: Contre-indications*, followed by *Métaquine: Indications* (2016)—two novels that must be read together.

## Floriane Soulas

*Les Oubliés de l'Amas* (2021)—novel

## Aurélie Wellenstein

*Mers mortes* (2019)—novel, science fiction/fantasy
*Le Désesrt des couleurs* (2021)—novel

## Samuel Zaoui

*Humaine machine* (2022)—novel

# SOURCES ABOUT (FRENCH) SCIENCE FICTION

NooSFere—a website whose goal is to promote French science fiction: https://www.noosfere.org/

*ReS Futurae*—an open-source, Francophone, international journal of high quality, dedicated to the study of science fiction in all forms and genres (novels, comics, graphic arts, cinema). https://journals.openedition.org/resf/

## Two academic books in French:

Bréan, Simon. *La Science-fiction en France: Théorie et histoire d'une littérature.* PUPS, Presses de l'université Paris-Sorbonne, 2012. (A comprehensive historical and thematic overview of French sf.)

Vas-Deyre, Natacha. *Ces Français qui ont écrit demain: Utopie, Anticipation et science-fiction au XXᵉ siècle.* Paris, Honoré Champion, 2012.

## Two recent academic books in English:

Buzay, Emmanuel. *Contemporary French and Francophone Futuristic Novels.* Palgrave Macmillan, 2022.

Lord, Christina. *Reimagining the Human in Contemporary French Science Fiction.* Liverpool University Press, 2023.

# Ooligan Press

Ooligan Press is a student-run publishing house rooted in the rich literary culture of the Pacific Northwest. Founded in 2001 as part of Portland State University's Department of English, Ooligan is dedicated to the art and craft of publishing. Students pursuing master's degrees in book publishing staff the press in an apprenticeship program under the guidance of a core faculty of publishing professionals.

## Project Managers
Maya Karkabi
Kyndall Tiller

## Acquisitions
Alena Rivas
Amanda Fink
Jenny Davis
Kelly Zatlin

## Editorial
Sienna Berlinger
Jordan Bernard
Kelly Morrison
Tanner Croom

## Design
Laura Renckens
Elaine Schumacher

## Digital
Cecilia Too
Anna Wehmeier Giol
Paige Brayton

## Marketing & Publicity
Yomari Lobo
Sarah Bradley
Tara McCarron

## DEI & Online Content
Jules Luck
Nell Stamper
Elliot Bailey

## Operations
Haley Young
Dani Tellvik
Em Villaverde

## Book Production
AJ Adler
Elliot Bailey
Corwin Benedict
Claire Curry
Jenny Davis
Alexandra Devon
Ariana Espinoza
Amber Finnegan
Kip Franich
Noraa Gunn
Kara Herrera
Julie Holland
Marielle LeFave
Isabel Lemus Kristensen
Savannah Lyda
Aurora Miner
Jazzminn Morecraft

## Book Production cont'd.

Agi Mottern
Mara Palmieri
Rachael Phillips
Abby Relph
Samantha Gallasch
Alexa Schmidt
Brittany Shike
Coriander Smith
Alice Stoddard
Isaac Swindle
Emmily Tomulet
Emma Wallace
Shoshana Weaver
Bradley Wilcox
Jennifer Wurtele